Seven years

Hurtling through space was an enormous tumbling rock known as MN4, that our astronomers named after an ancient Egyptian god of destruction.

Asteroid Apophis was the talk of the year that every scientific community on Earth was aware of, although its flyby in April 2029 was to be nothing more than a spectacular celestial event; but as warring nations were locked in global conflict, our civilization was unprepared for the devastation that followed in its wake.

Several years after governments fell and society dissolved a ragged pack of survivors stumble upon the buried truth, revealing what circumstances had led to the aftermath that ensued, leaving them to question their continued struggle to salvage what few splintered shards were left of our world that would forever define humanity's bitter legacy.

Titles by Michel Savage

Faerylands Series
The Grey Forest
Soulstorm Keep
Sorrowblade
Ivory

Shadoworld Series
Shadow of the Sun
Veil of Shadows
Shadows Gate

Outlaws of Europa
Rebels of Alpha Prime

Hellbot • Battle Planet

A Couple of Zeros

Forgotten Future

Broken Mirror

Project EVE

Witchwood

7

ഇ൝ഌ

Broken Mirror
Apophis 2029

Michel Savage

Enter the Grey Forest

www.**GreyForest**.com

Broken Mirror – Apophis 2029

The Grey Forest
P.O. Box 71494
Springfield, OR 97475

www.GreyForest.com

Cover art by Michel Savage

ISBN: 978-0-9719168-5-2

First Edition: Oct 2016

Printed in the United States of America

0 9 8 7 6 5 4 3 2 1

Doomsday

Throughout human history, there have always been premonitions of an Armageddon where humanity would meet its final demise. In the past millennia there have been countless wars, famines, and plagues that have brought great suffering and tides of death across the globe. It is this realization of our own mortality which drives those few among us with the strength of spirit to uphold the belief that we, as human beings, can better ourselves even in the darkest of times.

What if mankind failed to exercise the level of ethics we use as a gauge to define ourselves above all other creatures with whom we share this world. Like a shattered mirror, in desperate times we strive to save what little is left of ourselves in every sliver and splintered shard. One could argue that the human soul is nothing more than a delicate shadow cast from our experiences and fragile emotions, and if we should ever be compelled by harsh circumstance to choose which fragments of ourselves we should keep and those principles we might choose to discard ...would you truly recognize the reflection left behind as your own?

Table of Contents

Daydreams

It was a bright morning on the docks, one could feel there was a faint chill in the air and a light breeze seen by their bundled scarves and tell-tale wisps of hair dancing around the trio of girls that stood staring out upon the cold sea. A British ship with high masts that needled their way into the blue sky was moored at the nearby pier, its brine-stained hull sunk low in the waterline with its belly full of cargo. Several dark-skinned men with colorful turbans hauled woven baskets filled with marvelous and mysterious spices, while their comrades stacked ornamental rugs on worn wooden carts as they unloaded the anchored vessel.

A few feet from the ship's ramp stood several men, alight in a whirlwind of urgency, one pointing out at some distant object of interest upon the far horizon. Burly men with sullied linen shirts dodged between the stacks of barrels lining the wharf as others of a grim stature stood idly by, caring solely for the weight of their ivory-handled cane or a golden pocket watch, each with their black sealskin top hats fashionably tilted askew. I then began to wonder what type of wax the elderly man had used to sculpt his long handlebar mustache, or if that tiny golden box hanging from a fine gilded chain at his vest pocket might be filled with exotic snuff.

I spied the gathering of the three young women at the edge of the pier. Each of the girls had a similar hue of hair, making me wonder if they were perhaps sisters or merely friends that shared an identical stature, as each one differed but by a shade in height. Their closeness revealed a sense of familiarity, as they seemed to lean together like three stones built within the same pillar against the salty ocean wind that wove their curled locks into a shimmering tapestry.

Though I could not quite see their faces, I imagined that the tallest girl was eyeing the prim young gentleman at the very edge of the dock, although I could have mistaken the subject of her gaze that may have drifted to the buff, clean-shaven young man who struggled with a coil of thick mooring ropes in his effort to secure a passenger boat tethered below them. As her height did bare the air of maturity, the next youngest of them in line stood in the middle; whom I imagined had her eyes shut with her face turned towards the morning sun as she breathed in the sharp fragrance of the sand and salty sea. It must have delightfully tickled her mind to think of the strange and magical lands that lie beyond those distant stormy clouds, which stood like sentinels at the very edge of the horizon of the rolling blue ocean that dominated the scenery.

Next to her was the youngest of the trio; brimming with the innocence of life and discovery, whose head was turned upward ever so slightly towards a lone seagull soaring effortlessly above the shore. The lapping waves crashed with the raw force of nature, like a lash of ecstasy disintegrating into a glitter of white foam upon the distant rocks; their resounding climax melting lazily back into the cold dreadful sea.

Time seemed to stop, as excited thoughts raced through my head, wondering whom these people were, their names, their families, and what their personal lives must have been like. I was curious to know if it was the expectations of their hopes and dreams that truly set them apart, or merely their capacity at playing the part of different castes, like actors in a play. Such as the two young men on the dock, for example; one whose calloused hands wiped the sweat from his brow as he labored at the direction of the poised gentleman beside him, whose perfumed handkerchief sat perched like a puffed rooster from his lapel pocket while a smug glare of arrogance glinted from his beady little eyes. For a passing heartbeat, it made me wonder what circumstances were at play that placed this odd pair in such two different worlds that made them so unequal that one man was cursed to suffer for the other's gain.

Likely, it was nothing more than the mere clink of silver coins and favored upbringing which had changed their course to distance them so. With a hint of a smile, I wondered for such a brief moment; which of the two men might the older girl eventually choose to share her affections?

The saddest part of this poetic scene was the marring of a small grassy hill at the lower edge of the dunes, where the girls stood in their pale quilted shawls. There, I could make out the tiniest of flowers in the purest white and yellows, swaying in the tender grass that all but dissolved into a mush of putrid streaks that fingered their way into the stain upon the broken concrete wall. The tender brushstrokes of the fine painting of that sunny seaside afternoon trapped in time so long ago was now decayed and marred as it hung by a single rusted nail, exposed to untold years of wind and rain. I felt an ache as I was torn away from that brief moment of escape and wrenched harshly back into the reality of the world around me, my brain kicking and screaming in reluctance the entire way.

I looked down at my shivering fingers, which were so numb that I could hardly feel them. The drip of water off my hair and down my face into my jacket, served to reminded me that I was soaked to the bone. Mentally, I was slowly losing it, and struggling with the fact I was likely suffering from hypothermia and becoming delusional as my vision faded in and out. I sat crouched with my back against the ruins of the cold concrete while staring out from the dark hollow of the shattered building around me towards the gray world beyond; now enveloped by a curtain of rain. For but a fleeting moment, I lost touch with reality once again, wishing I could disappear into that marred and broken painting; to be anywhere but in the here and now.

Sunset was fast approaching and through the pelt of the heavy sleet, I could hear the Weepers approaching from behind. It was not surprising these diseased creatures would chase me this far beyond their nest; considering the rampant starvation which had engulfed every nation across the planet since the event. The doctors named the syndrome KRI, but survivors knew it as "Cry", the aggressive virus the scientist had titled the MN4-Kriotin Hemophilia disease was highly infectious. Its pseudonym made a measure of sense because essentially anyone who became infected with it exhibited signs of severe depression in the final stage of incubation, as their eyes would literally well up with tears of blood leaving stains of dark streaks streaming down their face. A shocking and ghastly sight that became all too familiar.

The effects of the first stage actually varied from person to person, but virtually all victims would display symptoms of acute dementia that progressively worsened, but one interesting side effects was that the infected subjects became colorblind, and their notable habit of converging into mobs and to hunt in packs. As much as people had fantasized the coming of some sort of zombie apocalypse in recent decades, actually calling infected loved ones as the "undead" was regarded as highly offensive by most. Though in untreated cases, the victims of the disease quickly reverted to an almost primitive state, leaving them uttering lamenting moans akin to shrieks and cries of anguish in their demented misery. Thus, among the public the term 'Weepers' was used to nickname anyone who became afflicted by the blight.

In an imaginative twist, survivors took advantage of this token symptom of the infected being colorblind and posted specially stippled signs on buildings and roadways; like a type of secret code that could only be deciphered by its subtle colors. If by chance, you were unfortunate enough to have been born colorblind, then you were pretty much shit-out-of-luck; however, it was an effective deterrent to separate the infected.

For those who contracted the pathogen, the loss of cognitive abilities usually varied wildly from case to case. The real problem centered around those who had succumbed to the contagion but were left intelligent enough to be dangerous. When the disease first broke out, the initial reports of dozens of such patients, rapidly became hundreds, which soon escalated to thousands of people who were swiftly ferried off to secluded quarantine camps. The surge of infection rates seen by hospitals and disease centers quickly expanded into a pandemic that had spiraled out of control.

It didn't matter much in the end. Clinics were not certain if the virus had mutated to become airborne or if the bug was solely transmitted by physical means. Blood and mucus contact was a sure-fire way to get infected, thus, the level of fear and propaganda helped birthed a zombie craze which had more than a superficial basis in fact and caused entire cities to implode as our social infrastructure fell into complete chaos. In the panic that ensued, even healthy people were shooting one another out of fright. During the hysteria, untold millions of citizens blockaded themselves in their homes with their family members who had already been exposed to the virus. Beyond the plague, countless innocent lives were lost as a result of frightened suspicion and reckless ignorance.

I could only guess that it was currently around early Spring of 2036. I couldn't be sure since I hadn't seen a real calendar in years, and just tried to keep track in my head after discarding hastily marked scratches I had collected on scraps of paper, which had ultimately lost their purpose. I always forgot how many days were in each month, counting leap years; but really, what the fuck did it matter anymore? Currently, every day was a *'just stay alive'* holiday, though given, some days were better than most ...this was not one of them. It was mid April, back in 2029 on Friday the 13th that the asteroid had hit, as if it were some sort of dark omen. In the aftermath that followed, our so-called modern civilization had thoroughly shit itself and done a mighty good job of it.

The clatter of a loose metal pipe rattling on the ground several yards away shook me from my cold-induced stupor. A wild human scream in the opposite direction informed me there was more than one Weeper in the immediate area and that they were closing in on my location. The heavy rain was to my advantage since they could not possibly track by scent in this downpour, and it would help to muffle any errant noise I might make. Still, it was alarming how fast the infected could move, but their defective vision as a symptom of the virus, made it far easier to hide in the shadows from these creatures.

Even when sane, the human species can be undeniably vicious, but take away all the inconveniences of exercising a conscience and you end up with a very nasty beast; and these monsters were clearly hungry. At first, reports of cannibalism among the survivors had been scoffed at, labeled as nothing more than the crazy rants that all the zombie doomsayers had dreamt up while cowering in their crappy bug-out shelters. As it turned out, the first incidents were entirely true; they started from a number of small townships which had been locked in isolation from any distant outlying communities. Due to a critical combination of both local Authority and Government imposed Martial Law, blockades of all connecting access roads and a suspension of shipments to their trivial little backwater towns; they had quickly run out of stored provisions. When food shipments that relied on our mass transit system had come to a screeching halt, people looted supermarkets and hoarded any available supplies they could get their grubby little hands on; but when those rations were gone, they turned to their cats, their dogs, their goldfish, and eventually on one another.

This was not lost on the infected victims who were once attended to, only to find their caregivers had turned tail and left them abandoned. One by one, all the Medical and Health Care facilities were overwhelmed and had pulled out their personnel in a hurried retreat as their quarantine camps became swamped with infected patients while their wards started bursting at the seams. The military hierarchy lost all control as their soldiers deserted their posts, either responding to the needs of their own families, or out of despair as the stock of respirators and fancy anti-contagion suits dried up. Sadly enough, wearing a protective suit actually made you a target for those desperate for the gear itself. Many times, soldiers would end up shooting the very civilians whom they were engaged to protect when they suddenly found themselves confronted and outnumbered by a scared mob.

Those who had been infected with KRI for more than a few weeks frequently turned barbaric with hunger that ravaged their deranged minds, much like a small child would throw a tantrum, they didn't know right from wrong; their brains didn't work that way anymore. I had once stumbled upon a pack of weepers who were feeding on the remains of an elderly man, even though his broken grocery bag full of soup cans lay scattered on the ground around them. They had forgotten what a can of food was, how to read, or even how to open them, it was as if somehow in their minds they had entirely lost who they were and only existed moment to moment in a primal state.

Weepers were filthy and wild, their eyes bloodshot with

crusted streaks of dried blood caked upon their cheeks. I vividly recall how one of them dug out the old man's eye and plopped them into its mouth, suckling the juices; I still shiver at that horrid thought which my disturbed mind refused to forget. Apparently, weepers don't like the way each other smelled, which was thought to be a pheromone block by the very pus that seeped from their eyes; the fact that they wouldn't attack one another was a compelling test to that theory. They were just poor sick people who had misplaced all sense of their humanity, and in a way, you could not help but feel sorry for them. Those survivors who claimed they no longer felt any touch of sympathy for them had already lost their own humanity on an entirely different level.

I crouched there, drenched in the shivering rain as the weepers approached. Realizing I didn't have many options left to me at the moment, and that if I was going to survive another day I would have to move now! Hiding was only optional if you had the high ground. The problem with being hunted by Weepers, was that they could go pretty much anywhere you could. One benefit was that their night vision was much, much worse, but the approaching dusk would only slow them down.

Just a few hours before, I had taken shelter from the approaching storm in an old farmhouse far over the hill. The woods here were thick and I always made an effort to avoid the open roads whenever I could. The farmhouse was a once picturesque cottage with a tall barn, its faded red paint peeling from the rotting wood. Nearby, an old farm truck sat in disrepair, its wheel wells had grown over with tall grass while its true color remained uncertain as its body was covered with a patina of rust from top to bottom. Several windows on the wooden hovel had been shattered and my wary ears detected nothing but silence from within. In all respects, the property seemed to have been left abandoned for several years.

Not one footprint or trace in the dirt showed any use of the front door. As dark clouds rumbled angrily overhead, I heeded their threat and dared to explore within; hoping for nothing more than to find a spot where the roof did not leak so I could get some decent rest until the following dawn. I was glad to find the door unlocked; the hinges creaked in protest as I made my way inside.

It looked like most homes I had trespassed upon over the years, a real mess. There were telltale signs that the residing occupants had left in a hurry. There was a sculpture of a small cast-iron bullfrog sitting on a shelf by the door to greet me. Looking upon this miniature icon it had occurred to me that I truly missed the croak of frogs found by the rivers and lakes; which is not something that one usually thinks about until it's gone. From what I had heard through many rumors was that such amphibians were among the first species affected by the virus and had nearly gone extinct across the globe. Crickets too, were rare, so much so that noticing a single solo chirp echoing in the night was as uncommon as a shooting star. Their usual chorus of evening song had been replaced by a blanket of eerie silence that spread throughout the night, smothering the darkness.

As disheveled as the house was, including the rank smell of musty upholstery, it was still far more inviting than being caught outside in a downpour, especially so since the eruptions of freak lightning storms were dangerously unpredictable. I didn't bother scrounging for food; if anything had been left behind, it had either putrefied or the bugs and mice had long since devoured it, and likely, other wild creatures had eaten those vermin in kind. Food was scarce as it was. Dysentery and malnutrition ran rampant in small towns and villages among people who didn't possess the knowledge nor the basic means to survive on their own.

After the event, it was an astounding joke how so many people tried to trade paper money, jewelry, and even gold or silver bullion in exchange for food; at the very least, the banknotes had the minimal use as toilet paper. Precious metals weren't so precious anymore if you couldn't eat, shoot, nor light a fire with them. However, though bartering weapons for food was commonplace, it became an even more dangerous endeavor if the unscrupulous person you were swapping items with decided to test out the given firearm right then and there; taking your life along with all your plunder for themselves. In this new world, everyone had his or her own definition of what honor actually meant anymore. Honestly, if a sticky or dangerous situation came down to a decision between me-or-them, I would tend to pick '*me*' also.

I stepped over the broken furniture that littered the main entry, bypassing what appeared to be the kitchen. Usually what you would find left rotting in people's refrigerators would make your stomach churn and was best avoided. Anything that could make you ill was a real risk; let alone a cut from a rusty nail as bandages and antiseptics were rare commodities these days. I remember the old documentaries I had seen in college about the 'preppers' as they were called everything from 'wacko's', to 'conspiracy nuts', to just plain backwood hicks preparing for the end of the world, and all the hokey shit they had believed would someday save their ass. A decade later, nobody was laughing at them when Apophis fell from the sky and turned our world into a spectacular clusterfuck.

Long before the asteroid arrived, the public rumors that were flung around was that the ancient Mayans had predicted the this calamity long ago. A great deal of gossip centered on all the corrupt insurance agencies and the scams they pulled on the unwary public, along with the rampant banking fraud that nearly destroyed the fragile economy which had set us upon this course. Life on a global scale would have actually taken an upswing if the soaring human population rate had not been so wildly out of control. A few nations began to implement mandatory sterilization for convicts and the mentally disabled, or even lowering themselves to offering bribes by promising monetary compensation for anyone who accepted voluntary compliance.

All the wasted effort was a frivolous social experiment, one which had failed horribly. Its condemnation was compounded after it was discovered that the pharmaceutical industries worldwide had been quietly and secretly adding anti-fertility elements into a number of popular medical prescriptions. When the media blew that story wide open, the drug companies turned around and blamed their conduct on the local governments, claiming they were only following orders; when suddenly overnight, all these conspiracies were swiftly silenced. The crash of the Net in 2026 was loosely blamed on computer hackers, and such accusations were quickly turned around and placed upon solar storms when the skeptics could not uncover any proof of sabotage and the allegations swiftly escalated towards any other type of scandal that could be dreamt up. The piles of unsubstantiated misinformation flooding the national news and media airwaves always pointed its nasty little finger back towards covert government involvement and their all too frequent efforts of going to extraordinary lengths to cloak their secret agendas. Shortly thereafter, the free internet world-wide-web, as it had been known since its birth, was replaced by a system called 'Smartwave', "*a new and infallible technology for our modern era of communication*," as the governmental propaganda touted.

The general population wasn't stupid, we knew all media was now being censored by automation, but there was nothing we could do about it. A wide belief was that anything named "SMART" stood for: **S**urveillance **M**arketed **A**s **R**evolutionary **T**echnology. Any public blog, chat, or dialog, or uploaded transmission was read, reviewed, deleted, or rewritten within nanoseconds. Of course, there were a few exceptions that slipped through the security net, and those rare incidents were either followed by tragic freak accidents that ended the life of the suspected perpetrators, which needless to say, were incidents that were quickly erased from downstream media sources, and thus, nobody would ever hear about it. News events were glazed-over under the thin disguise of an open and free-speech media. Truth be told, it was a method of media whitewashing that had actually been in practice for well over half a century.

Half a decade after Apophis struck, there was a lot of confusion about some relevant but missing facts when the asteroid event happened in 2029. It was one of those puzzles that slowly gnawed at the back of your mind; over the kind of absurd conduct by those in authority, that it was beyond anything we could fathom. Considering, that with all our given technology, how did our space laboratories, astronomers, and all our scientists manage to fuck up so badly? Who was to blame for such astounding incompetence, was merely water under the bridge at this point. Whomever or whatever group of sneaky secretive spooks that had been responsible were likely already long dead, or held up in a claustrophobic military bunker somewhere, frantically yelling and bickering with one another as to how they had nobody left to order around. Then again, maybe that loose analogy is merely unsubstantiated paranoia, citing our inability to admit that sometimes "*shit happens*" and people will always be looking for someone else to blame for their current state of affairs ...but then again, there's always a chance that '*shit happens'* by design.

I clicked on my light as I entered the farmhouse; my solar-charged flashlight was one of my prized possessions, which had saved me from breaking my neck in the dark more than once. Thick clouds moved in from the approaching storm as the door rattled behind me. The interior of the building took on a grim but familiar air, the kind you sense when roaming such domestic ruins as you sift through peoples shattered lives. I try to push back the distressing thoughts about that, which was hard for me, and always has been.

I would always find myself thinking about the people who had lived in the vacant buildings I explored; judging what tastes they had in their decorations and for what possible occasions long past they had collected their forgotten memorabilia and personal trinkets they had chosen to leave behind, now scattered among the ground like so much insignificant garbage. My mind would be driven to wonder about the child that once wore a small sweater left crumpled in a mound upon the floor. Sometimes I would come across old family photos, as prints were rare since most modern images were digitalized on battery powered displays, and were now forever lost. It was a swelling ache I felt inside that deeply saddened me to think the people I saw within these discarded photographs were now dead, or worse, had become infected and lost who they had once been.

Oddly, there were no pictures on the walls within the farmhouse, just a few crappy shelves and empty broken frames lying on the floor. Even in old abandoned buildings, you still have to be careful of your step or rotting timbers that were merely waiting for someone to put a few pounds of pressure in the wrong place. In some cases, I had seen Mother Nature entirely reclaim old settlements; with trees sprouting from rooftops, branches, and vines muscling their way through weakened brick walls that had crumbled apart in surrender to the invasive greenery.

Whenever I found an uninfected rat or two, I would consider myself lucky and make a quick meal of them. Some wildlife still survives in the deep forests, though most are so deformed and blighted with abnormal growths that no sane person would dare consume them no matter how easy they were to catch or how hungry you felt. It was just not worth the risk, no matter how well you might cook such tainted meat.

The Kriotin virus affected more than just the human race; many other species fared far worse. Almost every class of mammal also contracted a form of the same disease, which physicians had first thought was an overly-aggressive form of rabies, which the MN4 virus was commonly confused with during the first few vital months of its discovery. When it became painfully obvious that the usual conventional vaccinations were failing in patient trials, they had finally linked the sickness to the alien debris and dust particles expelled from the asteroids mass and its fallout that was filled with irradiated organic molecules, which had already dispersed throughout the Earth's lower atmosphere after the initial impact.

It was common knowledge that for eons, comets and asteroids frequently deposited such cosmic proteins and bacteria upon our little blue planet as they've done since the dawn of time, which in some scientific arenas were accepted as the original building blocks of life here on Earth. Apophis itself was no different, and there were no rules to say that whatever alien germ was hitchhiking on that lump of rock had to be benign or compatible with our ecosystem. Hell, we were long overdue for another biological plague anyhow, and it was certainly more interesting than influenza, or a watered-down version of a bird, swine flu, or another rampant Corona virus, which was nothing more than a fart in the wind compared to this typhoon.

Contracting KRI wasn't specifically fatal, and actually, fewer than half the people who were infected with it became dangerously violent, a majority of the patients simply regressed into something akin to severe autism or a dysfunctional depressive state rather than anything close to being manic or schizophrenic. The bulk of victims were usually unable to care for themselves and would waste away if left unattended. This category of infected became confused and unresponsive, they could not feed nor clothe themselves, or had any recognition for others. Survivors would often see them wandering the streets in an incoherent daze or huddled in dark corners, twitching in fear at every little sound. It was a horrible way to die.

At first, there were scattered rumors of a vaccine, but it wasn't a cure for those already infected. As it turned out, even that empty promise was a crap-shoot, it was just some antigen in its test phase created out of pure desperation to sate the public fears. Unfortunately, the virus was constantly mutating. Its genetic markers would change so that an antibody might work one day but not the next. Sometimes, entire families were wiped out in a matter of hours because they had a genetic weakness within their DNA at that given phase.

Some people never reacted at all as though they possessed a natural immunity, although their luck was short-lived, for those scarce few became the subjects of grim experimentation by cruel doctors who were both desperate and pressured by their local authorities to find a cure. Most often, the immune patient ended up as a dead guinea pig sliced up on a shiny steel laboratory table. It wasn't long before you realized that your best bet was to just keep your fucking distance from anyone who either looked infected or exhibited early-stage symptoms.

The early signs of infection were the real problem, given the catastrophe that affected everyone's lives. Most people were depressed as it was, and all too frequently innocent survivors who were unable to handle the stress, or were already crying over dead loved ones, sometimes ended up with a bullet in their head despite the fact they weren't actually infected. People were scared and all too willing to pull the trigger out of fear.

The whole world had gone crazy ...not that our species hadn't been insane all along.

Rain had begun to pelt the dirty glass of the windowpanes as I continued my exploration of the house, at least it would be a test if the roof would hold its own and keep me dry until morning. The first rule of surviving on your own is to scout out an entire building to make sure it was safe to be in. Unfortunately, near the end of the hall, I stumbled across a dark descending stairwell and vented an audible sigh of regret upon finding it.

"Well, shit," I whispered to myself in hesitation, knowing I had to investigate, though I really didn't want to.

It wasn't that I was afraid of the dark, but I spared no personal love for cellars since they most always had only one point of entry or exit. For a brief moment, I juggled the thought of sleeping in the barn outside instead, but by the condition I had seen of the rotting exterior and gaping holes in its roof, there was no way I was going to spend a dry moment out there in this storm. Besides the fact that one of its large doors was hanging askew from its frame with no means to secure it.

I set my flashlight on to its brightest setting and descended into the gloom below as the tattered floorboards creaked under the weight of each step. I spied odd ends of furniture and broken boxes, which were tossed about as if a whirlwind had passed through the room. This cellar was unusual, as its dimensions extended far beyond the footprint of the foundation of the house above; appearing to be nearly twice as large. Most likely, it doubled as someone's bug-out shelter back in the day and had been raided at some point by scavengers moving through the countryside. Still, I had to investigate to see if it was safe. Besides, there was always the remote chance I might find something of practical use which had been left behind; a coil of rope, or a can of fuel, pretty much anything that could come in handy for bartering or of use in a time of need.

It was when I turned the edge of the stairwell at the bottom landing when my heart suddenly stopped. I was used to seeing dead bodies, but what I saw before me left me in shock. In the narrow light from the lamp, my eyes pieced together the image of desiccated human arms and legs that intertwined in a layer of filth. As hardened as I was to such scenes, I still jumped when I saw a leg twitch, then an arm, and the huddled pile of Weeper's slowly began to stir. One after another, they wriggled up from the tangled mass to shade their bloodshot eyes from the glare of my flashlight. One of them hissed in annoyance as it peered into the blinding light just as their putrid stench hit me like a brick wall. Lying there coiled in their own feces, more than a dozen infected began to shamble to their feet. Flying up the stairs, I ran faster than I ever had in my life.

All of which events happened nearly an hour ago since I had disturbed the nest of weepers, which had chased me relentlessly through the wet forest. Duck and hide techniques are efficient enough when trying to escape their pursuit most of the time, but from the gaunt looks of this hive, it was rabid hunger that kept them lingering on my trail. No matter how much ground I gained, they would not give up. I assumed I had lost most of them among the thick layer of trees and rocky terrain but there were still a few stragglers I could not seem to shake.

It was by sheer luck that I had stumbled upon this collapsed office building, and realized I might stand a better chance if I found a way to barricade myself in rather than running blind through the sheets of rain during a violent electrical storm in the open. That is when I dove behind a massive broken pillar for a spare moment to catch my breath, shivering from the cold. As I huddled there in exhaustion, I peered across from me to notice an old oil painting of a merchant ship by an ocean dock with three girls standing near a grassy shore; the damaged canvas sitting crooked in its cracked frame that hung upon the far wall where its corner had been exposed to the rain; washing the paint from the image. Time seemed to stop for me in such moments; it was the way my mind seemed to cope with the stress of the nightmare my life had become, and what little sanity I had left to cling onto.

Apophis

I cannot count how many times I have asked myself if it was worth it all? Honestly, I don't actually think there's anyone who didn't ask themselves that question a hundred times over since the day of the impact. Understandably, there were no rulebooks to go by and very few 'intact' families had managed to survived this long; everyone knew the definition of loss in one form or another by now. Watching a close family member or friend turn into a dysfunctional cretin or a raging lunatic was tough, but showing sadness or distress over their suffering would only put you on a watch-list under suspicion of also being infected. Any emotional signs of remorse or sadness mirrored the early-stage symptoms and people would treat you like you were a rabid animal until a medical diagnosis could be administered to test your health; that is, if they didn't shoot you stone dead first.

Due to these symptoms mimicking emotional grief, the human race quickly drifted into becoming callous and unfeeling; which in many ways, made us worse than the poor victims who contracted the disease itself. In its wake, mankind lost an important sliver of its own basic humanity.

I gathered my strength and scrambled up the side of the shattered wall, finding the smooth concrete was dreadfully slippery in the pouring rain. Daring to look over my shoulder, I caught a glimpse of one of the weepers standing in the muddied clearing staring back at me. Whether its gender denoted it as a he or she was unclear, for its skin was covered with grime and tangled hair. It just stood there in a hunched pose as if in pain, and I could feel its glare wash upon me as a low growl issued from its broken lips. Frankly, I was astonished that they were able to pursue me this far through the storm. The human sense of smell pales in comparison to most animals, especially so in such harsh weather; but they might have retained their more predatory traits that enabled them to track my path through the woods. In my haste I hadn't exactly been as quiet as I had desired, snapping several branches as I pressed through the forest undergrowth and losing my balance more than once in the slick mud and brambles.

I was guessing there were two, or perhaps three of them still on my tail. There was no guarantee what would happen when they eventually caught someone. Sometimes a victim would just be stripped of their food and belongings, or might be beaten senseless if their prey struggled. In the rare cases, they were killed violently and their bloody bits and pieces consumed if the infected were exceptionally hungry. Our species were scavengers after all, and have been since the dawn of time. Regardless, any type of physical contact whatsoever signified a high chance of contamination, so when you saw a Weeper, you either hid or ran.

There were more than a few isolated cases where gangs of survivors assembled hunting raids to clear out the dangerous weepers who had escaped their isolation camps. Ethically, in my point of view, the infected were still people and it made me sick to my stomach whenever I saw them shot down in cold blood or the callous executions of the ones who were clearly unthreatening and harmless. Some people accepted it as a form of mercy but it was outright murder in most cases, especially when they put down the children. As far-gone as they were, there were still those who looked scared in that final moment before the end, as if it was some vile act of betrayal by their own species. After the government staff had abandoned the clinics, hospitals, and quarantine camps, everyone began to assume there was no actual cure, nor would there ever be one.

Truthfully, it is that loss of hope that weighs so heavily on your shoulders and of not knowing what tomorrow will bring. All I knew at this moment was that I didn't want to die like this; cold and wet in the middle of nowhere. Understandably, for most people the thought of catching the disease was even worse than death; cursed to be left alone to survive like a crazed animal or waste away as your mind turned to mush and losing all sense of who you were.

The suicide rates across the globe skyrocketed and continued to climb after the outbreak. In many areas there were survivor camps run by religious groups who preached empty hopes and offering salvation. In such instances, these fanatics were more dangerous than the disease itself. I even heard strange tales of newcomers in their midst who would argue with them why any God of theirs would allow this blight to befall them, only to end up murdered in their sleep for their blasphemy.

Personally, I never fell for the steaming pile of fraudulent crap they fed to the mindless masses. Religion was for the weak who desired to blame their actions on anyone or anything but themselves; or to wield as a personal excuse to harm another human being under the guise of some holy cause, as if to justify their disgraceful conduct. People killing one another over *'make-believe'* was a type of insanity I didn't want anything to do with.

* * *

In an adjacent building far above, a dark figure was watching from an open balcony, a hooded image that clung to the shadows, only outlined by the brief flashes of lightning that crackled through the dark skies. He watched the drama unfold below as the lone survivor was scrambling through the ruins of the office building towards a fenced field, with a pair of weepers in close pursuit. From his position, he could see the creatures were cornering their prey who was currently fleeing towards a dead end. From the 4th floor of the building that loomed above, a crack of gunfire resounded and the flash of an aiming laser glistened through the heavy rain, taking down a third weeper that had emerged from the dividing tree line.

* * *

Hearing the shot, I was startled and lost my footing; painfully twisting my ankle as I stumbled and cut my hand upon the broken concrete. Suddenly, the bright flare of a laser sparkled in the puddle at my feet and I ducked for cover behind a pile of rubble. I tried to peek through the cracks, aware that there was someone in the main building above placing me in their sights. I quickly realized that the sniper had thought either I was one of the diseased or that I was an easy target for pilfering my supplies. Stuck out in the open, I had no place to go.

Doubling back to the forest meant that I would have to take

my chances with dodging the group of weepers on my tail, and after nearly a full hour of running, I had no energy left to continue playing cat and mouse with them. My prospects of making it this close to dusk were close to zero. A few yards ahead there was a large fenced area that opened up beyond. Next to the gate, I could tell there was a small opening that had been jarred loose, inviting me a way inside. From there I could find shelter on the ground floor of the building where I had spotted a large pair of double doors moments before.

Jumping out from behind the broken wall, I sprinted for the hole in the fence; strafing as I went to avoid the sniper but a shot rang out as a flash of green light traced the ground in front of me. The bullet ricocheted off the cement just a few feet from my head, sending stinging shards of stone into my face. Whomever it was on the trigger had been waiting patiently for me to show myself. In a panic, I crawled back under cover from the gunfire just as I heard the familiar growl of the weeper that had followed me onto the upper wall. As a distraction, I leapt out and faked a jump out towards the fence once again, and pounced back in the opposite direction towards the corner of the building where I saw an open balcony. Another shot cracked the air as I made my way to the edge of the wall, my twisted foot throbbing in pain.

Almost losing my balance, I came upon a sudden drop-off. With too much momentum pulling me along, I leapt for the top of a loading truck that sat with its rear towards the wall. Hearing a metallic thump behind me, I turned to find that the weeper had also scrambled its way on top of the roof of the truck behind me, struggling in its fevered attempt to gain its footing on the slick steel. A quick glance told me that I had grossly misjudged the height of the balcony above. It was much farther away from the edge of the trailer's shell than I had calculated.

At this point, I realized I was cornered and didn't have any choice. If the creature behind me got close enough to touch me, the game was over. I almost faltered as the stab of pain shot up my calf when I took a running leap for the balcony, my numb hands grasping for the exposed rail. It was just too slippery, and time seemed to slow as I dug my nails into the metal, it was too slick with water and the pack I had on was far too heavy. I gasped for air as the rain pelted my face in the fleeting moment when my grip finally slipped free, knowing I likely would not survive the fall to the hard pavement below.

As gravity was pulling on every ounce of my being, my attention from the dark void looming below was turned upward towards the sheets of pouring rain that pelted my face as streaks of lightning lit up the cloudy sky. A strong arm had grabbed mine; I went dizzy, fearing my worst nightmare had come true and that I had finally been caught by a weeper. To my surprise, I could still hear the infected creature growling in anger behind me, its bony hands swooping in the air just a few feet shy of my rear. A gloved hand pulled me up to the edge of the balcony from where I hung in limbo, as I came face to face with someone wrapped in a heavy mask and goggles holding a sniper rifle as they rested the barrel upon my shoulder.

"Don't look at it, keep your eyes down and hold still!" A man's voice ordered.

I turned my head into the railing as instructed, and the kick of the rifle jabbed into my collarbone. Holding me up with his left hand on the edge of the rail, he had fired with his right, using my shoulder as a muzzle rest to get a proper aim. Seeing its prey was about to escape, the infected ghoul had made a desperate jump to grab my flailing legs; a ploy that would have worked if not for the force of the rifle blast that split its head wide open, sending its lifeless body skidding backward across the top of the truck. Its blood sprayed upon my back and across the balcony.

"Fucking filthy creatures," I heard the figure mutter to himself, "Keep your hands where they are, and don't touch the blood!" he warned, "I will pull you up." the man stated as he laid down his rifle and took my other hand to help me clear the edge of the rail. In a daze, I stood there for a brief moment, a bit stunned that I was still alive. The shock of the moment wouldn't stop there.

"Don't move, you're going to need to strip." he demanded as he secured his rifle and stood back while wiping some bloody muck from his goggles with a rag he threw to the ground and proceeded to do the same with the scarf which had covered his face.

"What?" I stuttered innocently, still startled by the turn of events; slowly coming to realize that I had been saved, only to be promptly robbed of my gear.

As his scarf fell away, it revealed the man had a slight beard, several days unshaven, but he left his goggles on. Leveling his rifle at me, he clicked off the laser sight with one hand but kept his finger squarely on the trigger.

"It's not what you think," he stated, though with a slightly apologetic tone, "there is contaminated blood on your pack and outer clothing; I need you to drop everything right here, right now," he ordered gruffly once again, "...you can keep your undergarments on," he added.

That would have been all fine and dandy ...if I actually wore underwear. As I undressed, he finally lifted up his goggles and I could see by the dumbfounded expression that washed across his face that he was not expecting to find a girl underneath all the layers of my gear and boyish exterior. I took care not to use my cut hand, which made it more of a struggle than an embarrassment as I stood there in nothing more than a soiled tank top and socks. Taking off my hat, my long blonde hair unfurled down to my waist. He just stood there gawking at me for an awkward moment.

"Is this good enough?" I finally asked as I rolled my eyes, "And I should thank you, I guess," I offered, still assuming he was the one who had been taking pop shots at me while I was down in the courtyard but he had still saved me from breaking my neck, "...If you don't mind, I'm hurt and tired, and it's *really* fucking cold out here!"

Presuming it was the freezing stutter of my lips that got his attention back to the situation at hand. He threw down his gloves in the pile next to mine as he checked himself over a second time for any splatter of blood from the dead Weeper. Once satisfied, he took one last scan of the open courtyard below as lighting crackled angrily through the sheets of heavy rain, then promptly escorted me inside the dark building.

"Try to watch where you step," he cautioned with a measure of concern, noting I was down to wearing mismatched socks, and even those were filled with holes, no less, "there's broken glass around here."

I was still shivering as we made it down the long turn of hallways, it appeared this had once been an industrial office building at one time; its adjacent sister structure had collapsed sometime in the recent past. It was dark in here and the waning glow of the setting sun had fallen fast due to the raging storm. The warm glow of firelight flickered at the end of the corridor where we were heading. Upon hearing hushed voices trickling down the hall, my host ran ahead and thankfully came back with a thick blanket to cover me up just before we turned through the doorway to be met with the startled gaze of several shocked faces.

All eyes in the room turned towards me. Nearest the door was a black man with muscled arms and an interesting array of dreadlocks nestled upon his head. His smile was followed by a girl with dark brown skin and long raven-black hair. Across from her, a middle-aged redheaded male with a buzz cut was whittling away at something in his hand with a pocketknife. Behind him was an older man with a receding hairline of ashen gray; within his sullen eyes one could see many years of hardship that had shaped his view of the world. To the far right, just out of the light of the miniature gas stove sitting in the middle of the room slept a young boy, curled up on a cot, fast asleep.

"Well, look at what the cat dragged in! I thought I heard some shots, was that you Thorn?" The man with the dreads inquired.

"Hmm, and not a bad catch at that," the dark-skinned girl turned to comment as the man sitting in front of the stove grinned in approval at her perverse sense of humor.

"She was cornered outside, there was a pack of weepers down in the yard," Thorn mentioned as he stepped into the room behind me. Upon this news, the older man stood up, clearly concerned at this report.

"How many are you talking about; and how did you get her inside?" he pried, realizing they had not come from the direction of the ground floor stairwell, all of which had been thoroughly blockaded. Thorn stumbled over to his cot and grabbed a clean scarf from atop the blanket, while he gestured for me to follow as he answered his companions.

"Just a few strays, I think; I didn't see any more," he remarked, "everyone, this is..." he paused, realizing that in his lapse of seeing me naked outside on the balcony, that he had entirely neglected to introduce himself or ask my name, "*what's your name?*" He whispered towards me while trying not to seem too obvious about it to the others.

"Uh, Caitlin," I answered through shivering teeth.

"Caity," he blurted back to the group, trying to seem nonchalant as if he had known my name all along; while he in turn, introduced me to the gathered rabble within the room. "Caitlin, this is Haiti," as he proceeded without further formalities while motioning to the black man who gave a wry smirk with a flash of his white teeth, "and Serena," turning to the raven-haired girl who couldn't resist the earlier sexist remark.

"Can I call her Cat?" Serena added with a hungry wink towards me as Thorn brushed aside the comment.

"Felix is our cook," he pointed over to the chubby red-haired man sitting in front of the tiny stove, which made his title appear a little pretentious. Behind him stood the older gentleman whose posture became slightly more relaxed after his initial stance, "Killroy, here, is a little older and wiser than the rest of us," Thorn added as a flavorless compliment, "I helped her over the balcony just above the dock," Thorn finally answered Roy, "and just barely at that," my host finished as he turned back to me with a faint grin on his face as he gently nudged me from behind in Serena's direction.

"And you are ...Thorn?" I had to inquire, which I thought was a slightly odd name. He just nodded back to me as the dark-skinned girl carefully took my arm to look at the cut on my hand. She guided me back to the shower room down the hall where they had moved a tub around to catch rainwater through the cracks in the ceiling above. I honestly didn't expect the showers to work when the girl turned the knob and helped me removed my makeshift robe, but water began to spurt, a little brown with rust at first but it cleared up after a minute.

"Get yourself washed up and I'll bring you some clothes, Kitten," which apparently was her pet name for me I began to realize; leaving me guessing that Serena was either extremely friendly towards strangers or that she was a brazen bisexual.

Stripping me of my blanket, she left me there, but not without a long sultry glance back at my bare ass. All I could do was hesitate, while wondering if she was actually being serious as I felt the warm water splashing at my sore feet. Stepping into the stream of the shower, I could feel my muscles begin to relax; at least it wasn't as unpleasant as the bitter rainfall outside. There must have been a water tank on the roof that fed these pipes which had retained its insulation.

Over the past several years, I had become accustomed to bathing in rivers or in the rain when needed, or gotten by with a soaked rag and pans of boiled water whenever the opportunity presented itself. I had almost forgotten how long it had been since I had a hot shower, but this lukewarm bath was still an unexpected privilege; even more so when I found a half-worn bar of soap lying on a tiled shelf, which I had assumed was for communal use. Turning off the knob when I was done, I stood there naked for a while and began to shiver again from the draft seeping into the room until Serena came back with something akin to a towel and an armful of clothes.

"Take these; you're a bit taller than me but they should fit," she offered while setting aside a small selection of garments. I could tell at first glance that she had grossly underestimated my height, in proportion to the offered attire. She was slight and a bit more on the athletic side, and not at all unattractive; but I could tell there was an ingrained attitude about her that might rub me the wrong way if we were stuck together in the same room for too long. Even so, I wasn't entirely ungrateful.

"Thanks," I added as an afterthought, "when can I get my own gear back?"

"Thorn said you got a bit of weeper blood on them, so they have to dry out completely for a full day before you can touch them again." she remarked.

Since my stuff was all in a pile out on a rain-swept balcony, I

figured it would likely not be sooner than later. I tried a few of
the garments on she had left behind, at least to keep me warm,
and hoped she wouldn't notice when I quietly tore a few rips in
the undersized shirt to stretch it out so I could breathe.

"Is that his real name?" I inquired out of mild curiosity to
make light conversation; as it was becoming ever more obvious
the girl was spending her attention watching me get dressed.

"Hah," she chuckled back, "no, no, it's something more
ludicrous like 'Jebediah,' I think, or one of those funny Quaker
names," she giggled, "we've been tagging along together as a
group for some time now. One night we found an abandoned
liquor storage and we all had the insight to burn our ID's after
having a few too many drinks while we crashed around a
campfire," Serena stated as she sat down, rubbing her wrist in
deep thought as her tone subsided into something a shade more
sincere, "so we decided, '*what the hell*,' there's no government
anymore and we can be who we want to be; so we made up our
new names." she sighed, and as she did so, I could tell her mind
was drifting a million miles away, "but my ID chip was
implanted like most people nowadays. All my medical records,
credit data, my work history, and related family..." she ended
with a faint whisper.

"Yeah, I was going to get one of those," I added to break the
awkward silence, knowing better at this point to not inquire
about her family since they were likely dead. It was a fresh scar
I could see in her eyes now, but these were memories we were
not able to shed a tear for ...at least not in public.

Her mood returned as dramatically as it had dissipated; which
was likely a self-groomed reaction. I followed her back as she
took a small detour to recheck the security of the barred doors
on our way back to the main room with the others. There was a
new makeshift cot waiting for me along with some cooking
utensils and a pack of dried noodles. Killroy saw that I was a
bit confused at first as to this solitary arrangement so he made
sure I knew the rules.

"Since you were exposed, you will have to cook your own
food for the next few days or so," he informed while keeping a
few steps distance, "and will ask that you don't touch anyone or

their stuff during that time, Miss."

Meaning they were keeping an eye on me, which was an understandable precaution. That is when I finally grasped that Serena's gift of clothing were actually hand-me-downs that she never expected to get back. I could see Thorn's gloves propped on sticks to dry by the propane fire, and turned to see him tucking in the little boy who was still asleep in the back of the room. It humbled me to realize that the score of events everyone had suffered stretching nearly the last full decade, as to just how hard this must have been on the children who would grow up only thinking this was how life was, and would never experience how the world used to be.

They would be calloused by the blunt hardships of the world around them, only to be cursed to having to hide it all inside. I imagined it must be like living within their own bleak emotional tundra while never being free to explore the joyful colors hidden in a world locked deep beneath a sheet of impenetrable ice, where no one was allowed to display feelings of sadness or sorrow. Thorn finally got up and came over to talk with me, though still keeping a notable distance.

"Who is that?" I inquired, nodding over to the sleeping child. Thorn turned a moment towards the boy with a heavy sigh as if my innocent question had just lit the slow fuse to a very long tale.

"It was about six months ago or so, I would guess, that we found him out by the edge of a city while making our way south, perched on the edge of a small abandoned camper," Thorn stated with a look of pity as he turned back towards me, "he was just sitting there all alone on the stoop as if he was waiting for someone to come home."

"No sign of his parents?" I inquired, though it seemed like a redundant question. Thorn just shrugged.

"Nope, and we don't know what happened to them either. He hasn't spoken one word since we met, and it was obvious he had been starving for quite some time," he added, "a few of us were worried that he might have been infected, as the symptoms, you know, are a bit similar, but he didn't show any physical signs beside his detached behavior."

"Maybe he's deaf, or possibly mute, and not able to speak?" I suggested.

"I don't think so, it just seems like he's in shock and doesn't know how to handle it. I've seen people respond like that before ...just not for this long," Thorn replied, "we checked out the trailer, but there weren't any photographs or anything to let us know his name, so we just call him, 'Kid.' He kind of picked up the nickname from Roy who yells '*hey, Kid, over here!*' at him all the time," he finished intimidating Killroy's deep voice as Thorn gave a foolish smirk while he motioned over his shoulder towards the older man.

"How did you find this place?" I asked while eyeing the dried noodles, the grumble from my stomach admitting I was sorely hungry. Noticing that, Thorn backed up, giving me a few feet within the zone of my courtesy quarantine which would last at least until tomorrow. He motioned for me to take the metal pot over to the stove and he graciously set down a canteen of water next to it for my convenience. Felix also stepped aside to make some room for me to cook as Thorn continued his story.

"We were all stragglers who happened upon each other down the road in one hairy situation or another," he smiled as if to welcome me to the club, "some of us have been together longer than others, and a handful of survivors we've known have already parted and gone their separate ways. We came upon this facility a few weeks back and it seemed like a good place to hold up through the winter storms," he managed to add, but with a certain lack of conviction in his breath.

"What was this place?" I asked as I finished stirring my soup while warming my fingers over the edge of the burners as the tiny blue flames licked their way up the sides of the pot.

"Ah, it looks to be an industrial building of some sort," Haiti added from the other side of the fire, inviting himself into the conversation, "although the office area seems to have seen better days," he noted, referring to the collapsed portion outside. It made sense; that was probably why there were so many freight trucks and a large loading dock below, and communal shower facilities for the drivers. Of course, this place did not resemble a Country Club, but I was just as interested in what it had been used for.

"Don't worry about it though, we scouted the property and blocked up all the doorways, so we're relatively safe here," Thorn assured me, "just try not to expose yourself in the day by standing in the windows, or use any lights in the outer area at night. It's better that nobody knows we're here, or to attract any unwanted attention," he added with a note of precaution; and it was good advice as I had also learned the same tactics for self-preservation over the years, "...but what's your story, Caity?" Thorn inquired with a soft grin, and he seemed genuinely interested to know.

"Yes Kitten, where are you from?" Serena chimed in from across the room. My sad story wasn't as complicated as most and was a tale that was all too familiar.

In my early twenties, I had taken off from the boring little town I had grown up in, to go to college out west. I had rushed around looking for a good job and a decent place to live in the rat race my life had become after leaving the security of my family. I was just striving for my own independence like any other child who breaks away from their parents, only to have mild regrets from time to time.

I was on my own at that point and had a long-distance lover I met a few times a year, as I never had the desperate need for a steady romantic partner, or having to constantly be responsible for placating myself to someone else's feelings on a daily basis. It was a lifestyle I had become accustomed to, because I would find it far too mentally exhausting if I ever woke up to find that I was tethered to somebody else that I had to answer to over every petty little thing. It just wasn't my style.

When the flyby of the asteroid was going to happen, every government and major news media assured us it was just going to be a harmless spectacle like Haley's comet, though it was promised to be a tad more impressive; being an only a 1 in a 1000 year event of its kind. Well, that it certainly was. The approach of the asteroid was broadcast worldwide but it was still considered a minor distraction, as mainstream media was overwhelmed with coverage of several petty incursions fueled by insanely volatile mixtures of political and religious wars, international tensions, foreign invasions, terrorism, forced occupations, etc. The list just went on, and on. It seemed like there were just too many people on the planet and not enough space for the human race to keep from bumping shoulders. Earth's population had tapped at over 10 billion, which far exceeded what the global census had predicted, all thanks to our mandatory health care laws pushing medical science and modern drugs that extended the average lifespan. Of course, the crooked pharmaceutical industry spitting out erectile dysfunction pills as though they were sex candy, which, fundamentally, resulted in people popping out babies as though they were going out of style.

Wars tended to act as the thinning of the herd, but not nearly as much as in the old days when people used knives, swords, or rifles; now encounters were automated by robotic war droids or remotely piloted drone bombers. In the countries that possessed the technology, real people were still pulling the trigger, but piloting a drone was still considered a chicken-shit way to fight a conflict. The over-bloated militaries around the world were too busy playing toy soldier to worry about caring for their own citizens and basic human needs. It's unfortunate how science leaned towards creating new ways to kill one another, but for the obnoxiously rich and the elite; that was where all the profit was.

I had just started college again after finding part-time work. Unfortunately, both AI and robotics had actually taken over a vast majority of the available jobs while I was growing up, which made things even more difficult for the unemployed. Aggressive trade unions began to spring up, meant to assure real jobs for real people; but it was a constant battle with large corporations to get them to comply with regulations that were typically never enforced.

The day when the shit hit the fan, I had been on the road out to see some friends out of town, after having gotten off late from work because my abusive boss had assigned me with a last-minute shift to work overtime. Back then, Apophis had been visible in the skies for weeks, however, the tall forest trees that lined the roads along my route obscured most of the night sky.

I was listening to my digital music since the radio reception was horrible in this area, so I was pretty clueless to the emergency broadcasts when I saw a bright pulsating flash which lit up the sky, followed shortly by a second surge. A ghostly blue wave crackled over the heavens for a brief moment and my electric car immediately cut out and went as dead as a doornail.

I found out much later that it had been a naturally induced EMP burst, which had rippled through the ionosphere, created by the detonation of the asteroid when it skimmed the Earth's atmosphere and broke in two. Fortunately, I had a few bottled drinks and a crapload of nutrient bars in my back seat, which I kept forgetting to put away since I was a tad forgetful at times.

My vehicle coasted to the side of the road and I got out only to find that my mobile link communications didn't work either. I waited for a long time out on that dark lonely road but nobody came. I slept in my car that night and didn't head out on foot until the welcome break of dawn that brought with it a strange wind. So there I was, playing pedestrian with a backpack full of diet bars, not fully realizing just how valuable they would become in the long days ahead.

A convoy of military vehicles, which had contained shielding from the electromagnetic pulse that swept through the atmosphere, began to cruise the highways and were picking up civilian stragglers that had been stranded along the roads. Ignorant as to what was going on, we were all a little dismayed when our convoy delivered us to a large military facility at the end of a dirt road out in the middle of nowhere. Apparently, there was a secluded training base along that particular highway that neither I nor anyone else had ever heard about, one which had never been recorded on any public map.

I was there for a few days with a handful of other civilians as we sheltered in a spare bunker during the erratic and brutal wind storms that kicked up in the days that followed, while the world outside went to hell. It wasn't long until one day we woke up and looked out the windows as we watched every last camouflaged soldier pack up and disembark, leaving us with orders to stay where we were for our own safety. Later that evening, our group heard a low hum echoing from the dark forest coming from droves of personnel carriers that arrived with scores of medical patients wearing masks. It was this new unit of officers in their spiffy white contagion suits that told us something dire was amiss.

They erected tables, then tents, then barricades, followed by barbwire as the few of us left watched from the exterior of this new containment fence. I was snooping around, when by chance I had overheard a pair of doctors during a hushed conversation, saying they planned to place all the civilians within the newly raised quarantine zone. With that concerning knowledge fueling my fears, I slipped out of the camp that evening under the strange glow of the aurora lights that peeked through the scattered clouds. These Northern lights were an entirely new weather phenomenon for this area as were the unusual lightning storms that seemed to erupt ever more frequently.

With little guilt, I was glad that I had been selfish over the weeks while in confinement and had taken the precaution to hoard my diet bars and a stash of canteens acquired by sleight of hand. The military rifle I had pilfered was a last minute-snag, an opportunity I could not pass up since fate had placed it within arms' reach when one of the careless guards had left to relieve himself in the can. I slipped away into the woods that evening, and have been on the run ever since.

Though the situation was looking bad, I was still alive and physically healthy considering the alternative, though mentally exhausted to a fair degree. The things I have seen and witnessed these past few years had molded me. It was the way society had fallen apart at the seams while average people had devolved into brutes willing to kill one another over a bottle of fresh water or a mere can of beans, had made me wonder what kind of future we were fighting for. The stories I could tell would fill a book. Maybe I would sit down one day and write one if there was anyone left to read it.

The Basement

I got the impression that a few of the members in this ragtag group were a bit less open than others; then again, it wasn't my place to pry. Whatever personal secrets or thoughts they had wished to keep to themselves were blotted out after they had discarded their past and assumed new identities. Some things were just downright hard to discuss, and to appear overly curious would only risk opening old wounds. I, like so many others, had been initially infatuated with reuniting with our families when the disaster occurred; no matter how much of a stretch from reality that might be. The hard truth was, the result of such a quest to pursue the fates of our loved ones would not end with an acceptance of what we may eventually discover.

Shortly after my escape from the quarantine camp, I had wandered into the outskirts of a small town, though I was wary about making contact with any hostile residents or accidentally stumbling within sight of any military personnel. After slipping into an abandoned home, I found several newspapers that recorded the world events I had missed during my isolation back at the camp. Actual newsprint was a rare thing to find as most people used digital pads for streaming information in our paperless society. I would occasionally find expensive phones and tablets tossed in the street like so much garbage, which had burned out and turned into useless bits of plastic and wiring by the massive EMP that had swept the globe.

The limited information I read therein stated how the MN4 asteroid had penetrated our orbit earlier than expected, and the official reports were that it had split into two sections due to a combination of atmospheric friction and Earth's gravitational forces. One half slammed into the Arabian deserts while the other came crashing down into the China Sea near the Philippines, with a majority of the loosely scattered debris showering over India. I recalled having seen a brief meteor shower on the horizon that first night as I sat alone in the woods in my car, but its view was mostly hidden by the tall woodland treetops. Needless to say, nobody was prepared for an aftermath of this scale. Impact on both land and sea combined into a colossal nightmare with devastating results. As it turned out, the dual electromagnetic pulse caused by both the asteroid sections, as they punched holes through the atmosphere, was merely the icing on the cake. In our electronic age, we had put far too much reliance on fallible digital technologies which had left us prone to such astronomical events. Apophis effectively turned off our modern civilization like a light switch.

Life was very hard that first year, especially so from all the fine debris kicked up into the atmosphere from the Saudi desert. Static storms covered the globe, frequently erupting without warning, especially in mountainous terrain. Out in the Far East, their populated shores were nearly entirely obliterated by tsunamis and aggravated earthquake zones which intersected alongside Indonesia. What the inland flooding had not destroyed, aftershocks did.

The initial death toll in that first week alone was stacked in the billions. Shortly thereafter came panicked rumors about radioactive debris, which only sparked further hysteria when the sickness was exposed. The enveloping cloud of the epidemic became ever darker when aggressive flesh-eating staph infections had turned public fears into utter chaos. Anyone with open or seeping wounds were at risk, and it was shown the virus could easily spread within shared living quarters, upon clothing, and even blankets. The overcrowded conditions of the hastily erected medical camps had provided an optimal environment for the disease to proliferate.

Such outbreaks were rare, but the panic it spread among the surviving population brought out the worst in people. Remove all rules and consequences from society and it will test the true character of your fellow man. In every single case these provisional medical bases had evolved into quarantine camps, and I made well sure to keep a wide berth from them whenever I strayed into their midst.

I once camped for several months with the remnants of a small family along a backwater village road, who had the blessing of their home being well-hidden from the main streets by the forested rim of a mountain. I traded my lodging by frequently scavenging for supplies in the nearby city and helping watch over their two little girls as their loving parents held onto their own fading measure of sanity. It was dangerous scouting the central streets of the city where the Weepers ran rampant, so I kept to searching the outskirts of town. This new pestilence had turned every metropolis into a mass graveyard. Dead bodies, or what scattered remains were left of the corpses, littered the streets. Fires burned uncontrolled, and I watched over time how once angry crowds that mobbed the urban avenues had slowly dwindled over the months into nothing more than a handful of cautious survivors warily picking their ground.

Nearly every store had either been looted or was a haven for infected rats and vermin that posed as much of a danger as the people who were afflicted. They ate off the dead, as did the birds who were not as vulnerable to the virus; but which in turn, infected any stray dog or cat that might consume their remains. With luck, I could usually find slim pickings among abandoned apartments and larger office buildings with private cafeterias. Clean water also became scarce, since you could not even trust the rainwater that might harbor the bacteria draining into the streets and gutters. Everything that wasn't properly bottled had to be boiled; making daily life a real pain in the ass.

Though the steep decline in population assisted in making those chance encounters of dangerous groups far less frequent, there was still the ever-present and growing hordes of the infected emerging from the outbreak. Dozens of times I came across the diseased who were alone, either huddled into dark corners or wandering aimlessly in a store or mall, grunting to themselves incoherently. Some Weepers just stood in place, as still as a statue as if they were an abandoned store mannequin, which made such encounters creepy and unsettling. Such confrontations were especially frightful if they went undetected and you accidentally stumbled upon one within arms reach.

Groups of armed survivors often went on rampages, screaming 'Zombie Hunt' as they picked off the infected one by one.

Unfortunately, even innocent bystanders weren't safe either and were frequently gunned down in the heat of the moment. It was sickening to witness such reckless behavior that only served to further spread the blight among the feral pets and hungry vermin that roamed the ruins.

One day, while charged with watching their little girls as the mother slept and father was out gathering firewood, I had been distracted while cooking them a meager meal only to come out to find the youngest child crouching within a shadowed corner of the yard while her sister was sitting at the dinner table inside. The child stood there in her faded white dress, quietly petting a dead squirrel, its eyes filled with blood and pus. I stood there emotionally paralyzed for a long horrified moment, shocked in silence while the little girl pouted while she caressed its furry head down to its limp bushy tail, as she hoped in quiet vain that the little creature was sleepy and might soon wake up; until I finally mustered the courage to speak, and told her in a cold-stiff tone to put the dead animal down.

I could not bring myself to wake the mother as she slept soundly in her bed, oblivious to what had befallen her youngest child; I bit my lip raw wondering how to explain how I had failed to protect her daughter. Their father was out collecting wood and would be back by daybreak, so I kept my distance from the adolescent and everything she touched until nightfall. I left a note for their father, scribbled in charcoal from a burnt stick I found in the fire he had built that morning. I simply couldn't bear to watch the misery that would unfold when he read it come daybreak. That very eve, I slipped away into the night while they were sleeping. The crack of a single gunshot I heard echo through their small valley in the early light of dawn, still haunts me to this day.

There have been moments in my life I wasn't exactly proud of, but I try to learn from my mistakes rather than ignore them. Far too many people who gave up every shred of hope went crazy. I tried not to be one of them. There were more times than I can count when I honestly entertained the idea of putting that gun of mine to my head, but something kept me from doing it. I was stubborn, like my mother.

Thorn and his odd cluster of rowdies had made a temporary home here within the industrial building but hadn't quite mapped out the entire complex at this point. There were still a handful of sections which had been blocked off by locked metal doors but I was willing to help with a bit of exploration if they needed me. As I slept, the elderly man, 'Roy', as Killroy's nickname, had kept a keen eye on me through the night. If I had shown the slightest sign of symptoms, I am sure he would have personally escorted me down the hall and pushed me off the balcony with a ten-foot pole.

However, he checked me again in the morning with a minor exam, flashlight in the eyes and inspecting my gums, and a short verbal test to see how coherent I was. Apparently, he had some minor experience in the medical field. At least he was kind enough to bandage my cut hand, which had begun to heal normally. Roy made sure to set some additional ground rules if I should choose to stay with them, one of which was to note the level of the rooftop water tank that was low and we were to keep our showers sparse. Followed by instructions not to take food or rummage through anyone else's stuff and promptly report anything unusual that could pose a danger to the group. Pretty much all of it was common-sense advice.

The little boy had awoken and Thorn brought the child a plate of food to eat. He looked a bit under the weather as if he had a cold, which Felix later confirmed while we shared the gas stove. Haiti was in a pleasant mood, eager to check more floors as he wiped down a few metal pry bars with a soiled rag. He commented how it was *'just like Christmas'* whenever they found a room with any amount of useful stash. Food, of course, was the top priority on the treasure list, but as the scavengers we had all become, each of us had our own set of values to the knick-knacks and equipment we might stumble upon. Basically, if you couldn't eat it nor use it for protection; it was usually considered worthless weight.

It was a vast change from being on the run. Here, I could keep clean and dry and not be constrained by the limitations of what I could carry. Thorn helped me set my pack items out to dry on a makeshift clothesline in the hall and he let me borrow a pair of rubber gloves to set them out, making sure I understood they would only be safe to handle once they had completely dried through. I appreciated their strict precautions; it was the only way they had survived this long.

It was Roy's turn to get some shuteye after having kept vigil over me the night before while Felix kept guard in the main room with the child. Serena and Thorn carried a few flashlights along with the crowbars Haiti had supplied; who was my assigned partner during this excursion.

They had only arrived here a short time ago, and there were still a few upper floors and the basement area below the shipping dock that were left on the list to be explored. A few were merely utility rooms that bore nothing but stagnant cleaning supplies and burnt-out wiring. I was glad to hear they had yet to find any cadavers, assuming the entire complex had been abandoned after the asteroid hit. We could glimpse ragged desk calendars still set to that blighted date as ghostly reminders of our cursed past.

Wire cutters and other tools were prized finds, as were anything that passed as a sealable container. Discovering sanitary towels or even toilet paper rose to the level of luxury items, but truly useful articles such as bleach for sterilizing had long degraded since it only had the shelf life of a year or less. Medical alcohol was the only true alternative, but had limited uses. It was humbling to see just how many daily household items we used to take for granted in the past could disintegrate so quickly over the years. Our modern society had become lazy and far too overly reliant on the conveyor belt of excess we lived by, which everyone so readily abused.

Remove global mass transit from the equation and life quickly comes to a screeching halt. Many people died because they had absolutely no clue what to do if a meal did not come from a deli or in a frozen tray from a grocery store. City dwellers fared the worse. When water stopped flowing, toilets ceased to flush and sewers backed up onto the streets; the reeking stench of it would drift for miles and only added to spreading more illness.

Frozen foods had rotted within days with no power to keep anything refrigerated, and expired canned food was a crapshoot for botulism after several years. Fuel for small generators became a rare commodity, almost as much as it did for spare parts when they would begin to fail. Years later, everyone had used up the last of their stashes and was left to endure hardships far beyond their wildest expectations.

On the top floor, we broke into a sizable office room that apparently belonged to the plant chief where we found money scattered around the floor. It was just useless paper at this point not even worth burning. I knew there were some people who resorted to using it in place of toilet paper; but money was incredibly unsanitary. Of course, old habits die hard, and during the first several months of the pandemic people continued to use paper currency for barter as it had always been before, without realizing that they were handling, in essence, a used napkin that had been touched by countless individuals who might have been exposed to the virus.

Paper money soon became a possible, if not prime carrier of the virus, which was quickly exchanged through many hands on an hourly basis. It was an oversight of basic logic that cost a lot of people their lives; and it wasn't until much later that people got a clue that they were helping to spread the taint among the survivors.

The fact was that most people were left without anything that could be used for tender since most everything that related to currency was done through debit cards and implanted ID chips. All that digital information had been wiped out in the EMP surge. With all the electronic money gone, a good many people who had once considered themselves well-off solely by the amount of digital capital in their bank accounts and the placement of the decimal points in their investment portfolios, had suddenly found themselves destitute in the financial collapse, and were left to beg and scrape just like everyone else.

It was pitiful to see how those individuals, who had valued themselves solely by their possessions alone, had let themselves become so entirely stripped of their character. Personally, I found it to be a fundamental disappointment in the human race as a whole, to realize that so many people lived such shallow lives in our day and age. Many individuals with that type of mindset became even more erratic and mentally unbalanced than the infected themselves, for there is nothing more dangerous than someone who has nothing left to lose.

Within the chief's office, an array of digital tablets were neatly stacked upon an array of color-coded shelves; their lifeless screens made them nothing but expensive paperweights since printed data was rarely ever used. There was a hologram photo of the plant's boss and his family hanging on the wall. They looked like your typical upper class; domesticated trophy wife standing beside her overweight husband, their two children wearing identical school jumpsuits. Their robotic nanny poised in the background merely as a status symbol to their peers.

The quartz display on the wall that would have brandished his name was now blank, all the electronic devices were damaged from either the EMP or their batteries that had corroded and destroyed their fragile innards. The only thing of notable value was a diagram of the factory levels hanging on the wall, which is where Haiti took a note of special interest.

"Hey, Thorn, come take a look at this," Haiti motioned.

We all followed in kind, wondering what it was we should be looking at. The holographic glass frame allowed a three-dimensional image of the building's interior layout to be viewed at a variety of angles. Such laser engraved glass was typically used by contractors and architects for prestige since they were fragile and had little practical use in the field. Haiti pointed to an array of large circular structures located in the basement. What they were was not quite clear. It was an area they had not yet been able to access since that section was locked behind a pair of massive security doors.

"Ah, that must be the area behind the bulk doors at the ass end of the lower dock, on the bottom level," Thorn responded, as he pointed to the hologram, "maybe its time we took a look down there," he suggested.

We slowly made our way down from the top floor, prying open any locked doors we passed along the way to see what we could find. From what I saw, their crew had done a decent job of barricading the facility from the inside, allowing only for a single hidden entrance and an emergency escape by a coiled rope off the second-story balcony. Their preparedness and foresight helped me feel a bit more comfortable, since they seemed to have a better grasp of sensible necessities than most groups of people I had met in the past. Shit could go wrong in a heartbeat; we all knew that from experience.

The lower dock angled in from the ground level, though any access via the storm shutters had been closed off. Several large hauling trucks were chaotically arranged within the garage as if they had been abandoned in a panicked rush. Blocked behind them was a large set of sliding double doors running nearly the entire width of the sizable carport. After an initial inspection, it was clear these gates were disabled and could only be opened by the remote switch located in a small booth to its side. However, without electricity, there was no way to operate it. The doors were too large and its gears were sealed behind the thick barrier wall. Whatever was inside was well protected.

After mulling over our options, we rolled one of the trucks out of the way and Haiti came up with a workable plan to rig the access conduit with juice by directly connecting a line to the electrical grid outside the lower building. It was the same fenced-off area that I had almost stumbled into when I was being chased the day before. Thorn finally got around to clarifying why he had taken the liberty of putting a few pop shots in my direction earlier in the courtyard; while humbling himself under my tempered glare.

"I had an eye on you since you exited the forest, and the group of afflicted that were in pursuit. When you climbed over that wall, I was trying to take out the Weepers whenever I had a clear shot, but saw you were about to run into the grid," he explained, "so I tried waving my laser sight in front of you as a warning not to go that way, but you were either ignoring the signal or didn't see it, so I placed a few warning shots at your feet as a final resort."

I recalled seeing a few transformers and wired scaffolding beyond the fence through the sheets of rain, but did not realize it was still active.

"You mean that power grid is still live, but how?" I inquired, knowing that electrical lines everywhere had been down for years, especially so in a place this remote.

"After a few weeks here we realized just how dangerous that section of the yard was, especially during electrical storms," Haiti answered for him over his shoulder, "it's like a lightning magnet and anything in range of it gets fried. Ole' Thorn here kept you from being barbequed," he smiled at me with his cheesy grin while patting Thorn on the back.

The mish-mash of steel and busted capacitors could hold residual electricity from a lightning strike for several weeks. Dangerous voltage would hum through the structure for days after being zapped by a thunderbolt. A few of the lights would still hum on, but most had been fried or popped from the frequent power spikes. They pried open the back access door to the grid area with a wooden rod to show me, pointing out a few smoking remnants of dead weepers that had recently wandered into that mess.

"It lit them up like a match," Haiti gleamed as if it had been a spectacle to behold, "Eh! Don't touch nuth'in, girl!" He warned as he quickly lifted my arm away with his wood pole from contacting the metal handrail just outside the hatch, "It'll still give you a good zap," he cautioned. I didn't want to get cooked, so I took a step back at his lead.

Though the storm had passed, I could still hear a low hum coming from the Grid and felt it in the ground at my feet. This place was still juiced up and we worked out a way to make use of it. We went back upstairs and pulled out all the excess wiring we could find. Felix came along to assist us, while giving helpful instructions not to bother with anything below a certain gauge of thickness. After several hours of labor, we had pieced together a cable starting from the access panel in the garage that led all the way to the outer hatch where Felix stood alone; all decked out in black rubber gloves, thick dark goggles, and a makeshift handle from a broken broomstick. I could tell he was not feeling so keen about being at the charged end; the nervous stutter in his speech gave that away.

"Ah, okay, you guys ready down there?" He shouted down the hall to Serena, who in turn gave me the verbal signal that I relayed to Thorn all the way down to the garage where Haiti stood waiting.

The dark-skinned islander had previously wired up the conduits under the panel. With a final shrug of his shoulders, he turned and gave us a thumbs up; hoping he had gotten the polarity right. Felix made the connection and angry sparks shot out the stray bits of wire down the line, we all jumped back, as did Haiti, when the panel in front of him erupted like a box of fireworks.

"Ah! Eee, Stop! STOP ya ginger-headed freak!" the black man screamed as he fell back, shielding his face, "Tell him to only make contact in short taps!" he instructed Thorn to relay up the line as we followed in turn shouting the orders back to Felix, who sat nervously at the smoking end of the hot cable, trying his best not to choke on the burnt rubber wafting from its tips.

Following his advice, the crackle of sparks shot down the wire where Haiti had fixed the connection in haste. With a clank and squeaking of metal, and grinding of dry gears, the colossal doors began to part. After resisting a few feet, the creaking metal began to stall and Haiti yelled back for Felix to halt. Felix disconnected the power cable and resealed the outer door, and the rest of us made our way back down to the garage where he was waiting. The group of us gathered close to peer into the dark narrow gap beyond the breach.

Thorn snatched his rifle, followed by Haiti, who grabbed his favorite shotgun while stuffing a large machete in the back of his belt. Serena donned a pistol, though she did not appear too worried about needing to use it. She contended that if this area had been sealed off like this for the past several years then there likely wasn't anything alive left lurking inside. We decided to take our weapons just the same.

My solar light had fully charged from sitting out on the balcony the entire afternoon, and we let Felix go back to clean the rank of soot and burnt scraps of rubber from his hands. The four of us could handle this alone, and we really didn't like the idea of calling it a night leaving this door cracked open without knowing what was on the other side. The trailer beds in the outer dock suggested that there was something big in there. We double-checked our gear and ventured into the still air with light steps. An eerie silence greeted us as we made our way inside, the kicking of every small pebble echoed off distant walls which lay shrouded in the darkness beyond the reach of our lights.

The ramp-way extended just a little farther into the basement until it leveled off. Within, we were faced with half a dozen tall stainless steel doors arranged in a semicircle. High above, I could make out a set of conveyor rails, their hooked chains retracted onto thick spools. It was a real mystery as to what they were for, as none of us had seen anything like this before.

"What the fuck is this place?" Serena blurted out, reflecting everyone's shared dismay.

Thorn wandered off to inspect one of the large rounded doors and tapped on a glass plate located next to it. There was a similar box beside each of the sealed doors. Using the butt of his rifle, he tapped the glass hard once, and smashed it open on his second try. He glanced over us and shrugged just before depressing the large red button that was positioned beneath the broken glass.

We were startled when its frame lit up and a loud siren wailed with flashing red lights above the door where he stood. Some sort of emergency back-up power connected to it was still in operation and we took several steps in reverse when the silver door slid out then folded up like a submarine hatch as thick steam seeped out around its edges. With a hiss, the door jolted to a halt, and after our moment of shock, we dared to peek inside.

A dim blue light pulsated around a sizable central dome, its edged speckled with polished silver bars. I was completely baffled, and by the look on Serena's face, so was she. Haiti ventured to step inside to get a better look at the device, brushing aside the mist of ozone with his hands. It took him a while to determine what it might be as he shined his flashlight into every crevice for a clue to how it worked.

"What is it?" Thorn finally inquired with impatience as he squeezed up next to him. Haiti tucked his finger under his chin in thought for a moment before speaking his mind.

"Ya know, if ya ask me, I would swear this was a hydrogen

generator," he exclaimed, tapping the side of the cone, "and this here is the coil." as it made a metallic 'thunk' similar to a water-filled tank when one of the many rings he wore touched the outer plate, "Them there are magnetic coils around the edge," he mentioned while pointing at the polished plates, "when engaged, this thing lifts itself up on a magnetic field so it can spin at high velocity while ionized water is injected from below ...or above, I can't tell which." he corrected himself while standing on his toes to inspect the top of the cone.

That could have explained why the system still had power and there was such a large transformer array outside the building. This complex was an energy bank. However, that hypothesis still left us confused.

"I thought hydro was made into a gaseous fuel, not electrical energy," I wondered aloud. Haiti looked confounded for a brief moment and then raised his finger as his eyes widened.

"You're right lass!" he smiled back, "The design of these creates wave energy meant for battery storage, but they must have some other secondary purpose." Haiti rattled on, though he still seemed confused about something since the piping in this room failed to present any answers to where exactly the hydrogen gas was being pumped off too.

Any industrial complex with such a dangerously flammable substance would have enormous external silos for storage, but there were none to be found in the area. Given that fact, and that we could not figure out what these large trucks could possibly be hauling in and out of this lower bay. We knew what we had found was incredibly valuable; the question was, how could we make practical use of it?

The men mulled over the thought that there might be an underground pipeline sending it off somewhere like a buried gas line. Fossil fuels had run thin during my adolescence, especially with petroleum, creating a serious energy crisis that peaked every few years and gravely strained the global economies in every nation. After that period, it seemed like more and more Resource Wars began to spark worldwide. Everybody was stuck in their old ways, as the global corporations that controlled the flow of energy had no desire to take a loss on their aged assets by going cold turkey and transitioning to new technologies and renewable energy.

Here, we were looking at proof of such scientific advancement right in the face. We were left a little baffled, wondering who had paid for this advanced military-grade machinery, and what the hell was it doing way out here in the middle of nowhere hiding under an unassuming office complex? We figured Roy might have the answer since he was the oldest of our group. There was only a single control nest in the upper walkway that throttled the conveyors on the ceiling, but there was no other additional passages beyond this room. We were all hungry and tired at this point, so we headed back up to the main hall with the rest of the gang to tell them what we had found. It had been a long day, and I was ready to get some sleep myself.

As we sat around making more dried noodles on the tiny stove we shared, each of us swapping places with our own personal cooking pots. Both Haiti and Felix threw around ideas about what this place had actually been, so I butted in and suggested the obvious; that we should recheck the manager's office on the top floor again for anything we might have missed. I realized that any digital data had been erased but there was always a possibility of finding something that might provide a clue.

The rest of them had already planned to squat here through the coming winter if food supplies held out, so it wasn't like we didn't have time on our hands to explore this place in depth. Oddly, we noticed there was no company signage outside the complex itself nor printed on the sides of the vehicles, but there was also a good chance any identifying information might have been on the adjacent office building that had collapsed. Thorn and his group had originally found this place by pure luck while skirting a frontage road; even given the fact that the forest had reclaimed most of the area. From the layout of the facility, there didn't appear to be ample parking areas that could actually hold a large number of employees which it appeared this place had been built for. Then again, it was impossible to estimate with any degree of accuracy because of the collapsed sister building was nothing more than a giant pile of rubble.

There was always the chance the staff workers had been

ferried here by a company bus or some other mass transit, but that was a long shot. Only a single-lane access road led out of the facility, which was now nearly obliterated by overgrowth. We sat around in the dim light of our lanterns, swapping stories about where we had once lived or places we had dreamed of seeing but never had the chance to visit. Such conversations as these between survivors frequently led to hushed moments when we wondered what was still left out there beyond the horizon and where our lives might take us, which ended with someone searching for somber words that would dwindle into inevitable silence. It was a hard question to consider, as if all our dashed hopes and dreams now only lived in the distant past with no real place left to linger in the present.

Thorn wanted to make it to the coast and joked about naming an entire beach after himself. Serena made the point that he should change his name again first, otherwise nobody would want to vacation there; which got a laugh from everyone. Felix wanted to travel to Asia, just to see if the old ways of the Buddhist monks had survived in their solitude. Serena dreamed up something far more exotic; to head far south to live in the jungle, a concept Haiti identified with ...as long as there was an adequate number of naked Amazonian women there for his personal harem, of course. Roy had thought the best chances for survival were actually to travel north and possibly team up with any groups of survivors and those with the skills to rebuild civilization, but finally did admit he might actually prefer to find a quiet cabin in the woods to live out his final years alone.

As for me, my dream was the most outrageous and even surprised myself when I lingered on the thought of it long enough. I always wanted to explore all the areas destroyed by the impacts, the barren coasts and the devoured shores, to trek the burning oilfields of the Saudi deserts and their lifeless dunes, which had been drastically transformed into a bleak alien landscape. The thought of all the dead had not entered my mind, I just wanted to see what life had survived, the plants and animals that had struggled and thrived through this calamity. In my own way, I would find that personally comforting.

Fallhaven

In the early hours of the morning before the break of dawn, we were awoken by a strange clicking noise that we could feel through the cement floor, a repetitive tapping that reverberated throughout the structure of the building. Even the young boy woke up, looking about bewildered. Roy was on his feet in no time with a cocked gun in his hand. Thorn and the rest of the crew looked just as confused as they hastily pulled on their pants and boots, all of us looking the worse for wear for this untimely arousal.

"What the fuck is dat' man?" Haiti blurted in his pigeon-English accent. Thorn checked on the boy for a moment, then grabbed his rifle and flashlight.

"What's going on?" I inquired softly, feeling just as groggy as the rest of them looked.

"We don't know, we've never heard anything like this before," Roy replied in a serious tone, "Serena, get to the balcony and check outside, and make sure to keep your light hidden," he ordered to the dark-haired girl who had switched on her flashlight. He glanced over to Thorn and motioned for him to join him as they made their way to the stairwell. Haiti got ready to follow in kind, but was advised to wait until Serena made her rounds in case she found anything unusual to report. I wasn't going to just sit here, so I threw on my boots to follow after the two men.

The three of us made our way down the stairs into the lower dock to determine where the source of the vibration was coming from. Entering the garage, we heard the metallic tapping echoing from behind the large metal doorway we had opened the night before. That got us worried. Creeping our way towards the portal, we shone our lights inside, their beams cutting into the darkness. The silver hatch Thorn had opened was still ajar but now a dim blue light inside was blinking where the metal cone sat. This was Roy's first look at the mechanism, so he approached it with due caution.

"That's the thing Haiti thought was a generator," Thorn explained to the older man as he stepped inside the small circular room.

"Are there more of these in the rest of them?" Roy asked with a hint of suspicion, referring to the adjacent silver doors that lined the lower dock. Thorn and I merely shrugged at his question.

"Don't know, we didn't open the rest; but I would assume so," Thorn replied. Both of them stood by the object trying to figure out the actual source of the sound and were suddenly startled when a ear-popping 'clack' from the cylinder resounded as it jerked sharply, which made the two men jump back a full two feet. It had appeared that the generator was attempting to spin but was meeting resistance as if the internal coils were stuck.

"Get out!" Roy shouted to us as we all backed away, "Close the door!" he screamed again over the partial deafness from the ringing in our ears. We all stepped out in haste as Thorn moved to the box beside the door and mashed the button again repeatedly with his hand, but to no avail.

"It won't close!" He yelled as the cylinder tapped violently again. Roy waved his light around frantically, looking for something when he finally spotted the control nest on the upper walkway placed just above the sliding doors to the dock. Finding an access ladder, Roy scrambled up to the booth under the red glare of the flashing beacon. Once on top, he fiddled with the control board and its affixed joystick he found there but was only left frustrated when he realized there was no power to the panel itself. Thorn and I looked on expectantly up towards Roy as the cylinder continued to rumble.

"It's no use, that panel only controls a crane by the looks of it, there is no bypass to reseal that cell," Roy yelled over the noise, while pointing at the generator containment door behind us after he hopped back down the ladder. We headed back out up the ramp to the upper dock where we could hear each other more clearly.

"You didn't find any other access points?" Roy inquired.

"Nope, that chamber appears to be a dead end. Should we

open the other hatch's and take a look inside?" Thorn replied. Roy shook his head in strong disagreement.

"I would advise against that, but we should scout the area outside of the building to see what else is behind there," he suggested, "but my guess is this section it's connected to is buried underground, by the looks of it," Roy stated as he estimated the dept of the lower section. Thorn nodded in approval, though with a certain degree of reluctance.

"Hey ...is that thing going to blow?" He had to ask.

"Who knows," the gray-haired man answered, "if that really is a hydro generator, it's not the water source we have to worry about, but if there is any hydrogen vapor that's built up inside that thing it might very well ruin our day and take this building down with it," Roy shot back with a grim look.

We quickly made our way back upstairs to find that Felix had finally awoken, as he had somehow slept his way through the noise of the disturbance. We saw Serena there sitting on the edge of a table as Haiti had taken over her post on the balcony outside. The thumping vibration continued from below.

"There's nothing out there, what did you find?" she asked.

"That generator you exposed last night is kicking around like a caged mule," Roy responded, "we need to get eyes outside to investigate what that thing is connected to out back."

He ran off to find Haiti several floors above, keeping guard. The old man's first worry was that the noise might attract unwanted guests to our location, which was exactly the kind of attention we were trying to avoid. Luckily, this complex was so remote that there was little chance of foot traffic by looters or wandering infected, however, low-frequency noise could travel for miles in all directions. Thorn had taken out the few stray weepers that had followed me through the woods here, and there was no sign that any others had roamed into the area in the following days since.

Thorn decided to recruit me to help him survey the space outside the rear of the complex. He kept watch via his scope on top of the roof at the rear of the building. Roy was kind enough to escort me out over the second-floor balcony by the strung rope while Haiti kept watch on top of the ledge. Roy was actually pretty fit for his age and seemed more critical in his decision-making than the rest of us. There was clearly something more disciplined about his character that made him difficult to approach on a friendly level.

After hitting the ground outside in front, I shouldered my assault rifle and we made our way around to the back under Thorn's line of sight from high above. There was a field to the rear of the building that had been cleared of trees. Here, the young vegetation had begun to set in, but there were no larger trees more than a few years old. Small bushes had sprouted around the area within a rusted barbed wire fence that had fallen into ruin. We kept our eyes on the forest's edge; relying on Thorn to give us due warning in case he spotted anything.

"What do you make of this?" I inquired, kicking what appeared to be an old rusted beam bolt half-buried in the ground. Roy tromped over to have a look, and that was when we began to notice that there were actually dozens of them scattered around, littering the area in a wide swath. They were easy to miss among the tufts of dried grass from any given distance at first glance. Roy seemed to be in deep thought for a moment before he dropped the metal bolt back to the ground.

"Hmm, it might be nothing, but keep your eyes open," he finally replied, stating the obvious as we had several open acres to cover. Something still bothered me about this wide vacant meadow that I couldn't quite grasp. Growing up in the countryside, I could usually tell when something was out of place. That is when it hit me; that this small fenced area appeared unusually level compared to the sloping hillside that eased next to it.

From the outside, we were glad to notice we could barely hear the pulse of the generator from below, but of course, we would much rather have it go dormant again. After asking Roy what we should be looking for, his guess was for anything that appeared like exposed piping or a junction box. If there was a pipeline of some sort below us, the contractors had done a damn good job of hiding it, or it had simply become camouflaged by all the overgrowth that had sprung up in recent years.

After finding nothing further of real interest, Roy and I began to make our way back to the front entry when Thorn shouted out to us from above. We turned about just in time to see a puff of dust erupt from the ground near the far edge of the field. I could not see it from this distance until the cloud of dirt finally settled. A tainted metal cylinder several feet wide had forced its way up through the soil. At first, I had thought it was a broken piece of pipe, but that thought was quickly subdued when a radiant blue laser spread from the shaft in all directions.

Roy grabbed my jacket collar and pulled me down behind a broken slab of concrete just before the light swept over us. It was a horizontal beam a few feet off the ground so it had no way of contacting Thorn who sat transfixed far up on the roof, several floors above us.

"What was that?" I asked Roy as he released my coat from his grip, while noting a similar look of worry had also crept over his chiseled face.

"*Shhh*, just keep quiet!" he whispered under his breath.

The beam pulsed as it scanned the area for half a minute, then abruptly shut off, but the cylinder remained transfixed as several panels on its surface popped open and shut. We stayed there hidden behind the toppled slab for several minutes, just peeking beyond its edge at the mysterious object. The thin slits in the stained metal core finally closed and it sat there silently for about five minutes before we heard a loud bang centered far below our feet. Less than a minute later, the tall metal pipe slowly slid back down beneath the surface and out of sight.

Roy grabbed me to make a run for the corner of the building as we made our way back around to the front entry. Haiti saw us and let down the rope again so we could climb back up. Seeing how nervous we were, he was a bit curious about what we had found.

"So what's the rush, something chasing you, man?" Haiti inquired, having no clue what had just transpired from the blind side of the building. Ignoring him, Roy climbed the rail and set off down the hall at a hefty pace.

"Was that some type of automated defense?" I hollered after him, but he didn't bother to respond.

I stayed behind and filled in Haiti about what we had seen, but that led to even more questions. Grabbing my light, I chased after Roy down the stairwell. There in the docking garage, we were surprised to find that the great sliding doors we had left ajar were now sealed shut. It was also obvious that the noise from the whining generator beyond had also ceased. We both immediately turned around and made our way up to the roof.

I was exhausted from running up the flight of stairs. Up on top, we found Thorn still crouched on the roof, looking through his scope at the location where the cylindrical object had disappeared. I sat next to him and he leaned over to let me look through the viewfinder, all I could see was a round indentation partially obscured in the soft shade of a nearby tree. There was no longer any movement from below, but both men wanted to keep watch for a little while longer.

"The access doors to the lower dock have been resealed," Roy mentioned to Thorn's surprise.

"What did you see?" I asked, still clueless as to what was actually going on here. Roy pointed out with a motion of his hand at the area below, and a suspicious detail in the surrounding landscape we could only make out from above.

"You remember walking down there; didn't you stop to wonder how odd it was that the ground was so dry considering it had just rained all night?" His hard words were meant as a rhetorical question. From our position up here, I could see what he meant. The wet ground outside of the cleared area was obviously darker with moisture separated by an invisible, yet distinct line, around its entire edge. Even so, I was still confused to what that suggested.

"There's something buried beneath there besides that generator room." Thorn realized as the area measured much larger than the floor plan of the lower docking bay.

"I would bet there's a bunker down there under the foundation, right below our own feet," Roy proclaimed, explaining that underground shelters were laced with drainage webbing to disperse moisture away from the subsurface structure. He was probably right; the visual footprint we saw below us was predominantly larger than the lower dock where we found those generators.

After keeping watch for another hour up top, we decided to rally back in the main room where we had set up camp. The little boy was sitting there patiently chewing on a ration bar while the rest of us discussed the situation. There were a few suggestions tossed around that we should abandon the complex and search for another place to lodge, but the winter storms were already at our doorstep, which was a serious concern.

Felix thought maybe we could do a little more exploring and try to contact someone in the shelter below; that is, if we found anybody still inside. Old man Roy pointed out that we had not actually seen anybody yet, and that the bunkers maintenance system might be completely automated. Even if we found a way in, there was no guarantee of what we might run into down there. Thorn and everyone else finally had to admit that the temptation of an entire bunker, that was possibly full of supplies, was worth the peril involved. Everyone in the circle had been through far too much over the past several years to walk away from such a prize ...if it existed.

Haiti kept watch through the night on the roof as the rest of us slept, dreaming of an entire complex full of food and untainted water. Maybe there were people down there, or maybe it was nothing more than an empty sub-basement filled with bare cement walls. We would find out soon enough.

We set off to find an entry point at first light. Upstairs in the executive office, we failed to find anything on the holographic chart that would explain what the hydro generators were actually connected to. Pipes from the circular array shown in the lower basement were directed vertically straight into the ground where they merely disappeared from the graph. After some digging around in the building, the men found a few shovels and a large crowbar stashed in the garage maintenance room and we decided to take another walk outside.

Serena and I kept guard after we made our way off the balcony and around the rear of the building. We cautiously made our way to the fresh break in the ground along the exterior fence. Roy was brave enough to tap on the circular metal plate that was now submerged a few feet below the dirt. He jumped back, expecting something to happen, but we all relaxed when it failed to react after several moments.

"Let's dig around this thing and see what we find," he ordered. Felix and Thorn swapped turns shoveling as Roy helped with an empty bucket to remove the soil from the hole. The ditch grew ever wider as they slowly exposed a metal plate, rimmed by a wall of reinforced cement, nearly twelve feet in diameter. In its center sat the edge of the cylinder we had seen before, that was embedded with sensors. We were all a little on edge, not knowing if the thing was going to shoot up at any moment and zap one of us. We took turns listening to the plate cover, but we couldn't detect any sound coming from below.

"So, now what?" Felix huffed as he leaned on the shovel and wiped the tired sweat from his brow, "Maybe we should just bang on this thing until somebody answers," he suggested halfheartedly as he raised the handle to strike the metal plate below their feet. Quick as an asp, Roy grabbed the shovel's handle to stay his blow. By the reaction shown on his face, it was obvious Felix was a little surprised at how fast the old man could move.

"How about if we don't act so rashly, and actually try to proceed with a measure of caution first, son," Roy shot back, with the derogatory tone in his voice to respect his age, "If there happens to be anybody down there, we don't want to give them the impression that we are hostile," he added while lowering the shovel back down gently, "...which could end badly for us if they do," he offered as a final resolution.

Thorn took a moment to confer with Felix, who finally admitted that they did not wish to trip a reactionary response from any automated defense system that might be in place. So far, digging the area clear of soil had not gotten us detected, and we wanted to keep it that way for now. At the edge of the supporting wall, Felix noted one side had a slanted edge and exposed what appeared to be the rim of a hatch after digging a few more feet down the exterior wall. After clearing to top section off, we discovered that the panel opening was simply too small to accommodate an adult-sized person. That was when the crowbar we had brought came in handy. Prying off the hatch, we discovered a mass of live electronics embedded inside. It actually took Felix less than a minute to crosswire the connections, and we all jumped back when the entire plate lifted from its seal as chunks of dirt fell within the open casing.

We stood back with guns drawn and waited in silence for a few moments while the dust settled, only to be startled once again when a section of the plate folded in to reveal a metal staircase that descended into the darkness below. Serena returned to our camp to grab some extra flashlights and gear for us to use on the descent down the shaft. Felix was a little reluctant to venture down into the pit, but it was clear that we would likely need his expertise if we came across any additional electrical panels. Haiti accompanied the dark-haired girl when they came back down, and Thorn scolded him for leaving the child up there all alone.

"Serena, stay up top and keep an eye on the boy while we take a look below," Thorn instructed her while motioning to his previous position on top of the roof, "we don't know how long this will take, but we will try to make it out before nightfall," he stated, which would be roughly another five to six hours. Haiti had his trusty machete stuffed in the back of his belt, and Thorn handed his rifle to me.

"Here, you and Serena will need my scope to keep an eye from the rooftop, and you two can trade shifts until we get back." he offered as an assignment.

"I'll go with you guys; I can handle myself," I stated firmly as I handed Thorn's rifle over to Serena in kind. All the men just stared at me for a moment as a hint of unwillingness to argue with a six-foot tall woman glinted in their eyes. Thorn seemed as though he was about to disapprove, but he eventually shrugged his shoulders in surrender and waved Serena off to her post. The five of us looked down the dark stairwell, wondering what we might find in the depths below.

A moist heat rose through the narrow shaft as we descended the tight switchbacks; all the while, trying to keep as quiet as possible. However, we were completely oblivious to the motion sensors we had triggered, which were deftly hidden on the landings between each set of stairs.

There was no hint of what type of structure this was, to reveal if it was either civilian or military made. There was always the chance it was a private complex but that was highly unlikely. In my travels, I had stumbled across more than a dozen civilian-made underground bunkers. They called them bug-out shelters, which were usually poorly designed and not much more than replicated bomb shelters from the dawn of the atomic age. It was ludicrous thinking, as most of those vaults were nothing more than glorified storm shelters that might have been sparsely useful for protection, from, say, a tornado, but undoubtedly useless from an actual nuclear blast or radioactive fallout.

It was beyond foolish to outright crazy how people would think they could hide their entire family in such tiny boxes underground. I had guessed that they gleefully imagined they would all sit there smiling while they ate their cans of beans and read a pleasant book, as they waited for weeks to months for the death and chaos raging above to subside.

Some of these 'preppers' had poured their life saving into these faulty shelters that were nothing more but claustrophobic death traps. There were actually companies that sold these family-sized coffins, where they would basically do little more than dig a shallow hole and plop it into the ground to be covered with nothing more than loose dirt. Little to no reinforcement or insulation whatsoever was ever installed; and in most cases, they even failed to pour a foundation.

After the asteroid impacts, when the earthquakes rattled the terrain and vast ocean flooding poured inland several miles to submerge the coasts; those tiny confined shelters would bury their occupants alive during an avalanche or mudslide, and could fill with invading seawater in a matter of minutes. Barricaded in a little hole like that with water pouring in through cracks and air vents, would be a horrible way to die. A tsunami or leaking rainwater would end up drowning their victims as their gear and supplies floated around their heads while they gasped for air in their last seconds of life, wondering where they had gone wrong in their planning. They simply didn't think to prepare for that eventuality.

I had seen this with my own eyes, passing across backyard shelters with putrefied bloated bodies floating among dank water. Even when someone had taken the effort and foresight to build a proper refuge, none of them took the time to disguise their white candy-cane air filters sticking up from out of the ground like a sore thumb or the obvious access hatchways they left in full view above ground.

I found several such shelters that had been forcibly entered and ransacked. Looters would stuff the only air filter to the bunker with a rag, and they simply waited for the armed occupants inside to either open the door or suffocate. With great effort, the doors would be broken in, and what was once a family of survivalists were now nothing more than a rotting pile of corpses curled up in the corners where they had smothered to death. The large cities were the worst hit as violent mobs of both Weepers and Scavengers took to the streets.

Survivors would barter food and supplies at gunpoint, as nobody trusted one another. There were always wild rumors floating around, of some military or government shelter complex somewhere out on the horizon as our salvation. It was a wild story that changed every time it was retold. It was a fantasy we kept alive by some twisted need for hope, that we could actually restore our blighted civilization. Such rumors were always quelled by those few citizens who had barely escaped the medical concentration camps with their lives, or fled their way to safety after the military had abandoned them. Underneath our hard exteriors, we all felt forsaken.

I was nobody special, just like everyone else trying to survive. I didn't have any specific training or military background. Years before the MN4 asteroid had graced our skies, I had dated a guy for a short while who had taught me the value of being cautious. I had always wondered what had happened to him after we parted and went our separate ways. It was practical advice he had offered that I now put into practice every day since the event; that 'trust' was something to be earned, not demanded.

Several flights down the stairwell, we came across a pair of sealed shafts decorated with large round hatches that apparently only opened from the other side. Yet further down, we discovered a similar pair, until our descent came to a sudden halt when we hit a steel cage blocking the rest of the stairway. Roy glared at Felix, who had found a loose steel nut and let it drop down the stairwell beyond the bars. The clank of metal echoing up the shaft subsided after several drawn moments.

"Well, it seems like its a long way down..." the redhead commented as he tried to brush off Roy's stern gaze.

"I don't think we're going to get through these doors," Thorn added softly, trying to keep his voice low. Thus far, we had failed to come across any signs that would designate what this place had been constructed for. Felix took a closer look at the hatches that were situated opposite from one another across the small platform.

"There are no access panels I can detect," he blurted, stating the obvious as he pressed his ear against the dull metal door, "but I can hear something inside," Felix mentioned as Roy and Thorn took their turn listening. It was like the sound of the wind, which didn't make much sense all the way down here. Luckily, Haiti had the sensibility to bring the crowbar along with us and he suggested that we should have a go at the metal bars to access the lower stairwell. There was no padlock on the gate, as it appeared to have some sort of internal lock; which certainly didn't make things easier for us.

We all took turns trying to widen the cage bars, hoping our iron crowbar was up for the job. After nearly half an hour of grief and strained muscles, we managed to get the bars separated wide enough to squeeze ourselves through, but just barely. Stripping off our packs and extra gear, we stuffed them through one by one; all except for Felix, since he was a little too chubby for the narrow gap we had made. Try as we might, we simply could not get the bars to bend any further to let him through the gap.

"Get back up top and help Serena," Thorn instructed him with a sigh of resignation, "we will be back up in a few hours no matter what."

Felix nodded apologetically, his plump love handles now bruised and a little worse for wear. We gave him one of our spare flashlights for the long climb back up top while he offered us a doleful look before he turned and ascended up the stairway.

Past the locked gate, we couldn't help but notice that the footing was constructed differently here, and clearly lacked the finesse of craftsmanship that was present in the stairwell above. My ears began to pop, which made me wonder just how far down we had traveled.

Roy estimated we had dropped over twenty stories below ground so far, which surprised me since I hadn't kept count. Going down was easy, and I was starting to dread the long climb back up. The old man came to a sudden halt and told us to hush for a moment as he held up his hand; it was only then that we heard the faint chime of a distant alarm. We had no clue as to where it was coming from until we reached the bottom of the stairwell, which ended at a landing in a large rectangular room where the cool moisture had pooled upon the glistening floor.

A single open shaft reached into the darkness, adjacent to it sat a large rusted grate that appeared to be an elevator door. By the amount of thick rust accumulated on its surface, we doubted it was still functional and would not entirely trust it even if it was. There was no other direction to go except to make our way down the narrow tunnel as the sound of the alarm rose in volume the closer we approached. We could see a dim yellow light flashing far ahead through the corridor, so we proceeded with caution until we came to an especially interesting room.

The ceiling opened up to exposed raw bedrock, as you would find in a cave, though the floors were cemented and there were rooms and passages lined entirely with glass suspended off the floor. As high up as they were, there seemed to be nothing within the glass chambers themselves. The flashing light came from a beacon mounted above a horizontal tube that was half-buried in the floor with an opening on one side, where at both ends there bore deep shafts into the wall itself. Surrounding us, a pair of yellow handrails lined the interior walls. It was all very strange, indeed.

"Ah, what the hell is this, man?" Haiti blurted; unable to contain his curiosity as his wide eyes scanned the structure in wonder. We strolled over and peered down into the tube, but it was far too low in height to venture within; at least comfortably.

Roy looked just as confused as I was; even Thorn was at a loss.

"Take a look around and see what you find," Roy bade for us to investigate the odd chamber. One thing I had to mention to Thorn, was that besides the flashing beacon, I didn't see any other hard wired light source in the chamber. On the far side of a curved partition, I found a handle set firmly on top of a narrow tube, and I called to the others. We were all a little bewildered since it did not appear to resemble any kind of control switch we had ever seen before.

"Well, we've come this far, might as well see what it does, eh?" The islander man suggested, as Thorn gave a slight shrug of approval for him to give it a try. Haiti grunted with effort as he tried to twist the handle this way and that, but to no avail. It wasn't until he attempted to pull on it that there was a hiss from within the pedestal and the handle itself slowly spun on its own accord. The honey-colored beacon above the tube suddenly turned a vibrant green and its flashing grew ever more frequent as we heard a rumble from the tunnel beyond.

That got us nervous, but no matter how Haiti tried, the handle would not depress back into its former position. He had activated something and it was now coming up the tunnel. The green light flashed faster and faster, until it turned a constant solid tone just as a large bullet-shaped cone, streaked with filth, nosed its way slowly from the mouth of the tube. The first thing that shot into my mind was utter dread, as what slowly eased into the chamber looked very much like a missile. I could see the others were also as worried since it resembled a warhead, and were wondering what to do next.

"Oh shit, man ...what did I do?" Haiti gasped.

As the long cylinder slid up to the platform, we could now see that it was tapered at both ends. It suddenly came to a halt and a panel along its length opened up to reveal what appeared to be four seats within; each pair back to back, laid out in single file. It was some sort of transport, like a mini subway car. The vehicle itself, seemed extremely confined for the given space inside. Just then, a broken voice from a hidden speaker blasted into the quiet room.

"Welcome...*krrzt* is your departure station to Fallhaven.

Plea...*krrt* present your green pass to the...*krrzzt*." A pleasant female voice spoke through the static of the broken speaker. After a long hesitation of silence, we finally realized it was a prerecorded audio.

"Fallhaven?" Thorn whispered to himself with a confused look in his eyes.

"What now, man," Haiti asked with a dash of excitement, "we goin' for a ride?"

Truth was, we were not entirely expecting this turn of events. Roy was hesitant to comment, although Thorn thought it was worth investigating. He argued that we didn't know when this subway car might be here next, or if we could ever get it to work again. Old man Roy volunteered to stay behind so he could go back and report to the others, as Haiti, Thorn and I, finally decided we would take the chance to see where this transport might lead.

"I really don't think this is a good idea," Roy cautioned as we each stepped in the vehicle and crouched into the tightly packed seats like sardines.

Roy went back over to the control handle we had used to call the car. He stood in front of the pedestal behind the partition as Thorn gave him the thumbs up. Thorn and I sat in the first section, while Haiti was in the other half enjoying some legroom. The seating was so cramped I had begun to wish I had been in the backseat instead; but before I could say anything, unseen sensors activated the panel which slid closed and sealed us in. There was thick muck smeared over the windows which we could barely see through, but we could make out Roy standing at the console. Just as he was about to give the handle another try, the lever depressed on its own before he touched it and the small four-person missile slid off down the tube.

"Oh ...shit." Roy marked with a worried glance towards the tram vehicle as it swiftly shot off out of view. Through the greasy windows, none of us saw him waving his hands frantically in panic as we disappeared into the darkness.

The vehicle came to a halt several yards into the tunnel as we heard a thick door slide into place behind us. This process was followed by a suction of air expelling the atmosphere from within the chute, which made our ears began to ring and the tube outside exploded into a blur as we suddenly launched. Shooting down the tube at impossible speeds, I could hear Haiti over the whooshing noise whooping out loud in glee. We passed through several lit sections, but the transparent panels were so covered with filth that we couldn't make anything out.

Our wild rollercoaster ride came to an end after what seemed to have been ten or so nauseating minutes later; we had no idea how far we had traveled. Our vehicle decelerated until it came to a halt once again, and we could hear a door sliding open just as the hum of the magnetic coils along the wall pulled us through into an open chamber that was brightly lit with a harsh green light from a beacon mounted on the roof above us.

The interior of the vehicle decompressed and I suddenly felt ill, like I was going to throw up my breakfast all over Thorn. He too looked a bit queasy himself; his face going a tinge pale, and by the sounds of it, Haiti, sitting behind us, was experiencing the same amount of despair. The panel slid open as we shielded our eyes from the bright light as the same alluring voice of the audio recording greeted us.

"Welcome to Fallhaven, please follow your assigned escort. All guests are required to obey the rules. Have a pleasant stay."

The Atrium

A harsh lingering stench hung within the room as we stepped out of the small transport cradle, wondering where we were. Similar to the station we had departed, this one also had glass rooms fixed high upon the ceiling that glowed with a strange light that appeared to be emanating from the panes themselves. Across the room, a humanoid robot sat poised in front of a counter, looking at us with its large lens eyes. At closer inspection, we could see it was permanently affixed into place at its post; its once pristine white plating now stained with dirty streaks of brown and black. Some violent force had removed its left arm as several frayed wires danced with errant sparks as it moved its torso in stiff jerked motions.

The rest of the room was in disarray as were the floors of the glass rooms hanging above that were littered with debris and clutter. There was a doorway that opened up to an adjacent hall that caught our eye, which had streaks of dark stains also decorating the walls beyond its edge. To our dismay, the panel on the transport closed after we stepped off the platform and the vehicle slid off into the dark tube; stranding us there. Haiti ran up trying to stop it, but there were no handholds to get a grip on the smooth skin of the vehicle. After it penetrated the small tunnel, a metal door swiftly closed behind it.

"Ah ...well, it looks like we're gonna be stuck here for a while, wherever 'here' is," Haiti remarked, the gleam of his usual smile absent from his lips. We were worried, not knowing how far we had traveled, or where, or what this place was except for its solitary name. Stamped across the top of the doorway in bold lettering was the title; FALLHAVEN.

"At least this place has power, maybe we should see if there is somebody here or something we could use," I suggested. It was the logical choice. As scavengers, we had survived similar unknown situations but we were currently at the disadvantage of not having a means of escape should things go sour, and having an open route of extraction was always the first rule of thumb.

Haiti drew his machete and took the lead through the entrance. I kept my gun ready as our trio ventured into the hall. Every so often, we would hear a faint shuffling or rattle echo down the corridor from unknown sources as we made our way further into the mysterious complex.

"Ya know man, this might be the place that's been sucking up the juice from those generators up top," Haiti offered up his theory, which made a bit of sense when we considered it.

It was safe to assume we had traveled several miles underground, but we currently had no idea in which direction we had gone. Thorn stopped to wipe away the caked gunk from a sign on the wall by another door, which read 'Infirmary' underneath the smear of filth. From the decrepit looks of it, all three of us began to assume this place had been ransacked and abandoned long ago. If there were any medical supplies in stock that hadn't expired by now, they would be of some practical value and this was the place to look.

There was a mixture of sentiment as we looked through the medical bay. We found scanners and sets of laboratory beakers, but most of the flasks had been strewn around as though the place had been deliberately vandalized. There was also some notably expensive equipment stacked within the lab that seemed mostly intact, but a majority of the machines were smashed or broken in one form or another. Thorn found a cabinet full of vaccines and stem injectors for inoculations, but the glass refrigerator was unplugged; which undoubtedly meant the drugs had long since gone bad and were now useless.

It didn't make much sense at all, since all these supplies were invaluable, and would have been packed and taken by anyone who might have originally evacuated this facility or by any number of people who would have scoured this place before us.

"Ut-oh," Haiti whispered aloud, just audible enough for us to hear, who was standing in a corner of the room at the edge of a gurney. Thorn and I wandered over to peer over his shoulder to see what he was looking at lying upon the floor. There, crumpled up in the corner was a decimated human cadaver, its skin dried and pale. It seemed like it had been there for several years. What was left of a torn white lab coat was stuck twisted beneath the corpse. There was a smudged nametag on the jacket, but nobody dared to touch it.

"I think its time we find our way out of here," Thorn admitted, as we began to get a grasp on the situation. Turning around, I nearly jumped out of my skin as a shadow passed across the bay door followed by the thumping of heavy footsteps as they faded down the hall.

"What the hell was that?" I blurted out in dismay. Regardless of the question, we needed to find out what or whom we were dealing with, and of course, find our way back to the surface in the process. Haiti leveled the long blade of his machete while clenching his grip on the worn handle anxiously.

"I'm not rightly sure we really want to find out," Haiti whispered nervously.

"We have to take a look; it could be someone who could help us..." Thorn suggested, though there was a fair measure of doubt rather than conviction in his tone. Warily, we made our way back into the hall and followed in the direction where we had seen the figure pass. Many of the ceiling lights along the hallways were broken or cracked, but allowed enough illumination to see by.

Every so often, we could make out handprints on the corners of doorways, made from the same filthy grime that marred the hallway floor and was splattered across the walls. If it were dried blood or feces, I would imagine it would have smelt worse than it did. Still, that stale odor reminded me of the dens of the diseased I had crossed before; the strange scent lurking in my nostrils gave me a bad vibe I could not seem to shake. Eventually, we came across a set of wide double doors, which had been propped open by several metal rods jammed within its hinges. Stepping through, we could see that it led into a large gallery beyond. Haiti motioned for us to crouch down as we crossed into view of the spectacle before us.

In all respects, it appeared to be an indoor amusement park, or what was left of one. A huge domed arena with a blue sky and wisps of clouds painted above it. Lining the area were rows of seats and what appeared to have once been stores and shops set adjacent to a ringed section of food courts, which now lay in complete disarray. It took a moment for our eyes to adjust to the change in lighting where we began to see hunched figures moving among the broken structures in the park. Some of them looked human; a few others, well, not so much.

"Weepers!" Haiti whispered to us over his shoulder as we hugged the entrance wall. The smell of them was more pungent here in the central hub where they had herded together. I spied two of the infected attempting to ascertain the function of a broken swing, as if in dismay as to how it worked. Another sat on the edge of a slide as if contemplating the danger of pursuing such folly. There was a particular one, however, placed in the center of the court that was the most disturbing of all. In the middle of the plaza squatted a large grotesque beast with mottled skin, and horribly deformed. None of us had ever seen anything like it.

"What-the-fuck-is-that?" Thorn breathed through tight lips, wondering if we should retreat. We could not quite get a clear outline of the strange creature whose features were hidden within its own shadow. It looked like it could be a man, but was so warped and misshapen that I doubted myself. We conferred for a moment, since we currently had no alternative avenues available to consider.

"I say fuck this, and try to see if we can get that jet-tube ride working again," Haiti spouted, "ain't no way I'm stay'in here with that *thing*, man!" His voice cracked while he pointed to the monstrosity.

"Unfortunately, the control gears to that tram were broken," I advised him, as I had specifically examined the apparatus at the same time he inspected the busted robot that sat in front of its operational console.

"Hell, man, we can look again and try to hardwire dat' shit up..." Haiti began to blabber aloud until Thorn motioned him to hush his excited voice. The truth was, without Felix around, we were as dumb as rocks when it came to splicing electronics.

Looking out across the room for options, Thorn spotted a brightly lit hallway with a blinking 'Atrium' sign hanging halfway off its hinges across the mall. Looking around for alternatives, it seemed our only option at the moment. Doing a visual headcount, I tallied only a half dozen Weepers, including that grotesque blob of flesh sitting in the center of the arena. We had enough ammo to take them out if we needed, but I suggested that we should practice a measure of stealth and make our way along the darkened section of the storefront on the upper platform. It seemed like a plausible route since the recreation area, where the infected were grouped, was a good twenty yards away from our position, and the weepers appeared thoroughly occupied in their own little world for the moment.

Sneaking along the edge of the shadows where the lights had been torn out of the ceiling, we carefully chose our footing among the filth; wary not to touch anything with our bare hands since this area was thoroughly contaminated. Smashed and broken toys, trash, and other paraphernalia littered the floor around us; all brushed towards the walls by the various pathways made by well-worn footpaths through the jumble of debris. Clearly, this place could have easily accommodated several hundred people back in its heyday as some sort of entertainment mall for the visiting occupants. What exactly had happened here was anyone's guess, but it was evident that whatever transpired over the years had come to a very sour end.

I did start to wonder though, since that body in the medical bay was still intact, it meant the infected here had not yet resorted to cannibalism to survive; which logically meant that there was still an abundant food supply in stock somewhere in this complex. Getting out of here in one piece was the first priority, but it would also be nice to have something to show for it. This place was a curiosity, and I could not help but wonder more about its past as my mind began to wander in thought.

I was shaken back into present reality when a scraggly face popped from the shadows of a storefront doorway as we were attempting to creep past. His deformed head was bloated with large blisters, and lurched in sharp jerks when he walked as it gave a hoarse gasp through several broken and shattered teeth.

We were startled to the point that I almost wet myself. Fear built up as the three of us turned towards the park area to see dozens more infected stand up from the shadows where they had been previously hidden from view. One after another they stood, and still a dozen more rose from the floor and remnants of broken tables; their numbers multiplying by the second. I stared at the horde who dully peered back at us with their ghostly eyes, and I began to feel a sinking pit in my stomach. Haiti was the first to react.

"Fuck this ...RUN!" Haiti spat as he took off like black lightning towards the Atrium door, his beaded dreadlocks slapping across his back. It took me but a few milliseconds to follow in kind, though it felt like the world was in slow motion. The diseased all stood there gaping at us for a few seconds in surprise. Together in unison, as if one body, from their mangled throats issued a low howling moan. It was a truly terrifying sound, and I could feel my own piss warming my crotch as we ran for the lit doorway that seemed like a million miles away.

'This was a really stupid move,' I thought to myself with a gazillion diseased mutants at our backs, and we had no idea where the fuck we were or where we were going. It was at times of flight like these that I zoned out, my subconscious taking over. Fleeting moments turned into dragging minutes as if I was watching myself from a distance.

I jumped over a shattered counter in a single leap as Thorn followed my lead behind Haiti, who was making a beeline for the open Atrium door. Out of nowhere, a Weeper lurking behind a counter window grasped out for my face. An uppercut with the butt of my rifle split its jaw as it flew backward. Ahead of me, Haiti yelled something incoherent as he whipped out his machete and took a wild swing at a mutant that jumped up from the lower platform as it reached out to grasp his leg. The creatures severed fingers bounced from his blade and tumbled in the air past my face. Thorn caught one of the creatures climbing out from underneath a shelf and used its head as a stepping stool to launch himself up over the counter I had crossed, its deformed face crunching into the floor beneath his boot. Their haunting and horrifying moans pounded like a dull drumbeat as we flew towards the light, as though it were our divine salvation from this unthinkable hell.

Thorn caught himself as he stumbled through the entry and I turned to see a ladder leaning into the corner of the door. Slinging my rifle over my shoulder, I grabbed it with both hands and rammed the edge of the ladder into the exposed handle, cleaving it into its mate on the latch. The door slid nearly shut, with the head of the ladder blocking the jam. Almost instantly, clawed arms reached through the gap as desperate howls and gnashing teeth followed in their wake.

"That won't hold them for long," Thorn announced what was glaringly obvious; each of us hoping there wasn't another similar mob waiting for us in the chamber beyond this foyer.

Hastily making our way through the short hall, we stumbled across the source of the bright illumination. Light beamed out from an enormous greenhouse that had grown wild over time. The ceiling and walls here were adorned with photo-luminescent arrays, most of which were in perfect working order. Here the air was wet and moisture beaded upon the walls to condense and rain down upon the plant life. Several pots and tubs were overturned, but the aggressive roots stemming from the foliage was unhindered. Deep greens of every shade towered far above us; I was so distracted looking up that I nearly tripped upon the thick vines scattered at my feet.

"Holy demon shit," Haiti blurted, "would ya' look at this, man," as he gawked at the indoor jungle around us, though he still took a moment to give a concerned glance back towards the mutant horde rattling the doors from down the hall.

"I wouldn't worry too much, I bet they avoid this place ...the UV lights hurt their eyes," I mentioned to them both, though, I was not so foolish as not to help our ethnic friend to seal the thick sliding glass doors behind us. In all aspects, this place was clear of the feces and filth we saw strewn around the weepers den. The infected had shunned this section of the facility, because of the ultraviolet light and the pain it caused to their altered eyes, which was an adverse effect of the disease. We gently brushed the plants out of the way with due reverence as we made our way through the garden, amazed by the stark clash of such exotic species and blooming flora existing so close to the putrid horde of weepers; literally just rooms apart.

For but a brief moment we forgot where we were, our eyes wide open in awe as we looked up to see tiny lights drifting in the mist as it flowed between the towering plants and hanging vines. It was like something out of a fairy tale; and we stood mesmerized by the delicate fireflies floating in the light breeze from a mechanical fan centered within the dome above.

"Bioluminescent insects. Most interesting, I wonder how they got down here?" Thorn inquired, as if grasping an afterthought.

Personally, I was captivated, for having found this little oasis deep underground. It made me even more curious as to where we were and what exactly this facility was supposed to be. Logically, of course, there was the large fan above, drumming along without pause, using this botanical garden as a source of oxygen to cycle throughout the facility. That, and the fact there was still electrical power here; either connected to those hydrogen generators, or were possibly combined with an array of active solar panels somewhere topside we had yet to see.

Before the world turned upside down, I had given some study into greenhouse domes for use on interstellar exploration. I was one of those nerdy kids who grew up wanting to be a space explorer. I even put in an application with the space agency for the international manned mission to Mars planned for 2030, which of course, got a proverbial boot in the ass just a year prior to its launch ...so much for my starry-eyed dreams of being an astronaut. I had still learned something about indoor solariums and CO_2 recycling needed for a sealed environment, and this fit the bill perfectly. Somewhere connected to the ventilation system there was a carbon scrubber, a type of molecular sieve to remove the excess waste gas within the enclosed habitat.

Unless there was an automated well, that meant that all of this water had also been recycled. It was too bad this place was infested with the carriers of the virus, otherwise it would have been the perfect place to call home through the coming winter. The artificial UV light help shed the gloom of being buried underground, I almost didn't want to leave the atrium.

"Aye, look what we got here, man!" Haiti burst aloud through the jungle of brush farther down the nursery. Thorn and I caught up with him as he climbed down off a stainless steel table with a handful of oversized bananas, looking quite happy with himself. We were astounded as we turned to find oranges and apples, including heaps of what appeared to be cherries and plums, their bright colors popping through the foliage. I was as glossy eyed as the men who were picking at the fruit, but it didn't take me but a moment to realize there was something odd and out of place. Haiti looked at me in astonishment when I slapped the banana he had just peeled out of his hand before he took a bite.

"Aww, what da shit, woman?" Haiti whined, sounding more than a bit peeved by my personal assault then to his growling stomach. I also stopped Thorn's hand before he took a chunk out of a plum. He just gave me a look of annoyance until he saw what I was pointing to on the floor.

What had struck me as strange, was that for this much fruit to be growing here that it would have had to have gone through several cycles of decay and pollination but there was nothing on the ground in the form of compost to suggest that. I had also noticed unnatural discolorations on the various fruits upon closer inspection. My suspicions became clear after examining what Haiti's squashed fruit revealed where it lay mashed upon the floor at his feet. A web of stringy blood-red tendrils laced the cores of the yellow fruit, which began to bleed where the haft was broken. Understandably, Haiti was entirely creeped out by this, giving a visual shiver of disgust.

"That is just *wrong*!" He ventured to peer at it closer, being careful not to touch the ooze. It made us wonder to what extent the MN4 pathogen had evolved which could have altered the vegetation and the mutations of the infected we had seen out in the central hall. "Ohhhh no; that is just wrong, wrong, wrong," Haiti repeated again with his offbeat islander accent as he vigorously wiped his hands off on the sides of his pants. All three of us paused to slip on our gloves as a precaution.

The oranges had tiny black spots on their skin, and the apples had a lacing of the same vein-like goo around their top stems. Strangest of all, I found several of the fruits on the various trees were concaved as if they had buckled into themselves; almost as if they were being consumed from within. As freakish as it was, it appeared as if the fruit spawned, ripened, and after it decayed, it was ingested back into the plant from the same stem from which it had blossomed; rather than the usual process via absorption of the root system. This was beyond bizarre ...it was downright spooky.

"Well, there goes lunch," Thorn tried to make light of the situation, but Haiti didn't look too amused by the comment.

"Aye, someone be screw'in with mother nature, man. It ain't right!" Haiti snapped back.

"We should check were that ventilation leads," I ventured to suggest, "There has to be an exhaust vent to the surface somewhere."

Both men agreed with my proposition and we headed out the opposite paneled door stationed near an array of active pumps that fed a fine mist of water into the chamber. Haiti was more than ready to get out of there before catching what he amusingly called 'freaky-fruit-itus' as he so despaired.

Once we got to the doors, we found a dull gray and orange sign, its once bright colors had long since faded by the exposure to the intense UV lighting. listed upon it was the emergency passkey for the electronic lock. Not feeling too confident about the meager barrier we had erected with that spare aluminum ladder against the raging horde in the central mall, we resealed the panel and tripped the lock behind us. The air here was humid and the round tunnel was configured with looping pipes, all of which were coated with a thick layer of paint. A dim blue light lit the way ahead and we noticed a strange aroma of ozone lingering in the air. At least this area was free of the tell-tale signs of the afflicted.

A vibrant hum of electricity, along with a slow steady drumming of pistons, echoed down the twisting corridor that soon branched out into several paths. Color-coded pipes lining the ceiling raced off in different directions of the complex, while we argued among ourselves which way we should go. We figured an engine room was a sure bet, so we followed the cycling clamor until we stumbled into an alcove filled with large metal cylinders. It took half an hour for us to explore the cold chamber to discover that the array of tubes were feeding liquid nitrogen into sealed cryogenic freezers.

"You mean there are people inside there?" Thorn inquired while he rapped on one of the large metal barrels with his knuckles. Its reverberating dull ring failed to fully satisfy as an answer to his burning curiosity.

"Most likely, or anything else they wanted to turn into a popsicle." I responded. It was one of those popular practices for the uber-wealthy back at the turn of the century for those few people who considered themselves God's gift to the universe and presumed the world couldn't survive without them, and were simply too arrogant to allow themselves to truly die.

It was too bad there weren't any windows installed on the damn things, I wanted to see inside. Then again, there was the possibility that there were more significant items stored in them, like perhaps a selection of plant seeds from across the world to be preserved for future generations, or chromosomes of animals from every imaginable species ...but most likely they were nothing more than just a collection of pompous rich-fuck corpse-sicles, which is where I placed my bets.

However, we did locate a console that explained in slight detail the color-coded bars across the ceiling that might lead us to where we wanted to go. The Orange bar had led from this room all the way to the greenhouse, however, on the diagram it displayed a White strip with the longest route that led to the rear of the complex. It was all very confusing since the chart only showed the pathways but not the exterior walls to give us a hint as to how large this facility actually was. Haiti joked around about pushing a few buttons and turning off a freezer or two, but I advised him that would be unwise considering we didn't have a clue as to the contents of each pod.

"Ah, I is just playing with you, girl; no need to get your panties in a twist," he kidded, not realizing I actually preferred not to wear underwear at all; but chose not to correct his attempted jest.

"It's just a guess, but this section of the structure seems to be all basic power and maintenance. Communications and living quarters appear to be divided among the other two sections," I pointed out on the pie-chart diagram in front of us, which was so boringly basic it was pathetic, "this white bar here guides across several floors, so it looks like it might take us closer to the communications area on this grid," I offered.

"That sounds like a plan to me," Thorn admitted as he patted me on the back in a friendly way, which I honestly didn't mind his affection. He wasn't bad looking, but I did giggle to myself for a second when I remembered what Serena had said, about his name being 'Jebediah' or some-such. He turned to me as I smirked.

"What is it?" He asked seriously.

"Oh, uh, nothing, just a sore throat," I caught myself while grabbing my canteen for a sip while I faked a cough. I kind of liked Thorn, and didn't want him to think I was laughing at him. From that point, I knew I had to cook up a way to find out what his real name was; at a later time of course.

We gathered our things and made off back down the hall to follow the white marker that trailed the top of the interlocking corridors; unfortunately, none of us had noticed the beading of moisture collecting on one of the specimen pods that Haiti had accidentally disengaged when he was goofing around at the controls moments before. Neither did we see the silent pulsing red light switch on the console indicating one of the pods had begun to thaw as we shuffled out the door.

Following the designated route, we made our way through several sets of connecting hallways that led us deeper into the complex, always checking every turn in case there were more infected in the area. We came across a few rooms filled with shattered debris, but nothing so obvious than simply having been abandoned in reckless haste. Further down we found a stairwell that descended around a vertical shaft which we had presumed had held an elevator platform at one time, but there was no call button that we could find anywhere along each level as we made our way downward into the abyss. At the bottom landing, the throbbing sound of machinery shook the walls with its faint rhythmic heartbeat.

The room opened up into a gallery where we finally found the elevator platform we had suspected the shaft contained.

Understandably, the three of us were a little disgruntled as using the lift would have saved us a lot of time and grief hiking those stairs all the way down here; however, it didn't take us too long thereafter to discover that its controls had been intentionally sabotaged.

"Aye, someone broke the damn lift on purpose, man; what gives?" Haiti blurted with mild annoyance as he pulled out cut wires from the buttons under the panel. There was no quick way to repair it. Just as we gathered to look over his shoulder and inspect the damage, two orbs emerged from the ceiling in front of the outline of a huge interlocking steel door. Each of the orbs had one camera eye which hung by a mechanical arm. From around us, the same pleasant female voice we heard back in the reception area of the transport car began to talk from a hidden speaker within the room.

"A code white emergency has been initiated. Please stand in a single file and present your ID marker to the sentry for verification then advance to the blue light. You may only proceed after your medical scan has been sanctioned. Failure to abide by these rules will result in sterilization," the disembodied voice warned. Her choice of words is what got us ruffled.

"Sterilization...?" I blubbered aloud, not really liking the sound of that. Haiti's eyes opened wide with dread, and began backing his way towards the stairs. As he did so, a pair of green aiming lasers from the orbs fixed upon him as a warning to stop his progress. Thorn came forward, looking around the floor, hoping to find what the recorded voice had meant by its reference to the blue light. Startling him for a brief second, directly above us a silver nozzle ejected from the ceiling from which a bluish holographic cone beamed out directly down onto the floor, creating a cylinder just large enough for a single person to stand in. He shrugged as he looked at me when one of the orbs lasers moved from Haiti to Thorn's chest and down to the center of the blue beam as if to guide him.

Thorn carefully stepped forward while the light washed over his body, while specs of dust in the air glittered in shades of indigo around him. Some sort of analysis scan began to flash up and down the hologram exterior until just as suddenly, it sputtered out. The mechanism lost all power; the nozzle above sparked for a moment in argument then died altogether with a low whine. Thorn just stood there baffled. The security orbs, however, were still fully functional.

"Warning," the female voice cautioned, "do not attempt to exit the perimeter until your medical scan has been sanctioned. Failure to abide by these rules will result in sterilization," their computerized host instructed.

At this, Thorn looked a little worried as both orbs centered their pinpoint jade lights glowing upon his chest. From each of the orbs the sleek round barrel of a phase weapon deployed. It was a commonly known military weapon that burned through things, armor, buildings, people; literally making a hole through them. All of us froze in place. Thorn glanced over to me with a worried look washed across his face, not knowing what to do.

"Something broke, the scan did not complete!" I screamed out at the computer that controlled the security defenses. Truly, I didn't know if the damn equipment had kicked out because it couldn't detect an ID chip or had merely short-circuited; either way, I couldn't just stand there and watch him get fried. Regardless, Haiti and I were next in line for an instant cooking if those security spheres when haywire. Considering the speed at which they moved, I had no doubt that we would all be cut down before we could even make it past a few feet to reach the stairwell. I thought maybe I could unstrap my rifle, wishing I hadn't slung it over my shoulders during the steep walk down the stairs, but I didn't want to make a foolish move and trip a hostile response from the sentries that would only serve to get us all killed.

"There has been a system malfunction, please stand in single file while the probe reboots, then present your ID marker to the sentry for verification and advance to the blue light," the speaker repeated. Luckily, as the nozzle flashed to reboot, so did the security spheres, which shut down and retracted back into their cubbyholes in the ceiling. This brief pause only lasted a moment, as the sentries once again began to reactivate.

We didn't stall for the precious few seconds we had been given and made a jump for the stairs, only to watch as a thick steel grill suddenly slid into place over the exit, blocking our way to the ascending stairwell during the reboot cycle. The security system had been effectively designed to keep everyone in or out during the process. Either way, we were screwed.

"Hey! Look over there," Haiti shouted, pointing to a corner of the chamber where a large duct panel had been removed. A tool of some sort lay next to the grill left leaning by its side. In haste, we scrambled for the only egress as the pair of orbs began to drop, their camera eyes whirring as they initiated their focus onto us once again.

Haiti made it through the opening first, as did I, while Thorn followed in turn. The metal-lined tunnel was uncomfortably cramped as we crawled our way into what appeared to be a ventilation shaft. The duct was fairly clean considering its age, although I could detect the faint linger of ozone from an ionic filter as we hit a stream of cold air that flowed in from an adjacent shaft.

"Where the fuck does this go, man?" Haiti asked, his whisper echoing down the tight tunnel of gleaming metal.

"Anywhere is better than going back there, pal," Thorn replied, as he wiped away the nervous sweat from his brow.

"*Shh*, you guys," I rose my hand to hush them while holding up my light to see where we were going; "do you hear that?"

We all fell silent for a brief moment while we detected something rustling in the far distance down the shaft, but we were unable to identify what the sound was.

"Ah, that's just the air blowing," Haiti was quick to respond.

"No, no, listen; do you hear something?" I inquired again, trying to motion him to be silent, but he kept shuffling around, as did Thorn. It was aggravating; I was sure I heard something faintly familiar, but they were right about the damn air and it echoing through the vent made everything more or less indiscernible. Advancing our way further through the pipes, a little while later the shaft opened up into a fair-sized room. It was still not quite big enough to stand in, but sufficient for us to stretch our feet and aching backs from all the crawling we had done. Arguably, we desperately needed a short break to catch our breath.

Above us, a circular vent sucked air into a vertical tube that disappeared into the cool darkness; while at our feet a wide tilt in the shaft led us even deeper. The way above didn't appear to have any handholds, and not even Haiti wanted to take the chance of trying to jam the vent fan with his machete and risk having its blade snap off and come spinning back at us. With little debate, we chose the slide downward; it was either that or face an ominous 'sterilization'.

We slid in one at a time, with Thorn taking the lead. He used his boots to try to slow his descent by bracing them against the opposing walls, but even that tactic had little effect and the slippery metal skin eventually won the battle over his lack of traction halfway down the chute. We heard an awkward 'thump' and a moment of silence until he called up to us that it was safe for us to come down. Haiti went second, and since I was the most chicken of the lot, I went last.

The bottom of the vent emptied onto a rounded mesh platform that ran the length of an interior circular wall. Thorn warned us to spread far apart and distribute our weight evenly upon it as he cautiously shined his light beyond the breach of the barricade. Haiti and I both gasped as we realized just how deep the chamber below us was, as our voices echoed off into the enormous pit below. If the bolts that secured the thin fence to the wall should snap or give way beneath our feet, we would have a long drop into the dark abyss.

The only option we had was to scramble on all fours and make our way to the far side, hoping there was another way out of here. I always had a fear of heights, and this situation made me nervous to the pit of my stomach. Even in the cool flow of air, I noticed beads of sweat trickling down my neck and dripping from my chin through the thin metal grate. Apparently, this slim fence was only meant as a debris trap and was never intended to bear the weight of a person.

Haiti froze for a tense second as a bearing snapped loose beside him and a section of the grate went tumbling end over end as it clattered to the bottom of the enormous shaft. He laid there as stiff as a board in complete terror while his entire right side hovered over empty space, his eyes slowly turning towards where I had grabbed him by his shirt to keep him from falling.

"Shitzzz!" Haiti muttered as he took a slow moment to compose himself and slid slowly back onto the supported section, "Thanks..." was all he could muster to say in a low humbled voice, his eyes shifting to me in a flash of gratitude. I could almost hear his heart racing as he edged up ahead towards the relative safety of the wall. Slithering our way across the chamber, we found a thin slit embedded into the cement shaft, designating itself as our only option of escape from this witless predicament.

The opening was so small that we had to carefully unstrap our gear just to wedge ourselves inside, which was a difficult maneuver considering we had no room to even sit up. We had to inch our way along on our bellies within the cement shaft until we were sore and exhausted. It was then that we finally noticed we were lying on a panel of smooth metal, which, unfortunately, had brought our path to an abrupt end. The air here had a certain pleasant taint to it I didn't readily recognize, yet it was something old and strangely familiar. I had some rope in my pack, but it certainly was not long enough to get us down to the bottom of the colossal shaft from this height, let alone would any of us trust tying the end to the thin hanging grate as our only available anchor. We were stuck and there was nowhere else to go.

"This doesn't make any sense," Thorn began to whine with a degree of aggravation while stating the obvious, "why the hell would this slot be built intooooo...." he mumbled aloud; never finishing his sentence as we all went tumbling downward when the flue panel beneath us suddenly tilted on its axis that was secured into the walls at either side.

It wasn't exactly a pleasant experience being wedged together by the force of gravity while a gust of thick air suddenly roared through the vent below us. All three of us were a jumble of limbs and backpacks and gear and guns as we cried out in agony at every jolt on the way down. I saw a bright silver grate rimmed with light rush up to greet us from below, and just as suddenly, it shattered into pieces beneath our combined weight when we smashed through it. The end of this unpleasant joyride was accompanied by a flash of blinding light and a loud crash as our sore bodies came to rest. The three of us laid there moaning with the wind knocked out of us.

It took a dragging moment to gather our wits while we were grumbling in pain, until one-by-one, we realized that we were no longer alone. Dazed, I looked at the cold white gunk covering my hands, thinking I was somehow grotesquely injured, only to realize it appeared strangely like a crème filled bagel. Without even thinking, I gave it a lick to see if it was real. Haiti found himself headlong in a tray of biscuits with a dozen or so little sausages on toothpicks stuck throughout his dreads. In a nervous jitter, Thorn sat up and hastily brushed off tiny crab cakes covering his chest as though he imagined they were enormous bugs for a startled second.

In that moment, it struck me that was the familiar scent of baked food I had smelled before, that was wafting its way up the exhaust vent of the air circulation system. It all made sense now; well, except for the dozens of people staring at us around the large room as they paused in utter silence with their mouths open in shock.

I couldn't think of anything to say in our defense for crashing their party, so I just gave a short wave and said 'Hello' in a tone of embarrassment as chunks of whipped creme flopped off my hands and into my lap. Several men in gray vestments rushed forward as a taller man with sandy gray hair nudged his way through the crowd before us. The wrinkles on his face didn't detract from the stone-like glare beneath his dark eyes. He wore an audaciously decorated white coat covered with a ludicrous amount of medals, making it look as though his outfit came from a costume store rather than being military attire.

"I believe you three weren't invited," he declared in a staunched tone with a heavy hint of accusation seeping into his words, and then promptly motioned towards the guards in gray to cart us away to the murmurs of the crowd around us. As we were hauled away by force, Thorn attempted a brief struggle, only to get himself zapped with a stun baton as a reward for his defiance. We were dragged out of the large hall, which had been decorated into some hack attempt to resemble a ballroom, with each of the patrons present dressed in lavish, if not entirely ridiculous, attire. Many of the onlookers peered over one another's shoulders just to get a look at us while they stared on in disbelief.

I was hastily dumped into a small room as the door locked behind me, without a clue as to what had happened to Thorn or Haiti. Still in a state of confusion, I didn't have to wait very long until an older lady with wispy white hair stepped through my door with a cloth in her hands. She gave me a quick look up and down before handing me the towel.

"Here you go, dear. Clean yourself up," she said kindly, "that was a rough spill you took there. Are you alright; nothing broken I hope?"

"Sorry about ...all that," I hesitated in reply, "we had no idea where we were or that anyone was down here," I mumbled as my shaken excuse while I checked my bruises from the fall. Luckily for us, they weren't serving shish-kabobs and hot oil fondue on that banquet table we had fallen onto.

"You will have to forgive the General, he is a bit eccentric and a little overzealous at times, considering that we haven't had guests in such a long while," she offered as an apology, "the guards didn't rough you up too much I hope?"

"No, I'm fine, Ma'am," I muttered politely.

"Ma'am? Oh, my, aren't you are the proper one," the old lady smiled, "you can call me Beatrice, dear," she offered as she led me by the shoulder over to a seat in an adjacent room after waving her hand over a sensor on the wall. The chamber beyond was lavish, filled with hand carved wood furniture decorating the area along with plush deep red velvet cushions. It was quite old fashioned, much like my host whose hair was neatly tied into a bun.

"I was wondering about my friends..." I began to ask, but Beatrice quickly cut me off.

"They will be fine dear. The men were taken to a different section of the facility," she stated shortly, "but luckily for you, Kane left you in my care."

"Kane?" I inquired in my confusion about her reference.

"Oh, yes, General Kane; but he prefers his military title above personal mentions," she grinned as she walked over and poured a hot cup of liquid from a dispenser set within the wall, giving it to me as she took a plate of breaded cookies from a shelf next to it. The aroma wafting from the steam was fantastic, as I recalled the almost forgotten scent of orange tea. My mouth watered, I had not had hot tea in as long as ...well, as long as I could remember. I politely took a few pieces of the spiced bread offered, trying not to appear too much like a ravenous animal while I devoured them in short order. Beatrice just sat there and looked at me for a few silent moments with what appeared as a measure of sympathy in her eyes.

"What is this place?" I finally had the gumption to ask as I wiped the crumbs from the corner of my mouth.

"You mean this facility?" she raised her hands and gestured over to a framed poster on the wall that had been used as an advertisement of some sort in the distant past, "It is, well, it *was* a fallout shelter of sorts; known as Fallhaven, but we just call it 'Haven' for short," she answered while a notable darker look in her aging eyes flashed over her face for a brief second before she turned back to me, "And where do you come from, dear...?" she inquired while leading on to my name.

"Cait, or Caity, if you wish," I blurted back. Unwavering, she looked at me with a raise of her eyebrow, as an incentive that she was still curiously awaiting my full answer, "we're from the surface above Fallhaven ...I think," I uttered finally.

"You mean you're not sure?" she inquired in mild jest.

"No, I mean we *are* from the surface but there was some sort of subway connection that took us here, and I'm not sure how far away that was," I tried to answer as best I could, though still a little fazed that she wouldn't know that. A slightly worried look washed over her face again, only to quickly fade with practiced grace.

"Oh my, what a journey you must have had," Beatrice began to embellish to change the direction of the conversation, and I too wanted to avoid that subject; not knowing what they would do to us if they discovered we had fought our way through a horde of the infected after our arrival at the rail station. I could only hope Thorn and Haiti also possessed the wisdom to keep their mouths shut, and kept that obscure fact to themselves.

"We, um, then we made our way down a duct system until we ended up here," I quickly chimed in to draw her off the subject, as I realized I had to be more careful about what I said.

"Oh, I see..." the old woman trailed off for a moment, "lucky for you then, as a bunch of those diseased animals broke into the compound and the rest of us have been trapped down here because of them for quite some time now," she explained.

"You mean there is no other way out of here?" I asked with a hint of concern choking my voice.

"Oh, I believe there was at one time, but it's been so many years that some of this fancy machinery doesn't work anymore and the other exits collapsed as a result of earthquakes. The General and his security staff keep us safe though, so don't worry your little head, dear," she smiled as she gave me a motherly tap on the head, and stood up to activate a button by the door. Shortly thereafter, another woman showed up, "Elise, here, will escort you to your guest room, which will be locked for the first few days of your stay, for your own safety of course," Beatrice noted with a dry smile as she motioned to the pale-faced guide awaiting me at the inner door, "We have a lot of curious people here that will only hound you with frivolous questions. Be assured we will all finally get introduced when the time comes, but you will have an opportunity to get some proper rest in the meantime, Caity," she offered as I got up and was placed in the company of the chaperone who escorted me out into the hall and out of sight.

Moments after the door closed in the old woman's private chambers, the ornately framed poster of Fallhaven lit up, and the image of General Kane blurred in through its display as Beatrice stood before it.

"So," the wrinkled face of the General asked with a raised brow, his dark penetrating eyes losing none of their effect over the flat screen, "do you think she bought it?" he inquired. In response, the old woman casually tilted her head with a look of numb disregard.

"Trust me, Kane; I know what I'm doing," she answered coldly as she nodded in assurance.

Masquerade

After leaving my hosts lavish quarters, I could not help but notice there were still a pair of guards clad in starched gray uniforms outside the door, blocking the entrance from whence my comrades and I had been dragged in so unceremoniously. My escort, Elise, showed me to a private room after winding through a maze of halls, each section had been color-coded to distinguish their designated areas. While passing one corridor, I got the brief glimpse of two workers scrubbing something like graffiti off the wall that I couldn't quite read in its entirety because they were standing in the way, my pause was noted by my chaperon who hastily turned me back on course towards our destination.

"May I ask about my friends?" I inquired.

"You will be reunited with them in due time, I would suggest that you be patient," Elise stated abruptly.

At the end of a hallway, I was pointed into a small room, observing at first glimpse that it had all the bare essentials and aesthetics of a prison cell. As stupid as it sounds, I was almost giddy to find a working toilet along with a sink and clean running water. Elise took a moment to demonstrate how to operate the sonic shower and where to dispose my current clothing, and she pointed over to the sanitary tan jumpsuit folded up on the counter they had left for me to wear. Following her stern guidance, were additional instructions that my meals would be delivered to my room twice a day. After my escort left, I gave a glance around the room while mentally noting that my guest unit was likely under surveillance; but if there was a camera in the room, I had to admit they had done a damn good job of hiding it.

There was no way to open the door from the inside, so I figured I would make the best of the situation by getting some overdue rest, but even that train of thought was difficult to accomplish as I kept worrying about what had happened to my

companions. Likely, they were also being detained for a set
timetable as a precaution to check us for signs of exposure to
the KRI virus under the guise of our complimentary guest
quarters, of course.

I noticed that there was also a similarly framed poster of
Fallhaven hanging on the wall as the only form of decor in my
room. It displayed a retro twist in the marketing design
boasting the shelter as the place for "*health & safety*" and "*all
the conveniences of home*" among other such highly inflated
claims. Apparently, though, it was all legit; nobody could deny
that this asylum had kept all their sorry asses alive and well,
while the rest of society had fallen apart at the seams in the
outside world.

I briefly remembered seeing advertisements for places like this
long ago, and it was common knowledge that they did not come
cheap. Some very well-to-do families invested their entire life
savings into reserving spots in these types of sanctuaries for
their own children as an insurance measure, rather than putting
their kids through college. In hindsight, of course, some might
agree it ended up as a damn wise investment.

I think it was back in the early 2020's that virtual reality and
holographic gamers were the new surge in technology. Almost
everyone you knew had an alternate persona they had rendered
in the digital world. In most cases, overseas resource wars were
purely fought with unmanned drones and robotic counterparts
so there was little human-to-human contact on the battlefields.
Unless of course, you were from a country that wasn't flush
with such high-end technological advancements and military-
grade hardware, which left their soldiers being forced into
combat against a faceless enemy.

In my opinion, I thought it was a pretty chicken-shit method of
combat by utilizing armed droids and bomber drones while
sitting in a safe little room far out of harms way. Especially so
since the worlds governments used the taxpayer's funds to
create these robotic innovations while using them to enter into
hostile incursions and initiated wars by invading and occupying
foreign lands without any form of public approval, whatsoever.

That is where the hallowed gamer community came in. Most

everyone knew that there was little privacy left in the real world and that tabs were being kept on everyone and everything from our bank accounts to copies of our digital messages sent across the net. Everything you did and said was analyzed or scrutinized by national security agencies, or all-powerful corporations for marketing purposes. Everyone had their personal life monitored in one fashion or another.

There were astonishing but believable rumors that surfaced every now and then from the media that supported those facts, but these rare occurrences were quickly silenced and white-washed from existence. Every government on the planet abused their ability to cleanly snip public information from the net communications as if it had never occurred; even people working in the field of media were far from candid about their jobs. It was a scary thought to think that everything said and done was being either scripted, censored, or controlled to a certain extent. Any negative publicity about the questionable conduct of the Government or their military personnel was promptly drowned out with a landslide of misinformation.

I remember back when I was in college and reading historical data about how tens of thousands of people would endure unpleasant and hostile weather simply to watch live sporting events held within massive arenas, and were frequently assigned seats so far out in the stands where they couldn't see crap. On top of it, the majority of the audience would actually pay enormous sums for reserved seats to suffer abysmal conditions of blaring heat, rain or snow, just to watch a bunch of ghastly overpaid sports players who were usually pumped up to their eyeballs with steroids just to dink around with a ball? It sounded nuts to me, but the history records proved it had really happened.

It was a fad of the times to pay personal income just to watch a small group of jocks run around on a field to play a game; fortunately, our society had progressed past such idiocy. Sports were originally invented for personal fitness that provided a degree of healthy exercise for such players, but it was tedious and excessively boring to watch for anyone who was fairly educated and cultured. Fundamentally, in our modern era, someone watching any type of sports events was akin to a spectator watching someone exercise at a gym. Truly, it was as boring as balls and lacked any entertainment value to those with a sense of intellect.

The fine line of friendly competition between schools, cities or countries were blurred when the tyrannical police state was introduced. Everyone had a much smaller picture back then of how the world actually worked, and patriotism was expected of all. Now that I think about it, there were a disturbing amount of war games marketed to the general public, which groomed them for real-world combat on battlefields, and many suspected that covert military departments were using these platforms to train their artificial intelligence programs to learn and compute tactical data for such scenarios.

The gaming community evolved into a different shade than the nefarious social networks that were so popular at the time. The governmental departments of our paramilitary police could eavesdrop on personal communications over satellite; targeting virtually anyone. However, they seemed to be clumsy, if not outright incapable, of intercepting online games where the players passed information and data among themselves in real time. It soon became clear that if government security agents were able to actually access and 'play' within digital arenas alongside other gamers, they would usually stick out like a sore thumb and were promptly booted from privately owned servers.

Furthermore, gamers had their own identities hidden through server jumps and the virtual world soon became the only place where people could converse with confidentiality or without fear of reprisal. It soon expanded into a unique niche that outsmarted the government spooks. The nosy authorities that be, tried to counter this by creating their own gaming servers to entrap members into their web of surveillance with the lure of cash contests and valuable prizes; but most of us were too savvy to fall for that ruse.

Like an idiot, I had no idea that that poster on the wall was a communication and surveillance device, until several days later when it suddenly blinked on with another background and Beatrice was there to greet me on its screen. I was so startled that I jumped.

"Good morning Caity," she gleamed as the lighting in my room began to gently brighten as proof she had control of my cement cage, "I hope you've caught up on your rest. A brief excursion has been planned for you today, please be ready in fifteen minutes to meet the Director." She smiled at me through the screen, giving momentary pause as if awaiting my reply but I was too dumbfounded to say anything until after the screen switched to display the countdown of a clock, giving me barely fourteen minutes to prepare myself.

I had washed my clothes by hand in the sink days before and set them out to dry. I did so against my host's repeated requests that I place my old attire in the disposal whenever they brought my meals, although I noted that she never once tried to actually touch them, nor to make contact with myself for that matter, which confirmed my suspicions that I had been held here for quarantine observation. Regardless, I donned the placid tan jumpsuit they had furnished and tucked away my old clothes in a dark corner behind the counter, beyond sight of the view-screen camera.

The door opened on cue when the timer on the screen ran out. This time, Beatrice herself was waiting outside the doorway, so I attempted to display a decent degree of pleasantries and small talk as I could muster for the moment. After responding in turn, she motioned me to join her as we made our way down the corridor.

"The General has granted an audience to learn a little bit about you, and hopefully, to find a place for you in our community, Caity." That shocking revelation caught me off guard and worried me more than a tad. Did they really have the mind to keep us trapped down here? I was sure our friends up top were starting to get concerned that we had not yet returned since several days had already passed in our absence. She handed me a clip to tie up my hair, which was now gratefully clean from using the hydrosonic shower, of which I cheated and used water from the tap to finish the job. Having steam and soap bubbles vibrating across your naked body at high frequency was a sensation I don't think I could ever get used to. Admittedly, it was a highly efficient use of water for such a mundane task, but in my own personal opinion, I found sonic showers to be a slightly unnatural and measurably unpleasant experience.

I accompanied Beatrice down the corridors with a pair of armed guards following in our step. I wasn't too terribly anxious to meet this brash Kane fellow again face-to-face, but admit I was actually curious as to how this group of people had survived so well for nearly a decade all bottled in like this underground. They must have had a vast amount of supplies in stock and resources to spare for such an extended stint.

Hoping as I was to see my friends; after being ushered through a set of steel double doors, a brief smile of relief crossed my face as I saw both Haiti and Thorn sitting at a large oval table before us. Across from them sat the General, with a smug gleam in his eye and a cheerless thin line upon his lips as he turned his glare my way which was surprisingly effective at quelling my spirits or making any attempt to openly greet my comrades.

Haiti's crazy dreadlocks were now replaced by a mash of hair that looked like a botched attempt at being cleaned without the advantage of running water. One would imagine that the sonic showers were not prominently designed for his type of hairstyle. Thorn appeared just as joyless, sitting there in his identical brown jumpsuit. Both of the men looked at me uncomfortably when I walked in, which swiftly set the mood in the room. I was assuming this was going to be an unpleasant conversation.

Beatrice sat me down next to my companions and moved around the table to take her position in a chair behind the General, while a pair of guards took their posts at the door. I really didn't know what to expect and began to get nervous from the heightened tension hanging in the air. Being under the spotlight like this really wasn't my cup of tea.

"Now that you are all here, we need to address certain issues about your continued residency here at Haven," Kane granted his stern words without meeting us eye to eye. A quick glance over my shoulder revealed my companions were just as disturbed by the General's statement.

By the way he carried his voice, Kane was the Alpha-male around here and he made sure everyone knew it. In short order, he assigned us various job duties and made it clear that we would only have limited access to certain sections of the facility until the day we earned such privileges that the other residents enjoyed. Apparently, the earth-toned jumpsuits we donned were status marks of the lowest level of stature one could have here within their improvised community. A pseudo-totalitarian society had evolved here over the years of confinement that relied on subordinates who were valued solely by their skills, position, and above all, loyalty to the General who was now Top Dog; and had been for quite some time.

Both of my male acquaintances were ushered off with a set of attendants who directed them to their new accommodations and were dictated their new responsibilities in the 'social group' as Kane had so titled it. When the verbal thrashing was over, I had a sinking feeling in my stomach, even though Kane abruptly ignored me altogether as he got up to leave the conference room. Thankfully, Beatrice, who had been quietly sitting in the background without uttering a whisper the entire time, came over to offer a kind hand to let me up out of my seat. I think she could see the sullen look in my blue-green eyes, and I didn't feel well to say the least. Honestly, I wasn't very good at handling sudden amounts of stress dumped upon me in such an unceremonious manner.

"Don't fret, child," the old woman murmured softly, "the General likes to assert his authority when need be, and you three haven't had the advantage of being aware of the numerous sacrifices and hard work that he has accomplished over the years to keep us safe, and towards our devoted communal environment we have all come to appreciate as a result of it. He just doesn't know you. His stern disposition will dissolve over time ...you will see," she tried to assure me, though it sounded more like a sales pitch the way she slathered on her praise of the unpleasant old bastard.

"Why wasn't I assigned a post?" I had to inquire with the older woman, as I was not quite sure why Kane had failed to address me directly as he had my two friends.

"Oh, I think it is because you might remind him of his daughter," she revealed with a sigh of sadness, "she would have been about your age by now, and I might say that you faintly resemble her too. The poor girl passed away a few years back in an unfortunate accident when a portion of the tunnels collapsed..." Beatrice added, although, with an odd turn, just as quickly as it was mentioned, she changed the subject; leaving me hanging with a mixed emotion of both guilt and relief, "Anyhow, he put me in charge of seeing to your welfare. He has a reputable habit of being measurably more stringent with the men, of course; but I will help you find your bearings here, as long as you are willing to comply with the rules," she ended with a pat on my shoulder.

I felt an itch in the back of my throat when she said that, I really didn't like this word 'comply' nor the slight inflection of how she had used it.

"Are there a lot of people living here," I inquired as she led me out the door and into the main hall; trying to make idle conversation to glean what bits of information I could gather.

"Yes, quite many, dear..." she trailed off and quickly changed the direction of the conversation yet again by intent, I noticed, "Oh, silly me, I almost forgot to show you the arboretum!" Beatrice announced as she turned us about and headed the other direction to a white-painted corridor lined with an array of piping. The chamber beyond was uniquely different from the stale environment of the rooms I had seen thus far. We stepped into an enormous cavity with rows of trees that reached high towards the ceiling, which glowed with a pale turquoise light. What struck me by surprise was the abundant use of fountains incorporated into this garden gallery, as one might expect that water itself would likely be a scarce resource for the inhabitants in such a confined ecosphere.

There were several other individuals mulling about wearing either green or blue suits. Some workers were attending to the plant life, while other pairs simply appeared to be enjoying themselves with leisurely conversation in areas around the park. The leaves on all of the trees seemed brighter than normal, to the point is was almost surreal. Then again, I figured it must have been the strange tint of the lighting. Still, it was impressive that they were able to grow all of this down here so far underground by artificial sunlight.

"Quite a marvel isn't it!" Beatrice boasted, although it was more of a rhetorical question, "This is the garden area where we like to take our personal time to reflect," the pretentious old woman confessed as she led us inside.

Hurrying along to keep up with her, I was momentarily distracted by the gentle song of a bird, and with a quick search, I finally centered in on a tiny speaker perched among the tree branches as its source. That discovery was a little disheartening, though I realized that these recordings playing the sounds of nature were merely being used to enrich the atmosphere within the nursery.

"I'm still not sure what it is you want of me," I uttered when I finally got my host's attention once again, "and when may I see my friends again?"

"You can visit them in the main cafeteria in the worker's section below during their meal break," the elderly woman responded, "but that will be several hours from now," she turned again towards a set of round doors that led to a brightly lit glass elevator, "but for now, there is something important I wish to discuss with you, Caitlin."

Her change of tone caught me off guard but I was willing to listen if there was something that affected me directly. I sure as hell did not want to stay down here trapped in this bunker, to rot away my life with the rest of these indentured servants to Overlord Kane. The problem was, there was the issue of not being able to make our way back through the vent system the way we had arrived, which had ended up being a one-way trip to nowhere. The population down here had electrical power and ample supplies, and they were still functioning with a measure of decency after all these years cut off from the rest of the world, so it was still worth investigating just how they managed this feat under such extraordinary circumstances.

It took me but a moment to decide to play coy and let Beatrice expose as much as she would allow, just to see what I could learn.

"Certainly, Miss Beatrice, what can I do for you?" I turned on the act of being submissive to her persona in an effort to help me glean whatever information I could about this facility. Though, on the other hand, I had no idea she was playing me for a fool.

"Our little community has suffered some losses ...a few minor setbacks recently," she revealed as we exited the elevator on the upper level of the arboretum, "and some fresh perspectives provided by a person like yourself, Caity; someone recently from the outside world would help us here immensely. Your insight would be invaluable, even essential," she explained.

For the first part, I could understand their dilemma. As a community of civilians under the rule of a military commander, who were in the unfortunate position of being trapped down here by the collapsed tunnels and a horde of infected blocking their only means of escape to the subway sections and access to the surface. However, as she explained their dire situation, her story took an unprovoked turn that I found personally distasteful. Beatrice wanted to address the community members of Haven to introduce me as a survivor from the surface, but it was like a kick in the teeth when she asked if I would be willing to twist the truth *'just a tidbit'* as she so eloquently put it.

The fact was, life up top was a hard struggle for survival, but there were certainly many options that could change that. Down here in the bunker, there were doctors, scientists, and engineers that could assist to re-educate and rebuild from the basics to help their entire community make a fresh start on the world above if they were allowed to leave.

I would suspect that the generators we had revealed in the basement of the building where my friends and I had set up camp, could be effectively rerouted to direct its voltage out to the exterior power lines. I could imagine if they set up a walled grid and devised a secured perimeter to keep out any stray infected, there was always the chance we could continue the fight and try to produce a real cure for the plague. There was no reason to wallow and waste away the rest of our lives like subterranean rats deep underground like this; that was a horrible thought. However, as Beatrice began to debate the beneficial points of their social settings, there were a few, if any, meager advantages to her opening proposal.

"So, as you have noted, Caity, there are many dangers out there, and admit the outbreak of the disease is still rampant," Beatrice confirmed after our hour-long discussion on the current state of the world, outside of her slanted comprehension of the one she and her fellow servants endured here.

"But, that might not be the case everywhere," I tried to argue, "there are many groups of survivors who strive to live normal lives," I contended, attempting to plead my point with her but losing the overall mark I was trying to outline.

"But you agreed that their lives were harsh and existence was day by day, without the stability or security of knowing what their future could be," Beatrice played against my own words, "life is safer down here, for the time being ...and perhaps in time we can try to rebuild society into a semblance of the way it once was."

It was a tough argument; one that had many sides, but one which placed their health and safety above their individual freedom. Truth was, the world above was a scary place to be, but Haven was also more than a bit frightening in its own way. In the end, I finally agreed to do as she requested if only to play for time.

As a reward for bending to her wishes, I was granted a new residence on the privileged green level. Worker status also had its rewards, such as ease of duties with better quality of meal allowances and personal accommodations. That bothered me to a certain extent but I didn't want to appear ungrateful. Beatrice gave the orders that provided me with an emerald green uniform to match my post, as there were certain regulations all residence of Haven had to abide by. Likely that was because of the oppressive hand of General Kane keeping everyone in their place. As promised, she directed an available chaperon to show me how to get down to the worker-zone cafeteria level during their meal break to find my friends.

Once there, I was appalled at the sterile environment of their commissary where the brown-suited laborers gathered.   It resembled a prison environment compared to most of the settings on the upper levels. It took me a few minutes to find my friends through the almond haze of bodies shifting through waiting lines at the service counter, who promptly fanned out to their designated seats with meal trays in hand. I couldn't help notice that my assigned female escort also kept a diligent eye on me as she stood by the door away from the crowd.

Haiti stood up and waved me over when I spotted them as we made eye contact. Thorn was also there with a smile on his face. They kept a firm grip on their platters as we sat down together, not wishing to lose their paltry meals. From what Beatrice had led on, down here food was used as a form of leverage against the workers; like a reward payment for their services and loyalty.

I looked at the slop they had been served, feeling guilty about the finer meals we were provided on the green level. Nevertheless, my companions appeared righteously grateful to have some decent grub that didn't entirely consist of anything out of expired tin containers.

"Here, try this Caitlin," Haiti gleamed as he offered me his drink, "they have fucking soda pop here man!" I accepted it and politely took a sip, not wanting to sour the mood of their meager feast if they knew I had been served a gourmet meal before coming down here to visit them.

"What is it they have you two doing, you both seemed a bit distraught back in that meeting with the Director," I asked.

"*Distraught?*" Haiti spouted in his usual booming voice, "Girl, we were rightly upset!" He bolstered aloud, but he tuned down his voice after noticing several people turning their heads towards his outburst, "That damn evil-eyed old man is bad news," he tried to whisper in my direction while referring to his thoughts of General Kane.

"Maybe, you should try not to draw any attention to us," Thorn advised harshly, so Haiti began to ease his initial excitement, "we were separated into solitary cells for three days until we saw you again back there. Are you alright, Caity?" Thorn asked with gentle eyes.

"Yes," I smiled back weakly, noting his concern, "same with

me, but I was put in the care of a woman named Beatrice, she was that older lady who was sitting in the back of the conference room. Have you two happened to have heard anything about her from the other workers?" I inquired as Haiti made a conspicuous note of my teal shaded threads.

"They assigned us duties cleaning up corridors through the maze of maintenance rooms down here, but no, we haven't heard anything about that woman; but I'll ask around if you would like," Thorn replied.

"Aye, if we can; people not too friendly to strangers down here," Haiti added with a shrug. I noticed that he had already started making a hapless attempt to repair his braids. His trial use of the hydrosonic showers had done a real number on them.

"So what's your situation?" Thorn inquired my way over the clattering roar of the cafeteria; which was a subject I wanted to discuss but there wasn't any degree of privacy sitting in this crowd and I was concerned about being overheard. We had no idea who might be listening. I didn't want to make it sound as if I was getting special treatment, as I actually was; but I didn't want to lower their spirits or spurn any loss of trust.

"It's like this..." I began, searching for the right words, "since we are newcomers, the General wants me to address the residents here and tell their people how hard and horrible it is living outside of this bunker.   Basically, they want to keep everyone in here in this ...this *prison* for their own 'safety' as they put it," I explained with distaste.

"Whoa," Haiti spat out, "sounds like a power trip to me. The Man, he don't wanna lose control of his servants!" He finished, pretty much hitting the nail on the head about Kane as far as I was concerned.

"And you're going to go through with this ...what is it called, a propaganda campaign?" Thorn inquired with a raised brow and a hint of disbelief.

"I, I don't know yet," I stuttered, struggling with the issue, "but I think we should, just to give us some time to figure a way out of here," I compromised, and it seemed Haiti approved of that idea with an eager nod. However, by his blank expression, I could not interpret if Thorn accepted my plan or not. He was hard to read that way.

As I sat there wavering on his hesitant response, a toned bell rang in the cafeteria hall signaling that the meal break was over and the room began to flood with the sound of clattering trays and the rumble of boots of the workers rushing to get back to their posts. Haiti and Thorn stood up reluctantly, mentioning they had to get back to their assignments and that we should try to speak again tomorrow.

"As a precaution, don't go talking to the other residents here about what it is and isn't like topside, okay?" I hurried to advised the boys before they rushed off, "We don't want to cause any waves and need to keep our stories straight while we figure a way out of this nuthouse," I pleaded. Both of them agreed firmly with that precaution, though Thorn seemed more concerned than Haiti about what direction this was going. In short, we were being coerced to influence Haven's residents by telling them a watered-down lie; but more importantly, not to influence the local tenants into asking too many questions that might fuel a revolt.

Over the next few days of us biding our time and gathering Intel, it was turning out that our initial suspicions were more correct than we had hoped. Not only was General Kane a power monger, he wasn't exactly shy about it either. He had obtained an unwavering reputation throughout the facility that bordered on indentured servitude, if not outright slavery, in regards to his expectations of the residents.

It wasn't any real surprise how he might have attained such a position of unquestioned compliance from the inhabitants, since anyone who was saturated with the standard military method of thinking considered everyone else, especially civilians, as their lesser. In respect, those holding the guns - made the rules. It made me nervous, wondering what would happen to those who had refused to comply. The residents here seemed to keep their distance from us, almost at the point of intentional avoidance as if they had already been warned not to get too friendly.

As the days grew closer to my appointed public speech, I began to gather that the main reason everyone else appeared shy about getting too familiar with my friends and I, was for a reason far more sinister. From the gossip we overheard, it began to surface that those who crossed the General were prone to disappearing; which would be a difficult feat to perform in such an enclosed facility. Anyone he didn't like, or might openly disagreed with him at one point or another, would ultimately suffer an unfortunate accident. However, there was never any definite proof of this rumored conspiracy, though I'm sure anyone who could have either confirmed such suspicions or been a direct witness, would have quickly learned to bite their tongue. Kane was feared, and rightly so. Down here, he wasn't just a leader, he was their Master.

Haiti and Thorn tried to garner as much information as they could about the facility and explore the maze of vacant corridors during the course of their maintenance duties. As it turned out, they learned there were several sections of the underground bunker that had been sealed off by the order of their illustrious General. Oddly, many of these unused sections had been marked as either collapsed or structurally unsafe, though neither Thorn nor Haiti had actually noted any such reported damage. What soon came to light was that nobody else except for the small handful of staff in the upper tier of administration was even aware of the hordes of mutant Weepers that roamed the upper levels, which blocked them off from the only avenue back to the surface.

They had all been lied to and were intentionally trapped in this place, but everyone victimized by this ruse had been told it was merely a safety precaution to keep looters out. It soon became obvious this wasn't going to end well if we stayed here. We had to find a way out of this insane asylum.

Working in the green level wasn't too terribly exciting, considering that Beatrice had me assigned to light duties that were removed from anything that might reveal the sensitive technical operations of their conservatory. I wasn't stupid though; from what I could tell by what I had seen of the system charts, was that their greenhouse biosphere relied heavily on the hydro generators up top, although that was only one of many such power stations along the grid that fed this bunker. Water vapor was currently being pumped in and recycled through the floral chambers and mated with enriched oxygen to create breathable air, and any excess carbon dioxide was used as a catalyst for the process during the exchange.

I was not entirely keen on how the hydro cells worked but noted that several of their power substations had been flagged as offline. Apparently, these had also provided electricity to the subway system we had arrived on, and the entire array wasn't currently working even close to half of the capacity as it had been originally designed for. While in preparations, Beatrice finally informed me that I would be expected to make a statement during an inauguration of one of Kane's new lieutenants; which was apparently a big deal for the locals since it provided a welcome break from the monotony.

She was kind enough to hand me a prepared speech fully dictating what I was supposed to say, and was allowed to adlib its contents to a certain extent in my own words; though it was an expectation that I covered its underlined content. When I took the script to my bedchamber that evening, I began to feel slightly ill. It was as if I felt hollow inside and slightly tormented about how unfair it was for me to have to lie to all these innocent people for my own personal sake. Here I was, letting myself be used as an instrument to further victimize and dupe these individuals into complacency, so they could continue to serve their superiors in their subjugated existence.

I didn't get any sleep that evening, though I had to struggle to keep my thoughts inside since I was pretty damn sure there was someone on the other end of the video-screen poster on the wall spying on my every move; so I read the scripted notes aloud for the sake of my eavesdroppers. The words were hard to say:

- - -

"Residents of Fallhaven, I wanted to thank you for taking my companions and I into your welcome arms, and for your most generous hospitality. As you may already know, the plague endures and the infected still roam the surface," at least the introduction was mostly true, "...we heard rumors of this safe house; the legend of Fallhaven, which was the only refuge of its kind. For years, we struggled in starvation, running from the rampant sickness and gangs of murdering looters who care nothing for human life. In our despair, we had nearly lost all hope until we found this refuge.

(instructions: *pause and turn to motion towards the General, who will be standing to your right*)

Our sincerest gratitude to General Kane for his direction and generosity, and for giving us a new home where we can feel safe, and are now able to lead fulfilled lives. With sincerity, I can assure you that compared to the ruins and wastelands of the world above; what you have built together here is truly a Haven for all.

(instructions: *wait for applause from the crowd, then humbly smile and relinquish the stand to General Kane - then step away to your left and take your position beside the guards*)."

- - -

At that moment several levels above, a small blinking light on the main cryogenic console switched from red to a constant blue, while a pool of moisture had collected around an immense stasis chamber ending its thawing cycle. Awakening from its frozen slumber, something very large and angry trapped within the cylinder started to smash its way out of its metal sheath; denting the thick steel walls of the incubator, trying to get free.

Michel Savage

Control

When Beatrice came to greet me the next day, I saw that there was still a pair of armed guards stationed outside my door. Notice of my upcoming speech during the day's celebration had previously been broadcast to the citizens of Haven during their morning announcements. No matter how frivolous or routine such observances were, they served as a distraction from the tedious grind of subterranean life and the reality of their regrettable situation. They were like animals trapped in a cage, and their Masters didn't want the civilians left idle with too much time to think about that fact or letting it germinate any foul flavors of rebellion that had been quietly brewing during their long confinement.

Of course, over the past several years, there had been a few sporadic revolts against his authority since their incarceration here, but Kane had learned to rule with an iron hand. Those that followed in his shadow were wise enough to know not to cross him. Too many people had disappeared under his watch. He knew all too well how to silence troublemakers.

Anyone who didn't approve of their Commanders' personal brand of leadership found themselves excluded from such concerns in short order. He had a skill for keeping even his most trusted accomplices unsure as to who helped him carry out his dirty work. As a man of many dark secrets, Kane prided himself on how he juggled his subjects.

Beatrice had learned to survive with a measure of personal comfort that her position allowed. Whether Kane had faith in her or not was entirely irrelevant, at least to him. The General trusted no one, that is how he kept his flock in order and his head above water no matter what circumstances might fall his way. It had nothing to do with logic or intelligence, it was all about knowing how to manipulate others; something he did exceedingly well.

It wasn't by chance either, that it was only his assigned guards who had access to firearms; he knew full well that those who carry the guns, make the rules. This was an old law of the land, above ground, or below. It also happened to be a hard lesson I had yet to learn. I was not entirely naive myself; but guilty of making a few of the same mistakes over again, more than once.

It was this aching lack of trust I had with Beatrice, the way she held her tone with me, the fake kindness, or her style of twisting a conversation towards her own interests and the way she cleverly shied away from any touchy subjects with her, was a practiced technique of avoidance. I saw through this; not at first, but the damp and murky shade of her character made me uneasy. Of course, I could just have been paranoid and made it all up in my head; but then again, I could also be as right as rain.

An hour before the ceremony was to begin Betty wanted to make sure I was up to the task of speaking to the residence of Haven without choking on stage. I had been escorted from my apartment directly to her chambers for my final review since she had desired to analyze how I was going to carry my words to the audience, and had me do a read-through of my speech. Being wary that I was likely going to be subject to such scrutiny, I had practiced the dialog a half dozen times the night before, if not for fearing to look like a complete fool in front of everyone. Nonetheless, she was more than willing to correct my style of delivery.

"That should be fine..." Beatrice breathed after a long pause while turning her attention away from my gaze as if to deny me any additional hint of approval or simply just to keep me on my toes. I picked up our teacups and took them back over to the dispenser for another serving of warm honey and lemon that she suggested I drink before we began. With practiced innocence, when I saw that she had left her back towards me for a brief moment, I set down both cups with one hand and pocketed two data cards she had placed on the edge of her desk; hastily left there in preparation for the affairs of the day.

I had no clue as to what they were for or what information they had on them, but I simply couldn't let the only opportunity to acquire some answers slip by me. They were small enough to carry unnoticed or ditched somewhere if circumstances dictated. I just needed a way to access them via a console or tablet when I found a spare moment. However, that would have to wait until after the evening's events when I could find a minute to slip away after performing my expected obligations behind the podium.

Without missing a beat, I placed our steaming cups of tea on a tray and brought them back to the central table where we had been sitting before she turned back towards me once again. I did not wish to appear too eager, but I knew that both of my friends would also be present in the crowd during the celebration. Honestly, I wasn't looking forward to acting out this ruse, but it was our only option available to fit in until we could climb our sorry asses out of this forsaken hole and back into the daylight. I calmly smiled at the older lady as she offered me some last-minute advice while I sipped my fragrant tea; just as I had mentally practiced the night before. I was merely mirroring her own act and willing to take the chance she was too pretentious to notice.

For the first time since my friends and I had literally crashed their party nearly a week ago, I got the chance to see the main conference hall in its entirety. A creative ensemble of fresh decorations had replaced its former scheme. Now golden streamers and a number of tattered and manhandled signs along with colorful banners glorifying Fallhaven, had been arranged around the large room. Across several tables lay an assortment of fancy snacks and appetizers which sat on silver trays, along with an entire gang of attendees serving as waiters.

Frankly, I could see how granting such delicacies and the occasional entertainment would keep the civilians sated for short spats of time, satisfying such basic needs on a purely psychological level. The laboring tenants of Haven were milling about the room, most gathered in small pockets of conversation; their status of brown, blue, and green jumpsuits rarely intermingled. As always, the staunch gray uniformed guards kept vigil like unpleasant mannequins. It was my initial impression that Kane had molded them with that attitude, keeping them intentionally impersonal and unapproachable to the residents.

The buzz in the room quickly died down when music began to play over the speakers. As if on cue, the lights lowered and the General stepped out into the spotlight onto a stage that was set above the ensemble of guests. I followed behind Beatrice who took the lead up onto the stage behind Kane, who was adorned in his outlandishly gaudy costume with all its glinting medals. With a quick glance up, I noted that they had fixed the vent on the ceiling from which we had made our embarrassing entrance several days before.

Kane took a moment to turn towards the crowd and acknowledged their applause, then took a seat behind the stand. As instructed, I stood beside the guard at the steps while Beatrice attended the podium. Her voice was amplified throughout the complex as she addressed the crowd, and she began her speech once their voices were quelled.

"Welcome friends," Beatrice started, softening up the crowd for my brief introduction before ultimately surrendering their attention to the General, who was hobnobbing with the new officer recently accepted into his ranks, "we have a few new guests with us in our Haven; a rare treat indeed. I would like to introduce you to one of our three recent additions to our family ...Caity," the older lady turned as she motioned for me to take the stand.

Moving to her spot, I noted the marking placed on the stage denoting where to stand so that the directional microphone embedded in the ceiling could pick up my voice. Once in front of the audience, I could now see just how many there were, assuming, of course, that most of the workers had been allowed to attend. A quick estimate appeared to be several hundred, likely many more due to the blur of color-coded uniforms that blended in the crowd. Gladly, I did notice that Thorn and Haiti had both managed to squirm their way as close to the platform as they could. Haiti gave me a wide silly smile and waved, though realizing that my every movement and word I would say had been carefully choreographed for me. Regardless, he didn't seem too offended that I didn't wave back to him.

I took a deep breath and steadied myself, knowing that I had to impress Kane and his minions in effort to be allowed any measure of leeway from the short leash my friends and I had been placed on since our arrival. I didn't want to screw this up. It was best to give him what he wanted for the meantime until we could figure out where we were. I did not like the idea of lying to all these people, but hoping someday I would have the chance to correct the glaring indiscretion I was about to commit and clear my conscience. Still, I felt a bit selfish; but I couldn't let Kane or his trusted cohort Beatrice get a hint of how my friends and I really felt about this place.

The evening before, I had a fuming bout of insomnia; failing to get any restful sleep for most of the night. I had been in turmoil, contemplating if we should just consider staying in the bunker. There was a measure of safety here, and the quality of living was far higher than any of us had experienced in several years. In addition, there was food, and lots of it; stowed in carbon gas packets that could last for decades. Theoretically, we could live out the remainder of our lives here in relative peace.

The downside was that there was a steep price to pay for that resolution, which had a gaping flaw that blemished its floral appeal. I thought long and hard about the sacrifices; to never breathe fresh air again, or see another sunset, nor any possibility of finding something better and merely settle for living under someone else's thumb, and forbidden to express how you felt ...or even know who you could trust for that matter. The constant eavesdropping and spying on every citizen within these walls and their lack of choice, made me want to claw my way out of here through the dirt with my bare hands if I had to. I finally had to admit to myself that I couldn't accept being caged like this.

- - -

"Residents of Fallhaven," I pushed myself to start as Beatrice placed her hand upon my shoulder, as either an act of encouragement or a subtle reminder of her control, "I want to thank you for taking my companions and I into your welcome arms, and for your most generous hospitality," Beatrice nodded over towards Kane for his approval as I continued. The thumping of my heart seemed louder than it should, while I struggled to calmly control my anxiety, "as you may already know, the plague..." at that moment, there was a dull thump in the ceiling which made me turn my eyes upward for a brief moment, assuming that the ventilation units had kicked in, "of infected..." I continued, as another thump even louder from above turned the heads of several in the crowd upward as tiny crackles of dust sifted down upon their heads, "still roam..." I paused as a rise of murmurs erupted from the crowd while another audible pounding sent a large crack racing across the facade paneling on the cement roof, directly overhead.

Someone screamed and the crowd scattered as chunks of concrete gave way to larger slabs that came crashing down onto the ballroom floor. One hunk of rubble smashed into the buffet tables, sending food flying into the crowd. The residents fell over themselves in panic, trampling their fellow tenants. The guards hurried to Kane's side, helping him up as they looked around nervously for an avenue to escape the chamber and avoid the hysteria of the mob. Another crash echoed from above, and I was thankful to find that both Thorn and Haiti had mounted the platform and were at my side.

Nobody knew what was going on. My first thought was that the machinery lining the bunker had finally failed in a most catastrophic way; or maybe it was an earthquake weakening the integrity of the supports. We were frightened. Thankfully, the few of us left on stage were out of harm's way of the falling debris and the panicked crowd. We watched helplessly as chunks of concrete and metal beams rained down upon the hapless people below.

Another violent blow cracked open a section of the ventilation, which smashed to the floor and we all froze in silent horror when we heard a deep chilling growl rise from beyond the crumbled breach. One of the guards pointed Kane towards a rear door, while my two companions and I chose to follow in pursuit. After all, those guards were the only ones with firearms and we needed to get our hands on more weapons. We rushed after the General and his retainers as they slipped past the screaming mob through a secured exit that had been kept locked by means of an access keypad.

Glancing behind us, as we left the shattered remains of the ballroom, a mutated creature with oversized hands pushed aside the broken vents above, and its large bloated face turned its aggression towards the shouts of terror from those who caught sight of the monstrosity. The grotesque giant reminded me of that twisted mutation we had seen in the center of the shopping mall several floors above. Obviously, this creature had somehow bypassed the UV chamber in the arboretum, and had forced its way through the ventilation system. Luckily, it appeared to be alone; for it wasn't accompanied by the hordes of infected that roamed the upper levels.

The sight of it caught our breath short. We were used to seeing the distorted faces of those who had suffered from the virus, but this was a freakish beast straight out of a nightmare. Thorn secured the door behind us as we pressed to keep hot on the General's heels while his entourage swept him to safety. Beatrice, herself, was also in a state of panic as she tagged along beside Kane, though neither of them bothered to look back behind them in their haste. The way they had so readily fled the scene to save their own skins without care or concern for their fellow tenants was deplorable, and revealed their true colors under all their fluff and pompous bravado.

Through a maze of halls, we fled through the twisting corridors, which finally opened up into a wider industrial section hidden in the rear of the facility. This area had been kept off-limits to the civilians and made me wonder why it hadn't been displayed on any diagrams I had seen before. The three of us kept on Betty's tail, lest we get lost. Bursting through a pair of doors, the guards fell in first to secure the room and failed to notice that my friends and I had been following close behind. We stomped in as the gray suits pulled their weapons on us while turning their nervous eyes towards Kane for instructions.

"Halt! This is a security section, the three of you are to leave immediately," the guard barked as he pointed his gun at us.

"No, wait a moment," Kane uttered, as he ordered the guard to stand down, "since they're already here, I can imagine these new members might be able to enlighten us to the situation at hand," he finished with a look that I could only perceive as contempt.

"Yes, I imagine they could," Beatrice cut in while taking a moment to fix her ruffled bun, "tell us the truth about how you really got down here past the infected on the mall level?"

It was a final revelation that these two were fully aware of the hordes of carriers on the section above. Kane promptly sat down at a console and opened a channel that echoed throughout the complex.

"This is a code orange; a lockdown is now in order for all tenants. All citizens are to remain in their quarters or report to your nearest emergency stations to await further instructions," at this, he hit a series of keys on the board and an emergency alarm kicked in.

"Are we going to escalate this to white?" Beatrice asked in haste, a worried look washing across her face. The General looked just as tense, giving her a shrug of disapproval to reveal that code name considering their present company.

"What does that mean, going 'white'?" I blurted out, not like being left in the dark. Beatrice gave a distressed glance my way, realizing what she had divulged.

"A code white means, Evacuation," Kane stammered. His words made my head spin for a moment, but apparently, this admission was of no surprise to the pair of guards in the room.

"Evacuate where, to another section of this complex ...or up to the surface?" I demanded, almost knowing what his answer was going to be. As much as Kane liked to present himself being self-composed in front of his men, I caught him biting his lip in apprehension to my question.

"There is a means to get topside, but I will stress it is not without a measure of risk," he finally admitted.

It took a minute for me to connect the dots; there was a way to the surface but these two self-appointed bastards had kept that fact a secret to the others in order to keep their positions of power. I just shook my head in disgust at the way that some people are such iconic examples of the worst in human nature. I was so angry I wanted to scream, though I struggled to keep a bit of equilibrium in the presence of my friends.

"We did actually arrive here through a subway system, as we said before," I granted in our defense, "but it was on a level that was filled with Weepers."

"Weepers?" Beatrice asked in dismay; her statement revealing just how long they had been holed up down here.

"Yes, it was a common term given by the media after the plague hit the main population and was used to describe anyone who has the sickness," Thorn exclaimed, while Haiti nodded his head in agreement. To me, it revealed that Fallhaven itself, and any other vaults like this, had been filled to the brim and locked up at the drop of a hat when Apophis fell from the sky. When you think of it, that revealed an astonishing amount of construction and supplies and a whole lot of preplanning that just didn't add up in my opinion. I clenched the data cards hidden in my pocket that I had swiped from Betty's desk, wondering what secrets they might contain.

Kane motioned to one of the guards to lock the door. As he moved to the keypad, I stepped over towards Beatrice and tugged Haiti's arm as I passed by him. It was obvious Kane had become so relaxed and insolent of the sheep he had turned his citizens into over the past several years, that he was not used to having anyone second-guess him. Within his usual cavalier attitude, he noted aloud why he was locking the door ...it was his measure of control just to watch someone sweat. It was a well-worn tactic he used to determine the level of weight and sway he had over an individual. Unfortunately, for him, that was the wrong impression to have about us.

"There, of course, is the matter of your cooperation and required silence in this affair," he disclosed in a smug tone as the guard tapped in the lock code, "After we address this breach, we can't have you going around and..."

Cutting him off, I had already predicted the rest of the arrogant nonsense he was blabbering toward us, and took the opportunity of his distraction while he was gloating, and I forcibly shoved Beatrice off her feet and into his lap. As tall as I was, I could put some weight into it and she went sprawling across the console in front of him. The old woman was taken entirely by surprise to this turn of events, as was the guard who turned to catch her, and was promptly rewarded with an uppercut jab by Haiti, who had taken my cue. Thorn had strapped the guard who had been occupied locking the portal while his back was turned; having used the belt from his brown jumpsuit to garrote the sentry around his neck, while bending his arm behind his back.

The guard struggled a bit more than Thorn was in the mood for, so he smashed the man's head into the console on the wall, where he dropped like a stone to the floor, unconscious. The keypad he hit with the unfortunate guard's forehead answered in dispute with a crackle of sparks. Kane and his companion unraveled themselves from their tussle at the console only to find Haiti and Thorn pointing guns at them, which they had snatched from the guards. The General was a lean man, but not so stupid as to fight those odds.

"...You can't let us go around telling everyone you've been keeping them imprisoned down here all these years," I continued with Kane's train of thought before he was so rudely interrupted, "just to keep them under your thumb, huh?" I spouted with revulsion.

The look on his face was priceless; a mixture of defiance colored with admission. They had been pulling the strings for so long they had entangled themselves in the weave of their own lies. Of course, he would have to kill us to silence us, or as we would shortly discover, something far worse.

We secured the pair of guards with their own cuffs and tied up the two self-appointed Monarchs to their chairs with our loose belts. Taking a spare chair, I sat down at the console they had been hovering over and inserted one of the data cards I had swiped from her desk. The first card was a process log of the names and number of people residing in the complex. Within the log was a series of highlighted names of deceased individuals; their duties assigned and date of ouster.

It was that noted correlation between the evictions and listed casualty dates which I found bewildering, and I could not find a cross reference to what it meant. Hoping the second card I had in my possession would provide some clues, we discovered it brought up a three-dimensional blueprint of the complex revealing how it was tied into the hydro generators on the surface. The subway grid affirmed its connection to several other similar bunker compounds much farther along the route. However, the ping status of their grid activity was dark. Apparently, Fallhaven was the only housing shelter along the entire system that was still in operation.

"Aye, bring up them schematics there," Haiti requested as he pointed to a section on the holographic map on the levels where we were located. Zooming in on the details, I could trace where we had come down from the surface and bypassed the ventilation, down into the main storage chamber the Haven residence had remodeled into their main assembly hall. It was from there that I followed the trace of the ductwork where that creature had broken through; back up to discover its origin. Backtracking a few twists and turns brought us to that odd cryogenic chamber, and out to the air filters in the greenhouse with the UV lighting system and those mutated fruit trees.

"Ah, that be the freaky-fruit jungle there," Haiti exclaimed with a shiver, "Hey, are cameras in those areas be work'in?" he inquired, noting the camera icons situated on the map. Following the station numbers, I brought up several live feeds from the halls; luckily they all seemed to be quiet except for what we found in the stasis room. Within, we could see that one of the cylinders had been cracked open like an egg, with gouts of steam jetting from its shattered pipes. That got us worried.

"What the hell was in that?" I demanded with a note of apprehension as the three of us turned from the holographic map and over towards Kane. The look in Beatrice's eyes said volumes as she stared unblinking at the broken container displayed on the screen. Kane raised his voice as he tried to posture himself with a reply.

"That, Missy, is none of your business," he spat back. Thorn stepped up to give him a punch in the face while Kane flinched from the expected blow, but Thorn withdrew on the last second and ended it with a slight jerk of the old man's chin instead.

"*Pfft*, you're not worth it," Thorn professed with disgust.

"Look, whatever you had in there is now running wild in the complex, and we need to know what it is and how to stop it," I urged, stating the obvious gravity of the situation. Beatrice was genuinely frightened; her eyes were full of dread.

"That ...that level was a test project for the MN4 mutagen," she stammered.

"Keep your trap shut, Betty!" Kane griped as he snapped at her from his seat while he tugged at his constraints. It was clear Beatrice was more afraid of dying or devolving into one of those atrocities than she was of the General, himself.

"This shelter was funded by the government to house elite members of the cabinet and their families," she admitted hastily, "as were the other similar facilities tied to this complex by the underground air rail. Shortly after the global impact, several scientists from the government were assigned to create genetics research labs to study the Kriotin virus."

"To try and find a cure?" I pressed, noting the direct connection from the arboretum where we had discovered the mutated plants.

"...It started out that way," the old woman finally conceded, but that slight admittance only kindled the questions to follow.

Switching back to the personnel logs, I found several recordings after a few minutes of digging; a number of them were from Kane himself. What they revealed made our stomachs turn. In almost every case, the notations that marked a resident's death were of someone who had been banished to the upper levels where the infected thrived. These were all victims of Kane's pride, of course; his condemning death sentence for anyone who crossed him or refused to bend to his will over the past several years of his reign.

"What kind of *thing* were they creating in there?" Thorn asked, referring to both the genetically modified plants and human mutations.

"We had several medical scientists assigned to our site that started filling the stasis chambers with experimental subjects. Not to cure them, but to exploit the disease," she added, "We suspected it was to use against foreign nations as a type of biological weapon."

Her claim didn't make a lick of sense since the world was already experiencing a shit-storm as it was; who in their right mind would want to make things worse?

"For what possible reason?" I had to inquire as I struggled to get the words out, while shaking my head in complete bafflement. Turning on a live feed in the lower decks, we saw the giant mutant had freed itself from the ventilation system and was now tromping through the halls of the compound, crushing the heads of anyone that stumbled within its reach.

"In case there were other countries that survived the epidemic in better condition than ours, idiot girl," Kane barked in with a shade of contempt, "anyone who produced a vaccine would have total control and the leverage to get anything they wanted. Every other country would have to concede to their demands."

Though his words had conviction, it was from faulty, if not entirely tainted logic; one that only someone with a warped and twisted military mind could conceive as remotely rational. Of course, the idea of it was entirely insane. I completely lost my composure.

"Are you two fucking deranged?" I screamed back at them, so much so, as to make both Thorn and Haiti jump with a note of surprise, "what kind of irresponsible nut considers forcing their authority or contemplating thoughts of domination while the world is falling apart around them?" I glared at them both for a heated second, "There are no boundaries anymore, or countries to conquer. If you had bothered to pull your head out of your ass and see what it's like topside, you would have noticed there are more pressing matters rather than rotting down here and playing Emperor Kane!" I finished, feeling exhausted. Nevertheless, in my furious rant I had made a point; everyone down here, including Kane, likely had no clue just how far the world and our collective societies had dissolved over the past half dozen years.

"Aye, there are no governments left to rule, lad," Haiti tossed in, with a kind hand on my shoulder to comfort me as he addressed Kane. Thorn pointed out all the dead zones on the connecting air rail and chimed in.

"Didn't you ever stop to wonder why the other shelters aren't responding?" Thorn asked calmly, bringing a sense of rational awareness back into the discussion, "So what exactly happened here that made you want to stay in this hole?" He petitioned, though deep down the three of us already knew the answer.

This facility, as were all the other bunkers on the diagram, were connected by hundreds of miles of underground tunnels via the subway system which was built several years in advance and in complete secrecy from the general public. It made us suspicious that the Authorities had already known the asteroid would make impact and had been well prepared for its aftermath. The contagion that it carried which had spread across the globe had likely been an unforeseen contingency, which had thrown a wrench into their plans; destroying any idea they might have had to force their continuation of government.

During their first year in Fallhaven, the scientists worked on a secret project to enhance the virus while the medical division was attempting to thwart the spread of the disease. They had a staff of botanists that began a branch of study using plants to concoct a cure by incubating the infection and eradicating genetic markers in the process, so they could introduce an effective antigen into the ecosystem. Of course, this research was manipulated and bastardized by the military scientists towards their own ends, being the curious little critters that they were, and threw any ethical considerations right out the window. They, in turn, fed these modified plants cultivated with the virus to their test subjects with alarming results.

These test patients mutated to a desirable effect but soon evolved to a point where they became exceptionally violent and uncontrollable, and were eventually placed in stasis chambers for continued testing under sedation. During a lapse of protocols on one fateful day, a single test subject escaped, which indirectly spread the disease among the staff. Unfortunately, for everyone else, those few scientists who became contaminated were the only technicians who would have been able to provide a defensive treatment. Everything swiftly went to hell after that episode, and those few victims with the enhanced KRI syndrome were sealed off from the lower levels, which left them imprisoned within the mall wing of the building.

No longer having the mental capacity to operate the subway system, the infected found themselves trapped within the plaza were unable to suffer the intense UV lights of the arboretum. In the beginning, those few Weepers were arguably well off, since there were vast storerooms behind the numerous deli's and restaurants, which contained a warehouse of food and water that could sustain thousands. Those first few infected slowly rose in numbers as Kane and his entourage discarded any undesirables in their ranks to the mall level.

Outright murdering someone was simply not his style since it would create the hassle of hiding the body, evidence which could later be discovered and the method of their demise would come under scrutiny. Therefore, a plausible option was to lock them in the plant nursery, where the victims would either eventually consume the infected fruit or take their chances trying to cross the mall to the subway tunnels. Even if someone actually made it that far, it would grieve them to find the tram controls had been smashed beyond repair by the feral weepers wandering the mall level. Overall, it was a grim fate.

In the meantime, the General and his accomplice took the opportunity to exercise control over their subjects as their self-appointed protectors. They then proceeded to mold and segregate the social order to their own liking. Kane and Beatrice told whatever convenient lie to the community to keep themselves in a position of authority and would decisively silence those that questioned their judgment. Down here, they were judge, jury, and executioner. While up top on the surface, these two old scabs were useless weight and nothing more than nonessential bureaucrats.

Kane liked playing God; he wasn't about to let anyone know there was a safe way to get outside where they would be far beyond his grasp. I was perplexed by this situation, and there were odd pieces to their story that just didn't seem to fit. I understood Kane's self-absorbed tactics, but I couldn't understand why he could be so utterly stupid as to allow those test subjects to live. Why hadn't he just sterilized the stasis chambers when he had the chance and be done with it, and remove the threat entirely?

"What possible rationale would prompt you to let those things live," I stammered in contemplation of the absurd ignorance of it all while I pointed to the giant mutant on the screen, as we watched as it lumbered on its rampage down the residential halls, "when you could have just unplugged those cryogenic units and remove the danger they posed?"

In response, the General looked like he was searching for his words, choosing what he preferred not to reveal, but Beatrice had self-preservation in mind and beat him to the punch.

"Those specimens were our only leverage for assistance when the Militia Commanders arrived," she blurted.

Their muddled sensibility slowly became clear; those giant mutated lab rats were insurance, a guarantee for a position in rank when they got out of here. The problem was, the military brass never arrived; and they never would. In recent years, Kane had been forced to tighten his grip while playing King over his subservient subjects far longer than he had originally anticipated while keeping one eye on the clock as weeks turned to months, and months turned to years since the beginning of the catastrophe. In a small way, I could understand their dilemma; but I had no sympathy for their brazen selfishness.

"We need to help these people," Thorn noted with urgency, breaking the rising tension in the air as he pointed towards the security feed while the monster continued on its murderous spree through the complex as people scattered for safety. Anyone it had not killed was doubtlessly contaminated with the virus and would turn in a matter of hours, further spreading the pathogen.

"How can we stop this thing?" I pleaded with earnest, as victims continued to be butchered on the security footage.

"Caity, there were several empty service avenues below the maintenance rooms on the bottom level," Thorn answered, pointing to the area on the map where the manual laborers were stationed. Most operational areas were for refuse waste and water filtering, but it was a convenient maze of pipes that we could try to redirect that creature towards.

"You think we could trap it?" I inquired with hesitation.

"Nah, woman, we could kill that thing if we could lure it to the grinder!" Haiti mentioned with a half-smile, pointing to the processor room. The Grinder was the pet name given to it by the staff, which was a huge turbine fitted with interlocking blades. Its function was to pulverize food and plant waste into fertilizer for recycling back into the tree nursery and organic gardens. The problem was that it was located several levels down and there were a lot of innocent people caught in between along the way.

"Lure it with what, exactly?" I was afraid to ask.

"...Maybe live bait?" Haiti suggested with a questionable pause. The absurd thought of that made Kane laugh.

"Ludicrous! Why even bother? We should make our way out of here while we still can," he bellowed in contempt at the idea.

"What makes you think there is any '*we*' in that plan, old man?" Thorn shot back, "I'm all for leaving your sorry ass here, sir!" He finished sarcastically with a salute; then adjusting his hand as it pulled away into a personal message of contempt while flipping Kane his middle finger.

"We have to do what we can to save those people. How do we get them to the elevator on the level above?" I demanded towards our two hostages. At that moment, one of the bound guards lying beside Haiti began to stir and was quickly silenced again with a swift kick to the head.

The displayed map showed there were multiple routes, though we were aware it was outdated as many sections were either inaccessible or had collapsed. It turns out that Kane's daughter was one of the rare victims of Haven who had died in an authentic accident, rather than by foul play. Kane would cooperate to save his own skin, though his contempt was unwavering.

"We will assist you on one condition; that we both come with you," the General demanded, nodding across the table towards his accomplice, Betty, as the sole addition to that bargain. As we figured, he didn't actually give a crap about the two lackey guards lying unconscious on the floor. In his eyes, they were expendable.

Reluctantly, Thorn untied Kane but kept his gun handy and sat him at the console. His first step was to turn off the blaring alarm, and when he did, the creature we had been tracking on the cameras gave a curious pause.

"Hold on, turn that alarm back on for a second," I suggested. When he did, the mutant became agitated again. Kane turned it off once more and this seemed to pacify the brute.

The deformed beast continued to advance its way down the halls, only becoming irate when some poor soul was unfortunate enough to come within sight of it. There were a few people who didn't jump out of its way fast enough, only to have their heads promptly removed from their shoulders.

"Can you turn that alarm on in certain corridors? Maybe we can lure it by use of sound?" Thorn suggested to his captive at the console. Kane set up a line of sight, where the embedded alarms could be disabled on a route towards the recycle chamber located on the bottom level.

"It's taking the bait," Kane conceded, "and what's this grand plan of yours to get it to jump into that machine?" He huffed at the entire idiocy of our proposal.

"As my friend suggested, maybe a bit of live bait would actually work," Thorn answered as he nodded in agreement towards Haiti. With that, Thorn grabbed the old man by the arm, "and *you're it,* Kane; time to earn your stars!"

Beatrice was quick to assist us and helped devise a plan to instruct any survivors towards one of the sealed halls, while Thorn and Kane found a route to flank the creature and make their way to the waste processing chamber and attempt to lure it inside. As insurance, Kane vowed he would only repair the bypass to the central elevator once he was back safely. As little as we liked the idea, Thorn finally agreed; knowing he had to at least make a half-assed effort to keep the arrogant prick alive. I instructed Haiti to stay in the control room to keep a guarded eye on Beatrice and the monitors, while I went to help guide the survivors to safety.

"Stay here and help us to the elevators once I get everyone into the upper mess hall," I briefed, while Haiti affirmed without argument. I was suspecting he would rather stay here anyways, judging by his quick response, "Exactly how is it that you plan on getting that thing in there, really?" I asked Thorn with a breath of skepticism, referring to the recycling apparatus. Thorn just shrugged with a lack of immediate concern.

"Eh, I'll make something up," he replied with a thoughtless grin as we gave him a worried glance in response.

As Thorn was yanking the old man out the door, I followed close behind. We only had two pistols, so Thorn took one, while Haiti kept the other to keep Beatrice in line or either of the bound guards awoke and decided to give him a hassle. My mission was only to gather anyone I could find and guide them back to the secured corridors.

We backtracked towards the exit to the Ballroom and took a side passage that weaved its way through multiple service tunnels. This section of the complex had originally been off limits and designated as a restricted area to the residents, so only Kane and his guards had ever been aware of the outer perimeters. Once we hit a junction with an access door out in the security hall, Kane entered the code to unlock it.

"Be careful," I offered to Thorn with an almost idiotic thought of kissing him right then and there, which I admitted, would have appeared overly dramatic. Looking like a fool, I caught myself leaning into him and quickly regained my composure. He just gave me a nod, though I might have imagined a puzzled flash in his eyes. I felt like an embarrassed ass at that moment but did a damn good job of hiding it.

Thorn escorted Kane around a corner and was gone from sight; looping their way past the creature's current position as Beatrice would guide us both on our separate objectives from the control room and communicate through the local intercoms. I ran off on my errand and it didn't take long before I encountered several nervous residents hiding among the rooms and behind counters. I simply could not go around knocking on every door and had to keep the survivors as quiet as possible, so as not to sabotage our efforts or distract the mutant from its immediate course.

Beatrice gave vocal instructions through the video screens for all of the inhabitants to make their way to the mess hall level and to meet me there. I led several terrified individuals towards the main hall, pressing upon them that it was vital they keep silent. Many turns later through the corridors, we crossed the carnage left in the wake of the rogue monstrosity. Blood and body parts were scattered everywhere, their gore painted upon the walls.

It soon became painfully clear that these people had been kept sheltered down here for so long that they had no clue about common protocols dealing with such contaminated scenes. I turned back to see one man step directly into a pool of blood, not realizing he had just tainted his footwear. I screamed at him as quietly as I could while advising everyone to avoid touching anything. Once we got past the gore, I had him remove his contaminated shoes.

This endeavor was going to be a lot trickier than I had imagined; finally realizing to myself that Kane might have been right. Anyone of these individuals might have inadvertently contaminated themselves already. Many were holding hands, carrying their children and supporting one another. It was this faultless human contact and compassion which had exasperated and ultimately escalated the transmission of the plague in the past; it was these logical precautions that they had lost all familiarity with.

My heart sank in despair while I was forced to pass up several wounded victims of the attack as they called out in pain, not realizing that they were now beyond all help. Even if I had my own firearm, I didn't know if I could bring myself to give them the only kind of mercy left to offer. This genetically enhanced mutant infected everything it touched.

As I passed a bank of desks in an alcove, a movement caught my eye. Calling out to see if anyone was there, a little girl poked her head out from underneath the furniture where she had hidden when the raging creature had passed this way. With wide scared eyes, she turned towards me, tears beading in her eyes. I motioned for her to be quiet and to come to me so I could lead her to the others.

"Don't be frightened, come on," I motioned gently for her to come to me.

"What about the monster?" the child blubbered fearfully, her eyes scanning the hall around her as she stood their poised and afraid to move.

"It's gone, but you need to come with me now," I urged while lying as best as I could, not exactly knowing where the creature was at the moment, "what is your name, little one?" I beckoned again for her to hurry.

"Hannah," she stammered, still shaken by the brutal events she experienced moments before. Her eyes now wandering towards the dead bodies strewn about the hall, with an anxious pout forming on her lips as tears dripped down her cheeks.

"Hannah, I need you to follow me, okay? We need to leave now. I can take you to your parents," I added, though quietly hoping that I wasn't unintentionally referring to any particular corpse lying broken and sprawled around the corridor that might be her family.

"Mm-kay," the girl whimpered softly, as she suddenly bolted towards me. Her arms were outstretched as if she expected me to grab her up the way her mother had always done. With her eyes locked upon me, she faltered and stumbled while she ran the wrong way around the partition and went straight through the mound of bodies littering the edge of the alcove.

I stood there horrified and almost blacked out with overwhelming anguish. The little girl had tripped and fallen to her knees, having caught her innocent fall by planting both her palms into a pool of infected blood. A mixed look of confusion and dread washed across her face as she held up her bloodied hands, warm droplets of red falling from her stained fingers.

Mentally, I wasn't there anymore; all I could see was the face of that little girl I had taken care of for that small family in the woods, all those years ago. The image of that innocent child petting that limp squirrel and the pus of contagion dripping from its dead eyes. At that moment, I relived the emptiness I felt as I fled that evening, leaving that poor girl to her fate. The gunshot I heard echoing through the valley of a parent shooting their child, and not knowing if they had all met their fate because I had been too cowardly, too emotionally weak, to do the right thing when the moment called.

I knew it would haunt me, and here she was, staring at me

again. Her face on another child; the pleading stare of what circumstance and destiny had brought her young life to such a sudden and horrible end. I fell back against the wall, something inside of me breaking. This small girl before me, crying tears that would soon turn to a weeping of her own blood from her wide innocent eyes. To lose everything she is, or will ever be, into something absent and pitiful.

An agony welled inside, weakening me as I took several steps back, one after the other until I had to tear myself away. There were others to save who still had a chance, though I had an overwhelming feeling that I had left a part of myself standing in that blood-drenched alcove, beyond salvation. I wanted to cry, to bawl my tears out as I ran away from myself, but I had become too groomed, too jaded to show a single tear of sorrow, for it had become a familiar symbol of death and our lost humanity in this forsaken world.

Sacrifice

Kane was led several steps ahead of Thorn, who encouraged him forward with a helpful prod from time to time. Beatrice directed the two men through the speaker system from back in the control room, advising them where they needed to turn as they tracked the creature via the security cameras embedded in the video screens peppered throughout the complex. The number of guards Kane had on staff were actually very few, which were the only personnel in the facility he allowed to carry weapons; the lethality of which, was greatly lacking as Thorn soon discovered from his overdressed captive.

"So, instead of going on this mutant goose chase, why didn't you just order a squad of armed guards to blast that thing? I know it's big, but a shot to the head should stop it," Thorn muttered to Kane as he gave him another push towards the lower recycle chamber.

"For all that attitude of yours, you're actually not the brightest crayon in the box, are you, son?" Kane snapped back at Thorn, attempting to insult the younger man, "You grabbed the first gun you could get your twitchy little fingers on, but you never even bothered to check the magazine."

Thorn froze in apprehension and quickly checked the weight of the pistol he held, opening the clip to see if there was any ammo. Suspicious for a brief moment that Kane might be manipulating him into some sort of ambush, Thorn visually checked the clip; and with a sigh, he confirmed that it was loaded but noted it was filled with a number of strange blue flat-tipped slugs.

"What the hell are these?" Thorn spat as he engaged the clip back into the weapon.

"Stun bullets," the old man replied, "it's not such a good idea to shoot any infected and take the chance of getting tainted blood everywhere, or to kill the occasional rowdy civilian ...it's bad for public relations," Kane smirked.

With a grumble, Thorn realized that Kane was correct for the most part. Using lethal force on the residents would likely raise the level of dissent among the community. Popping a Weeper now and then at a distance had its uses, but firearms did splatter infected material that could be a liability in such close quarters as these. These stun bullets had a unique sheath that was designed to create a high electrical charge as they left the specialized barrel. These weapons had a much lower velocity than a regular firearm and were not designed to penetrate, but they could certainly deliver a decent amount of voltage to drop most anyone. However, they were devised to work on someone normal; and it was assumed that the deranged mutation they were chasing failed to fit that bill.

"Still, why not just get a squad of your men and stun the fuck out of that thing?" Thorn suggested, offering his two cents of wisdom.

"The frozen specimens were engineered to have a unique physiology. I highly doubt their nerve impulses would even be affected in any manner to stop it in its tracks," Kane replied, "you might only tickle that thing with these non-lethal weapons, or end up really pissing it off," Kane offered back.

That being the case, it wasn't really relevant at the moment if they were going to provoke the creature any more than it already was, since it was engineered to be hostile to begin with. The created mutation was an organism designed to go on a rampage behind enemy lines; there was little thought put into what would be done after the biological weapon had served its purpose, other than termination. The fact that the government scientists had actually taken a living human being and turned it into that lumbering atrocity, made it perfectly clear exactly who the monsters *really* were.

"We've drawn the target into the lower level and it has entered the recycling chamber. You two need to get down there and barricade the doors," Beatrice advised over the intercom screen on the wall nearest them.

"Where is Caity, now?" Thorn replied to the video board, checking to make sure she was safe.

"Caitlin is mak'in her way through the main level and getting the survivors to the elevator," Haiti's voice came over the speaker, "she's do'in okay, man," he consoled his friend, which satisfied Thorn's concerns for the moment.

"You two don't have any time to lose," Beatrice cut in with urgency, "I don't think we could lure that thing back in there once it realizes there is nothing down in that section," she added.

Both men hurried though the chamber hall until they came across the stairwell that led down to the reclamation conveyor known as the Grinder, they used for processing compost. What was a matter of concern was that when the huge beast had made its way through the entry to the machine room, it became apparent that the creature had taken an intense disliking to the double doors, one of which was nearly torn entirely from its hinges. This did not bode well for their planned attempt to lock it inside. Thorn ran to the nearest video screen and addressed the control room of this troubling development.

He could hear Haiti and Beatrice bickering with one another as their ethnic friend argued the question as to how they were supposed to subdue that creature with only a single pistol between them. The old woman suggested they should use the recycler as a distraction. The sad fact was, they really didn't have a clue what to do after getting that monstrosity past the bulkhead doors to the bottom level if they couldn't lock the doors and entrap it, and merely hope it would stumble into the recycler. Thorn was starting to get nervous about their choices and he didn't relish the idea of being torn limb from limb like a rag doll.

"Well, it looks like this is going to be a one-way trip," Kane smirked, noting Thorn's hesitation, "I would assume you're going to need my help on this one, young man," he added with a crass undertone as he held up his bound hands to have them untied by his captor.

Thorn pondered his choices for the moment and finally untied the General, who rubbed his wrists as a wry grin grew upon his thin lips. While Haiti and Beatrice squabbled about a course of action over the speakers, their verbal quarrel eventually died down as they brought up a schematic upon the video panel in front of the two men. One of the split screens showed the security camera footage of the hulking creature wandering down into the refuse chamber.

"We just activated the recycler drum. You need to get down there and somehow blockade the stairway to keep that thing trapped within that chamber, or lure it into the machine," Beatrice advised curtly.

"Betty, what are we supposed to do in there; politely ask it to jump into the grinder?" Kane added with sarcasm.

"Don't you have any real firearms stored somewhere down here we could use to kill this thing?" Thorn inquired, "Where did you store our weapons? We could go grab those and try to put a few holes in its ugly head," he finished, satisfied with the logic of his proposal.

"Most of the lethal weapons are locked upstairs in the depository, a level above the control room but our head of security is the only one with the key," Kane replied from behind him, "we don't allow the residents to carry anything harmful to themselves or others."

"...Or to your authority," Thorn snapped back. Kane just rolled his eyes in response to the allegation, further agitating his soured opinion towards the old bastard.

Thorn wanted to suggest that Haiti secure their weapons from storage and have is friend run them down to their location, but he actually didn't like the idea of leaving that devious old woman in the control room entirely unsupervised. He could just imagine all the hassle she could cause in their effort to escape if she was left to her own devices. Thorn started to realize his own mortality in a way he hadn't felt before. Walking into a dead-end chamber with nothing more than a few non-lethal shock bullets against something as powerful and unpredictable as that overgrown mutation started to pass the very fringe of outright stupidity.

Back near the auditorium, Caitlin had made her way through several blind corridors searching for any survivors that hadn't found their way to the central cafeteria. Many of the residents were duly hysterical, having been shielded from the horrors that had mercifully passed them by over the past several years.

Frankly, Caitlin was wondering how these people would adjust to the harsh life and psychological shock that was awaiting them on the surface, in comparison to the pampered life they had become accustomed to here. She turned around when she heard someone calling her name from an open room.

"Caity!" A familiar voice echoed, "In the room to your left," the voice instructed. Cautiously wandering into the room, she found Haiti's excited face peering at her through one of the video screen posters embedded in the wall, "We tracked your location on the security system monitors and this was the nearest console," Haiti explained.

"Where is everyone," I asked, "were Thorn and Kane able to trap that creature?"

"Not yet," he answered with a sour look, "that thing ripped off the damn doors to the recycling chamber. It appears that everyone left in the bunker has assembled at the cafeteria near the restricted access doors and are ready to leave. They are all look'in mighty worried too," he finished as Beatrice came into view of the camera.

"We need you to guide the residents to the elevator," Betty mentioned.

"Can't you just open the access doors from the control room and let them through?" I inquired. Betty fiddled for a moment at the control board and glanced back with an annoyed look on her face.

"It appears as if the automated lock has been manually disabled. There is a backup switch to engage it again on the bottom level," Beatrice replied.

"Can't you reach Thorn and Kane, and have them do it?" Caitlin asked, shaking her head at the logic of the situation. Wondering why Beatrice hadn't mentioned this earlier?

"I just tried to reach them both, but they aren't answering. It appears they are already in the processing chamber and we don't want to further antagonize that monster or allow it to get out again," the old woman answered. Caitlin shook her head again at the irony of the situation. They had just directed a rampaging mutant into the one chamber that held a reset switch vital for their escape.

"Uh-huh, that's just great," I muttered under my breath.

"The problem is, there is only one console in that chamber and if we use the communication board to reach them it could very well draw the creature to their presence," Betty admitted, "and we can't risk the chance of it damaging the junction box that resets the security doors." Unfortunately, this situation put me in the uncomfortable position of having to intervene.

"You have to go down there, lass," Haiti budged into the camera view for a brief moment at the old woman's noted annoyance. After he fell away, Beatrice came back into focus.

"We directed you to this residential room because it was the private chambers of our head of security, who keeps an emergency weapon under lock in there." Betty advised.

"Are you sure he didn't already take it with him," I asked as I scanned the room around me, finally finding a weapons locker tucked within the wall.

"Fortunately for us, it appears our officer in chief was one of the first victims of the attack," Beatrice mentioned as a flash from the security footage showed the individual she was speaking of, left mangled in a blood-spattered mess painting the floor and walls of the ballroom with and entire arm missing from its crumpled torso.

"Unfortunate for him, I'd say," Haiti's voice butted in over the microphone.

"One moment," Betty commented "...the log file shows that there should be a spare keycard located under the drawer of his desk. That should open the weapons locker."

Searching under the desk, I found the key snugly fitted into a hidden plastic sleeve and removed it. It took me a moment to find the magnetic slot where the card fit in, and I popped the lock. Wary of how useful this card might be, I slipped it into my pocket. The weapon nestled inside was huge, a bit on the side of overkill.

It was a Centurion IV, military-grade ion blaster. These things were one of the latest phases in weapons technology. Instead of crude bullets that relied on an internal combustion shell to deliver a projectile, this used electrically charged laser light to deliver a pulse of energy. Honestly, I was afraid to pick it up, not knowing what its capabilities were or the kick it might have. The small white lettered operational instructions printed on its side were obnoxiously curt and mostly what I would consider gibberish. All I cared about was where the safety button was and how much ammo it had. I discovered a power switch that gave a satisfying hum when I flipped it on, but the glowing red readout on the edge of the scope meant nothing I could decipher; leading me to guess that it must have been made by a foreign manufacturer.

"Where is this recycle chamber?" I inquired while turning back to the screen with the enormous sleek black weapon in my hands. Haiti's eyes widened for a moment when he got a glimpse of the gun, and the screen quickly brought up a diagram of the floor plan to the lower tier. Two levels down, I found the access stairs and main corridor that skirted the plant nursery that Beatrice had shown me on our first tour. I headed out into the hall and swiftly made my way towards the basement.

Kane and Thorn literally tiptoed their way down into the bottom level, occasionally freezing in place every time they heard a loud crash or metallic crack echoing up the stairwell.

"So, what's the plan, hero?" Kane pried, with what would have passed for sarcasm if he hadn't been so serious.

"Is that the recycler?" Thorn asked the old man, referring to the loud mechanical hum that filled the air ahead of them; expecting that the General would recognize the sound.

"Could be," he paused in response, "I have no reason to come down here where the staff does their dirty work," he blurted. Thorn rolled his eyes to Kane's obvious insult of the shelter residents as if they were mere serfs for the Emperor of Fallhaven. The two men reached the landing as it opened to a deep chamber of tightly knit pipes and vents. Stretched along either wall was a metal grillwork of flooring plates that set above a bundled mass of conduits that filled a wide canal. Here and there, a tangle of pipes wove up from the central canal to their mated sockets in the ducts high overhead.

Thorn thought he saw something move among the layers of pipes at the far end of the chamber, and motioned for Kane to keep quiet as he ducked down next to the recycler. The processor was a massive mulching machine. It appeared to be an enormous rolling pin armed with layers of teeth married to a similar smaller cylinder. Anything going into it was guaranteed not to come out in one piece. The deadly machine was mottled with streaks of rust and swathed with blotted stains from its years of overuse; it was truly a haunting monstrosity of marred and blemished steel.

An inhuman grunt spurred the men to take cover as they wondered just how they were going to taunt the creature into the crusher. Recalling that this lumbering beast had been biologically engineered, Thorn began to wonder if there was a remote chance that the creature might be more intelligent than everyone had presumed. Normally, contaminated individuals had varying degrees of reaction to the virus, though it was usually the astute ones that ended up being the most dangerous and unpredictable. Some weepers lost all their sensibilities and were unable to even turn a simple doorknob. In most cases, it was usually that short period between initial infection and the full turn of the illness that they were the most erratic.

Thorn chewed on the thought that this oversized mutant might not be as mentally disabled as most weepers tended to be, if so, then they were certainly in for a world of hurt. They had managed to lure it down onto the bottom level by utilizing the speaker system and exploiting its attraction to noise; but after getting a glimpse of the true size and weight of this behemoth in person, Thorn realized that their plan was probably futile. There was no way they could physically knock it from the platform into the teeth of the recycler; and since the doors to the processor room had been thoroughly mangled, there was no way to keep it caged down here. They had to figure some other way to put this thing down.

"There's a ramp lever on the far side that lowers the safety rail," Kane whispered to his captor, while pointing at the inset panel to their far right where there was a spacious nook in the block wall, "one of us needs to engage it."

Thorn considered Kane's plan for a brief moment, figuring the kinetics of it were in favor of getting the beast to fall into the loading belt if the safety rail was out of the way.

"I'll trigger it, you stay here and keep watch," the General suggested. With a note of hesitation, Thorn let Kane call the shots for the moment since the control board he was pointing to looked more complicated then just a simple switch. Nodding towards the old man, he signaled him to make his move towards the wall as they crouched below the level of the rail while the creature lurched around the maze of pipes at the far end of the room, grunting in anger over the loud hum of the spinning grinder.

The giant beast heaved itself onto the center walkway and began making its way towards their position. Thorn motioned for Kane to hurry while he kept his eyes on the approaching monstrosity. It then occurred to him that something was amiss, regarding what advice the General had so casually mentioned just moments before. If he had never been down here before, how would Kane know that there was a lever that activated the guardrail in that niche? Glancing back towards the panel, he saw Kane slip into the alcove and disappear like a proverbial snake in the grass. Rushing over to the nook, Thorn just caught sight of the panel closing across a hidden door.

"Bastard!" Thorn blurted as he hit the panel with the butt of his gun in aggravation, regretting his lack of judgment for having trusted Kane in that idle moment. Thorn shortly came to realize the level of that mistake, as his errant clamor caught the attention of their unwelcome guest lumbering towards him. The beast pushed its way through the bent pipes that groaned and hissed in its wake, its loud footsteps coming closer to where he hid in the recess.

Beyond the false door, Kane made his way to the secondary reserve control room, which had been his destination this entire time, and he swiftly entered the security passcode while Thorn had been distracted by the creature. With a smug grin, he plopped into the console chair in the shelter's backup control room and flipped the power on, bringing up the security camera feed to the recycler room outside. Kane switched on the intercom as the monster heaved its way towards Thorn, who was now trapped in the small alcove on the other side of the panel door.

"I suggest that you relinquish your weapon to my cohort, young man," Kane stated with a grim stare to Haiti over the camera he brought up on his monitor, which was now connected to the main control room where Beatrice was being held. Haiti looked a bit shocked for a brief moment, as they were both viewing the same feed from the Recycle chamber where Thorn was but a moment away from imminent death.

At that point, a shrill tone pierced the air over the line and the enraged beast ceased its rampage and began to turn docile. Kane took his hand off the button on his console and the tone ceased as the creature's mood resumed, and it once again began to advance on Thorn who was aiming his stun pistol at the creature. Once again, Kane activated the tone and the mutant went limp; proving beyond all doubt that he had control over the creature's response.

"I wouldn't shoot it if I were you," Kane advised Thorn over the PA system, who nervously twitched his gun, "you can't stop it with that, let alone harm it. You'll only get yourself killed," he stated firmly with his usual arrogant undertone, "that was a modulating resonance you heard, which is digitally encoded to control these engineered mutations. It only works for a short while, so I suggest that you do as I say," he warned Haiti, who took but a few seconds to release his handgun and the console over to Betty's control, having disarmed her captor.

"I have his weapon now, General. Are we activating plan B?" Beatrice inquired.

"I believe that would be the best option, considering the current circumstances," he pondered with a raised brow, "this isn't the most optimal timing but we have no other choice. Go ahead and release the shaft," Kane ordered.

Back in the main control room, Haiti sat in the corner as the old woman held the gun on him while activating the console. It was now clear to the islander that the secret secondary control room Kane was using had been previously erased from the base schematics, which is why they had not noticed it before sending them down there.

It would make sense that an astute mind like Kane's would

have a contingency plan in place. He certainly had enough time down here to arrange one, and had pulled it off right under their noses. Over the com, Kane ordered Thorn to drop his weapon and to move out towards the door, reminding him that Haiti was now their hostage. Not fully realizing where Caitlin was within the complex, he had assumed she was with the survivors at the evacuation shaft.

"Wait a minute, woman. Are you tell'in me that you let all those poor people get killed when you could've stopped that creature any time you desired?" Haiti blurted out in a mixture of astonishment and disgust, while Betty waved her gun at him with one hand as she busily punched in a backup protocol on the control console.

"Shut up!" She snapped back while activating commands on the screen, "...And no, we couldn't access our auxiliary control room which overrides the system; it only works one way," she stated with a hint of guilt, "the mutations were groomed to respond to an embedded signal while in status, which is far above the capacity of normal human hearing. There was only one such accelerator beacon that we had in stock, so we decided to keep it secured in the spare chamber."

"An accelerator beacon?" Haiti blurted aloud, "like some sort'a dog whistle to train them?"

"Yes, something ...something like that," she babbled back in haste as she activated the surface lift.

A grinding deep within the structure could be felt through their feet as the stairways of the main shaft unfolded from the walls and the doors unlocked to the evacuation chamber. Survivors who had gathered in the main cafeteria rushed towards the opening gates to a circular cell positioned at its center. The scared and wounded inhabitants of Fallhaven poured into the chamber, carrying what little they could; guided by the old automated system that instructed them to keep calm. Caitlin, however, was not with their group.

General Kane was playing a dangerous game, but his plans for Fallhaven had gone awry. While they were all imprisoned within the bunker, he alone had maintained power and control. If everyone was duly released to the surface, there was nothing from keeping these discharged citizens from detaching from his command; since he could not possibly have enough loyal guardsmen that could act as a substitute for these thick shelter walls. Their freedom was not exactly in his best interests.

Contemplating that, he made an executive decision and prompted a fallback program set on a timer before exiting the secondary control room, one that was untraceable to the main control chamber where Beatrice was stationed. Kane detached the accelerator beacon from the console. It was an oblong cylinder with a battery drive that was small enough to hold in one hand; knowing he had only moments to get back outside the vault door. He could see Thorn waiting for him at the stairwell entrance on the security feed.

With a new wave of confidence, Kane released the panel hatch and picked up the gun were Thorn had laid it down. The mutant stirred briefly after the tone had ceased blaring over the intercom, but the device resumed its tone from the General's hand as he held it aloft like a singing torch to ward off the monstrosity. The mutant quaked in response, reacting as if it had been drugged. Kane kept the pistol pointed at Thorn while glancing behind him with his beacon held in the other direction to keep the creature at bay. It took only a split-second for Caitlin to step into the room behind Thorn, her sleek centurion rifle in hand, aiming it at Kane who reacted by wavering his paltry gun at them both.

"Don't do it," Caitlin warned, the ion blaster warm in her hands as she felt the energy pulsing through its barrel. Kane had no intention of relinquishing himself to his captors again. He shot a bolt of electricity towards them from the stun pistol, missing as he stumbled on the grating beneath his feet. In response, Caitlin pulled the trigger on her weapon.

A blue beam of light lanced out like a glowing string of death, cutting through the rail by his side. Kane jerked away as the laser grazed the beacon in his hand, sending shards of sparks flying from its ruptured battery. Caitlin was surprised by the sudden weight of the rifle as it discharged, which had activated an internal gyroscope comprised of spinning magnets, pulling her aim low. The weapon itself became heavy when fired, which was far from expected.

Having nearly been seared in half from the laser; the beacon bounced to the ground and off the grated floor as Kane stumbled back dangerously close to the spinning claws of the recycler, while he watched the sonic beacon dance its way into the spinning blades until it was finally crushed between its metal teeth. The old man caught his wits and stared at the last sparking bits of the beacon mashed within the gears of the machine, realizing all too late what dire consequences that would spell. Caitlin and Thorn looked on in dread as a large shadow loomed over Kane from behind him as he turned. The behemoth was a twisted horror of tormented flesh, infused with a vicious alien virus and equally perverse human engineering. Its touch, its taint, its very presence meant death; and Kane's dulled eyes were aware he had been a party to its creation.

The hybrid creature snarled, its disfigured eyes devoid of any discernable emotion as Kane raised his gun in pitiful defense only to have his wrist grasped by the creature's thick misshapen hand that promptly ripped his arm off at the elbow. Sinew snapped as strings of flesh resisted. White glossy bone spattered with blood as the severed arm twitched, firing the pistol repeatedly. Kane fell back, the grinding teeth of the recycler beckoning to call his fate. The mutant threw aside the twitching arm as if in disgust and roared at the old man who cringed beneath its glare.

A thin shaft of blue sunlight bit through the air and sheared through its chest, causing it to stagger as if were experiencing pain for the first time with a sense of bewilderment. With pleading eyes, Kane turned towards the two companions while Thorn bolted forward and grabbed him up. The three of them rushed up the stairwell as the creature howled from below.

"We must hurry," Kane whispered feebly from the loss of blood as Thorn took a stark moment to bind the stump with a strip of cloth. Not sure if the creature was merely angry or mortally wounded, they heeded Kane's advice and made their way towards the evacuation chamber on the level above with the rest of the evacuees.

Through the blood-spattered halls, it became ever more clear that those injured by the mutant's attack had begun to turn, which was an infection rate far accelerated than either of them had ever witnessed. Those few maimed citizens who hadn't been initially killed in the rampage, began to snarl like animals as their red eyes welled with blood. Dragging along the impaired General between them, they had finally reached the cafeteria only to find its disheveled remnants entirely empty; all the Fallhaven citizens had already made their way to the escape lift. A communications terminal on the wall suddenly blipped on with Beatrice looking quite pale as she saw Kane drenched in his own blood. She put down the gun she held on Haiti, and her demeanor changed to one of submission.

"So it's over..." was all she said, a pool of relief settling in her eyes. We were all left a little dumbfounded by her response.

"We can sort this all out later, but now we have to get to the lift with the others and get the hell out of here!" I proposed, trying not to lose my mind in the desperation of the moment. Beatrice turned herself over to Haiti and we gave them a few minutes to arrive at our location on the lower level.

Frankly, it troubled me, and I was trying to fathom why Betty had reacted the way she did and surrendered to us so readily. As gruesome as Kane's injury was, at least it was clean from infection. The only part of him that had touched the mutation was now lying somewhere on the floor of the recycle chamber. That monstrosity was still loose as far as we knew, and we didn't wish to wait to face its wrath if it should follow us back up to the main level. We needed to get out of this hellhole and back to the surface. When Haiti and Beatrice rushed into the cafeteria, the older woman addressed us directly while Kane was left moaning in a seat beyond as Thorn attempted to bind his arm with a tourniquet.

"The escape lift is ahead, I've already activated the emergency protocol to take us up," Beatrice managed to advise the group as we all made our way to the central chamber.

Ushering us through the gated doorway, we followed in the footsteps of the surviving residents who had previously made their way to the elevator. A repetitive banging echoing towards us through the corridor drew our attention and we hastened our pace with a breath of caution. The lit hallway emptied into an enormous circular chamber with red blinking lights threading their way towards the surface along the chimney far above. In the center of the room, a large enclosed cell sat on the circular lift, its doors firmly sealed.

Peering inside the windowed slits, we could see the noise was coming from several of the citizens standing within who were desperately trying to break their way out. Beatrice stepped up to the glass and got the attention of one of the gray-clad guards inside, who quickly rushed over with a wild look in his eyes.

"What happened?" Beatrice demanded to the guard in slight confusion as to why they had locked themselves inside, "Open the doors!"

"We can't!" the uniformed guard yelled back through the thick glass, "we're locked in here," he answered, nervously jerking at the controls to the sliding door, "we didn't know where you were, so we followed protocol and directed everyone inside and followed the instructions given by the automated program over the speakers. Once we got inside and activated the lift, the doors sealed shut, but now they refuse to open!" He blared back with a nervous look over his shoulder. Behind him, we could see several dozen people in their multi-shaded jumpsuits milling about and attending to the injured.

Something wasn't right here, and the telltale look of confusion on the old woman's face showed it. For some reason, the emergency escape lift was not operational and she could only imagine there had been a failure of the gears. Scanning the systems panel by the lift entrance, she could see that it was getting power, however, it wasn't working. Beatrice spun her head as we all did in turn towards the source of the low painful chuckle coming from Kane, who stood leaning against a nearby support post; a deep red stain dripping from the binding at his severed elbow.

We turned back with a snap toward the elevator as we heard a wild scream, then another; and a symphony of chaos started to arise beyond the sealed doors as we watched through the small windows. It was an inevitable chance that at least one of the survivors had been contaminated during the mutant attack; but we had no idea just how quickly the engineered virus from the creature could spread and turn their hosts. Several shots from a stun pistol lit up the enclosed room, silhouetting frightened people dashing for safety, each strobe of light framing a shadow poised in terror.

The government scientists had accelerated the infection stage so it would become more effective when introduced into a hostile environment on foreign soil. The mutagen was created as a weapon rather than as a means of research for a cure. Beatrice vainly fiddled at the hatch lock, trying to reroute the directives to get the doors to open; but it was Thorn who pulled her away as the screams from inside escalated. It was simply too late for them. It was a hard call, but at this point it was safer to keep the doors sealed. We quietly turned our attention back to the wounded General, who had slumped to the floor where he sat upright with his back against a support pillar as a perverse smile drew upon his bloodied lips.

"What did you do?" Beatrice finally accused as she stepped towards the pitiful man while clenching her balled fists.

"You," he muttered between labored breaths, "...you can't do this without me. Haven could not have survived without my guidance. You know that, my dear," his weary eyes raised to meet hers.

Betty spun back towards the console to note something she had not seen before. Kane had initiated a lockdown. Nobody was going anywhere. Stomping back towards Kane, the glare in her eyes showed she had little sympathy that he was bleeding to death.

"Why would you do this," her voice rose to a shout, "stop this, open these doors and save those people!" she demanded, but her plea didn't move the stubborn old man in the slightest, his expression grim and unruffled in the face of her distress.

"I have manipulated these people to do my bidding for all these years, and every moment you have been by my side," he muttered, exposing her own guilt, "not once have you spoken out in their defense to save anyone, ever. All you cared about was your own position and minor power, which you earned through loyal service ...service to me and *my* wishes. Now that

I'm no longer in control, here you are Betty, turning your back on me for what - these lowlife scavengers?" He motioned towards us with a feeble wave of his hand.

"I'm ashamed to have done the things I did for you Kane, just to survive," she muttered with a tear in her eyes, "I only used you to get through this disaster alive, but you twisted it into something grotesque. All you cared about was to be the petty king of your own little world."

"No, my dear," he laughed bitterly, "I used you body and soul. You could never have endured their suffering on the lower levels or survived the years of menial work at your age, let alone, out there upon the surface. Don't insult me by pretending you didn't enjoy being at my side or feigning disgrace to this pitiful lot, just to trick them into trusting you now that the tables have turned," Kane muttered with a labored cough, his harsh words implicating her.

Honestly, it was hard to read Beatrice. It made us question if she surrendered simply to play us after she saw that the General's plan had backfired. Was she the type of person with the lack of character who would turn on anyone at any time just to save her own skin? Those were the qualities of a coward, someone more dangerous than Kane could ever be by being so entirely unpredictable. Within the shooting glances my friends and I cast between us, we were all sharing the same thought. Haiti pulled Beatrice away when it appeared she was about to strangle the wounded man. Though unfortunate as the given circumstances were, we still needed him.

"Is there anything we can do, maybe reboot this system if that's possible?" I inquired with a small measure of hope. Grudgingly, Betty made her way back to the elevator control panel while trying to phase out the screams of horror still echoing from the growing numbers of infected attacking those who were trapped inside the elevator car.

"The stairwell to the surface has deactivated to allow clearance for the lift chamber," she noted while pointing up towards the folded walkway sections above, as they were positioned along the walls, "I could try to reset whatever he did to the elevator by shutting down the power entirely to this section, and that should open the doors to the elevator so we can rescue our people," she ended with optimism.

We peered back through the windows only to jump back in startled fright when a mutated Weeper leaped towards us, its distorted face pressing against the glass. Whoever they had once been, they're mind was now quite gone; reflected by the frenzied gaze in its wild eyes streaming tears of blood. This clearly wasn't the usual plague, for the blighted victim's face and hands were bloated and mottled with erupted sores.

"We can't have those doors opening on us. This mutated strain appears highly volatile," Thorn warned as he pulled me aside so we could speak out of earshot of the old woman while we tried to debate our options at the moment.

"Look, I know she can't be trusted either but we can't go back into that complex with that monstrosity running around, let alone that this entire facility is thoroughly contaminated by now," I struggled to reason with him as Haiti looked at us both with a note of concern in his worried eyes.

"You ain't gonna let that crazy woman open those doors are ya, girlie?" Haiti inquired with his broken dialect, while referring to the screaming madness ensuing on the other side of the hatch where the diseased were attacking one another. Not failing to note that we were limited to defending ourselves with nothing more than a single stun pistol and a laser rifle in our possession; all I could do was affirm the unquestioning desperation of our situation.

"Actually, Haiti ...I'm afraid there's no other way."

Daylight

There was only one way to purge the lockdown protocol Kane had initiated, by dead booting the power through the emergency terminal. It was something Beatrice knew how to do but had never tried before. Arguably, it was a dangerous move, as the system would release all hatchways on the lift upon shutdown, which would free the weepers trapped within. The only smart move I could think of was to board the elevator.

"Ya'll crazy; there ain't no way we can go in there, woman!" Haiti argued while giving me a piece of his mind.

"Not '*into*' the elevator, but on top of it," I offered in defense of my plan as I pointed up to its flat ceiling, "we can use a maintenance ladder to mount the roof of the elevator chamber and ride it to the surface when the system reboots."

"And we will be well out of reach of the infected, it's actually not a bad idea," Thorn answered back, attracted to the plan I had come up with.

"Can you reset the power connection?" I asked while looking over to Beatrice; she nodded, followed by a smug glance towards Kane who sat on the floor drenched in his own blood.

"Yes, I think I can. Though I'm not sure how long it will take since we've never actually done it before," she agreed, though there was a tint of worry in her tone. I could see the sorrow in her eyes as she glanced through the glass into the interior of the lift, silently grieving all the poor souls within who had been baited by Kane's heartless treachery.

I gripped the Centurion rifle, not quite sure how much juice this thing held or how long it would last. Bullets you could count for peace of mind but this damn thing could entirely drain in the next shot, or the next hundred; I had no clue as to what its energy capacity was. We found a work ladder on casters that would suffice and rigged it up with a rope to loop around a nearby support so we could pull it far enough away to clear the gears after we mounted the elevator. Beatrice crouched down and worked under the control panel until she seemed to have finally found what she was looking for and promptly yanked apart a coupling, then quickly plugged it back into its mated socket. The moment she had done that, the lights flickered and the female voice of the system's computer came on over the PA system, giving us a countdown of five minutes until a full-scale power reboot. Haiti hopped over and assisted the old woman up the ladder. Once we were all on top of the lift, we struggled to draw the rope pulley in effort to remove the ladder from the rooftop where we stood; dreading the pandemonium that was about to ensue as the countdown progressed.

Having thrown down the rope over the side, which had been tied to the rear of the wheeled ladder, our eyes widened in despair as Haiti pointed towards the maintenance ladder which had begun to slowly roll its way back towards the elevator platform where we had mounted. We had failed to notice that the floor of the chamber had been constructed with a marginal grade towards the center of the shaft, where trace water leaks would be drained away through the gutter beneath. As the timer counted down to the last minute, we watched in dread as the tiny squeaky wheels of the stepladder inched its way back towards us ...then suddenly, everything went black.

A choir of clicking tones and tension wires echoed through the chimney as we all glanced upward into the elevator shaft. Slowly, the lights began to snap on one by one from the ceiling down towards us as we heard the hydraulic release of the lift doors opening below our feet. From within the elevator, the infected began to flood out and around the chamber, surrounding us on all sides. As the final lights clicked on at the ground level, we saw the outer room filled with the twisted mutations trying to claw their way to our position on top of the lift. It was disturbing how quickly the hybrid virus had made them turn; their wild diseased eyes were now gleaming from the reflected spotlights with vengeful hatred.

Luckily, they could not quite reach the top of the roof, but there were those that were bold enough to climb over the other weeper's shoulders in their effort to access the canopy. Thorn fired his stun pistol, as did Haiti, towards those few infected that had managed to gain the ledge, only to be dropped after absorbing several direct shots. To our despair, a few errant mutants began mounting the rolling stepladder that was now only a few short feet away, their added weight quickening its pace towards the edge of the roof. I took aim at one with the laser rifle but the shot cut low, disintegrating one of the ghouls shoulders and causing it to flip forward; blocking the wheels. With only a few sparse feet to breach, it did not take long for several more of the infected to mount the ladder and risk the leap over to the canopy where we stood.

Beatrice huddled in the center of the dome alongside Kane who recoiled in horror at the nightmare that had befallen them. We concentrated our firepower where the mutants were jumping onto the roof, and in a strange dreamy moment, the world around us paused as a grinding boom echoed down from the shaft above. Even the enraged infected hesitated as all eyes, human and mutant, turned upwards as a crack of heavenly light pierced from the surface hatch far above. I saw many of them waver as the first beam of sunlight raced down to wash over us, filled with dancing particles of dust suspended in the thick air. For a brief moment, they all stood there basking in the light as if some residual memory of their former selves held onto the splinter of that distant dream of a blue sky they had almost forgotten.

That fading respite lasted for but a brief second as their glowing eyes turned back towards their vulnerable prey. I took that precious time to cut down a few of them with the rifle as Haiti and Thorn joined in on the defense. Then began the hail of dirt and lumps of rubble that rained down upon us, falling from the widening breach of the hatch doors above. Stray chunks of rock smashed in the heads of a number of weepers who were unfortunate enough not to dodge the shower of earth shooting down the shaft. In a jolting lurch, the entire chamber began to rise; leaving the remaining mutants that had been pouring from the ladder to claw and shriek their fury from the rising elevator walls as it ascended out of their reach.

With a few final shots, Thorn put down the last of the wounded weepers as we all peered upward at the circular hole of the sky above us. Our eyes had become so accustomed to the dim lights of the bunker that we squinted at the enveloping landscape as the lift rose ever higher. We stood at guard in the center of the roof when it finally breached the surface plateau.

A broken field enveloped by steep hills met us as the lift jolted to a halt. It was an odd depository for any survivors meant to escape Fallhaven. I had forgotten that the subway system had routed us far from our camp, where our friends waited for our return. As we had just departed a hidden facility, I could understand that the evacuation site would also need to be well hidden. Any building or complex over the elevator shaft could have collapsed and blocked the exit. All the years of wind and weather along with a lack of maintenance topside had piled up a layer of accumulated dirt over the escape hatch, which apparently was intentionally camouflaged in an attempt to disguise its presence from spy satellites.

Thorn suggested that we check the interior of the elevator for anything usable or extra weapons that could have been left behind, though it was ill-advised to touch anything within the contaminated area. It would be several days until the residual remnants of the virus would dry out enough to die off; and that estimate was only a wild guess, as we had no idea of knowing whether this bioengineered pathogen followed the same rules as the original disease.

Haiti hopped off the roof and we helped ease Kane onto the ground where he stood leaning beside the doorway. He stood there with a strange gleam of hate in his eyes. With a grunt of pain from his severed arm, he slipped inside the elevator chamber while Haiti was distracted helping the others off the roof. As the former administrator, Kane possessed access codes to the core systems of the bunker, and had resolved himself to reaping vengeance against his captors. In his pain-stricken mind, it made perfect sense to leave them all to rot topside and make his way down back into the bunker and be a man who was still in control of his own destiny. He had other plans, devious plans that Beatrice had only barely suspected.

General Kane was once a lowly subordinate to the original supervisor who had been assigned to the Fallhaven facility.

Kane was no mere grunt but was capable of being shrewd and conniving whenever he felt that he was being passed over for promotion to positions he desired. The catastrophe had broken him mentally, and one day he just snapped. He did not like being told what to do, and was sick of following orders. An opportunity to bolster his status finally materialized when a number of the project scientists were transporting a key subject to the cryogenics chamber. Petty officer Kane took it upon himself to sabotage one of the test patient's stasis cells when no one was watching, and he quietly slipped out the door.

It was of slight inconvenience that his treacherous plan had to happen on the community mall level where a majority of the ration supplies had been stored, but it was worth the sacrifice in his deluded mind. By locking them within the foyer level of the subway system, in one fell swoop he had rid himself of his belligerent Supervisor and a majority of the bureaucratic staff, and was now free to fill the empty chain of command as he saw fit. His treason did come at a small cost, while having to weed out the few members of Fallhaven that might expose his crime, so he saw to it that any witnesses met the same ghastly fate in his effort to tie up any loose ends.

A thermal blast charge placed in the proper place had sealed off the upper deck from the residence below. Kane made up a cover story to present himself as their savior, and further elected himself their acting General of security. It was unfortunate that his wife had died during the original catastrophe as a victim of the outbreak that followed, and that his only daughter had been an unintended casualty of the tunnel explosion that he himself had engineered, which had collapsed to a degree far beyond his calculations. Kane was a broken man, his soul was black and poisoned, but his warped sense of self-entitlement was a lifting burden within his own twisted mind.

While Haiti wasn't looking, Kane slipped inside the doorway and began fiddling at the control board to retract the lift. With a hum, the gears clinked and the others still up on the roof glanced at one another in alarm; wondering if the elevator mechanism was beginning to fail.

"Hurry, everyone off. Jump!" Thorn yelled, as Haiti helped

pull the old woman off the roof. Thorn and I leapt as we toppled to the ground, just as the gears of the lift jolted violently. Glancing over to the doorway, we saw Kane standing inside the elevator at the control board as his face quickly turned from a sense of glee to one of aggravation as the compartment doors failed to cycle shut.

"That little bastard, I'll..." Thorn trailed off as a dark shadow crept up behind Kane, its distorted features reaching out to envelop him within its claws. The old man gave a brief yelp of surprise as the mutant bit into his neck, realizing too late that he should have checked the chamber for any residual passengers. He mashed his fist onto the panel once again and the doors began to cycle shut as he tried to wiggle free from the grasp of his attacker, as warm blood began spurting from his neck.

I got to my feet and took aim with the laser rifle, trying to get a clear shot past Kane, taking but a moment to realize that there was no reason to do so. Kane had been bitten, the mutant gene now contaminating his body; there was no surviving that. Kane suddenly leapt out of the doorway with the weeper clinging onto him from behind, and grabbed the muzzle of my rifle with his one good arm.

"Save me!" He pleaded weakly as if every last visage of his betrayal would be somehow forgiven. He grasped again further up the muzzle as I stared into his scared eyes, the swirling fear and desperation glinting there like a man convicted to his fate.

Suddenly, the hatchway shut behind him and the elevator began to descend. Kane lost his balance on the loose dirt that crumbled beneath his footing at the edge of the shaft. I stood there for the briefest of seconds, which seemed to last an eternity. Thorn held onto me from behind, screaming something incoherent as time slowed. Kane's bloody hand gripped onto the barrel of my rifle as his body dangled over the edge, the raging mutant still clinging onto his legs, gnashing its teeth and raking red tears into his back.

A beam of hot blue light burned through his chest just before I released my hold on the rifle. Kane and his assailant tumbled into the darkness below as a trail of bitter smoke from his seared flesh drifted upward into the light. As he fell, the old man still gripped onto the muzzle of the rifle as if it was his only salvation. The thick hatch door covering the shaft drowned out the sound of their bodies hitting the rusted roof of the descending elevator below. We scrambled away from the collapsing edge as the silo doors slammed shut with a cold finality. While the reverberation in our feet took several long minutes to subside, we looked at one another with tired eyes, realizing with a heavy breath that we were finally free of that maniac and the madhouse called Fallhaven.

It still distressed me to think of all those people I had known, who had surrendered themselves to one egocentric man and forfeited their freedom just to survive another day. All that time they had spent enslaved and their countless sacrifices were for nothing. It made me wonder how many other similar vaults around the globe lay hidden like this one, and all those people it sheltered who were just hiding from the inevitable. What purpose did their lives have if only to end like this?

I suddenly felt sick and hurled up what little was in my stomach on the parched ground beside me. Thorn came to comfort me as Beatrice and Haiti stood dazed at what had just transpired.

"Are you okay, Caitlin?" Thorn motioned with a gentle hand on my shoulder as I sat there on my knees; embarrassing myself with the puke dripping from my lips. I finally stood up and gathered my composure and we all checked ourselves for signs of contamination; any clothing or gloves with trace amounts of blood had to be discarded immediately. The men gathered up dry brush and made a fire to burn the infected clothing since we didn't want this hybrid strain getting loose, or chance what harm it might do if it got released into the ecosystem.

Wearily, we gathered ourselves after making the bonfire and made our way around the hills towards the welcoming sound of a stream. We only had a pair of shock pistols with a few charges of ammo left. I was grieved to have lost that energy rifle, but it wasn't worth taking the chance of being infected by all the tainted blood Kane had smeared upon its muzzle. Regardless, we weren't going back for it, nor were there any controls topside to speak of that could call the lift again even if

we tried. We were stuck up here in the middle of nowhere and were determined to find our way back to locate Roy and the others. The problem was, we didn't know where the hell we were or which direction to go.

We had to keep an eye on Betty, as the old woman was the only one left in the group who was a liability and lacked the endurance for surviving on the surface. She had spent nearly the last decade being fed and clothed, and using others to toil for her needs. That life came to a sudden halt with the end of Kane's reign. She had been at his right hand for more years than she could remember, having exploited the residence of the shelter to promote her position and control, just as Kane had done for his own self-interests. Now that it had all been swept away, she stood there gazing out at the cloud-filled skies, watching the sunset over the hills for the first time in what seemed like forever.

As darkness fell, the night air was starting to become bitterly cold and their small ragged band was ill-equipped for the seasonal weather with only thin jumpsuits for covering. With no rations or warm clothing and only their wits to rely on, they had little chance of surviving for more than a few days if they failed to find supplies and better weapons. An abandoned building would do well to protect them from the elements come nightfall, but they would be at a serious disadvantage if they ran into a horde of Weepers.

Haiti attempted to give the old woman some pointers for surviving in the wilderness and how to scavenge for supplies on the road, but it seemed of little use as Betty didn't appear to absorb even half of what he was saying. At least the conversation helped pass the time as we tried to find adequate shelter before night finally fell and left us stumbling in the dark.

The river we had heard echoing from the distance grew louder as we circled the barren hills. Below us, we saw what looked like an old mill at the corner of a lake, and we caught a glimpse of a road between the forest trees that sprouted along the riverside. The problem was this scenery looked nothing like the landscape around the facility where we had left our friends. We inquired with the old woman if she had known how far the hydrogen generators were from Fallhaven, but she claimed to have little to no knowledge regarding the full extent of the underground network.

"Most of the citizens who lived in the bunker were wealthy enough to have purchased a spot for their families, or had either government or high ranking military connections as a guaranteed reservation to reside there," Beatrice relayed as we made our way down the edge of the hill towards the lake, noting it would be wise to reach the cover of the trees before the sun fully set, "the rail system connected several such shelters across the country; some far larger than ours I was told," she stated.

"How many shelters?" Thorn inquired, just as boggled as both Haiti and I were at her claim; admitting to her that none of us had ever gotten wind about such an extensive underground network.

"Oh, and you wouldn't, dear," the old woman snapped in reply, "there were over two dozen I knew of, and there were probably many more. These facilities were top secret, and not available to the common folk," she ended without perceiving the flagrant insult towards her present company.

"So you're saying that this rail system crossed the entire section of this country, and its existence had been kept secret from the public ...how is that even possible?" I asked, just as shocked as my friends were to this revelation. It was a tall tale we would have not believed had we not seen it for our own eyes.

"Yes, quite so. Many tracks intersect, and there are parts of the subway system also extended beyond foreign borders into neighboring countries. The transport network was designed to function independently by vacuum pressure in the event there was a failure of the electrical grid," she answered, "There were actually several redundant power stations, much like the one you mentioned, where you had descended to gain access to the subway system," she added, "they were originally constructed over the past few decades beneath several key military bases and crucial governmental facilities, including some that were hidden under private resorts. All paid for by the clueless taxpayers for these black budget programs that were funded without a trace of their expense."

This really burned us. The common citizens had paid for all these extremely costly and lavish programs from their own toil and labor, but were never intended for use by the general public. It was a perfect example of the elitists skimming off the sweat and tears of others.

"I find it hard to believe they built all that for the event of a war decades ago?" I breathed, disgusted with what I was hearing as we hit the tree line and cautiously made our way towards the abandoned mill.

"That's what I thought when I saw Fallhaven for the first time, its entire underground ecosystem had been planned out and the bulk of supplies had been carefully stockpiled by their engineers," Beatrice admitted, "but we began to suspect that it had been created specifically for the catastrophe caused by the asteroid, not some frivolous war."

That admission stunned us. My friends and I shook our heads in disbelief. A plan of that nature carried out on such a grand scale as this had been scrubbed from all internet and news media sources, so that everyone in the general public would be kept in the dark. We weren't blind nor stupid; we had seen the propaganda videos about the inevitable consequences and fallout in the event of international thermonuclear war, but it seems the powers that be, had full knowledge of this approaching calamity and were only interested in protecting their own sorry necks. Clearly, everyone else was considered as nothing more than collateral damage.

Their contingency plans failed on the first tier, when the KRI virus introduced itself into the environment. The government and military entities had only been prepared for heightened levels of devastation resulting from earthquakes or tsunamis from the impact. The electromagnetic pulse that threw most of the world back into the Stone Age, was a quaint surprise but the alien pathogen that spread like wildfire, was the cherry on top of the cake. They had grossly underestimated the responses required on a fatal level.

Had the public worldwide been informed of this fate, many

more might have been better prepared for the cataclysm that followed, but there was also the calculated chance of widespread panic and unbridled chaos that could have destroyed our civilization long before Apophis ever entered Earth's orbit. Humanity had a regrettable habit of being selfish and self-destructive on its very own. Thus, on one level, the secrecy made sense; but on another, it was a complete moral failure. Personally, if it had been my sole choice to make, it would have been better to let everyone have a fighting chance. Certainly, things would have likely fared far better than the way they had turned out.

"Oh my, you believe in people too much, dear," Betty declared, "from what I've seen in my long years, survival has no sense of ethics or honor, young lady."

I didn't want to place any value in her harsh words, even when I knew what she had said was entirely true on many counts. Maybe I didn't want to hear the truth, realizing it hurt too much so I kept it at bay. It was my one character flaw, which made me hate myself at times. Like a bigot, I would ridicule others for not facing reality, yet was guilty of acting the same way most of the time. I only tried not to notice when I was doing it.

As vulnerable as we were, we took every precaution as we approached the old mill, even though the daylight was fading fast. It was widely reported that mammals, in particular, were the most susceptible to the MN4 pathogen, so even the smallest rodent could be a carrier. I had also seen cases were wild deer had aggressively attacked people as if they had gone insane. The truth was that most mammals which became exposed to the disease would pace about aimlessly or curl into a ball and starve to death as if they were in a paralyzed trance, having lost all concepts of instinct and self-preservation.

Earth had been long overdue for a plague, but the magnitude of this disease was of the likes humanity had never seen before. It was astounding how many people died from committing innocent mistakes to outright acts of stupidity. Cats and dogs were one of the most dangerous of all the factors, since most everyone wanted to save their damn pets during the successive evacuations, which only managed to spread the germ beyond any scope imaginable. It was an all too common occurrence when some idiots would try to smuggle their stupid feline or tiny rat-dog because they were small enough to carry in their coats or conceal in their bags, even though they knew it was a risk, only to end up infecting their entire family and others while locked down in quarantine.

Burn barrels were set up in lines to such camps. Every so often you would come across one while scavenging around; finding a burnt dumpster full of charred pets. The horrible part is that these poor animals were usually tossed into the incinerator cans while they were still alive, for fear of getting infected blood sprayed on the handlers if they were either shot or clubbed to death first. It was a horrible sound to hear, especially for a child who would see their beloved pet thrown into a glowing fire; its grisly cries as it burned would forever haunt their dreams. Unfortunately, it was necessary measure to fend off the spread of the sickness.

Birds appeared to be immune to the alien virus, as did most every reptile, so doctors turned to those species for research and experimentation. Fish were also a suspected carrier, which seriously dented food stocks in the early years of the outbreak when stockpiles of meat were being incinerated as a precaution. Enormous greenhouses popped up in an attempt to help curb starvation when the paranoid doctors and scientists instructed people to turn to vegetarian diets, just to be safe. Although, as it ended up, they were just grasping straws out of desperation and didn't really know what the fuck they were talking about. The people wanted reliable results from the government experts but instead, they were fed endless lies and misinformation in return, just to sate them.

At least, that is what they told the public. The truth was that most all suspect canned foods and stocks were actually confiscated by the government departments and health organizations; but instead of being disposed of as they had claimed; those supplies were rerouted and hoarded in giant storage facilities and distributed to secret military bunkers like Fallhaven. Actually, it was an ingenious ploy which effectively robbed food stocks from the public right under their noses with their unwitting consent.

At least this Doomsday turned out better than it would have in the event of a nuclear holocaust, along with the radioactive winter of ash that would have encompassed the planet. Even the dire devastation of a colossal solar flare that would have scorched the planet with cosmic radiation would have killed off most of the plant life. Those apocalyptic-style movies were great entertainment, but reality was far more somber. The dinosaurs and such reptile species once had their day in the sun and were taken out by a rogue asteroid, and now mammals were getting their dues.

Approaching the lakeside, we edged our way towards the old wood building. Surrounded by a rusted fence, the mill itself was in decrepit condition. There did not appear to be any breaks in the barrier, so we let ourselves in through the front gate while noting that the lock had already been cut. The wood was worn and the warped floorboards creaked under our feet. Considering the age of the building, we soon realized that any attempts at making a campfire here might risk the whole structure going up in a ball of flames.

Chains dangled from the high ceiling above piles of cut logs, which were now cracked and split from years of exposure. Investigating the service rooms, we were lucky to find some canned food which had sat unmolested in a dark cabinet. Many places I had seen over the years had been infested by rats and mice, and noted that such vermin could chew through almost anything if they were hungry enough. Thorn knew the method of opening a sealed container without the convenience of a can opener, by grating the lid edge on a flat brick. It was an odd find since most packaged goods had pull tabs for easy opening, which pointed to the fact that these canned goods were likely older than most. The contents seemed edible enough; in fact, I don't remember cold beans ever tasting so good. We were all so hungry we didn't bother to complain.

Haiti couldn't believe our luck when we found an actual oil lantern with some kerosene still in it. It took longer than we had wished to spark up some dry sawdust, which was plentiful in this place, just to get the wick lit. The lamp was smoky from the old condensed oil, but it was a welcome relief from the darkness. Betty turned to look out towards the lake in its eerie stillness while we all sat staring at the flickering lamplight in the center of the mill; wondering what tomorrow might bring. She had been locked away in that bunker for so long she had forgotten the chirp of crickets, the sound of river life and the buzzing of dragonflies. The dark waters lapped upon the support posts below the side of the building that overhung the shore of the lake. The four of us bunked next to the small bay which overlooked the lagoon. We were so tired and worn out from the morning's events, that proper protocol would have been to keep an eye on one another for symptoms but we were so tuckered at this point that we didn't seem to care. The truth of the matter was, if any of us had been infected during our escape from Fallhaven, the mutant germ would have exposed itself by now. We were finally free of that place, and that was all that mattered.

We woke to the soft drizzle of morning rain. A light fog rose off the top of the glassy surface of the lake, though the fine mist quickly faded with the break of sunrise. It was a pleasant change from the artificial lighting of the bunker and the recycled oxygen we had to breathe, compared to the cool crisp air of daybreak. The pleasantries of nature were interrupted by the grumble in our bellies for lack of food, since we had all split the mere two cans of beans we had devoured the night before. Haiti found a few empty pans and collected sparse amounts of rainwater before the showers stopped, knowing better than to drink from the river without boiling it first.

After checking the perimeter, we finally got ourselves cleaned up and groomed to a small measure of comfort and took account of our situation. Thoroughly searching the small mill, we found an old logging map of the area composed of elevation markers, but it did show a few access roads. Thorn pointed something of interest on the upper corner.

"Those buildings look like logger's cabins," he blurted out.

"What is that?" Haiti was quick to respond with interest, as was Beatrice, who was certainly looking the worse for wear from having slept on the cold floor for the first time in her life;

and chose to join us at the counter table where we had the tattered map rolled out.

"It's similar to a mining town, only it's a temporary settlement for their staff that work at the lumber site. A section of the woods is cleared out and they build housing for their crew," Thorn stated.

"Hell, that should be worth searching," I concurred, although it was mostly my empty stomach talking for me, "and it looks like its secluded enough to be off the beaten path."

"I agree, it's certainly worth a look," Thorn admitted, "I once worked on a firefighting crew one summer for the Forestry Department, and those camps are usually kept well-stocked since they operate so far out in the country," he smiled, "it might give us a chance to re-supply."

"Unless it has already been ransacked," Haiti interjected, while I noted he had slowly started twisting his hair back into dreads whenever he had a moment to spare.

There was always the risk of running into armed survivors, which were many times more dangerous than the infected. Anyone who made it this long through such hardships had learned the art of guile and strategy, nor would they just welcome any wandering dandy into their camp with open arms. It was unfortunate that so many people had devolved into heartless scavengers who had no value for any other human life but their own. At least Weepers weren't prone to trickery or deceit, which were a few endearing human qualities that earned its own sense of value under such circumstances.

The infected had a habit of creating dens in places that had a supply of nourishment nearby, or a sparse measure of protection from the weather; which is why you could find them huddling together in piles to keep themselves warm. One thing was certain; whether you crossed paths with survivors or a horde of infected, both were a real risk. If we were to have any chance of finding our way back to the others of our group, we needed better gear and supplies. There was relative safety here at the mill with the only one access door we had blocked and the surrounding exterior gate was intact; though, once outside the perimeter we were open game. With that in mind, I folded up the map and took it with us.

Out in the forests away from the deserted towns and ravaged cities it was easy to forget that anything had ever happened to the world. Most coastal ranges had been entirely decimated from the first piece of the asteroid that splashed down in the ocean, causing tidal surges that reached many miles inland. Here in the landlocked woodlands, little had been touched and there were still an abundance of wildlife. It was strange to see how little difference mammals had made in the ecosystem when they had been suddenly removed from the food chain.

Mother Nature found other ways of dealing with the unbalance but it was humanity, itself, which had created the largest disturbance in its struggle to regain its place back upon the top rung. After the initial impact and destruction subsided, there was a brief period of confusion worldwide when dolphins, whales, seals and a list of other sea mammals began to wash up on beaches around the globe. Marine biologists were clueless as to the cause until the KRI virus was verified to be carried by infected waterborne mammals, which had traveled with the ocean currents. Their usual migration paths had been upset and the crazed creatures ended up on distant shores where they had never been seen before. Their beached carcasses only ended up spreading the disease to far-flung reaches of the earth.

The ocean itself became a nightmare for seafarers trying to flee the ravages inland, thinking they could escape the outbreak. There were sparse accounts of rabid whales attacking huge ships, and on many accounts they were successful in destroying smaller boats. They became the sea monsters of old, giants of the deep that terrorized harbors. It was a mortal risk to take out a small craft into open waters, and with the abundant food supplies of the ocean depths, there was no way to know their numbers or where the aquatic beasts might strike. Mankind learned once again to fear the seas and what lurked beneath their dark mysterious waters.

The briny depths were a world away from this thick mountain forest, but even here, packs of infected squirrels or hordes of mice could turn a peaceful woodland hike into a scene of nightmarish horror. If you let your mind wander on the risks and dangers, paranoia could drive anyone to the brink of insanity. Survivors dealt with their stress in different ways, some better than others. Mine was to fade away into daydreams from time to time to escape reality; I really didn't know how to control it. Perhaps I had already lost my mind long ago.

It was depressing thinking about what once was, and how it was all lost. The family or friends you knew had disappeared or had died as you watched, but there was always this spark of hope that lingered in those chosen few who refused to give up on life. Surviving wasn't actually about finding food and shelter, it was about being tempered enough not to let yourself be broken. It was almost spiritual if you were inclined to look at it that way.

Trekking through the forest towards this hidden logging camp, we began to smell smoke wafting through the trees; the faint tinge you get from a wood stove. We followed the haze to its source as we approached upon the border of a small camp, identical to the one shown upon our map. Ahead of us through the tall trees, we saw several rough log cabins with rusted metal roof sheeting. To the far left in a partial clearing, we noted three chairs with people sitting in them around a smoldering campfire, over which hung a kettle pot on a spit.

This was a mixed situation, as it was certainly better than finding a horde of hungry weepers infesting the campsite, but armed survivors could be even more-so unpredictable. On separate occasions, both my friends and I have tripped across lone camps where being unknown posed a risk of being shot on sight out of fear of being a carrier of the virus; or simply gutted for any supplies you might be carrying instead. People could be desperate in the most vicious of ways. Human life meant little if you had something that could help someone else survive one more day. Food, ammunition, clothing ...it didn't matter what. In any circumstance, a safe haven would be strongly defended against trespassers.

Of course, we would have much rather found the place deserted but there were people here who could possibly help us, so we had to take a chance to find out if they were hostile or not. Haiti was the cautious one of the group, noting that we should approach quietly to get some Intel and find out how many people were here before we went stumbling blindly into their camp. He scouted ahead and took a covered position with a clear view of the campsite where the three individuals sat in their chairs, unmoving. Hands cupped to his ears, he listened intently for about ten minutes and quietly crawled back to us under the cover of the brush.

"I don't get it, man," he whispered with a hint of confusion, "they is all just sitting there, not talk'in about nuth'in at all. Something ain't right," Haiti confessed.

"Did you see anybody else?" Thorn inquired, but the island man just shook his head.

"Ain't no lights on in the windows, and that fire is mighty low. They isn't stoking it nor speak'in a word between them. They are just sitting there doing nothing..." he trailed off with a wrinkled brow.

We did not have much time on our hands, as the sun was beginning to cross over the canopy and darkness fell quickly in the forest. Betty suggested that we sneak up from the backside to one of the cabins and peek through the windows. The problem with that was with our limited munitions, and getting caught skulking around, would likely be considered an act of aggression. Most survivors had little patience and a hair-trigger for that kind of suspicious behavior.

It was interesting to note how having the world turned on its heel could dissolve social fabric so quickly. Being overly friendly was viewed with suspicion in most circles or could just as swiftly get you killed in the wrong crowd. Human nature was a saucy bitch when it came down to the have and have-nots, or those egotistical few with a sense of entitlement who believed they deserved more than others. Then again, that pretty much sums up the past several thousand years of human history now that I think of it.

As we were debating our plans, in an unforeseen move, the old woman got up and stomped out of our hidden cluster and headed straight towards the group of strangers sitting by the campfire.

"We don't have time for this..." were her only words as she

trailed off with a gleam of impatience in her eyes. That kind of attitude could get us all killed, but she was just out of arms reach as Haiti lurched for her a little too late; who was just as startled as the rest of us by her reckless conduct. We took cover again behind the trees as Betty stepped into full view inside the clearing. Had we the chance, we would have sent a scout to circle around first so as not to give away our initial location, but Beatrice didn't possess that measure of tactical training nor common sense. Before this moment, it all fazed us that her ineptitude in real-world situations might eventually become a liability to us all at some point. Obviously, that point came a lot quicker than we would have realized.

We stood breathless as she plodded her way towards the campfire, calling out a greeting as she approached. The reaction we expected would have been for the group around the smoking coals to jump up fully armed at the announcement of their surprise guest, but oddly, they just sat there unflinching. The three of them remained sitting as she got several steps closer to them and it struck me that something was seriously wrong here. When the old woman was only a few feet away, she slowed down and turned back towards us with a look of concern crossing her face. That is when we heard a shot crack the air, which echoed through the forest.

Dirt kicked up as a bullet ricocheted in front of her and the old woman froze, cowering to cover her head, then a grumbled voice called out from the tree line. The position of the buildings deflected the words so that it was impossible to be certain which direction the shooter was speaking from. Whoever it was, they were well trained in laying traps.

Beatrice had walked up on decoys, mannequins fitted with pants, shirts, and jackets, all stuffed with a skeleton of leaves and branches, finished off with hats that shadowed the faces crudely drawn upon tarp cloth. A great deal of effort had been taken to make them anatomically correct and posed to be believable at a distance. The firearms lying next to them were rusted props, though the burning fireplace was the jewel of this elaborate ruse. By my guess, the sniper was in the canopy somewhere due to the angle of the shot, but from the direction of it, I couldn't even begin to guess.

   Beatrice had walked straight into an ambush, likely one that the sniper had prepared just for us after having detected our approach long enough beforehand to have lit the fire; knowing we would have smelled the smoke and be lured in its direction. The old woman had done an immaculate job of giving away our obscured position in the underbrush. There was no ignoring the instructions we were given, lest we sacrifice her and chance a hasty retreat into unknown territory.

   "The three of you come out in the open, or the woman dies!" the rough voice demanded, echoing off the cabins and through the trees, making pinpointing its origin impossible.   Thorn, Haiti, and I, all shared a quick worried glance.   Without hesitation another shot rang out, this one merely a breath away kicking up the moist dirt at Beatrice's feet as she jerked in fear.

   "I won't ask again. You have five seconds to comply or the next one goes through her head!" the stranger warned. We all held our breath, wondering what to do at this turn of events, "Five," we speculated for a moment if we could escape behind one of the buildings or split up and take our chances, "...Four," only to realize that the buildings were actually too far in the open and the sniper already had the initiative, "...Three," we could flee and just leave her, which would be a real shitty thing to do, but the old woman had walked right into that trap of her own volition, "...Two," then again, we had no idea how many other snipers there were with their sights trained on us, so with a sigh of resignation, we stood up to expose ourselves, "...One!"

   "We're coming out," Thorn yelled out from behind the brush as we made our way out of cover. With our pistol held up in the air with our hands, as the three of us strolled into the clearing to surrender. As we got closer to where Betty stood, we saw the decoy mannequins ourselves, embarrassed by our stupidity.

   "Oh, they are good..." Thorn blurted under his breath in admiration of the trap.

   "Keep quiet and throw down your weapons," the mysterious voice instructed from beyond the veil of fog sifting between the dark maze of trees. We complied, hoping that our captors weren't as desperate as we were.

After a long moment, three masked figures emerged from the mist, each wearing goggles and ragged camouflage ponchos. Their gear was light, except for the high tech scoped rifles they carried. Any additional weapons they may have had were well hidden beneath the loose cloaks they wore. Thinking about it, I guess we looked outrageously out of place wearing our one-tone jumpsuits and were starting to realize we should have taken a measure of effort to blend into our environment. Any scout must have seen us coming from a mile away, allowing them ample time to bait this trap.

"Who are you, and why are you here?" the figure on the right demanded, their voices seemed mechanically altered by some device wired in the mask filters they wore. Beatrice just looked at us with sullen eyes, feeling a bit guilty about her mistaken display of bravado that got us into this fix.

"We found a map in the mill over by the lake and thought we could find shelter here," I answered, hoping the truth would settle their suspicions. The sniper on the left stepped forward and took our weapon that was lying among the pine needles where we had dropped it; and eyed its function with noted scrutiny. Holding the pulse pistol up for their comrades to view for a brief moment, before stuffing it beneath the hidden folds of their cloak.

The sniper in the center looked us up and down for a few seconds with tinted goggles hiding any expression as to what they were thinking. Slinging their rifles in turn, they removed their masks; admitting we were a little surprised to see that they were all women. The oldest of the three with brushed raven-black hair spoke first.

"She asked you a question!" the female demanded towards Thorn, while eyeing our strange attire. We were not quite sure if we should tell them about the complex we had escaped from, or if its mention would be problematic for us. If pressed about Fallhaven, our story of what had transpired in the underground facility would likely not be believed in the slightest; so I kept my mouth shut.

"Our clothes had become contaminated, so we took these ones we found in a storage building a few days walk from here,"

Thorn spoke up in my place, noting just how suspicious we looked wearing our mostly clean uniforms and complete lack of gear out here in the wild, while armed with nothing but a weak stun pistol as our only defense.

"Did you come in contact with any Ghouls?" The other one inquired, who was a quite attractive dark-skinned girl with shoulder-length hair. I assumed that was their nickname for the infected victims.

"Do you mean Weepers?" I answered, "No, we're not sick."

The girl in the middle was younger than her comrades, with matted dirty blonde hair and freckles, who stepped forward, taking a device that looked like a penlight that had an intense blue beam, and shone it into each of our eyes. Satisfied that we were safe, she put the UV light away back under her poncho.

"It will be dark soon," she noted with unease, "Ava, get them inside and keep an eye on them," the young girl ordered the woman with the wavy black hair; who promptly pulled out a dangerous looking automatic pistol from her belt and issued us towards the nearest cabin. Meanwhile, the other two women began kicking dirt into the pit and smothering the smoking fire at the center of the seated decoys.

"No sudden moves, and we'll get along just fine," Ava warned with a motion of her firearm towards the building. By the way these three women carried themselves, we suspected they had military training. It was obvious that their weapons were high tech, especially in comparison to the average citizen. Their firearms were clean and well oiled, and not of standard design. In fact, their outfits and gear were well matched for the woodland environment, which made me suspect that they had been located here for some length of time. Ava ushered all four of us into the cabin where we found stacks of crates and boxes of various sizes, along with a few cots and a sparse but ample assortment of laboratory gear.

Moments later, the other two women barged in and locked the door behind us. They toured the room and made sure the thick curtains were shut tight before lighting the oil lanterns that sat upon the tables; they also kept their pistols handy just in case we were having second thoughts about our capture.

"That is Kel," the young girl motioned to the dark-skinned woman across the room, "...and Ava," gesturing to the one who led us into the cabin, "and I'm Tasha," she finished coldly as she watched us with her intense pale blue eyes. Haiti stuttered in first with an introduction.

"Aye, they call me Haiti," he gave a half-cocked smile, "this is Thorn and Caity," he mentioned nodding towards us both, "and this here is Beatrice," he finished.

"Betty will do," the old woman suggested to our captors with a thin-lipped grin, "and what about you ladies," she added, "how did you come to be here?"

Tasha stalled in her response for a slight moment before she took a step forward. There was something mature about her far beyond her age; which in a strange way, made her appear slightly more seasoned than her fellow cohorts she commanded.

"Shortly after the asteroid broke apart in the atmosphere, recovery efforts began from the decimation of the resulting earthquakes and tsunamis near the impact zones, including the global storm fronts created by the debris that was kicked up into the atmosphere. The authorities found themselves in the middle of a battle against the MN4 plague that created these ...these diseased ghouls, or 'Weepers' as you so put it," she offered with a gesture towards me, "my father led a mercenary backup team for the local military. It was only one of several that took up the slack of the failing militant divisions that were assigned to quell the unrest and reassign the civilian population."

"...Reassign?" Thorn questioned suspiciously with a raised brow, that not being a word any of us would have used, or of an agenda we were even faintly familiar with.

"It was a term used after full-scale Martial Law was imposed to divide and corral civilians from quarantined sections into designated temporary camps, depending on their skills or influence, per se," she added by rubbing her fingers together, as a gesture of money being the source of influence she was referring to, "The homeless and destitute were acquired and sent to razor-wired fenced shelters in the red zone and assigned to work brigades to fortify those camps that required manual labor, while anyone newly infected was expedited to the nearest hospital detention facility for sterilization."

"You mean..." Thorn began.

"Yes, *that* kind of sterilization," Tasha cut him off in mid-sentence, as she made a gesture of a throat being cut, "Civilians who had fled the cities to escape the outbreaks were placed in similar facilities, which began to thin the resources available for the military response to a dangerous level. Thus, security contractors, such as my father, were hired to perform special operations assignments as an additional arm of the acting authority," she confessed.

"You keep on mentioning your father, is he here?" Betty spat out with a snip, wanting to speak to someone in command, rather than this smart-mouthed teen.

"That was six years ago, along with several other squads who ran these operations for the special forces, we believe he died during one of those runs," Tasha added with a harsh glare towards Beatrice, and just as quickly, she broke her gaze without a hint as to what she was thinking.

"Who is left of your division?" I had to ask.

"Just us," Kel answered from behind where we stood as she opened a latched crate and pulled out a handful of vacuumed packed rations, tossing one to each of us to catch. We were so hungry that we didn't even bother to read what was stamped on the silver foil. I ended up with something that tasted like tuna fish, although it didn't appear like any fish meat I had ever seen.

"Have you three been here all this time?" Thorn inquired in disbelief.

From the exterior, the buildings looked quite unused, and from what he could tell of the interior room they occupied, it didn't appear to be either. There were certainly stockpiles of rations, supplies, and other gear, and who knows what else was in the stacks of bins crowding the small cabin. With proper training and precautions, it was possible they could have survived here for that long, but something seemed a little out of place here.

"Originally, there were twenty-four of us in our squadron, but we are all that is left," Ava answered in return to Thorn's question.

"A few months after the impact, my father was heading a

convoy escorting a military scientist and his secret package to a nearby base. They had secured him here during a bad storm on one leg of the trip before they disappeared," Tasha informed her guests, "it wasn't long thereafter that we were overrun by a handful of scavengers, which in turn, had drawn a large horde of infected to our detachment that were likely attracted by the gunfire during the engagement," she paused as her eyes drifted for a moment in thought, "only a handful of them survived, the rest of our team were lost over the years during scouting missions or isolated incidents while traveling to our winter camps."

"You mentioned a secret package," Haiti had to ask, in response to our collective curiosity.

Tasha strode over to a wide table at the edge of the room where a square metal box sat, and she unbuckled its hinges. After carefully unfolding its side panels, we were all shocked to see what lay suspended within the glass canister beneath the protective outer case. Within it sat a jagged stone, scorched and melted from atmospheric entry, mottled with patches of crystallized slag. We could see a small-engraved plate attached to its base. In the dim light of the lamps, the four of us made out what it read at the same time, Apophis MN4 #99942.

"Is, is that a piece of the...?" Haiti began with a nervous stutter, but Tasha had a notable talent for finishing other people's sentences.

"Yes, but it's only a small fragment of debris from the core of the asteroid that rained to Earth during the initial event," she answered, "it's safe while it remains sealed within this shielded case," Tasha assured us while she patted the top of the capsule.

This warped stone came from the hunk of rock that was the cause of all our sorrows; and it was a mixed feeling of both anxiety and awe to grasp that only a thin sheet of glass lay between us and this small piece of Hades itself; which had caused this global pandemic and turned our world inside out.

Deception

I had once read a story written several centuries ago about a pirate crew that had been chased by a Man-of-War sailing ship, crewed by soldiers of the Kings Crown. These marauders were outmatched and outgunned, and knew if they were ever caught that every man would receive the gentle kiss of a noose upon his neck. In an effort to escape their pursuers on the high seas, the pirate ship turned its heading straight into the squall of a violent storm, facing the risk of losing their own sails. During the storm, these two opposing vessels had become separated for a brief time but after the gales subsided and the rolling seas calmed, the chase began anew.

The Admiral of the King's ship kept pace with the enemy vessel on the horizon, as their own military warship was the larger of the two and had more sail yard to catch the wind. During the pursuit, the military ship passed a lone vessel with folded sails that flew two flags high upon its mast. Flapping in the salty wind were the blazing colors of yellow and black, designating the solitary vessel as a plague ship. Upon their approach to the craft, they noted there were no hands on deck, only the lifeless gray bodies of its crew seen slumped across the rails.

An hour before, the Admiral had watched through his spyglass when the brigands had passed this vessel on the horizon during their pursuit, and observed that the pirates slowed as they neared the blighted vessel but had immediately raised full sail to escape the pestilence of the accursed ship. It was prudent of the Admiral to continue the chase at hand, and he gave a wide berth to the dead ship as they continued their advance upon the fleeing pirates. It was far into the day when the Kings navy finally laid its grapple onto the ship of the delinquent cutthroats that flew their ragged black flag of skull and bones.

The soldiers at arms were confused as to why the vagabonds weren't following orders to stand down, nor had they fired their cannons as the gun ports were propped to the ready. After many tense moments, it wasn't until they boarded the vessel to find that several corpses had been strung to the lines and wheel, propped up by a tangle of dowels and rope. The pirate crew had vanished along with their manifest. They discovered the Captain's quarters had been stricken bare, along with all the galley's rations. Within the ship's belly, they found no sign of bounty, stolen or otherwise; and scratched their heads in confusion when they realized they had been chasing a ghost ship across the open sea.

It took longer than it should have to concede how they could have fallen for such a ruse, which took its time to soak into the white talc wig of the admiral and his boggled men. The present cadavers left behind had all been tied up like puppets on a string to be used as decoys, while the sails had been unfurled and the rudder fixed on a wide curve from the plague ship they had left adrift many leagues away. The entire crew of rogues had abandoned their own vessel for another, though the Admiral was bewildered at the boldness of their most perilous strategy to risk taking the deck of a blighted ship, for to do so, they surely must have been the most desperate of men.

Now safely beyond the horizon, the sun had set upon the ocean where a lone plague ship lay adrift in the rolling seas. The pirate crew exploited the sailors bodies from the merchant ship they had captured several days before, and transferred what supplies and rigging they could onto their newly acquired vessel. The brigands made use of the poor chaps they had relieved of their lives and cargo by propping a few corpses upon the decks in various assumed positions of death after rubbing their exposed skin with ash. They then made use of the remaining cadavers, which they placed on their own ship and secured them to the riggings; and further completed the deception by placing a pair of false quarantine signal flags on the high mast of the merchant ship they now held.

The crew of marauders hid below deck while a skeleton crew crept back aboard and baited the Navy vessel with their rogue ship, after having set a course to graze by the stationary merchant vessel once the military warship gave pursuit. The pirates had the advantage of distance while the meager crew secured full sail and braced the wheel before they hastily abandoned ship and swam to the concealed side of the fake plague boat, and discreetly climbed aboard upon nets left placed at the open cargo ports on the blind side of the hull. Whereupon, seeing no activity on deck upon the decoy ship, the King's Navy was led off on a merry chase.

I remembered that story, because it was based on false flags and relied on a great many assumptions. Even as wild as they had seemed, it was perfectly plausible that the course of events had happened exactly as it was written. You see, the Pirate Captain had prior knowledge he was being hunted, and finding a lone merchant ship between unfriendly ports, he saw an opportunity to devise this most devious plan.

Their presumptions relied heavily that the timing would be right and the Royal Navy ship would arrive where it would be expected; and that the wind would allow him to use his own vessel to intersect with the one he had left adrift with his supplies and men many days prior. This also assumes his crew were loyal enough to him not to commit mutiny at the first opportunity and take the decoy ship for themselves once he was out of sight.

It also laid a great deal of risk that the pursuing military vessel would fail to board, or even fire upon and scuttle the plague ship as they passed it, while the pirate crew hid quietly inside. It also assumes that the soldiers wouldn't notice anything suspicious and call the bluff. Lastly, it further assumed that the King's authority would be so eager to catch the fleeing pirate ship, that they would become reckless, if not shortsighted, in the heat of the chase. The situation even trusts that the makeshift rigging would hold and that the Navy wouldn't catch the wayward ghost ship too soon and see through the hoax, and turn around to seize the small unarmed merchant craft before it disappeared into the starry night.

This was an actual historical account. The story, being slightly elaborated or not, spoke about how to view strategy from two entirely different perspectives. For one, the thin-lipped Admiral had grievously underestimated the bravado of his foes, with no way of knowing the shifty pirates could manipulate their assets at hand. Secondly, it was a sound decision on his part to keep in hot pursuit on the trail of the pirate vessel before they could escape into the darkness of nightfall, especially while his naval ship clearly had the greater speed and were gaining against them as the sun waned towards the horizon. And three, in that time period, anyone in their right mind would avoid a diseased vessel left adrift. Fears of sickness were high in that era, and men in service were acutely aware of their own mortality.

Given the circumstances, the Royal Navy acted in arrogance, and followed proper protocol by giving chase to their quarry just as they should have. They avoided an afflicted ship in kind, just as the pirate vessel had, or so it appeared. The Admiral also chose not to waste time and ammunition to sink the derelict ship because of his priorities, considering the tight window of opportunity of wind and weather to pursue his foe. However, most readers of this tale would shake their heads in dismay that the King's soldiers had actually cornered their prey while they played possum on an unarmed ship left adrift. The Admiral had them, but had let his adversary evade capture because of the complete efficiency of the misdirection awarded by the ruse. The lesson in the end, was that it was all about appearances.

Now I looked at this narrative in a different way than most. In my point of view, the Royal Navy in the storyline could be seen here as representing our modern Military. The marauders could be regarded as Citizens and Survivors, in replacement of the outlaw pirates as described; and the basic reason they got away was that the Government was far too presumptuous and eager to exercise its control. Our modern police state pushing their overly oppressive authority was always too bloodthirsty and eager to make a bust, too hungry to make the kill, too impatient to scrutinize the situation or question the facts, and far too narrow-minded to calculate the outcome as to those they would harm. Straight down the chain of command, the soulless minions in our government, along with our overly aggressive law enforcement and military personnel, blindly followed orders and usually made no effort to think for themselves; and got sloppy.

This is what I thought of Military soldiers and Mercenary lackey's, like Tasha's father and his crew, who were usually too small-minded and only concerned with saving their own skin and that of their kin, rather than honoring their oath to protect the public at large. In the first years after the asteroid strike, it was those who were wearing the uniforms and the badges who had revealed themselves as the true danger amongst us. They abused their authority, confiscated firearms, food rations, and supplies from the destitute civilians who were merely trying to survive. It showed just how ugly mankind can get by asserting who had the right to live, and by exercising one man's will over another by nothing more than a mere uniform.

Although I detested their type, I had to give Tasha and her companion's due credit when they offered to let us have the classified files that accompanied the meteorite sample. After a few minutes of shared reading between us, I finally got the documents into my hands and was left bewildered by what lay within those ivory pages. They revealed references to a counteraction, resulting due to the asteroid impact, not from it. These documents referenced another mysterious file as its companion for further relevant data. However, after searching through the folder several times, there was no other paperwork; the additional file it spoke of was missing.

"What does all this mean," I asked our female captors, "and what is this mention of a 'VEIL project' resulting in a code orange?" The two older mercenaries kept silent, letting their younger colleague bear the weight of explaining the situation to their inquisitive guests.

"As you can imagine, this ore sample is biologically volatile," Tasha noted to the rock behind the glass, "but it appears from the information that you hold in your hands, that this is not its normal state," she breathed, adding to our confusion.

"What are you talking about?" Thorn responded.

"I'm no scientist, but I've read that document a hundred times over, and it looked to me as if the dormant microbes within the sample were originally inert and harmless in their natural form, but had somehow gone through an acute viral mutation once they had been irradiated," she added.

"Irradiated by what?" Haiti chimed in as Tasha strolled to the other end of the table and unrolled the map she had confiscated from us.

"The answer to that question is here," she whipped back, pointing to the upper corner of the chart where a small region of the map had been left blank.

"There's nuth'in there..." Haiti barked in response.

"Actually, it's common practice to void out military locations and base facilities on civilian maps. There is *something* there, alright!" Tasha snapped back with a pen in her hand as she marked in a string of buildings to update our map. Tasha and her crew had scouted the area around this site for many years. On several occasions, they had considered abandoning this camp to locate other survivors but their decisive factors to remain in the area was that they had a significant store of food and ammunition stashed here, which they had been unwilling to part with. However, those supplies were beginning to dwindle near their end. As they revealed, most of the containers stacked about the room now sat entirely empty.

"My father's squadron had been on strict orders to protect this package," Tasha noted as she gestured to the meteorite glinting in the flickering light of the lanterns, "it was supposed to be a key sample used to help break the genetic code of the virus."

We could understand her analogy since the untainted original DNA chain would provide vital information in formulating a viable antidote. The base organism in its pure form could reveal clues as to how its structure reacted, including testing of any biological and environmental conditions as the primary catalysts which triggered the resulting mutations. In the right hands, its possible applications towards aiding the medical response for a vaccine were literally invaluable.

"But if that's the case, why..." I stammered while the blonde girl kept in character of anticipating our questions.

"...Why haven't we delivered it already, in my father's stead?" She asserted, "Simply because we couldn't," she answered after a noted pause.

"It's a full week trek to get there by foot," Ava added, "its not the distance, but the harsh terrain that presents an obstacle."

"A few years back, it was our plan to honor the people we lost in our squadron and finish the mission, but here," Kel advanced to the map and pointed to the road as it extended into a cliffside, "...the tunnel has collapsed, and carrying that sample between the three of us across that steep ridge would be far too risky," she noted while outlining the high cliffs surrounding the base.

With a glance back over to the rock sample, we understood they weren't really worried about themselves, but about the danger of either losing or damaging the capsule in its fragile case. The box-shaped container was not exactly the most convenient shape to be transported by hand.

"What happened to your convoy vehicles from the original escort?" Betty finally nosed herself into the conversation after appearing uninterested from its inception.

"Those trucks had built-in shielding from the magnetic pulse, as most military vehicles do, but our team couldn't shield themselves from a mountain crushing them," the dark-skinned girl answered. I guess Tasha could tell by the tilt of my head and look in my eye as to what my response was going to be, so she answered it for me without hesitation.

"It becomes rather obvious that the fragment is here," she noted to the meteorite as she patted the top of the case, "while its transport convoy was stopped there," Tasha granted. The circumstance did start to look suspicious once she pointed that fact out.

"Your father left the rock sample here on purpose?" Thorn began to pry with a puzzled look.

"I was only ten years old when the event happened, and like most people, we scrambled to save our families. My father would only accept the mission on the condition that he could take me along," Tasha revealed, "he was a hired mercenary, but he wasn't stupid. He didn't trust anyone and wasn't going to leave his own daughter in the hands of their inept child care services, especially after seeing the horrific conditions that existed at their quarantine camps. Honestly, my father didn't have much confidence in the military industry either. After a heated debate with their lead scientist we were escorting, he left me and a few of his crew here while he advanced to the target site to deliver their science technician but he never returned," she conceded.

"We waited here as ordered for as long as we could until we finally decided to send out a scouting party," Ava explained, "with no working GPS devices since the satellites had been knocked out, we only had a single mission map to track them by; which we lost when the soldier who was carrying it had been jumped by a mob of infected out on the roadside. The ghouls took more than a few of us that day," she added grimly.

"Luckily we had enough supplies here and were snowed in through the first winter. It wasn't until we took a full inventory that we found this specimen sample tucked under a pile of boxes where it had been hidden," the young girl answered, pointing back to the jagged stone.

"So, you're saying your father intentionally left the meteorite behind?" I reiterated with a mild measure of shock.

"Apparently so, along with a short note he left for us relating his concerns that there was something amiss, from what he had gleaned from the lead scientist during their dispute that fateful night; and he chose to make a personal resolution, if not a tactical decision, based on his suspicions," Tasha added.

"We heard the rumble in the mountains that evening, but it wasn't until the following year after the spring thaw that we discovered the collapsed tunnel road to the base. We don't know exactly what had happened except that there had been some type of explosion in the underpass. Considering the circumstances, we suspect the detonation was intentional."

Tasha's companions continued to outline how they had once made their way to the cliffs above the isolated base in their effort to seek some answers but had failed to pick up any radio traffic in the area. They discovered there was still electrical power to the base when they had last seen it, although it appeared there had been some type of incident which had damaged one of the buildings, and that several rogue infected had overrun the grounds.

It would have been suicidal to go back there, and far too risky to haul around that frail sample container on such a dangerous climb while not even knowing if there was anyone left alive at the base to deliver it to; so they hunkered down and waited for help that never arrived. The two adult women cared for and trained their commander's daughter to shoot and to hone her survival skills over the years. Much like her father, they were advanced techniques she seemed well adapted for.

On many occasions, they had attempted to hotwire several abandoned civilian vehicles they found along the roadside, only to find that their operational components had been fried. The laboratory base was located in the middle of nowhere and they were blessed to have this logger's camp to call sanctuary. It was located far off the main roads where no one would know to look, and few infected ever wandered into the area. They soon learned the effective use of camouflage and that nesting in the trees provided the desired advantage of both observation and safety from the afflicted and predatory animals.

However, supplies were running low as of late, and they had scouted as far as they could to find a way out of the forest and were now facing the choice of abandoning this isolated camp and the dangerous prize they protected during the harsh winter months. It became clear to us that we were all in the same fix. Stuck here in the backwoods it would take several weeks by foot for us to reach the nearest town to re-supply, and even that would be a risky endeavor. Towns and suburbs were always filled with weepers, which made them dangerous to explore, and actually finding anything of real use was always a gamble.

We agreed that stumbling across the importance of this artifact could not be ignored. We had the choice to either bury it and try our luck by fighting our way through unknown territory and hope we found another camp along the way, or get to that laboratory on the base and look for the answers that might resolve this outbreak. All the while, Beatrice kept mostly quiet and only glanced once at the stone remnant, hiding a tiny spark of fascination behind her somber eyes. I could tell something was spinning in her devious mind. The old woman was adept and cunning as much as she was unpredictable, and I suspected she had knowledge of Project VEIL before she had ever stepped foot into Fallhaven.

It was a long night with our new companions. They were well aware to keep the noise to a minimum and the windows blacked out so as not to attract any nocturnal creatures. Even though their vision was handicapped in darkness, it was from dusk that the infected were most active when it was easier for them to sneak up and catch their prey. As humans were not a species with natural defenses, they utilized primal instinct as a means to an end when left devoid of the raw intellect to fashion even the most basic of weapons.

The mental capacity of weepers were greatly dulled. In the control studies performed on diseased patients during the outbreak, medical scientists observed those infected who had fully-turned revealed that the transformation to their colorless eyesight was balanced by an increased sense of hearing. Few, if any of them, still recognized what a can of food was, but even those that lacked the articulate physical skills to open such a container without due violence and usually resorted to smashing them open by the use of brute force. Their sense of pain was lessened greatly, which is why it was so difficult to take them down. They suffered wounds like any person could, and would eventually bleed out if left untreated, but it was as if their primal instincts and adrenaline were set into overdrive.

We were lucky that the virus only turned a small fraction of those infected that ended up to be so dangerously violent. If that had not been the case, then mankind would have been overrun by a plague of homicidal mammals of every species. After all these years, their numbers had dwindled drastically as those patients who were infirm or docile usually just wasted away, either due to starvation or exposure to the elements. Those Weepers who had become stalkers were fearsome. Actually, it was scary to think of what people were truly capable of when beset by rabid insanity.

Still, precautions had to be taken as any wildlife that was capable of becoming tainted through a septic infection or by consuming a corpse could eventually transform into a brutal adversary. Tasha and her companions looked as if they had had their fair share of such encounters, even though it took a measure of convincing them to count us as assets instead of a liability. In the end, we were glad we had crossed paths.

Although Betty had seemed reluctant to reveal her past with the party, we shared our back-stories of how we came to be in the middle of this secluded forest. For the next few days, we prepared to investigate the base across the valley with the assurance that we could first arrange an excursion to find the few friends we had left at the abandoned hydropower plant. There was always the chance that they might have moved on, or worse, came looking for us in that underground facility. In either case, we had to find them and let them know what had happened to us.

With our current company, the supply of available rations were running thin and was now being used up at twice the rate with our presence. They had tried hunting before, and their skill with their high-tech sniper rifles would make it an easy chore, but there was no guarantee that any game taken down wasn't already tainted with the disease. Since the outbreak, many survivors had turned to a pure vegetarian palate by growing what they could in gardens to eke out an existence. Those efforts were limited to their location and time of the season unless they had the means to construct a greenhouse, which was necessary due to the enduring overcast and frequent storms. The fact was that most canned foods usually went sour a year or two after their marked expiration dates, and we were now past that timeframe by several-fold.

The three mercenary girls had limited luck with fishing in the lake near the mill until infected rodents began to raze their traps. Diseased beavers being the worst of the culprits, which were critters designed for both land and water, and could chew through anything. After their fishing nets had been destroyed, it became obvious they were fighting a losing battle. None of the girls really wanted to risk setting up additional netting in deeper water at the peril of being attacked by the waterborne rodents.

The pressure of our situation urged Beatrice to reveal there was a small chance that the subterranean transit system might be connected to the research facility beyond the collapsed road tunnel. After suffering several days of her silence on the matter, we began to wonder what else she might have withheld. As our plans progressed, Tasha, Ava, and Kel acknowledged that it would be far safer for us to infiltrate the target base if there was any way to access it through an underground conduit. With a measure of reluctance, we agreed to revisit the transport system, as our only known access at this point was back where we had left our friends at the generator plant.

At least now, we had new gear and weapons, and the seven of us had a better chance to make the long trek. Kel had already pieced together several map portions seized from their supplies and attached it to ours from the mill. They had made a crude drawing of their master chart which had been lost during a previous encounter. As their navigator, she had an idea where the power station might be and how to find it.

When I had initially stumbled upon Thorn and his crew, I had just been following the ridgeline of the western mountains through the forests, as I had learned it was prudent to avoid open roads and towns unless I happened to be in exceptionally desperate straights at the time. Thorn and his friends had come up from the south when they had chanced upon that building in ruins as an escape from the wet regional weather and violent electrical storms. This was fortunate, since we believed we were currently stationed far southwest of where that facility might be.

Beatrice gave us but a few assurances that the tube rail transit worked by a sealed vacuum system and would not allow contaminated people to wander into the tunnels as far as she knew. Understandably, Tasha and the girls were stunned when we mentioned the enormous mutants that we had seen, but we chose not to comment on the experimentation which had been performed at Fallhaven. That secret research had been the cause of the particular conflict between the young girl's father and the head scientist the day before he had disappeared. She was already aware that something sinister and underhanded was going on long before we had ever met.

It was during the first year after this viral blight had hit the public and the exceptionally harsh winter that followed, that the world began to fall apart at the seams. Radical tensions erupted between nations in the midst of the ongoing crisis. Political conflicts ignited while governments were struggling to gain some kind of control over the rising global dilemma as the plague continued to spread.

Back in Fallhaven, sitting high on their pedestals, Beatrice and General Kane were privy to classified data, which was crucial information they would do anything to protect from leaking out to the residents. In such confined environments, knowledge was power and they did not want to provide the tenants with a reason to revolt. The vast underground shelters honeycombed throughout the countryside, all of which had been built long before the asteroid impact. Honestly, it was spooky how quickly the military had responded in a show of brute force to corral citizens under the guise of humanitarian aid.

People who went into the camps never came out. They had been pressed into receiving phony inoculations as a cure that had never worked. All able-bodied citizens were turned into chain gang slave labor to build defenses for the military bunkers while armed uniformed soldiers stood around watching under the pretense of their protection. However, it was those same military guards that readily abandoned the civilians whenever swarms of the infected attacked, or merely deserted the civilians in empty camps when they had received orders to retreat. Any real government officials were never actually seen in person except by video while they were asserting their control and offering empty promises to the masses.

Now we knew where the elite had all fled to; giving their aired speeches from behind the thick walls of exotic shelters like Fallhaven. The social landscape had been scarred long before Apophis punched a hole into our atmosphere. Money bought elections, while heads of government entertained the public with their mindless banter. Throughout all the posturing of the authorities, the civilians themselves, were only concerned that they would be safe and healthy, and tried to recover their sanity through these grim times.

Officials allowed banking cabals to reap financial credits from the public coffers in return for their own slice of the pie. The corruption was rampant; but unfortunately for them, so was the virus. It brought the military and government to its knees, and all the while, they were keeping up the masquerade to the very end that everything was under control; when the reality was that they didn't have a clue as to what the fuck they were doing, and never did.

Whatever their game plan was, it crumbled from lack of disclosure. They treated civilians like children that needed to be protected and somehow forgot that they, themselves, were the parasites feeding on their host and ended up killing them off after sucking a lethal amount of blood from their citizens. In the end, it was the protected who became the prey, and it was those wearing the badges that were the real terrorists instead of the phantom ones they fabricated and pretended to defend everyone from in order to justify their inflated presence. When the Authorities opened the floodgates and sent out their jackboots to quell the fear and civil unrest, it was all by design to place citizens under their ward and keep them scared into a system of eternal and unwavering compliance.

Unfortunately, that tactic backfired when the cosmic disaster ended up having a few extra surprises of its own, which came to light in the aftermath. Here, nearly a decade later, I wondered what could have been done differently that would have made a more constructive or positive difference. Our world went to shit, but was there a way we could have kept the pile from being so deep? Some might argue that a measure of transparency would have helped alleviate much of the unnecessary turmoil and grief. Countless lives could have been saved if we had only been fed the truth, rather than erroneous propaganda.

I spent many long nights playing the "what if" game in my head. Thinking about it made my brain hurt, but I was still confused as to why these hidden bunkers were kept such a secret or the reason more weren't constructed, or why any form of warning wasn't issued to the public. There had been so much death to endure these past years. One could imagine the seething contempt seen within the bloodshot eyes of these poor victims infected with the MN4 pathogen. It was almost as if you could even envision that all the primal fury and rage of the deranged Weeper's was an expression of their hatred for what their life had become, having been left abandoned by everyone and the world they had once known.

Thorn and Haiti were especially concerned for their crewmates we had left behind and were all too eager to cooperate with a plan that would let them be reunited. I was on their side, but wary about having to enter the subway system again for obvious reasons. For the time being, we agreed to join forces with the three militants as long as it was beneficial to both parties. In this undertaking, we would get our friends back and possibly some questions answered along the way.

After another day's rest, we were fully packed and ready to hit the road. Even though Kel's map was a little blind, since our route brought us off the edge of its chart, we could still navigate to the wide valley where we could follow the exposed power lines to the hydro station where our friends had held up camp. After locking up the cabins, we made our way out into the early morning mist with Ava, who was wearing a custom backpack frame they had jerry-rigged to hold the delicate rock sample.

We advanced quietly down the hill and past the lake on the far side of the Mill towards a ridgeline that passed along the river. Kel took the opportunity to educate us on the use of hand signals for silent operations, in an effort to thwart making any unnecessary noise while communicating. It was clear that these girls knew what they were doing. They provided us with real firearms to replace the paltry shock pistol we had, which was nearly useless against a diseased animal or person. With mild affirmation, we did not allow Betty to carry one since we still held a measure of distrust over her conduct. She appeared content with that decision and chose not to argue the fact with our new collaborators. It was good to be wearing clothes fit for the trail again instead of those demeaning work suits from the bunker. Even the old woman accepted a change of attire and donned a camouflage poncho to help us blend into the scenery.

We made it up to the far ridge before nightfall and set up within a rocky enclave in an effort to hide our campfire light from any wary eyes lurking in the valley below. We were exhausted from the trek since Tasha was adamant about taking the high road instead of the marked trails below at the base of the mountain. After so many years, even well-established trails had pretty much grown over and returned to the wild. It only served to remind us how Mother Nature was quick to erase any evidence of our trespassing as we scarred the land wherever humans had chosen to tread.

A hot meal was welcome, and at least the weather was decent for the night. Under a curtain of broken clouds and scattered stars we let our minds wander, wondering what other giant rocks were out there looming in the blackness of space that might foretell our fate. The silent stars twinkled as they always did when I was a child, staring up into the heavens and wondering what was out there. Some might see the irony of getting such a rude and unmistakable answer from the cosmos.

"So, how did you get that unique name?" Thorn asked Kel as we settled around a low fire. Haiti was on first watch to keep guard, but we were high enough on the ridge to be out of the general range of any predators that might be lurking below the rim of the mountain.

"It's just short for 'Kelly'," she answered with a weak smirk, breaking a few shingles off her tough exterior.

"And Ava?" he inquired again, motioning over to the dark-skinned woman who was bedding down for the night across from them while Tasha sat quietly nearby gazing into the fire.

"It's actually Aleah, but don't call her that. Ava is her middle name, and she's not very fond of her maiden name," Kel warned.

Thorn took her advice to heart. People were even more particular with their identities these days, for it was either seen as a symbol of individual integrity or a form of escape. When a person failed to care either way, their psyche was usually devolved into a negative and abrasive mentality. Authorities of most nations were infatuated with tracking everyone's identity in the past, it was almost an emotional need to withdraw from those conforming chains that labeled us as to who we were solely by our bank accounts, birth certificates, hospital records, or job history and credit scores. But in the end, all that bullshit didn't matter anymore.

"And you...?" She inquired back. Thorn knew that his chosen

name was more than a bit odd, although, it was not as corny as some he had heard since the collapse.

"Ah, well..." he seemed a bit embarrassed, "Thorn was my handle in the underground community, back in the day when live-stream gaming platforms where our nosy government security agencies couldn't monitor public communications. Due to the limitations surrounding voice deciphering programs, they couldn't sift out the sound of all the sound effects, music, gunfire, magic spells, or whatnot in online gaming worlds, even if they could trace the routes through the millions of independent servers when anyone logged on," Thorn admitted as he held up his arm to show where he had a small scar from the digital ID chip implant he had removed, "The Government could track any given person in public by the location of your computer IP or cell phones; but those same tracing bots were stonewalled in the gaming world. Apparently, the overload of erroneous information blinded them. It was the only way the public could hack a bit of our own privacy back," he smiled.

"But, what did 'Thorn' stand for," Kel inquired, "was it a name of a online character you liked?"

"Ah, nothing of the sort," he admitted, "I was a bit outspoken at times, and usually went on a rant to the point that I became a thorn in their side every time I called out an obvious bigot or some loudmouth making an idiot of themselves with rude and invalid arguments," he revealed with a guilty smirk. Thorn related he had been an avid dissident for many years, helping organize protests through the only means of secure communications available to citizens at the time. In all their untouchable glory, the Authorities did not take kindly to activists, even in small measures.

"Well, I guess those days are long gone..." Kel replied humbly.

"Ah, well, I might argue it's the same shit hitting a different fan, the way I see it," Thorn grinned as Kel shared his quirky sense of humor.

The wind was sharp as it howled across the ridge but gently subsided upon the rising light of dawn. Taking the high road was a considerably harder path to follow but well worth the effort if it decreased the risk of being spotted by a pack of weepers or chancing an encounter with any infected wildlife. The hours passed without much comment between the companions as they made their way through the mountain pass until one of them noted a column of white smoke in the distance just before noon. Its presence acted like a beacon that guided our path, but it wasn't until the following morning that we determined that that the source of the plume was coming directly from the abandoned Hydro Station where we had last seen our friends.

Bridging our way down to the lower ridge, we spotted the power lines that snaked through the overgrown forest to the structure itself. A level of dread began to well within us as we drew closer. Thick clouds of steam were rising from a newly collapsed hole in the rear of the building, which was directly above where the turbines were located.

The stormy winter skies prompted us to make our way to the building in haste, as lightning strikes were sure to follow. We advised our new colleagues to stay clear of the fenced electrical grid as we made our way to the second-floor balconies by climbing the roof of the trucks at the loading entrance. Once inside, we began to see the extent of the damage done by the blast of steam that issued relentlessly from the rift in the rear of the structure. Vapors flooded through the lower halls as they clung to the ceiling in drifts of eerie fog.

It was a measure of sadness we felt when we arrived at the upper floor and found that our old camp had been abandoned. Serena, Felix, Roy, and the young boy were gone. Only a few bits of gear had been left behind, which we interpreted as a sign that they had departed in some degree of urgency. Haiti was the one who found a rough scribbled message on the wall from a can of spray paint, left lying nearby on the concrete floor.

"Aye, look here, they left us a message," he noted.

The dull red paint showed a circle with several slashes made through the edges; dictating a secret code they used to leave directions for one another if they ever got separated. Personally, I thought it was a brilliant idea but had nary a clue as to how to interpret it.

"Emergency, leaving, zero clicks, will wait two weeks," Thorn read aloud.

"What does that mean, 'zero clicks'?" Tasha inquired.

"It means they are still nearby somewhere," Haiti glinted back with a smile. However, we were unsure as to exactly how long we had been away, and more importantly, when the turbines might have blown. They might be long gone by now.

It was disappointing, but our mission still stood and we needed to get to the service entrance and into the catacombs of the rail system far below. We would have to make our way down to the ground floor and around the back of the building. The three mercenary women wanted to scout out the chamber with the hydrogen turbines but a wall of hot vapor blasted through the door of the parking garage when we pried it open; causing us to rethink the necessity of that endeavor.

The fog was so thick that it would be impossible to see, let alone the violent fumes from the blown-out metal gate made us realize that it might be an unwise decision to investigate further. Apparently, there had been a catastrophic failure of the magnetic turbines, but water was still being pumped into the broken system. There would be no way of telling what caused the generators to reach critical mass until the water source itself was shut off.

There was little debate as to what to do next. Our only avenue now was to traverse the stairwell down into the subway system where we had first made our way to Fallhaven. Exhausted as we were from the day's trek, despite putting up with the noise of the raging steam, we realized that the building itself might not be structurally safe to settle there for the night. Making our way through the upper floors, we found the spare escape rope flopped over the second-floor balcony. One by one, we made our way to the parking lot as everyone kept cover with their weapons drawn during the approaching dusk. For a moment, Thorn and I were distracted by something as we stood near an abandoned car while Tasha was rappelling down the rope.

Suddenly we heard a low growl from behind us, just as we turned and saw a weeper perched upon an overturned car only a few feet from our position. It was hard to tell its gender, as the infection was so far advanced that its head was nearly bald and covered with scabs with only traces of gray stringy hair. Its eye sockets were now entirely blackened from which streams of dried blood were painted upon its cheeks. Its teeth were cracked and broken and we could smell the stench of its fetid breath as it hissed at us.

As conditioned as we were, Thorn and I froze in fear at the sight of it leering so close to us before we could bring our rifles to bear. Ava, who was acting as our lookout on the balcony, did not have a clear enough view as the creature sprang in one inhuman leap to pounce upon us both. A shot rang out of nowhere and the creature flung head over heels backward to the other side of the vehicle. We glanced around in utter shock, as did Ava herself, who had not fired her rifle. Tasha clung anxiously to the rope, ready to climb back up out of reach to the balcony above as Thorn jumped on top of the hood of the car with his gun in hand. On the ground, the weeper lay crumpled in a pool of blood, having taken a clean shot to the skull.

On the far side of the collapsed ruins of the adjacent building stood a figure perched high up in the rubble of broken concrete. Seeing his ragged cowl fluttering in the evening breeze, we recognized Roy as he lifted his goggles. A wave of relief washed over us as we advised Ava and Kel to lower their weapons. Killroy disappeared back into the broken building to emerge on the ground level. We ran to greet him as the others were climbing down to join us.

"Nice shot, I owe you one," Thorn smiled as he grasped Roy's arm to shake it.

"We almost gave up on you," he nodded towards Haiti and I, as his gaze passed over Thorn, having noticing we had acquired some new company. He motioned towards Beatrice and the mercenary girls as they approached the reunited companions.

"What happened here?" I inquired to the billowing steam from the back of the complex while the other women joined us.

"Well, that is certainly an interesting story that's going to have to wait. That shot I took might attract other infected in the area, and we don't want to be stuck out here this close to nightfall. The others are camped out in a pump house we found just beyond the tree line over there," he advised while pointing towards the rear of the building, "let's get there while we still have some sunlight before we get soaked," Roy affirmed as we followed his pace towards the dense forest brush just as the evening rain began to fall.

The pump house was small but well hidden from view; and ended up being even far less spacious, as it was filled with large pipes that snaked their way through most of its interior. A loud cycling hiss drummed through the lines as the aged metal creaked and groaned in defiance, making me wonder just how safe it was to station ourselves here. Serena sat in the far back of the pump house, who appeared a little worse for wear, as Felix was tending a wound on her side. Her eyes widened upon seeing us, but were quickly shadowed by a painful smile. The small boy sat silently while huddling in a corner, barely acknowledging our arrival as we bolted the thick metal door behind us.

Thorn introduced them to the group while Haiti went to check on Serena and help Felix dress her bandages.

"Where the hell did you go?" Serena coughed, clearly in pain from her injury that bloodied her side.

"Are you going to be alright?" I asked with concern, offering what I could do to help.

"Ah, don't worry about her, this little bitch can handle more than this scrape," Felix grinned while wrapping fresh cloth as Serena issued him a slight glare in return.

"Glad you could make it back, ya lil' bastard," Roy laughed as he removed his gear to take a seat by the makeshift burner lighting the room while Tasha and her friends set down their rifles to join us, still donning their ponchos.

It was a long evening trying to get comfortable in the limited space as we bedded down and caught up on recent events that had transpired below in the Vault. We informed them about the deep rail system and the tenants of Fallhaven, the mutant weepers, and General Kane, and the fate of the poor civilians who met their deaths by his hands. This led to the introduction of Betty, who sat oddly detached from the conversation, and over to the pair of soldier women, including Tasha, who had a special air about her that the others also noted.

Both Roy and Serena had scouted the stairwell a few days after we had disappeared in their attempt find us, but to no avail. A full week after we had disappeared into the bowels of the complex below, there was a system fault in the basement that shook the whole building. They went down to see what had happened in the turbine room, which had lit up with red flashing lights above every one of the generator cores. Not long thereafter, a series of steam explosions shook the foundation, and a piece of shrapnel caught Serena as the blast ruptured the parking garage door.

They were forced to escape the hot steam that found its way to the upper floors and were rightly concerned that the rest of the building might collapse at any moment, so they abandoned camp. The exterior power grid had collapsed and they had stumbled across this derelict pump house on the edge of the property. They each took turns as spotters while awaiting our return. It was lucky that they had given us a few extra days; otherwise, we may have never seen them again.

"So what's the plan now?" Roy asked, noting the desperate situation they were currently in.

"Well, believe it or not, we are going back below with our new guide," Thorn answered, while motioning towards Betty who sat despondent and plainly worn out, as the old woman was not used to the physical rigors of travel we had endured over the past several days. Her once bold and snappy attitude had been distinctly dulled; even so, we still did not fully trust her.

We opened the secured metal box, which Ava brought into the middle of the room for them to see, the light from the alcohol stove glinting menacingly upon the mottled surface of the asteroid fragment as she lifted off its cover.

"We have to get this chunk of rock to the research lab," Tasha noted to the others while unfolding our wrinkled patchwork of a map and pointed to its location, "to find out what happened there and why they were so desperate to get this ore sample."

Razorback

We were grateful when the morning sun arrived and we could finally crack the door open to let in some fresh air. The pump house had become stuffy with the lot of us all crammed into such tight quarters. I got very little sleep myself since I was constantly awoken by the bumping metal and hiss of the pipes, which left me less than happy to see the arrival of dawn. I couldn't help but notice that a few others in our group were also grumbling as well; each of us a shade cranky from the lack of a proper nights sleep.

We checked our weapons and packed our belongings to begin our return descent into the underground labyrinth. None of us were too keen on the idea either, especially our friends, after hearing our tall tales about hordes of infected and enormous mutants. We were also a tad concerned about bringing a child into that type of danger, but we certainly weren't willing to take the chance of getting separated again.

The harsh evening storms had dissipated and a light drizzle filled the day, the shimmering rain glittered in the beautiful morning light. Dew washed the dust from our boots as we made our way to the hatch and into the dark stairwell beneath the surface. From the silo entrance, we had a front seat view of the blown-out walls from the adjacent turbine room where the hydrogen generators had been set beneath. From within, a monstrous column of steam billowed up into the sky, almost appearing as if it were feeding the clouds far above.

Felix had the bright idea that maybe some of the valves in the pump room might be able to shut off the flow of water to the generators and stop the process, but a few of us also thought that might be riskier than doing nothing at all. Besides the fact, that if there was even one turbine still running underneath all that debris then we wouldn't want to take the chance of cutting off the only available power supply to the transportation tubes in the rail system below ground. Beatrice was adamant about leaving the generators alone and we readily agreed to take her advice since she had far more knowledge of the subterranean tram system then all of us combined.

We snaked our way down the long ghostly stairwell as system lights flickered while errant echoes taunted us from below. With our small band making slow progress, it was nearly an hour before we hit the first pair of shafts. The large round hatches had been previously sealed when we had first passed this way, but they were now propped wide open. Farther down the stairwell, we could see that the other pair of hatches on the level below had also been left ajar.

It was now the old woman's turn to lead the way, and we followed in Betty's steps as she entered the first shaft we crossed and into the massive tunnel, which eventually led us to an anti-chamber with a familiar design. Here, another set of alcoves sat with a robotic effigy sitting at a counter, its circuitry was dark and was apparently without power.

"This rail should take us to Brookhaven," Beatrice mentioned while wiping away the dust from a system chart on the wall. Kel unfolded our map and laid it beside the frame; we all noted how the color-coded lines met up with our destination when they were superimposed.

"Brookhaven is here, but how do we get to the Lab topside on the other side of the mountain?" Tasha inquired to the elderly woman while she referenced the chart.

"Here," Beatrice pointed, "at the Brookhaven terminal we have to cross to the blue route that will take us to the end of the line where the Laboratory is stationed above it."

"What are these cross-sections on the route just before our stop?" Ava inquired with interest towards the additional markings, which apparently, had been crudely drawn onto the diagram prior to our arrival here.

"I'm not quite sure," was all the old woman could muster, "but we need to take these tubes to Brookhaven first," Beatrice affirmed as she made her way over to the first bullet car and cracked open the hinged door. We were troubled that these rail cars could only hold four of us at a time, and we realized we would have to split up. Looking at the map, we saw that there were several other bunker communities that interconnected along the route. We began to consider the possibility that there could also be thousands of other survivors who had been left isolated in their separate shelters all along this subterranean network.

"Beatrice, isn't there a chance that Brookhaven and these additional stations on the map here, Sundance, Springwood, and all these others, might still have people residing in them?" I inquired with a spark of interest as I read the chart. Everyone was hopeful that there were still people who had survived out there, though trusting they had been under better management other than the likes of Kane's regime. There must be untold stocks of food, clothing, and medical supplies, while hoping we could retrieve some useful provisions to take back with us.

"All I know is that several years ago these other communities went silent one by one, and the citizens of Fallhaven were the last ones left on the grid," Betty replied with a serious look, and we could see the note of surrender in her eyes as she spoke.

"By chance, could it possibly just have been a break or failure in the communication lines between the shelters?" Ava inquired; noting that the bunkers were pretty far apart from one another.

"I seriously doubt it," Beatrice answered bluntly; "each station command can monitor power flows to the others along the system grid, which allows us to regulate power consumption. Some of the shelters mysteriously dropped off the system charts overnight, while some stayed static for weeks with no response until they also went dark."

"There's no telling what we might find," Thorn cut in, "it could've been the result of a collapse from an earthquake or maybe they were overrun by infected that somehow got below as we had seen them do," His words were harsh but rational. If we went chasing these wild theories we might just waste our time running into dead ends or find ourselves in deeper shit than it was worth.

"We will send the first scouting party through and return to relay what we find," Kel suggested.

"The rail system doesn't work that way," Betty snapped back, "each car kicks forward in a sealed vacuum tube and is followed by the next. Currently, it appears that all the terminal communications are down," she mentioned while motioning to the dead console radio.

"So this is a one-way ticket," Tasha clarified for us all.

"Well I hope this piece of crap still works," Roy smirked as he made his way to the tube car, "I'm calling front seat!" He grinned while he stomped over to the vehicle, just like one of those pricks at a carnival who would always shoulder their way past everyone else in line just to get the best seat on the ride.

Kel joined him, as did Haiti and Felix, who personally struggled to get his girth into the tiny seat in the rear. Betty frowned as she tried switching the console on, only to have it whimper back at her in return as the voltage failed. The four of them sat in the tiny car trying to glare at us through the oil-streaked windows as we tried to fiddle with the controls to get the system working.

"Well fuck, maybe it doesn't have any more power," Thorn scowled as he referred to the destroyed hydropower plant on the surface above, whilst Roy could be heard mumbling to himself at the front of the closed car, losing his patience.

With an electric whine, a dim green light blinked on weakly above the rail and the car began to slide forward as it picked up speed and disappeared into the darkness beyond the breach. We could hear Roy whooping in joy, just before a curved plate closed over the tube to seal the vacuum pressure.

We realized that there must be at least one turbine still running back up top, though it was clear that the power supply had been severely crippled by the damage it had sustained. Hopefully it wouldn't fail entirely on us along the way. Personally, I couldn't imagine how anyone could traverse down the tube line without a tram car considering the way it had been constructed. Either it was a gross oversight and the result of bad engineering or the system had been intentionally designed in that manner to restrict foot travel. However, in hindsight, such a design would certainly act as a security measure, which would isolate each of the shelters if there were an outbreak along the network. This worried us more than a tad, as there would be no escape if the rail car came to a stop at its destination, leaving us only to be greeted by a horde of deranged weepers.

"Are you okay with this?" Thorn asked gently while he put his hand on my shoulder just as a new bullet car slid in from the rear of the rail. I looked back at him softly, considering how empty my life had been lately without a kind touch.

"Well, there's one way to find out," I grinned with my goofy smile as I stowed my rifle into the seat of the secondary car while Thorn and Serena slipped in the rear with Tasha. I hated myself for a moment, blowing my chance to kiss him just then. I was such a chicken it wasn't even funny. I had always found myself having to act tough just to sneak past that bit of awkwardness.

Ava was holding the boy's hand while he stood there as quiet as a mouse, always staring at the floor and never meeting our eyes if he could avoid it. Betty, Ava, and the boy would follow in the next car; the controls allowed a few seconds after activation before the tram doors locked shut. We waved at them like idiots going on a family vacation, mostly for the child's sake; but I doubt he even noticed. It made me wonder if he was autistic, which would explain his detached behavior.

I felt sorry for him, but I guess all of us did in their own way. There was little to no future for children in his condition within this new world. His was a similar symptom to the infected victims who would simply be left to die on their own. In a way, I guess the only difference was that we cared. It was this lingering sense of responsibility we held for another human being that let us continue to cling to our virtues. However, in reality, that distorted sense of hope either made us compassionate or it made us weak.

This rail line was on low power and zipped along much slower than the first ride we had taken weeks prior. I started to become fearful of what would happen to us if the transport lost power halfway through the system, sticking us like a cork in a bottle. There would be no way to open the doors, and I certainly wasn't going to assume there would be breathable air in the vacuum chute. With that thought bouncing around in my head, I found myself getting slightly anxious to get this unpleasant ride over with and getting myself out of this small cylinder as soon as humanly possible.

There were slight moments of paranoia when the subway car almost came to a standstill. It was an aching amount of time that dragged on before we finally slid into the landing platform at Brookhaven station. Honestly, I was a bit giddy to get out of that cramped seat to a place where I could stretch my legs. We made a quick scout of the terminal as it took another twenty minutes before the last transport arrived at our location because the tram system was running on low power.

Within this complex, there was a constant drip of moisture echoing down the empty halls. We counted a few locked doors while we had waited for the final tram car to arrive, but we didn't want to make too much noise breaking the doors open if they didn't actually lead in the direction we were heading; so we figured it would be better to wait until Betty arrived so she could guide our way. We found a significant amount of mold growing on the floor of the landing that made the air here stuffy and unpleasant to breathe. If there were infected running loose here, we certainly didn't wish to rouse any that might be hibernating in the blanketing darkness that lingered beyond the dim glow of our flashlights.

I was skeptical about our ability to reach the Laboratory, considering that if the tunnel on the roadway above had been collapsed by design, then whoever was responsible would certainly not have likely missed applying the same tactics to any subterranean access. We had already been sidetracked a great deal over the past few weeks, so I didn't want to jinx us somehow along the way by being overly worried about every inch of progress we gained. Betty headed straight to a covered booth in the center of the chamber that Roy had already broken into. There was no robotic attendant poised within this particular stall, as it had been designed solely for manual use by human personnel.

"The blue line is a restricted transport," Beatrice mentioned as she pointed across the divide to the wide metal doors branded with a large military seal, "this control box should bring the access car to take us the rest of the way."

Throwing the switch within, we waited patiently as we heard a metallic click in the mechanism but there was no juice flowing to the device itself. In all sincerity, it made me wonder just how stupid of a design this was for a redundant system that apparently relied so heavily on electrical power, which did not make much sense for a catastrophic scenario considering that the purpose of this subterranean network was to sustain itself in an 'Aftermath' event. Whatever wiring was being used for the subway tubes by the damaged hydro station power lines, it apparently wasn't connected to this secondary system.

"Crap!" Was all she uttered aloud, and it was almost funny the way the old woman said it.

"Well, have you got another plan?" Roy inquired since she was acting as our guide for the moment.

"We have to get past those doors," she snapped back, "it's just a common railway car, not one of those vacuum tubes," Beatrice added.

"You mean the tunnel beyond is large enough to traverse by foot if we need to?" Kel asked as she peered inside the small booth at the both of them.

"Yes, we can take one of the transport cars if it has power, but I guess we could walk there if we had to," she answered.

However, there was a small problem of note. While hopping across the grated bridge to the broad sliding doors, both Roy and Tasha noticed that there were gun turrets embedded in the ceiling to either side of the entry point. That got us a tad worried, for if we managed to get the power switched on in this section, then those robotic gun ports might become a serious problem for us.

"We should disable them gizmos there while we can," Haiti suggested, and we couldn't fault his logic.

There were scraps of concrete and metal bars we could jam into the rotational gears to keep the turrets from spinning, but it was Ava who suggested it would be far safer to simply disable them entirely by removing their wiring and visual lenses.

Being the smallest of the group, Tasha was the one we slung up by a rope we were able to grapple into the niches along the roof. They had fashioned a pulley made with a few carabiners to hoist her up while I tried to help Felix and Thorn figure out a way to unlock the door to the blue line. It was an aggravating search in the dark until we finally stumbled across a lone access panel far around the backside of the hallway that circled behind the main doors. Betty mentioned that the other locked corridors led to extensive walkways to outlying engineering terminals, but it would be wise not to try and tamper with them as we loathed the idea of making too much noise in these hallways. Any sound would be amplified and give away our position to any Weepers in the area; also considering that the others were a bit spooked by our stories of the horrifying mutants lurking down these dark halls.

Both Kel and Ava were helping Tasha with her chore of dismantling the turrets while the other men were keeping watch for trouble. Betty assisted Thorn and I with opening the access panel that led to a small winding duct beyond.

"Damn ...it's never easy," Thorn sighed, as he and I were clearly too tall to fit into the small vent, but Beatrice was of slight enough stature to give it a try.

"This looks like it goes into the ventilation and out into the rail line on the other side," she mentioned, "give me your knife and I'll take a look."

"What do you want my knife for?" Thorn asked while focusing a suspicious glare towards her as he placed a guarded hand onto his utility blade.

"If there is a locked grate on the other end, how do you expect me to pry it open ...with my good looks?" Betty snapped back in a condescending tone, as we both almost smirked at her wrinkled face.

The old woman was worn and tired, and we could tell she was losing her patience at this given moment, but she did have a point. Going in head first, there would be no way to turn around or attempt to kick open a panel on the opposite end. With little argument, he handed her his blade and a spare flashlight. Betty got down onto her belly and jimmied her way into the ductwork; she slowly wiggled around a corner until we lost sight of her. Several minutes passed until we heard her muffled cry that she had found another panel and her weak attempts to get it open.

Within the tight vent, Betty had slid her way over to the opposing wall and almost snapped the blade while trying to wrench the locking clip open from the inside. She finally busted the latch on the panel, which swung open with a creak. It was as dark as death in the tunnel beyond as she crawled out of the duct and back onto her own feet. The air here was cold and there was a strange stench to it that left her feeling light-headed. Stumbling backward over a loose block of concrete, she found herself falling into a pile of splintered muck.

It took a dizzy moment for her to realize what she was looking at as she held up her hands from the fall; the shredded clothing and broken bones lined with tattered flesh. Turning her flashlight, she gave a startled scream as the twisted faces of the dead glared at her through their rotting sockets. Dozens of cold gray bodies surrounded her, and for a terrifying moment of panic she thought she saw them move. Having disturbed their embrace, the pile of corpses fell upon her.

Grisly arms flopped upon her shoulders, and a loose head rolled into her lap as tattered clothing veiled her face. The old woman jumped in fright to break free of their grasp, frantically shining her light around to escape the horror. It took several moments for her weak heart to settle down from its rapid pulse as she heard Caitlin and Thorn calling at her from the other side of the vent.

Scanning the area there were corpses everywhere piled up at the end of the tunnel, at their stage of decay it was impossible to tell if they had been innocent survivors or the infected. On a side track sat a rail car in stasis, several yards off the lead turnstile. She found herself on the other side of the broad metal doorway where there stood an identical booth to the one stationed in the main terminal, though this one had several sets of handles poised within. Stepping into the booth, with a hasty guess she gave one a pull.

At first, nothing happened; just a familiar click of connections meeting without the electrical power. Looking closer, Betty saw a key slot and fanned the light around until she found one cadavers wearing a uniform. Timidly searching the corpse, she found an access key hanging from its neck. With a harsh tug, she removed it and placed the key within the slot in the booth and activated the mechanism. With a whir, the power pulsed on as sparks flew wildly from the bottom of the panel. Beatrice had an idea to herself while standing there in the cold dark, perceiving an opportunity to take this last railcar to her freedom and leaving her captors far behind.

For a brief moment, Thorn and I looked at one another with concern as we heard electricity spark through the wires in the hallway beyond the vent, met by a sudden yelp from one of the girls around the corner. Tasha had dropped to the floor with a thud as the turret she was trying to dismantle spun around with its gun ports open when an automated female voice came over the terminal speakers.

"This is a restricted area, please present your identification badge for scanning," it repeated in a loop as its turret gears were jammed with its own wire sockets Tasha had just yanked out moments before. It was lucky that she had done so, as the obstinate machine began to fire its pulse laser after the timer elapsed. Since the turret box was jammed facing one direction, it was unable to deploy the sensor device locked within its housing; regardless of the fact that nobody actually had an ID badge to begin with. Firing half-cocked, the three girls dove for cover as the broken turret began to spray laser fire over their heads while the motorized housing fought the blocked mechanism until its gears finally locked up and it misfired once within its own shell, whereupon the entire unit exploded in a violent ball of flame.

Shrapnel shot through the air as the turret cup bounced to the ground with a clatter. Kel could be heard cursing as she gripped her bleeding calf, after being struck from a scrap of metal that had torn through her leg from the blast. A puff of black smoke issuing from the dead turret now clung to the ceiling like an ominous cloud. Ava looked just as rattled as Thorn and I turned the corner. Fortunately, the rest of the crew had been scrounging through the other half of the station landing for another access point during this mishap.

We all glanced at one another with apprehension when we heard the rail train on the other side of the thick door hum to life and start off down the tracks in the adjacent tunnel. Instead of finding a manual handle for the door, apparently that bitch, Beatrice, had decided to take off on her own. Thorn and I felt a twinge of remorse on that ill decision to trust the old hag.

"What da hell was that all about?" Haiti jibed with his usual accent, just as a familiar female voice chimed to life from the speaker overhead.

"Redundant security protocol initiated," the computer whispered calmly, "back-up ordinance is now online." With that brief notice, the secondary robotic turret dropped down and a single red eye deployed from it and cycled opened while it turned its attention towards the stunned group of friends.

"This is a restricted area, please present your identification badge for ...*krrt*!" it began to order as everyone took the first two seconds it was busy blabbering orders, by drawing their own firearms and putting several dozen rounds into its exposed wiring harness before the security system could finish issuing its warning.

We all stood there waiting in frozen silence until we were satisfied that the turret was dead, before everyone relaxed and lowered their smoking weapons.

"Where is the old woman?" Roy asked as all gazes fell upon me. I flashed a pathetic glance to Thorn who gave a nod towards the metal door.

"I knew we couldn't trust that withering cunt," Serena spat, while we heard the railcar disappear down the tunnel. Roy stomped back over to the central security booth and threw the switch within. We all just about jumped out of our pants when a tiny hidden third turret dropped from the ceiling between the pair of crippled security guns. We lowered our twitching firearms when it just turned out to be a rotating strobe light.

With the power now activated, the sealed panels took several moments to cycle as locking clamps disengaged and the doorway slid open. Beyond was a single tunnel; a small booth could be seen hugging the wall to our right alongside a large pile of decaying bodies heaped in the far corner by a small open vent. Many of the overhead lights were still in working order and lit up into the far distance until they blurred out of sight down the long tunnel. There was something left unsaid that was eating away at us this moment, considering the ruckus we had just made blowing up those turrets and activating the door siren. If there were any nests of infected within earshot, they would certainly be heading our way.

"Well, it looks like we're walking," Roy moaned, as we headed off down the rail shaft at a quickened pace.

It took but a moment to bandage Kel's leg, but the wound slowed her down noticeably. That pile of bodies at the end of the tunnel concerned me, not knowing if they had already been dead and dumped there like so much trash; or if they had been survivors who had tried to escape, only to be left trapped and abandoned. The truth was, a whole lot of shit had gone down over the past several years that would never be answered, nor would anyone be held accountable for. It made me worry about what direction the human race was going. Would we rebuild a better world, or just end up repeating the same mistakes all over again that led us to where we were now?

It was a damn long walk down that musty tunnel as our boots kicked up dust and our broken stride echoed off the walls. We kept our pace up and an ear out for anything unusual, and were finally greeted by a loud hollow 'bang' that streamed from the far end of the shaft. We quickened our pace towards the sound.

"Dis is a long fuck'in tunnel..." Haiti heaved with a labored breath. We all concurred that we needed a break soon, especially Serena and Kel, who weren't in the best condition to keep up at this clip.

Felix had taken the meteorite pack in an effort to assist Kel from further injuring her leg with the load. The bleak overhead lights gave an eerie glow to the hot mist floating high overhead while the condensation that streaked the walls glittered with an unearthly tinge. It was possibly my nerves, but something felt terribly wrong down here, giving us all an unshakable sense of unease. After what seemed like an hour, we finally noticed a faint blue glow up ahead with errant sparks lighting up the tunnel walls. It wasn't until we reached the last few dozen yards that we realized what we were looking at.

"Holy shit!" Felix uttered, as the rest of us gaped at the

cluttered destruction before us. A railcar with bold white lettering spelling out the word 'Razorback' hand-painted along its side, had jumped its tracks and crashed into the middle of the tunnel, its bottom wheels facing us. We could not approach it due to a deep rift splitting the tunnel where the rails had snapped off halfway over the chasm. The lights were still on inside the rail car, and a few of us thought we could see a shadow moving within. Roy took a closer look at the edge.

"What could cause this, an earthquake?" Thorn inquired under his breath in wonder. The break in the cement foundation cleaved straight through, perpendicular from one side to the other leaving it impassible by foot. The distance between the broken rails and the back end of the train car would be barely reachable with a running jump, but not for someone who was injured. Even then, one slip on that skinny smooth metal bar hanging over that dark rift, and down you go.

"Blast marks," Killroy answered, "there, and there," he pointed out to either side, "It appears they attempted down here what they did topside to the mountain tunnel," he declared, which was conclusive to the previous events Tasha had told us about.

"It makes sense," Ava answered, nodding to Tasha, "they blew the pass to blockade access to the Lab. We should have guessed they would have cut this one off too."

"How are we going to make it over?" Felix asked, nodding towards the two injured girls and the child.

"That's a risky fuck'in jump..." Serena added as she looked down into the chasm, calculating the odds as she kicked a small chunk of broken concrete over the edge. It clattered several moments later, still falling, "...and it's a long fuck'in way down too," she added with the same color, not caring about her foul language in the presence of a child. With all modesty, Serena wasn't exactly what you would call the motherly type.

"It looks like they just intended to blow the rails, but there was a natural fault or cavern below this section and the whole damn thing caved in," Roy noted, "hand over some of those bandages," he motioned to Thorn, who was carrying their medical supplies. Not knowing what he had in mind, we watched as the old soldier gingerly tested the longest rail

hanging over the chasm and straddled it to wrap adhesive
bandages across the length of its end. After a moment, Tasha
seemed to recognize what he was doing, but Haiti hadn't quite
caught on yet.

"What's all that for?" He injected with curiosity.

"It's just some added tread; I don't want to slip on the last step
and make an ass of myself," he smiled back at the dark man,
who nodded in return at the sensibility of it.

Wrapping a rope around his waist, Roy jerry-rigged a crotch
harness like a professional climber and counted out several
loose coils of rope. I was starting to get impressed with Roy's
knowledge of preparation and the amount of versatility he
displayed. Though Tasha was young, she seemed to agree with
his methods. I got the impression that they were both birds of
the same feather.

Felix and I gritted our teeth as Roy paused for but a moment
and took a running leap off the edge of that skinny metal rail.
He spanned the gap, and landed with a thud on the tip of the rail
car, barely catching the rim where the heavy metal wheels were
set.   It was a hard landing and we could tell that he had
bloodied his hand on the sharp rigid edge.

Having secured the lead end to the rail post, he cinched the
rope tight on the cars rear handrail and tossed the spare yardage
back over to our side of the fissure. It only took a few moments
to follow Tasha and her friends lead by tying our packs and gear
onto the ropes to be slung over to his side. It was a practical
precaution so we could avoid having to risk losing our supplies
from falling into the pit, resulting from something like a sloppy
toss from one side to the other. Let alone, we didn't want any
extra weight on our backs while making that kind of jump. The
other girls were slight and athletic, but I was taller than most
and not really the acrobatic ninja type as it were. Admittedly, I
was more than a little nervous about making the jump myself.

Both Thorn and Ava made it over first with enviable ease. We
were roping up Felix after having secured the meteorite sample
to swing it over when we heard a strange rumble that got
perceptibly louder from the far end of the tunnel. Roy took a
few steps up to peer into the train car to find Beatrice lying

crumpled and unconscious near the front end. Looking up towards the tunnel, it took him a long moment to decipher the source of the commotion and he directed Thorn to grab the binoculars from his pack.

Thorn and Ava were busy rifling through the knapsacks when Roy gave a silent stare back at us across the rift, when his face lost all color and turned a pale white. From around the edge of the derailed train car trickled in the forerunners of a stampede of infected. Their heads were bobbing like a massive tide of diseased flesh. Roy motioned the others to crouch down as he pulled his handgun from his belt, but regrettably, all of our rifles were still bundled up tight with rope from being strung over the chasm just moments before.

The first few Weepers hadn't seen Roy or the others as they rounded the edge of the rail car and saw us standing on the other side of the rift, staring back in complete confusion. Like idiots, we didn't think to send out a scout, and most of our firearms were now bound together and out of reach on top of the train car. Tasha started firing from a backup pistol she carried in her waist belt, which captured the immediate attention of the leading handful of the swarm. They ran straight for us like mindless dolts, right over the edge and into the chasm while their arms swam in the empty air as they fell into the blackness. The boy hugged Haiti closely while the creatures charged for us and fell into the dark fissure below without pause.

On both sides of the rail car they were funneled at a choke point so the ones behind had no clue what happened to those in front of them, and promptly leapt gnarling and screeching as they glared insanely at us with their wild bloodshot eyes. Those stark few who paused at the rim of the crevasse before them, were unceremoniously nudged into the abyss by those weepers who came running up from behind; being far too occupied with propelling themselves towards the sound of gunfire.

Some might call it luck, but it was also distressing to watch countless numbers of sick people plunge to their deaths without even the mind of knowing what they were doing. Tasha emptied two full clips before she was out of ammo, and Serena was down to throwing loose stones to try to distract those few left as the mob began to diminish. The few dozen at the heel lost the momentum to hurl themselves so recklessly over the edge. The remaining weepers then turned their attention towards our three companions atop the railcar, and began to clamber towards them in their mindless rage.

Roy fired, counting his shots, but half of them still missed as the bullets ricocheted off the steel hull of the train while Thorn and Ava scrambled for the packed guns. Dread filled us when one of the diseased turned their scrutiny towards the rope that stretched across the void to our side and the exposed meteorite pack that hung there in limbo in between us, where it sat swaying dangerously over the rift. The blighted creature that was attempting to scale the rope to reach us on the other side, jarred the wobbling box containing the rock sample. Both Tasha and Kel grabbed for Haiti's machete to fend it off, only to realize that they took a dangerous risk of cutting the rope and losing their precious cargo.

Still harnessed to the far side of the lanyard, fat little Felix was being tugged and swayed by the creature who was grasping wildly at the rope for any given handhold, pulling Felix off balance towards the jagged edge of the fissure. I grabbed his arm to help him, but he just turned to me with a look of surrender in his eyes and pulled away from my embrace to my utter confusion. Another weeper was clawing for Ava on the edge of the train as she fumbled for a handgun from her pack, only to have it slip off the tilted edge of the train and disappear into the black pit below. Seeing she was being overwhelmed and had but a scarce few seconds before she would be within the ghoul's reach, Felix did something chancy and outrageous.

As he was being pulled towards the edge by the creature jarring the meteorite container, Felix took a running jump off the edge of the rail and a mid-step on the head of the weeper hanging in the middle, kicking him squarely in the face, which in turn, launched his bulk towards the brute antagonizing Ava on the other side of the breach. He grabbed the ghoul by its legs, and with a look of shock upon the creatures crazed and twisted face, they both fell into the depths. We were all stunned by his desperate stunt and gasped as he abruptly dropped beyond sight over the edge.

It was only a few startled seconds before we heard him kicking and swearing from the bottom of the taut rope, which was still tethered to the handrail of the train. Freeing his rifle from the bundle, Thorn finally came to bear and took measured shots at the last half dozen weepers trying to mount the train. The kinetic force of the sniper rifle jolting a few over the edge of the rift. In the moments that followed, we scrambled to help Felix after clearing the last of the creatures from the broken lip of the fissure.

"Hey, hold on Felix!" Thorn yelled into the darkness below, while Haiti set the boy aside to help Serena try to find more rope. The line began to dance violently as the thin rope scraped dangerously thin on the jagged edge of the fault. From the shadows below, a horrid face leapt up and clung to the meteorite box hanging on the lanyard. Out of bullets himself, Roy scrambled for more ammo in his vest. On the edge of the rift, up the line crawled Felix, blood from deep gashes on his neck and back painted his shirt in scarlet. He had a crazed look in his eyes, not from the alien virus, but in a personal vendetta against this creature which had condemned him to his fate.

Felix ignored Ava's hand reaching out for him and pushed himself off the edge with a thrust of his legs, swinging over to the last weeper clinging on the pack. The fall down the chasm had been cruel, as the thin rope snapping his torso hard with the extra bodyweight it carried from the infected attacker. The creature had mauled him to make its way back up the breach in a desperate attempt to save itself. Felix knew he was already dead, but he wasn't going to let this afflicted bastard hurt his friends. The alluring taste of revenge is all he felt in this final moment.

The thin rope, the fragile box and its delicate and deadly stone fragment, the gnashing and bloodied creature and Felix with all his weight, pulled the line taught beyond its capacity. Strands snapped as the line began to fail and Thorn brought his riflescope to his eye to take aim; but stalled when he suddenly felt a firm hand fall upon his shoulder.

"You can't risk hitting the container," was all Roy said, and Thorn knew he was right; if he missed and shattered the rock or the capsule, it could infect us all. With resolve, he lowered the weapon.

It was all over before we could grasp what had happened. Felix pulled the quick release on his harness with one hand as he grasped the creature's wrists, and with one aggressive blow, he head-butted it from behind. Stunned by his attack, Felix was able to pry both of the weeper's hands free from the container and they both fell into the chasm, swallowed by the unforgiving gloom. A few dull thuds, and the rattle of falling stones, were all that followed to tell of his untimely end. Felix was gone.

Bouncing by a thread on the ripped line was the meteorite container, left barely strapped to the pack by a few frayed cords. With great care, we hauled our dangerous package to the end of the train car and secured it. The men quickly reloaded their firearms and scanned the tunnel for yet another wave, but were instead met by a cold and eerie silence.

We repaired the rope and continued to rappel the rest of our crew over to the train, some of us were still lingering in a state of shock. It was a lesson learned that you could never let your guard down. We were one companion less, and the wiser for it. Once we got repacked and sheared the rope, we made our way over to the front edge of the car and looked down through the window at the source of all our grief. There on the floor, Beatrice began to stir, looking a little battered and drained.

"Ohhh, what happened..." she moaned, mentally taxed from her concussion. She was fortunate that the front windows to the car had not broken through, or she would have certainly succumbed as a victim to the infected horde. One of the boys jimmied the sliding pane open and we all glared down at her with disdain while she gazed back up at us meekly. Up top, we all glanced at one another, wondering which one of us was going to shoot her first.

Failsafe

"Well now, Betty, give us one good reason why we shouldn't just drop you over the edge of this chasm here and call it a day?" Roy muttered to the old woman who was busy collecting her dignity. At first, she glazed her puppy dog eyes with innocence, trying to garner some sympathy from the lot of us; though she was entirely oblivious to the bloody massacre we had fought through only moments before while her sorry ass was unconscious through it all.

"I don't know what you mean," she began faintly, "I was trying to get the doors back there open and I must have hit some switch that started the train and it locked me in. It took off and I couldn't stop it," she blathered as an excuse.

Of course, we didn't believe a word that came out of her mouth, even though it was still a viable story. With that lingering doubt, it would be hard to kick her off the edge of the rift; besides, she might still have information we needed to get into the Lab. Roy turned away at the mention of her alibi, grumbling to himself with a furrowed brow. He and Thorn began to discuss the audacity of her claim while out of earshot from the old coot, who sat in the stalled train with a look of worry creeping upon her wrinkled face.

We had to consider the factors that Roy brought up as relevant. Since it had taken us almost an hour to reach this spot after we had heard the train crash, then it would be logical that the location of the Lab was still another hour away if that's equally how long it took for the horde of infected to reach us from that location. Technically, that chasm would have kept them pretty well contained from the rest of the subway system; but that also led us to believe the Laboratory had entirely lost quarantine. If we ran into the number of weepers that were in that mob again, next time we would not have a convenient ravine to save our asses.

We needed Beatrice, at least for now. As much as we wanted

to chuck her into the pit, she was the only one among us that knew what to expect when we got there. At least we had not been on that train when it had jumped the rails, or likely more of us might have been dead or broken in ways that would have been disastrous when the infected swarmed upon us. Fate sure works in mysterious ways.

We had all our weapons loaded and were now carrying backups, as there was really nowhere to go if we got overrun by another wave of infected. Any retreat back to the fissure would end there, and we had no wish to join Felix at the bottom of that dark abyss. I was not entirely religious but I had caught myself praying under my breath as the next hour dragged on while we helped our injured companions reach the end of the tracks.

Grudgingly, we helped Betty out of the train and tried to pry as much information as we could out of her. She began to clam up more than usual since she was becoming suspicious that her usefulness was swiftly coming to an end. She certainly hadn't made any friends with that stunt she pulled by hijacking the train, and without any valuable advice to offer, the old woman knew she would be colored a liability; which was not a pleasant title to have in our current world. People who proved to be a risk to themselves or fellow companions were either dropped like a hot stone or put down like a sick dog.

Beatrice was wise enough to realize that she wouldn't last long out here on her own. She had been all too accustomed to the high life as one of the elite, living in her preferred status back at Fallhaven. While she had been there, she didn't have to do a lick of work, just say a word or point her finger to get others to do her bidding for her. Out here, she was nobody, and Kane was no longer around for her to ride on his coattails.

I wasn't truly ignorant. I figured Betty only did what she thought she had to do just to survive in these given set of circumstances. I could imagine many would have done far worse. The fact was though, that she could have done far better. Unfortunately, people do not usually remember the good things about others, but instead, tend to dwell on their faults. Agreeably, that kind of attitude creates needless drama, but is also quite effective at distracting others from your own flaws.

More often than not, human beings were apt at being psychologically unbalanced on any given day.

The truth of it was, I did not want to think about what I would have done or how I would have personally handled things if I had been in her shoes. I might have very well made the same mistakes as she had. It simply was not healthy to dwell in that level of self-judgment in this fucked up world. There was no point in it really.

It wasn't as if we could run to a convenience store anytime and grab a bottle of liquor to drown our sorrows, or watch a few videos to escape from reality for a little while as we had all been groomed to do in our past lives. We had to deal with our own shit, and dealing with other people's shit kind of came with the territory. Those that weren't flexible in that methodology usually led very short and lonely lives. In my own way, I felt sorry for the old woman. It wasn't like she had many choices left to change her direction.

I realized now that Betty had simply been grooming me as part of her personal crew back at the shelter; but she had been kind. It wasn't like we had any measure of compassion in our world today, and it was far too easy to be baited by even the smallest gesture of decency; even though the ulterior motives could be quite the contrary. Thinking about it now, I really didn't see much better conduct by most people I had known throughout my life, even before Apophis had struck; which, I admit, was a sad thought.

There was almost no notice before we hit the end of the line. Beatrice had informed us we would arrive at the terminal but she had not been very elaborate about what to expect. What we had all been apprehensive about discussing was that none of us had ever seen a murderous mob of weepers that large and in such concentrations since the beginning of the outbreak.

We had expected to find heaping piles of trash and human feces. Usually, you could tell were a group of infected had nested by the lingering stench of it. Here at the terminal, there was no evidence that revealed any of the diseased had been loitering in the area. The depot itself was curiously clean of their trace. We were all boggled, wondering where that raging horde had appeared from.

The end terminal of the rail tunnel did have a strange design to it that left our questions unanswered. A large circular steel frame that resembled an old-fashioned bank vault masked one entire wall. Several parallel stairwells to either side of it led off to a gate on one side, while several steel pockets that fanned around it had us guessing what they might be for. It was truly a bizarre example of architecture that left us baffled.

"It might be a heat sink," Haiti said aloud.

"A what?" Roy asked; a bit confused by his flat statement. Tasha stood beside him and put her hand to her chin as if judging a work of art in a gallery.

"Yes, I see it. It could very well be..." she concurred with the island man to our further bewilderment.

"I'm sorry, you lost me," Roy snapped back, a little annoyed at the two companions. Thorn agreed quietly as did I. The rest of us were getting agitated with Beatrice who was keeping tight-lipped the closer we got to the lab.

"What is this," I asked her kindly, trying to get the old woman to cooperate as we motioned to the strange attachments. We were stuck here on this side of the chasm anyhow if we couldn't find a way in. I attempted again to be diplomatic, trying to clarify to her that pushing our patience any further wasn't exactly in her best interest at the moment.

"That's the main entrance to the laboratory facility topside," Betty finally blurted out while waving towards the gigantic circular door, "and that gate leads to the cargo conveyor."

Her curt comments plainly left us unsatisfied. Searching the entry to the vault, we found no access lock, although there did appear to be a telltale socket in the cement floor where a control board might have once been; but which had been detached and removed. Tasha discovered a panel above the conveyor door that was a complete bitch to pry apart; but after half an hour of cussing while applying a good measure of brute force, we finally managed to bust it open.

Haiti had some limited expertise to bypass the lock on the gated hatch, which swung down to allow us entry. That was when we were hit by a wave of foul odor that divulged where all those infected had originated from. Even if the railway had been intact and Betty had made it down here alone, she would have still been stuck here without us.

"It appears as if a redundant electrical system released this door to the conveyor the same time the rail car was activated on the other end of the line," Roy mentioned as he scanned the circuitry map on the back of the panel we had snapped off.

"Aye, dis here transportation is all automated, man," Haiti agreed as he peered over Roy's shoulder.

"Personally, I would rather go in through the front door," Serena commented while holding her nose, trying to pinch off the reeking stench drifting from the interior. After conferring with Beatrice, it became painfully clear that there was no other way in. This facility had been specifically designed to allow for secured entry and it was obvious the back door had been locked down tight. We had no other choice, and would have to gain access through the cargo port.

The interior of the cargo bin was awash in red light from the numerous emergency beacons lining the corridor. A number of us tied scarves over our faces to ward off the horrid smell wafting through the corridor. A wide conveyor belt led the way inward, and apparently, this system could accommodate large amounts of cargo containers for transport from the terminal floor to whatever loading bay they had at the end of this line. In all honesty, we were not exactly comfortable entering such a confined space that had only one known exit.

The hard red light made it difficult to distinguish outlines at any given distance, and if this is where the infected had come from, then there were likely more wandering within. Turning on our flashlights would only manage to draw attention and make us walking targets. None of us wanted to be boxed in or find ourselves surrounded in such tight quarters.

Betty wasn't much help at this point, as the cargo conveyor was just a glorified baggage trolley and claimed she didn't have a clue where it went. Roy was getting aggravated with the old woman when she attempted to be elusive about the layout of the complex beyond the large bulkhead doors in the depot. It had been nearly a decade since she had been locked away in the confines of Fallhaven, so he tried not to get too pissed about it when she said she couldn't remember. Thorn didn't know whether to believe her either; and truth be told, neither did I. Beatrice had made a life of being a manipulator after all. Sometimes I found myself feeling ashamed for the way we were treating her, but then I had to wonder if she was just putting on an act and playing me to feel that way whenever she glanced in my direction with that doleful look in her eyes. It kept eating away at the back of my mind though; wondering how she been familiar with this Lab if it was a classified military facility?

Maybe she had just been on some tour of the entire system as a presentation to the egocentric elite who had given themselves a free pass for their god-given right to survive above all others, which was at the expense of the lower class citizens who had actually paid for this complex network. Whenever I thought about that, it made me angry.

Tasha was finally getting to complete the mission her father had never finished by delivering the meteor sample. We all wanted to know if it truly contained some type of biometric information that could be used to create a vaccine for the plague. It wasn't as if we had anywhere else to go. After Apophis had struck Earth, the following haze of wars and riots that erupted from the impact event had destroyed what little was left of our supposedly civilized world. When the MN4 virus reared its ugly head, nations were already locked in bitter conflict while they blamed one another as if it were an intentional act of aggression spurned by one country or another.

Tensions rose while treaties dissolved and international borders became a wild free-for-all while soldiers of every flag were occupied shooting at one another as the disease spread its poison across the globe. Unfortunately, a huge amount of resources and healthy lives were wasted while the human race was trying to kill itself instead of helping the sick and working together towards a cure, until it was far too late. Those countries that were too busy accusing their rivals for the fallout quickly dwindled away into silence as their populations succumbed to the malady. Now the meek had inherited the earth in the form of weepers.

Here I was with a bunch of other ruffians, risking our lives to bring a little chunk of rock from space to an over-bloated military lab in the middle of nowhere, and without a real fucking clue as to why. It was all too depressing when I let myself dwell on it. Daily life had gotten so desperate that nothing made sense anymore; it was so preposterous that it was almost laughable.

The conveyor aisle was mostly clear of debris until we hit a laser wall. Several horizontal green laser beams fanned from one side of the wall, and we had to cautiously test it with an object it might burn through. We were relieved to discover it wasn't a high energy security barrier at all, but some type of advanced scanning device for incoming containers.

However, the second we broke the beam a horn sounded, and we all froze in place. Moments later, the noise of machinery whirred and the conveyor we were standing on began to lurch forward. Even though it was a gentle tilt, Kel almost lost her footing because of her injured leg. The rest of us readied our weapons as we were transported through the conveyor system.

The noise of the running equipment would be enough to get the attention of any of the infected that might be left in the tunnels, and we would be fools not to expect another horde to swarm upon us at any moment. We bit our lips as anxiety set in. I began to feel lightheaded as we nervously anticipated the oncoming mob.

It struck us that the conveyor belt floor was moving inward, rather than in the direction of the train tunnel, and it began to pick up enough speed that would exhaust anyone trying to counter its pace. Wherever we were heading, this was going to be a one-way trip unless we could shut the conveyor down. Roy barked for us to be ready as we were quickly approaching a light up ahead.

Several large windows were glazed with a bright green light that bled into the red washed transit belt, and we stood with our mouths open in awe as we passed within its glare. Through the grime-covered glass glittered the countless spotlights of a massive Superdome. Our conveyor lined across its upper edge, gently curving along the wall of the enormous structure.

Beneath us were several cranes and building platforms, including an indescribable jumble of scaffolding jutting like a forest of black spikes silhouetted against the floodlights. The sheer scale of the site was impressive.

"What the..." was all that fell from Roy's lips. It took a long moment for him to turn his attention back to Beatrice, who also appeared a touch astonished while she stared with wide eyes out into the construction pit beyond.

"What is this place, really?" Tasha asked, beating Roy to the punch. The hold below us was so enormous that several dozen facilities the size of Fallhaven could have easily fit within its circumference. It must have taken decades to build this hidden complex under the remote mountainside. Our transit belt was slowly approaching an isolated tower, which fanned out from the interior wall to overlook the arena. Things were about to get interesting.

"All of this ...is the Veil project site," the old woman finally admitted, "it was to be the central command for all the base shelters linked to it."

"And what about the laboratory?" Ava asked in response.

"What about it?" Betty shot back with a cavalier tone, "It's all interlinked, I have no idea if anyone is still in control of this place. The automation is still working to some degree, but I don't know who ...or if anyone at all is still running this place," she finished with a glazed look in her eyes.

"Where does this conveyor belt actually lead?" Thorn demanded, grabbing her by the arm as if to affirm that she would follow the same fate as us all if we were overrun by another mob of weepers.

"To a cargo bay I would assume, young man," Betty chastised Thorn as she jerked her shoulder back out of his grasp to retain what little sense of dignity she had left.

We braced ourselves as the belt approached the upper echelon and a wide steel door opened after we passed through another laser wall that detected our presence. The cargo room was unremarkable except for the interlaced storage rings that lined the walls. There were several toppled containers knocked askew upon the floor noting that this section of the facility had been left abandoned in a hurry. It was not a good sign.

The only way out that we saw, was back through the conveyor system that led to the train terminal. That huge mob of infected that attacked us must have used this to escape, which was the way we had just entered. We had to be on our toes if there were more of them wandering about. This facility looked like it could hold many hundred or perhaps thousands of personnel staff. If they had all been turned by the KRI virus then a significant percentage of them would be hostile and dangerous.

"How do we get to the laboratory topside?" Tasha inquired, as we all drew our attention back to Beatrice.

"Sure, I'll be your tour guide," she remarked with an unusual sense of humor lost upon us, "don't go wandering off, children."

"Maybe she hit her head a little too hard back on that train," Thorn whispered under his breath to me as we let the old woman take the lead.

The doors to the cargo room were wide open. The facility had power, but it was intermittent in places that apparently had suffered significant electrical damage. We advanced quietly through a series of confusing hallways, noting blood smears and scorching from weapons fire that decorated the walls. Some serious shit had gone down here at one point and ended in a bad way. There were no corpses though. That worried me more than if the place had been left littered with them. They had either been cleaned up and disposed of or entirely consumed. There was no way to tell by the mess left behind. Someone had put up a fight, and we had no idea who the victor was. That horde that attacked us in the tunnel made me lean towards the darker side of the two scenarios.

"Come on, chop, chop, boys and girls," Betty snapped at us as she headed straight for a transit elevator and motioned to usher us inside. Roy advised her to keep her voice down, considering the overwhelming evidence that this place had been overrun by the infected. Oddly enough, her attitude was flippant, as if she didn't give a damn anymore. Roy shed us a glance that said he wouldn't mind just cutting the old woman's throat if she put us in jeopardy again, shaking his head in displeasure while he quietly fumed as we stepped into the broad elevator.

"This might not be the best idea," Tasha offered, referring to taking a lift up to a floor where it might be a serious tactical disadvantage not knowing what lies beyond the elevator doors when they finally slid open. She had learned not to take unnecessary risks, and her two comrades agreed with her.

"How high do we have to go up?" Roy asked Betty before her hand could reach the control panel to pick a floor as he moved to stand in her way.

"How rude," the old woman blurted as she stared him up and down, her behavior starting to become even more erratic than usual. She was acting very strange and we had all noticed it.

"How many floors up to get to the laboratory level?" Roy demanded again from her.

"It's too far to climb. Besides, I have no clue where the stairs are here," she spat back in contempt.

We could tell Roy was getting weary with her attitude and was making mental notes if he was willing to take the risk of letting the old woman continue to be so reckless with all our lives at stake. She might know her way around this vast facility, but that blown rail system and the removed control panel at the back door screamed that this place had been put on lockdown for a reason.

"Look, lady, I don't know what your game is, but you're starting to become a liability," Roy clarified to her. We all stood by his statement. Our group was tired and exhausted, and we were not in the mood for swallowing her psychotic bullshit anymore.

"Maybe we can find the lab on our own," Tasha remarked with a glare towards her. Betty waved her hands in surrender and finally said something reasonably sane.

"Okay, fine," she muttered aloud, "the laboratory is only four stories above ground, but I assume we are..." she paused as she wiggled her head around Roy's body to take a glance at the control elevator panel, "thirty floors or so below ground level at the moment," she answered directly, "...so, if you all want to walk and take the scenic route, you go right ahead; but I'm taking the damn elevator," she declared stubbornly.

We couldn't presume why she was acting so saucy all of the sudden. It could have been as Thorn suggested, that she was suffering from a concussion as she wasn't being her usual self. Maybe a few screws in her head had gotten knocked loose back in that train wreck after all.

We discussed the situation with Serena and Kel, who would both be hampered by their wounds if we took the stairs some thirty to forty stories up. It was a better plan since weepers didn't have the mental capacity to operate the lift, and that we would be inviting thirty times the risks of confrontation at every floor if we took an emergency stairwell. Without much debate at that fact, it did make more sense to use the elevator, as long as it didn't break down and leave us trapped. Roy stepped aside and let Beatrice have access to the panel. Oddly, the panel lit up the moment she put her hand close to it while she punched in her code. Just as strange, we also noticed that the floors weren't labeled. She put in a numeric sequence followed by depressing one of the color-coded keys, and the doors chimed shut.

The rest of us were mildly amused when soft elevator music started to play as the lift began to ascend towards the upper floors. Haiti smirked, while Roy seethed. I enjoyed the rhythm on a personal level though, because it was a nice tune. It made me wonder if the reason for elevator music in the first place was to distract you from dwelling on the reality that you were willfully risking your life by stepping into a small tin box set over a deep shaft, that was being held secure by nothing more than a thin cable. On the other hand, perhaps it was to take your mind off the effects of claustrophobia for those who suffered from it.

On the ride up, we heard banging on the doors as we passed several levels. Other floors had severe electrical failures that sparked the panels as we crossed, and we heard the lift stabilizers grind in anger beneath our feet. With nervous relief, the car finally slid to a gentle halt as a recorded female voice came over the speaker: "Blue Level," while the doors slid open with the sound of a chime.

It was clear something had gone awry even on the upper floors, where we found equipment and packages strewn everywhere. Long shadows cast through tall glass windows that let in the light of the setting sun as it neared the horizon. At least there was no sign of blood splatter or weapons fire here; the place was merely trashed.

Beatrice marched out in front of the group and turned back to us with an awkward smile, then promptly headed out towards a central hall without taking any tactical precautions. There were clearly infected people wandering this facility, yet she acted as if it didn't matter in the slightest. The old woman strolled to the main foyer and spun around once more with a hand on her hip and a furl in her brow as if she was wondering why we were all still standing at the elevator door, poised with our weapons drawn.

"I swear, if she gets jumped, I'm not saving her wrinkly ass..." Roy grunted. Truth be told, we all were beginning to agree with his logic.

"Are you coming or not?" Betty chastised from across the room. Timidly, we checked our corners and did a visual sweep, realizing that there weren't any telltale signs of weepers on this level. "Trust me, this is a secured level," the old woman urged, "there is nothing to worry about." Needless to say, we didn't put much value in her words.

"This section does seem quiet," Thorn finally affirmed after a drawn moment.

We were still on edge after our last encounter in the rail tunnel, but it was getting tiring lugging around our weapons on the draw. We were wounded and drained, and were attracted to the idea of getting a chance to recoup. Kel's leg needed to be rebandaged, and a few of us were getting more than a tad strung out from hunger, so we decided to play along. Betty led us straight to a sizable rest area that appeared to be a staff breakroom.

We plopped down on the stiff couches and rifled the cabinets for anything to eat. Unfortunately, there wasn't much present to impress anyone as it had all been previously looted. The mercenary girls took their time to give some medical attention to Serena and Kel, while I roamed back out to the main hall near the elevator. In a rare break in the clouds, the orange glow of sunset cast its warm light through the lobby.

Looking down at the entrance through the glass, it appeared we were now several stories above the ground level. Outside there were lighted pylons and a wide curved yard full of military trucks parked in a jumble. It was hard to make out any details in the failing light, but I was relieved not to see any infected wandering within sight. Even if we were able to jack one of those trucks, there was still the matter of the collapsed mountain tunnel blocking the only road out of this place.

Someone had locked down this facility and we all wanted answers as to what had happened here. Tasha, I assumed, would want them the most since her father had disappeared somewhere on this base. We barely got the rock sample here in one piece; now we just had to figure out what to do with it. Distracted by the view and with the shadows casting behind me, I was startled when I heard a voice speak just over my shoulder.

"Nice view," Thorn noted as he took a step beside me.

"I really miss seeing the sunset; being stuck down in the dark like we were, really wasn't for me," I admitted, "I grew up on a ranch in the boonies, and when I finally moved out to a big city the first place I got was this tiny basement apartment," I giggled out loud in embarrassment, "I don't even think it was actually legal for them to rent out. It was like a boiler room, where all the water heaters for the rest of the apartments above me were right beside my bed, and it only had one teensy window that wasn't even at ground level. Oh, jeez..." I smirked.

"That bad, huh?" Thorn offered with comedic sympathy, "Well, I can understand not wanting to live underground. It was hard enough for us when we were stuck back in Fallhaven," he granted with a cute smile.

"Yeah, that apartment I had was like a cave ...but it was *my* cave," I smiled faintly while he gave particular notice, "It was a space of my own. That was a strange time in my life," I reflected with tearful honesty.

"...And this isn't?" Thorn answered back with a questionable smirk.

We both giggled to the point it was infectious until we couldn't seem to stop. That sense I had of feeling stupid and awkward around him melted away just then. I looked at Thorn in the scarlet light as the sun hit the horizon ...and we kissed. It was over before I knew it, and I wondered if I had hallucinated what had just happened. I was facing him and our hands were touching, but the sudden sound of gunfire echoing up the hall snapped our attention back towards the break room.

We didn't say a thing as we shot a single worried look to one another before we made a dash for the corridor. Like an idiot, I had left my rifle in the breakroom with Ava, who was at the task of cleaning all the weapons. Thorn drew his automatic pistol and we swiftly made our way down the hall. Just as we were a few steps from the entry, shards of metal and plastic sprayed out of the break room as we covered our faces from the sound of the blast. Wires and bits of gears sparked errantly amongst the debris on the floor when we finally rounded the doorframe.

We found Roy's limp body lying slumped over the central table with a smoking hole burnt into the back of his skull, while Haiti lay mortally wounded in a pool of his own blood by the door. Kel stood on the opposite side of the table, nervously holding a shotgun; its barrels still smoking from the blast. What looked like a large mechanical box sat sparking between us in the middle of the room. Serena was sitting up on the couch staring at us in disbelief while Ava lay sprawled across the floor, wildly grasping for gun parts as she tried to assemble a workable firearm.

"What the fuck was that?" Serena wailed, having just woken up and suddenly left gawking at Roy's corpse and the blackened hole burned through his head. We rushed to help Haiti who was gurgling in his own blood. There were two neat holes in his side, causing him to bleed out.

"Hold on Haiti, we'll patch you up," Thorn assured, trying to assess his wounds; though blood oozed through the deep punctures with every breath he took.

"Aye, dat fucking robot, man; what kinda shit is that?" He muttered weakly while he coughed up blood, its red staining his white teeth. He looked dazed, his eyes rolling in pain.

"What happened?" I asked, trying not to lose my head. Kel reloaded her weapon as Ava handed her another pistol, which she quickly reassembled just as Tasha came running around the corner to the breakroom. She looked just as stunned as we had been when we stumbled upon the frightening scene.

"Some sort of Lab robot came rolling in here and shot a laser into Roy's skull, then stabbed Haiti with its pincer when he jumped on it," Kel answered in shock.

"Da fucking thing was quiet, man, we never heard it coming," Haiti coughed again, his breath getting shaky, "it just rolled in here without any warning and killed Roy ...and fucked me up real good too," he sputtered while trying to sit up. Thorn tried to get him to lie still while searching for something to wrap the wound. Haiti held onto his hand tightly, his grip tensing for a brief moment; then he gently collapsed. Haiti was dead.

A look of anguish washed over his face as Thorn turned to me. The little boy, who had been cowering in the corner, gingerly stepped over to Haiti's body, touching his limp arm with a mark of sorrow. They had personally been closer than the others, and Haiti had always been kind to him.

It took a short moment, but the rest of us finally came to the realization that Betty was nowhere in sight. The wheels began to turn in my head. She knew about this facility because she had been a member of the laboratory team at one time. How the panel in the elevator only seemed to work when she got close to it made me suspect she had a chip implant that allowed her internal access. She had known the code for admission to this particular floor and was acting so cavalier once she got here because she knew this place was her own territory, where she would have the upper hand on us.

"That bitch, Betty, said she needed to use the restroom and left down the hall. Roy told me to keep an eye on her, so I tried to follow her," Tasha stated, "I lost her when she entered a room down the end of the far corridor, but the access button wouldn't work for me after she went inside," the girl revealed with a tone of regret.

"She must have locked it from the inside," Serena mentioned from behind, referring to Beatrice sealing the door.

"I don't think she needed to," I added, "I think Betty has an embedded ID chip that allows her access to any security points on this level," After revealing my suspicions, the rest of them agreed, and my analogy made perfect sense to Tasha. We should have seen this coming, but the old woman had played us all too well.

"She probably sent that automaton in here to kill us all," Kel accused, pointing to what was left of the robot, "I knew we should have dropped that crazy cunt back at the pit," she admitted heartily, implying to the chasm under the derailed train where we had lost Felix. Grudgingly, I had to agree. Beatrice wasn't just a liability, she was unpredictable and dangerous.

Thorn was just as shaken as Serena, seeing both of their comrades lying dead without any forewarning. They had all been through a lot of close scrapes together. Roy's maturity and tactical knowledge had been of great value to their team, and even Tasha had admired him. It was disturbing to think that with all his training and combat experience that he was taken down so easily with a single shot. He didn't even see it coming.

"Gear up. Ava, watch the door," Tasha instructed while we got the rest of the weapons together.

Betty was still out there, probably playing the same game she had back at Fallhaven. Likely, she was sitting behind a control board watching us on some hidden security feed. Mobile laboratory robots had some lethal capacity present in their set of tools. They were armed with steel clamps that could crush bone, including scalpel lasers, which had the ability to sear through living flesh; as in the case of Roy's grisly execution.

The robot's reactions were quick and they were equipped with quiet servos, which made them silent stalkers. We had to find Beatrice and either get her under control, or put her down. Serena stayed behind to guard the boy and the meteor sample.

"Follow me," Tasha advised as Thorn, Kel, and I made our way through a series of switches down the white-tiled hallways, checking our corners as we went. We finally arrived at the door where Tasha had followed the old woman. The sign inset beside it was labeled: 'Tracking & Phase Development'. The activation panel would not react to our touch, only confirming my suspicions that Beatrice had an implanted chip with full security clearance.

There was no way to pry the door panel open, and if there was a way to access its wiring, we couldn't seem to find it. As tempting as it was to bang on the door to cuss at the murderous bitch, we realized that kind of outburst would be entirely futile. However, that did not keep Thorn from doing so in his anger.

"Open up Betty, you damn..." Thorn yelled, beating the sliding steel door with the butt of his gun. He never finished his verbal threat, as to our utter surprise, the door promptly opened.

I didn't know whether to be puzzled or impressed. Tasha looked just as stunned, but she wasn't going to waste the opportunity to get inside. Tasha was a mark smarter than I had given her credit for, considering her age, while I watched as she took a spare ammo clip and wedged it into the frame slot to jam the door open, to keep it from closing on us.

"We might need a way out," she advised, explaining her precautionary measure to keep us from being locked inside.

Within the rectangular room were stacks of blinking panels, most of which looked like data storage computers. A few robotic arms whirred behind panes of glass of several dozen sealed cases, moving countless numbers of test vials containing mysterious substances. At the far end of the room sat Betty, alone in a chair looking at multiple digital screens. I thought Thorn was going to shoot her right then and there as he raised his scope to aim at the back of her head. He stalled when she merely glanced over her shoulder and quaintly answered his rude summons to be allowed inside.

"Welcome to my old workstation, come take a look at what I found," she declared.

With a note of vigilance, we slowly approached her to see that she was unarmed and not seeming to be a threat, "I hope you don't mind me getting distracted by all this mess, but it's been a long time since I've been back here," she added; completely oblivious to Thorn standing directly behind her with his rifle pointed at her, while seething to put a bullet in her skull.

"Why did you kill them, Betty?" I had to ask mournfully while placing a hand on the muzzle to lower Thorn's rifle from the back of her head. She turned around, looking a little baffled, then casually spun back to her task of monitoring the array of screens before her.

"What an odd question ...what do you mean, dear?" She babbled innocently while distracted by the data flashing on the screen before her.

It slowly became clear that Beatrice had no idea what had just happened in the breakroom, and admitted to us that she had no control of the laboratory robotics in the facility. Contrary to her past actions, we started to believe what she was saying. She took a moment to bring up a status screen for the facility so we could see what had transpired here. Data began to stream across the board about the lockdown with bold red letters that lit up on the screen as they blinked: *'Failsafe enacted.'*

Cypher

"Why were you in here and how were you able to open that door?" Tasha demanded, giving Beatrice the third degree.

"I have clearance," Betty replied, tapping at the hidden chip in her wrist, "everyone who had worked here has them."

"You told the others you were heading for the restroom but ended up locking yourself in here instead ...whatever this place is?" Thorn retorted while scanning the robotic arms whirring behind the glass in multiple containment lockers. Each of the automations were tirelessly filling jars of liquids in test tubes in one size or another, and replacing them on slotted trays.

"I passed by this station where I once worked and couldn't help but take a peek. It is not my fault you couldn't get in. I opened it when you knocked," Betty countered in her defense.

Tasha gave us both an incredulous frown, noting though that her side of the story was entirely credible. The question was, who the fuck sent that robot to lynch us in the first place? It appeared that Betty had an answer for that.

"I was just looking over the project results from the past several years when you dropped by," the old woman answered, "Apparently, when the failsafe was initiated, the mobile assistant automations had been assigned alternate programming to act as sentries," she read from the emergency status displayed on the board before us, "anyone who wasn't authorized with embedded clearance would be considered as a trespasser, and..." she trailed off as Tasha finished for her.

"...Anyone trespassing on a military facility would be subject to the use of deadly force," the young girl noted. Tasha had seen how touchy defense personnel could be when she was growing up. Many times, they tended to overreact with too much testosterone whenever push came to shove.

"Wait a moment. So you had us walk in here knowing we would become targets?" I had to inquire, bewildered by what Betty had just admitted to.

"This facility has many levels of automation, and for one, Caitlin, I had no clue that the system failsafe had already been triggered," the old woman stomped back in response to my damning accusation.

"Well, you could have taken a wild guess!" Thorn spat back, waving his hands around the place, noting the containment lockdown and the hordes of weepers roaming the massive facility. He did have a point.

"Thank you for the attitude," she replied with a rancid tone towards Thorn, "but I had no idea the lab automations could be programmed in that manner; hell, I wasn't even sure my own clearance would still work on the upper levels after all these years," Beatrice admitted.

It took some convincing but Tasha upheld the old woman's excuse, and that it wasn't exactly uncommon for upper Military Admin to enact hidden protocols whenever shit hits the fan. It took some digging, but Beatrice was able to bring up the files on the VEIL project and what had transpired here at the facility after the impact event. Tasha was attentive to this information; secretly hoping that her father hadn't become one of the infected wandering the base. If she ever found him in that condition, she knew what he would want her to do.

International governments and the military complex had been preparing for such an event well before June of 2004, back when asteroid MN4 had first been discovered. Within the files, we found an inventory log recording the several thousand asteroid flybys over the past century alone that had the same prospect to cause a similar catastrophe. Apophis, itself, was only about as broad as a twelve-story building, but that was big enough to punch a hole through Earth's atmosphere and devastate a small country if it hit land, and could cause widespread tsunamis if it made contact with the ocean. Nobody would have guessed it would do exactly that by breaking up and striking two separate zones on both land and sea.

A collision with Earth had been a theoretical possibility, but the narrow odds were disturbing enough. Scientists on the MN4 project calculated the asteroid's trajectory would bend during its first flyby encounter in early 2029, as a result of Earth's gravitational pull upon the celestial body. Their ability to see where the asteroid itself would go after extrapolating its orbit was fogged by the lack of credible data. Astronomers noted that it would be premature to predict if Apophis would cross into our orbital path again after it swung around the sun for another encounter exactly seven years later, to the day, in 2036. The only way they could be sure was by calculating the data during its near-earth pass, and on its return trip back into tracking range. As anyone could imagine, that simply wasn't good enough for the heads up high. They demanded results for an alternate resolution to the problem, whether it really existed or not; and prompted an assurance that asteroid MN4 would never become a viable threat to the planet; which seemed like a humanitarian endeavor on its shiny surface, but it was solely motivated by their desire to retain control over the population.

Most nations had been locked in Resource Wars at the time of the impact event, and tensions had been running high among the public and politicians. There could be notable benefits appearing to act as a Savior in the eyes of the world forum and social media, and it would be a tremendous financial and strategic advantage to use the alleged menace of Apophis as propaganda and leverage towards their own ends. Upon that premise, the VEIL project was formed as a semi-secret black budget program and was sold to the public and rival nations as their only salvation.

The classified files we read within revealed the roots and true purpose of this enormous facility we now stood in. To reduce the range of the asteroid's trajectory into Earth's orbital path, it was proposed that they could help nudge the floating rock out of the danger zone. The sooner they gave the asteroid a gentle push, the farther it would veer from its collision course.

Beatrice brought up a visual model covering the details of the project hardware. Upon the central screen displayed the specs for a space probe. It was a very advanced and expensive spacecraft that was designed to shoot out towards the approaching asteroid to land on it and deploy a wide reflecting screen. This device would deflect solar radiation in small enough amounts to gradually change its trajectory and push it off its projected path towards our planet. The sooner it was deployed, the wider the range of safety to distance the celestial object from ever intersecting Earth's orbital plane.

All of us except Betty were frankly baffled by this revelation. All these years of preparation for this event had been kept under wraps from the eyes and ears of the civilian population, and apparently, any leaks had been stricken from the media. It did not make much sense to hide such an important venture, one that seemed like it would have gotten overwhelming public support; yet, it was entirely censored.

"So, unbeknownst to the public, they sent up a rocket to shove the asteroid in another direction. For what logical purpose would they keep that a secret?" Kel inquired of the old woman, who seemed to be just as interested in the information.

"Obviously, something went terribly wrong," she answered, "and the fewer people who knew about the program, then the general population would have no one to point their fingers at to blame."

Betty made a valid point. It was just another evasion of liability game our government entities chose to play; one which had been groomed by decades of poor judgment and incompetent leadership. Had Project VEIL actually been a success, they would have promptly stepped out into the spotlight to take all the credit for saving the world. Instead, somebody fumbled the ball. I was disgusted by the thought of it, but it was still a viable answer. However, what we discovered buried beneath all the data deep within that file log did not sit well with either of us. The Veil program was merely a sub-project for its top secret sister program; a military space station.

Now all the pegs started to fall into place. The military and government elites had a backup plan and needed a convenient excuse for the vast amount of funds and hardware that were being consumed on this colossal enterprise. Over-budget costs and emergency funds were all too common on such ventures. Tasha had a point to make after viewing the files, a question that would linger on our conscience.

"So, what was the purpose of keeping this facility operational after the failure of the probe?" she asked Beatrice who was busy ogling the screen. We did not like the answer. She brought up the computer audio to dictate what had happened here at the Lab site since her evacuation to Fallhaven, along with Kane, those many years ago.

"The Veil Probe was launched eight months prior to its estimated intercept date with the celestial target. Echoes from the planetary radar telescope revealed the asteroid's precise distance and velocity for rendezvous with the potentially hazardous asteroid 99942 known as Apophis," the monotone computer voice dictated, "the probe landed and successfully deployed its reflective panels, however, the subsequent results of radar observations revealed that the predicted solar radiation that was calculated to help reduce the risk of interception with our orbit, had instead, aggravated the trajectory by increasing the rotation of the solar object."

We looked at one another with exasperation, realizing that the massive amount of resources and costs that had been incurred to prevent the chance of this disaster, had instead, guaranteed it. The computer files continued to display the outlandish failure on the screen before us in vivid heart-wrenching detail.

"Unforeseen by previous data forecasts, the resulting intervention of the probe amplified the target asteroid's dynamics and trajectory, to a point that it significantly elevated the probability of impact," the computer affirmed, "upon entering our orbital plane, MN4 was subject to Earth's gravitational pull. As impact was now imminent, the Project chief and assigned Commanders had initiated a surrogate backup plan, by detonating the thermonuclear payload embedded within the Veil probe as a last resort, thereby attempting to disintegrate the target. This course of action failed to pulverize the object as expected, and instead, created two main shrapnel bodies that retained their critical mass upon entering the stratosphere."

A new screen opened up as the other faded, this one showing the celestial event from a view in space; recorded by satellite footage with superimposed graphics detailing the following repercussions across the globe. Apophis had split into two projectiles shortly before punching sizable holes into Earth's atmosphere. This resulted in a pair of electromagnetic pulse waves that encompassed the entire planet; sending our civilization back into the Dark Ages. Several military installations retained equipment and vehicles which had been specifically constructed with protective shielding for such an event but not of the magnitudes we had encountered. The civilian population was not prepared in any form for the catastrophic impact of a peak EMP wave. Many populated areas were subject to a double strike that devastated most regions as all electronic components were demolished and the power grid severed. Our modern world had become far too reliant on such vulnerable technologies.

As it turned out, the computer data revealed that this was actually a similar risk we had faced daily from our closest star, the Sun, in the form of coronal mass ejections. Errant solar storms have occasionally razed the planet for billions of years throughout Earth's history. The difference being that we have built a civilization reliant on such a frail infrastructure. Everything from power plants to global communications suddenly stopped working, and we all ran around like chickens with our heads cut off, looking like complete fools.

At zero hour, there had been massive blackouts where people took to the streets, sparking a level of chaos that quickly escalated into wide-spread looting and riots. There were no operational wideband communications or working navigation as commercial airliners fell from the sky. Ships at sea became lost, as the EMP burst had not merely been aimed downward towards the planets surface but had also fried every satellite and positioning systems in close orbit. Any effort at celestial navigation soon became futile as the atmosphere quickly clouded over in the days that followed from the dust and debris kicked up from the land impact created by the first fragment of Apophis. It was an aftereffect akin to a nuclear winter that endured for years to follow. Raging electrical storms soon followed in its wake as global weather patterns were disrupted on an epic scale across both hemispheres.

Like I said, the shit hit the fan, to put it mildly; and life these past few years had been a real challenge for everyone on the planet. With no power nor backup systems, hospital patients on any kind of life support quickly expired. Billions of people fought for food and shelter in the failing climate, making life beyond unpleasant at every degree   ...then came the MN4 plague in the form of the irradiated Kriotin virus.

The towering amount of data displayed on the screen was almost too much to ingest. The classified sister program of the cover VEIL program was named MIRAGE; a tag named used as a mirror site for the protective shelters. Apparently, Mirage was the secret space station reserved for the top crème of the elite class. It was a designated command post to oversee the entire project and guarantee the continuity of government. This information made us wonder what the hell they have been doing up there in orbit all this time while the world went to hell.

"That's interesting..." Beatrice noted as we all stood gawking at the screen while trying to absorb the information that had been thrown at us. Fundamentally, it was difficult enough to swallow how our space program had fucked up so badly and directly caused the asteroid to hit us, but it made the situation relatively far worse to realize that a group of arrogant assholes had saved their own sorry butts by jetting off to the safety of orbit, while everyone was left to rot on the surface.

"What is it?" I inquired to Betty's unfinished remark, as we watched while she tapped on the control board.

"There seems to be no communication from the space station. All transmissions have gone dark," she noted.

"It's possible they could have ran out of food and air up there after nearly a decade," Tasha mentioned, "it serves them right!"

It would be an ironic turn of events if that were the fact. The EMP that sent us back to cooking by campfire and the global storms that darkened the skies were petty hardships compared to the viral outbreak that swept the planet and almost wiped out our species. We had enough grief in our lives, but learning that we did it to ourselves was icing on the cake. Holy fuck, were we stupid.

"*I can guarantee you that was not the case...*" a strange voice came over the intercom in the room. Even Beatrice turned and

appeared surprised by the interruption. We had assumed that
the base had been abandoned long ago, but apparently, there
was someone else still here.

"Who are you?" Thorn called out to the hidden speakers in the
room, yet feeling at the disadvantage when he couldn't find
them. We knew cameras could be embedded within the screens
displays; it was just unnerving knowing someone had been
watching us all this time.

"*I am your host, and it has been some time since I have had
proper guests,*" the man's voice offered, "*my sincere apologies
for the recent deaths in your group, but the automations are,
well... automated,*" he smirked with distasteful humor.

"What is it that you want?" Tasha demanded as she gripped
her gun tightly. She wasn't keen to being put on the defense by
an unseen foe.

"*It's not what I want, young lady,*" he answered abruptly, "*but
what I can provide.*"

We looked at one another with a hint of apprehension, not
knowing what we should do next. Thorn tapped Beatrice on the
shoulder with the muzzle of his rifle, motioning her to get up
from the console, not knowing if she was somehow a party to
this new contact.

"Who is that?" he whispered to her threateningly, trying not to
be overheard. Respectfully, they were still standing in front of
the screens that picked up every word he said.

"*You may call me Cypher. I invite you to let us get better
acquainted and will offer to provide you with answers to many
of your questions,*" Cypher granted, "*I have provided security
access to the top floor. If you would, please bring your other
two companions from the 3rd floor breakroom,*" he instructed.
With that said, the door to the secured room opened as a prompt
for us to depart.

Clearly, this mysterious host had some measure of control over
the security systems. With the recent deaths of our companions
weighing on us, we wondered if this 'Cypher' fellow could be
trusted at any length. We didn't want to walk into another blind
ambush but we were here for a reason, and he was offering
answers.

It was an odd feeling walking down that corridor back to the break room. We were still in a daze as we disclosed what we had just learned to Serena. The young boy had calmed down to a reasonable level, having cried himself to sleep over Haiti's death. We assembled and shuffled over to the elevator, still wary of any robotic threats that still lurked within the halls.

The elevator ride was far longer than we expected for only going up a single floor. Finally, the door chimed as the female voice uttered "Green Level," over the speaker while the doors slid open. The room was stark white with a jumble of makeshift panels, which had been scavenged elsewhere and reassembled within this chamber. An uncomfortable tension hung in the air, and the elevator door suddenly slammed shut behind us after we stepped out. When she tried to open it again, the controls were unresponsive to Betty's implanted chip.

The large panels were attached to a set of gears, that swung open to reveal a wide glass wall; beyond it stood our host.

He was oddly dressed in a mix of a modern lab coat, which had been retailored to resemble something from the renaissance age. An entire top floor of the building had been cleared and repurposed as a living space. Makeshift curtains had been assembled to decorate the windows in an ornamental design. Bits of plastic and data disks had been patchworked into the windowpanes to faintly resemble a stained glass trim.

Scraps of lab equipment had been remade into the visage of candelabras, each adorned with bright lights to simulate flickering candle flames. Similar to their construction was an enormous digital fireplace that overwhelmed the rear wall with its lavish decor. Our impression was that our host had gone a little off-kilter trapped up here all these years in solitude. Our initial presumption was pretty close to being on point.

"Welcome," Cypher gestured with a faint smile. He was not terribly tall, though clean-shaven and appeared slightly gaunt. The strange fellow certainly had an odd look to him that befit a recluse. He carried himself well as he casually strolled over to lean on a desk chair that had been modified to give it the illusion of a high back. It was all strangely pseudo 18th century, including his eccentric gait.

We were baffled by his initial presentation, but kept a tight hold of our firearms, not knowing what his game was. As we twitched uneasily with our weapons, several robotic arms unfolded from the sides of the room in response. We turned in defense as their metal clamps extended towards us.

"What's this all about?" Thorn demanded as we raised our guns to fire. The metal arms kept at a distance for a moment as their multiple appendages spun and whirred.

"There will be no need for those," Cypher gestured for us to lower our weapons while he flashed a shameless grin, "I can assure you the glass is quite indestructible."

"You don't look familiar," Betty mentioned, trying to recall if she had ever met him in the years before the cataclysm. Cypher just shook his head.

"No ...I wouldn't," he shook his head at the old woman's comment, "I was assigned here after you left, Beatrice," Cypher noted to her directly. She was surprised that he knew her name, "Your staff file was flagged the moment you entered the main facility. I've been keeping tabs on you and what you have been researching, dear."

"What are you still doing here?" Kel asked as she gently tapped on the thick glass that separated them. He smiled back and raised his hands to his secured quarters.

"It's a mere safeguard against contamination," he explained, and I have everything I need and more than enough idle hobbies here to keep me entertained."

In a facility this size, we could imagine that he had ample food and water to last him the rest of his life. Instead of risking the contagion, he had chosen to seal himself off. Cypher confessed that he had been here since the day of the catastrophe while most of the personnel had been evacuated to the numerous subterranean shelters along the rail system. Only a small exclusive staff of scientists had been left here to secure the laboratory habitat.

Our questions were many as we tried to piece together the information which had been revealed on the computer from Betty's old station, along with Cypher's own first-hand account. It was Tasha's inquiry to her father's disappearance and the consequential collapse of the mountain tunnel that won our host's foremost attention. Being of strategic importance, a squadron had been left to guard this facility, which explained the cluster of military vehicles strewn across the entrance outside the base. He proceeded to explain the purpose of her father's mission and how it had come to an abrupt end.

"A convoy had been assigned to escort one of the lead scientists along with a secured meteorite fragment excavated from the surface impact site," Cypher began as he took a seat in the tall chair facing us, "Unfortunately, there was an alleged mutiny within the ranks of the security contractor and we failed to acquire the sample specimen," he concluded, while we kept silent that we were already aware of this knowledge.

"But what did they need the sample for, was it to create a vaccine?" I asked on Tasha's behalf. Cypher gave a long drawn out sigh as if it was a subject he would rather forget. We had lugged that rock all this way here at our own risk. Tasha had brought the capsule with her since she did not trust letting it out of their sight nor did she wish to leave it unattended in the breakroom during this introduction.

"The fragment was a primary specimen for the military branch on the blue level," he finally admitted as we turned our attention to Beatrice, whose face flushed with mild guilt, "as you can tell, we were quite secluded here from the ravages that affected the global population, and this site was kept secret in an effort to keep it from becoming a target of infiltration or possible air strikes from foreign rivals," Cypher related.

"I'm a little confused. Why would anyone want to attack this compound in the first place?" Tasha inquired with our joint interest behind her.

"It would be nothing to do with the failure of the Veil probe, I assure you," Cypher declared, his eyes lingered on Betty when he spoke, "nor anything to do with the secret space station that was constructed at this site, but it could certainly be over concerns about the exploitation of the virus that would make this complex a target."

It wasn't until that very moment when he revealed this crucial position that we could finally put all the pieces together. The scientists stationed in the upper levels of Fallhaven had been researching how to enhance the virus for military applications. Cypher further went on to disclose that the automations working around the clock in the Phase Development lab, where Betty had been stationed, were not creating biological test samples as a remedy for clinical inoculations, but were instead, tailored to intensify the original pathogen for use as a adaptive agent for adoption towards bio-warfare.

"I've made several attempts to shut down the program that has been running on the blue level for all these years, but I was locked out of its system and unable to affect the termination of that stage of operation," Cypher admitted, "since its integration is deeply rooted into the core system of the complex, and doing so would require that I cut all power to this facility that protects me," he explained as he got up and walked to the large pane window to the outside world. The sun had already set, but its soft glow was still settling in the cloud-swept sky that painted the distant horizon.

"The files showed that the Mirage program space station was unresponsive to hails, and there was no activity displayed from the orbital," Thorn stated to the man behind the glass about the data the lab computer had revealed earlier. Cypher nodded solemnly at his remark, his pattern of behavior changing to a callous attitude.

"And there wouldn't be either," he acknowledged with an almost whimsical flare, "As the original launching platform, we had full access to remote systems on the station, of course. I took it upon myself to induce a certain level of ...intervention." he finished with a pause. We weren't quite sure what he had meant by that last statement, and he could read that confusion by the bewildered look that spread across our faces.

"What did you do?" Beatrice spoke up, a serious tone seeping from under her breath. Our self-elected host casually wandered back to his chair, leaning upon it in thought as he placed a hand to his chin. We were all a little disarmed by what he said next.

"The final transport of our top branch Commanders to the orbiting station was postponed by a few last-minute glitches and unforeseen mechanical setbacks. When our Administration here failed to acquire the meteor sample for their project research of the alien virus, they decided to initiate an emergency launch to evacuate the top members of the governing body to the Mirage orbital," he pointed above in reference to the space station still circling the Earth, "with a little ingenuity, a single person could override a few key systems, push a few buttons and abort the launch mid-flight with a kill switch ...*kapooow*!" he added with a dramatization by using his hands to represent a rocket in flight and then exploding along the length of its journey.

"You blew it up?" Ava intervened, to clarify his theatrics.

"Not the station, mind you ...although I do admit that it had originally crossed my mind," Cypher granted to our dismay, "Unfortunately for them, at the last moment they chose not to include me on their exclusive VIP list, so I taught those arrogant fucks a little respect!" he admitted with smug resonance. The evil grin he wore proved that he still found an ample amount of amusement from their demise after all these years.

"You just ...just, murdered them?" Beatrice spat back, exposing the true color of her loyalties to everyone in the room. Cypher stomped up to the glass and gave the old woman an ugly glare, stepping out of character for the first time. The unbalance of his genius coming to light.

"Murder ...murder? Those self-serving aristocratic lumps of human filth deserved worse!" he spat back in anger, "I've had a great deal of time to contemplate their conduct over these past several years, and I would do it again a hundred times over! They didn't care about the world they had destroyed from their bungling, their only selfish concern went towards surviving the aftermath of their negligence," he affirmed.

His words rang true. The elite branch of our ruling government and military had grossly mismanaged the recovery operations and conspired to weaponize the virus, rather than concentrate on cleaning up their own mess. It was about securing their power, even after proving they did not possess the ethical strength to wield it. Then they tried to jump ship when they lost control of the situation; it served them right.

There were still a few dozen personnel on the space station at the time, but by remotely overriding a few airlocks and purging the atmosphere in selected sections on the station, Cypher was able to vacate the entire platform of its staff. The man was a touch psychotic, but intelligent. It was a dangerous mixture.

The phase development lab on the blue level a floor below us had been allocated to replicating the MN4 virus for genetic splicing into various compounds. The automated machinery had continued developing research samples nonstop for the past several years. Not trying to create a cure, but revealing ways to manipulate the pathogen into various strains for military applications. Beatrice had been a part of the original research staff that had helped develop the monstrous mutations at Fallhaven. Those test creatures had been secured in cryogenic freezers for future study, until the day they had eventually lost control of the containment lab. We all knew how that had worked out for everyone.

They had been aiming to regulate a half-life to the virus in an effort to utilize the microbe as a weapon on foreign soil or against any resistance met by their new regime. Instead, the initial mutagens were blended with a brew of experimental pharmaceuticals, which ended up being wildly contagious and further resisted all forms of controlled degeneration. Their grand idea of spreading a designer disease that would be rendered impotent over a set time span had eventually backfired on them in a spectacular way.

Even more disturbing, was Cypher's revelation that these genetic research facilities had been attempting this same scenario with every known viral outbreak over recent decades. Whenever a new disease or epidemic had been detected within any given country across the globe, those instances had actually been the first steps of many in the biological test-phases related to this Mirage project, which had been birthed to create a designer virus. However, it wasn't until the introduction of this exotic alien germ that there existed a truly potent and viable candidate for their covert agenda for population reduction and control. They had been creating and testing bioweapons here under clear violation of international treaties.

We had to agree on one point with Cypher, that the world was a better place without our high-ranking officials running the game. Not only had they entirely botched the mission to prevent an asteroid collision that would likely have never happened in the first place, but they had also added fuel to the flames by trying to forcibly manipulate and gain global domination through treachery and intimidation. It was beyond reckless ...it was madness.

While we were arguing with Betty about her involvement with such an immoral agenda, Cypher tapped a few buttons on the arm of his control chair. A mechanical arm on our side of the glass wall reached out and snatched up the covered capsule that Tasha had set beside her. We all turned just as a separate clamp uncovered the soiled cloth, unveiling the meteor sample held within. Cypher nodded in contemplation for a silent moment before cutting the tension in the air with an audible sigh.

"Ah, I had been wondering what this little item was that you were so carefully lugging about; its contents had been shielded from the cargo scanners by its lead lining, I would presume," Cypher stood debating for a second with a finger to his chin, "Is this what I think it is?" he inquired to the young girl as she clung tightly onto her rifle with a scowl of defiance stamped upon her brow.

"My father was the hired escort originally assigned to deliver your head military scientist and this meteor sample to this facility all those years ago," Tasha revealed to Cypher as his eyes lightened up at her words, "as you already know, this package was never delivered."

"Until now," Cypher corrected as his face glinted brightly from behind the glass while he gazed at the container. Beatrice took a stand in front of the box in defiance, as if blocking his view of it would somehow sway his mind. The robot arms simply moved the container higher above her head and closer to the transparent wall where he could view it in greater detail, "A very dangerous gift indeed," he smiled while admiring the celestial shard containing the microbes that had forever changed the world we knew, "so enchantingly beautiful, yet so deadly," he exclaimed while his eyes swept down to meet Tasha's glare, as if to complete the meaning of the metaphor.

"What happened to my father?" Tasha spoke flatly, her blue eyes turning as cold as steel at that moment. She had suffered through many sleepless nights for an answer. We all quelled our jabbering among one another to hear his response.

"As I mentioned, there was an incident of insubordination between the military personnel and the contracted mercenaries who were hired to deliver this most valuable package," Cypher began with a nonchalant wave to the small stone as he turned once again towards the window on the far side of the room; his voice amplified through a hidden speaker to us at a constant volume from wherever he stood within his protective cell, "when the authorities in charge at the time discovered that the armed escort had delivered their Scientist but had left the rock sample behind as a bargaining chip, and began demanding answers, the situation quickly escalated into a firefight after they were informed about the true nature of the Mirage project," Cypher finished with a long breath.

"But why were the tunnels blown, it seems a bit extreme for a lockdown," Tasha argued.

"When the mercenaries held the head scientist hostage as leverage, they apparently didn't appreciate the bits of classified intelligence disclosed to them that revealed the purified sample of the asteroid was actually going to be utilized to develop a bioweapon, rather than a cure. They had a pretty ...let's say, *volatile* reaction to that information and took drastic measures to seal off the base," Cypher related, acknowledging that her father and the rest of his squad had fought back and collapsed both points of entry to the complex.

The road through the mountain was destroyed, which effectively blocked all ground-based vehicle exits, and they took measures to sever the subterranean train rail below ground. Power to the base was being supplied by the hydrogen generators through sealed conduits in the underground tunnels, so they ultimately failed to shut down the facility completely as they had initially planned. However, their heroic move crippled the continued function of the base and all but a few helicopters left in commission, which they promptly disabled by the use of explosives. During the insurrection, the base was irreversibly damaged and key sections were compromised, which eventually led to a breach in containment of the biochemical agents. To avoid exposure, the incident initiated an emergency evacuation of all top officials by launch to the orbiting space station.

Prior to that incident, Cypher's aerospace division quickly lost any continued value after its failure to mitigate the asteroid, and it was not long thereafter that the true purpose of the Mirage Station was exposed to the present personnel in its entirety. Having helped design the guidance systems for the transit vehicle, Cypher took measures into his own hands for having been left behind, in the form of exacting swift vengeance.

He admitted that Tasha's father had died during the revolt. The containment of the base led to the entrapment of those personnel left here on the site, who had eventually succumbed to the disease. During the chaos of the initial clash with the mercenaries, there were a few of the original staff which had escaped via the underground rail system to the outlying shelters; many of them unknowingly spreading the MN4 contagion on their persons as they fled to the other bunkers along the underground subway system. It was ironic how all the precautions set in place to protect the underground facilities had been jeopardized by the fleeing faculty themselves, who had good reason to mask their personal involvement with this highly illicit operation from the rest of the shelter residents.

It was a grand failure. It never ceased to amaze me how mankind could be so arrogant and small-minded, and could never seem to grasp the larger picture or see anything beyond their own posturing. With their top officials slain in the catastrophic failure of the launch vehicle, the rest of the military staff tried to escape the facility on their own, and one by one, each of them had succumbed to their due fate. Many of the workers still lurked here in their infected state, mentally deranged and aimlessly shambling the corridors in search of food; staring listlessly behind their dull bloodshot eyes as the virus coursed through their veins.

Cypher had used his knowledge of the station and its computer system overrides to have the robotic automations help him construct a containment cell on the top floor. He had more than enough rations and supplies available for him in storage that would have sustained the thousands of workers that had once staffed this facility. He then devised an elaborate system for disinfecting any goods, and programmed the failsafe sequence to target anyone who either lacked security clearance or was infected. Confined here in solitude, Cypher lingered for the past several years, alone in his ivory tower.

He watched in earnest through the security feed during the mayhem that ensued around the base as the contagion had spread, and the once few weepers, quickly became many. This led to a problem that he had been working on, ever since he had imprisoned himself in his gilded glass cage. The power levels that maintained his elaborate system relied upon had become compromised over the span of time; and he needed to shut down the debilitating energy drain from the automations working feverishly in the biotech chamber on the blue level below. He was certain by the old woman's reaction to his tale, that she would be less than cooperative to assist him towards that ultimate goal.

These past years spent trapped inside his glass box had not gone entirely wasted for Cypher, while he worked diligently crafting a wild plan. On the launch pad in the underground bay, there sat a prototype shuttle that had been used as a model for the personnel transport created for the high officials. During his time incarcerated on the top floor, he had reassigned the robotic units in the bay to finish construction on the smaller model and to make it flight worthy. All that was left to complete his venue was to divert the excessive power being funneled away by the untiring automations in the Phase Development Lab, and have it diverted directly into the hydrogen cells on the launch vehicle. Cypher was an egocentric engineer who wanted to take his place among the stars as he felt he had deserved, and he was going to persuade his current guests to help him achieve that end.

The Run

Though his paranoia was clearly validated, Cypher took great measures to keep from putting himself at risk of meeting the same fate that had befallen the rest of the facility staff. He had seen how his coworkers had been mercilessly mauled and slaughtered and turned into the walking husks of their former selves. The dread of it kept him awake for days on end while he devised layers of security to guarantee his safety and remove any chance of exposure.

Former workers on detail at the base had been moved to the outlying shelters shortly before the comet strike, personnel such as Beatrice, who had been relieved of her duties in the blue level as the research tasks were left to be compiled by automation. Millions of chemical recipes and DNA strands from the infected hosts of this new disease had been left for the computers to analyze and sequence. When the mercenaries revolted against the research base, they had left the system crippled and slowed its progress. With no more active staff on duty, a failsafe lockdown of the contagion samples was left unhampered to continue its programmed functions without interruption.

The security system was protected by an encrypted firewall that Cypher was unable to access from the floor where he had imprisoned himself. After a great deal of probing, he revealed there was an entirely separate data server connected to the phase development lab, one which was heavily shielded from changes to its initial protocols. It had a direct power connection to both the redundant and reserve power source as a safety measure to keep it in operation. These were the very test samples that had been supplied to the military labs and cryogenic chambers, which had been relocated to several resident shelters along with the scientists while they secretly worked on infected humans with experimental drugs.

The power coil which carried electricity to the blue level was engineered to be foolproof. If the development lab should ever accidentally lose power, then the specimens which had been mixed and stored in refrigeration would be compromised. Years later, without human intervention by the outlying labs, the robotics had accumulated thousands of stacked samples, which were currently drawing excessive amounts of electricity from the crippled power supply. Because of the recent energy drain, the top floor systems were starting to get buggy, so Cypher had applied all his efforts towards the repair of the prototype ship. However, he found that remote control of the robotics in the launch bay had its limitations.

The service drones he had reset as sentries currently patrolling the halls of the laboratory wing kept the upper levels free of any wandering Weepers, but there were still countless numbers of the infected left roaming the facility. Understandably, Cypher did not wish to become one of them. By chance of her arrival, the functioning chip implant in Betty's hand granted her clearance to certain security operations they might come across. He only had to manipulate her to his will.

Cypher kept the core sample in his possession, counting on the fact that it could be used as leverage against Beatrice. With Tasha accepting solace to the fate of her father, the rest of us were stuck in a situation we had little control of. Getting to the lab had become a one-way trip and there was nothing here to keep our interest. Cypher had promised us answers but what he had offered still left us feeling unfulfilled.

Having sequestered the entire top floor for himself, our host agreed to let us return to the level below. Though Beatrice tried, she noticed her security chip would no longer override the controls to the elevator. Cypher had partial command of the facility except for access to the shielded systems in the Development lab. We returned to the break room in remorse to find that the bodies of our friends had been removed and their blood sanitized from the scene. With a measure of worry, we searched the entire floor and finally found Serena and the mute child at the far end of the Foyer, both huddled under blankets asleep in a dark corner.

"Are you two alright?" Thorn asked as he gently nudged

Serena awake with his hands, speaking softly enough not to wake the boy cuddled up next to her. She seemed a little shaken but recovered enough to answer.

"After you left, another robot entered the room and removed the damaged one we had destroyed, then it came back and took the bodies of our friends," she shuddered, "It didn't attack us. I was alone there and didn't know if shooting it might provoke it and I was worried the boy might get hurt, so we left the room to find a safe place to hide," she finished.

We disclosed what had happened upstairs on the top floor to her and of our eccentric host with whom we met. Tasha and her friends had retired back to the break room with Beatrice, as she found she was now unable to open any other doors on the blue level. Apparently, Cypher was able to block her access to the station's computer to keep her in check. I left Thorn there while he shared our tale with Serena as I walked back to the window to look out at the evening sky. I stood there peering at the dark swirling clouds as lightning flashed far in the distance.

It had been a long while since I had seen the stars, as there were only rare times when the clouds would part in the evening hours. Perhaps that is why I kept moving, always on the go; trying to find a better life for myself where there weren't hordes of weepers or people killing one another for mere scraps of food. There was no way to escape that world anymore; maybe I was just searching for another place where I could finally see the stars once again.

Suddenly, an intercom crackled on from a miniature video board on the far side of the room. A familiar voice issued from it, calling my name.

"You are the one they call Caitlin," the hushed voice hailed from a distance. With curiosity, I strode over to the sound to find a palm-sized viewing panel on the wall meant for video intercom use. Cypher sat there framed within the small digital screen.

"Yes," I answered in confusion, "...what do you want?" I inquired while feeling a little bewildered as to why he was contacting me in secret.

"I have a proposition for you, Miss," Cypher submitted with

feigned politeness, "to help you and your friends ...if you will do a favor for me, that is," he offered. I was listening. There wasn't much any of us had planned for after escaping this place if we ever managed to get out of here alive. Topside, the facility was placed beside a river gorge with high cliffs that circled the perimeter. The mountain tunnel was permanently blocked, and since we didn't have the gear to scale the high cliff walls that encompassed the facility, there was no way out but up. I did not realize until this very moment that 'going up' would be an option. To my complete surprise, Cypher offered to take us with him during the launch.

It seemed like a bizarre gesture. One that I wasn't sure if I found appealing, but I didn't want to speak for the rest of the crew. Sure, I had always wanted to visit space as a child, but I sure as fuck didn't want to stay there forever. His offer didn't come without risks, there was a great deal we would have to do.

"Why are you asking me, and not the others?" I inquired with a shrug of my shoulders as if I was a nobody. It simply didn't make sense to me, since I didn't exactly come across as the leader type.

"It seems to me that you and Beatrice appeared to have a history together," Cypher explained, "I have your image and data on file from your short stay with her at the Fallhaven shelter," he confessed, having hacked her personal files.

I really shouldn't have been surprised. The rail network had connected the bunkers to one another, so it would be safe to assume there was a data cable secured to each facility from the main research base. It was clear to him that we did not share any love for the old woman and Cypher wanted me to ask the others of my crew if they would accept his offer. Those whom agreed, he would grant passage to the Mirage orbital station if they so desired.

"And what about any of us who don't want to go, even if we do decide to help you?" I had to ask.

"The prototype vehicle was originally designed as a shuttle, rather than a simple rocket booster," Cypher countered, "that is why it was a 'prototype'. The final version was too large for that additional feature and had to be reengineered to the revised specifications. That means I can drop off anyone within a thousand-mile radius before leaving the atmosphere; as long as I have time to alter the flight plan, of course," he answered with that annoying signature grin of his.

His offer actually wasn't a bad one. He would give us as many supplies as we could carry and even locate an abandoned bunker or two within flight range for anyone who wanted to stay behind on the surface. Personally, he squabbled to question why anyone in their right mind would turn down the chance to live on the orbital station considering the current global conditions; but he was a man obsessed with science. I found the thought of living the rest of my life in a sterile vacuum under artificial light and filtered air entirely abhorrent. There was no replacement for the feeling of the wind in my hair and the earth beneath my feet, and being able to travel wherever I wanted; it was a sense of freedom I valued above all else.

Grudgingly, I agreed with Cypher that I would present his offer to the others, but that I couldn't make any promises. To this concession, he nodded and ended our brief conference with a tribute to have a robotic unit bring us purified water and prepared meals to the break room. With a click, the screen went black and I was left to ponder this new situation.

I advised Tasha and the other women that supplies were being delivered to us just moments before a robotic automation arrived, which made them jump out of their skin. Thorn enticed Serena and the child back to the main room where we ate the best meal we've had in years. Even the grub at Fallhaven had paled in comparison to the finer quality of this cuisine Cypher had presented. The administration here had apparently spared no expense of the taxpayer's money when it came to acquiring lavish personal perks for themselves, and considering the given circumstances, Cypher had been living quite well.

"Wow, fucking champagne!" Serena touted as she took another swig straight from the bottle. We had all lost our grip of lesser etiquette somewhere over the years, some of us more than others. The smile fell from her face when she set the bottle down, only to linger in silent thought as her eyes were drawn to the spot where Haiti had died. The breakroom was probably not the best place for us to stay, considering, but there were no other tables in the main foyer. Our host hadn't considered that we would not forget our fallen friends so easily; but in his limited psychosis, Cypher was likely unable to fathom how strongly it would affect us on an emotional level.

Beatrice sat alone at a second table, feeling shunned for her previous involvement with the viral outbreak and her former connection to this classified facility. The fact was, she had a lot to be ashamed of, but she was just one of many government workers who shared that guilt. However, in light of it all, the unexpected feast which we had been gifted had significantly helped to lift our spirits. It had been a good play on Cypher's part to offer us this carrot as a peace offering, especially so after suffering the whipping stick that took the lives of our two friends earlier that day.

I had to find a way to speak with each one of them in private in an effort not to reveal our hand to Betty about the proposition Cypher had made. Of course, Thorn was first on my list. We had some quality time to make up for as it was. I took his hand and dragged him out to the windowed foyer while Tasha and her girls heckled us under their breath. It was all in good fun.

"I'm sorry about what happened to your friends, Thorn," I whispered, savoring a shared moment together once again. He still looked shaken by the thought of what had happened earlier.

"Yeah, I'm going to miss Haiti and his funny accent, he was always upbeat," he glanced away with a heartbroken smile, "and though Killroy was a hard ass, he knew his shit," he turned back with a flash of shame over his choice of words in my presence, "...I mean, he knew his stuff," he apologized, not wishing to seem crude. I thought it was cute.

Like the rest of the crew, we were all exhausted; it had been a very taxing day. Our heads turned when we saw Beatrice exit the break room with a blanket and head down the hallway towards the Development lab. Feeling unwelcome, she was going to spend the night there alone. Cypher actually let her in, noting he could keep an eye on her from the security cameras if she managed to get herself into any trouble, so we were not too worried about it. It was probably for the best and was by design of our host that gave me the opportunity to openly speak with the rest of our companions without Betty overhearing. I just wanted to clear things with Thorn first.

While I was holding his hand, I told him how Cypher had contacted me through the video-com while he was tending to Serena, and of the offer he had made us. I explained how Beatrice fit into that equation, but the less she knew about it the better. The plan made sense to Thorn as I spelled out the details. Little did I know that Cypher was listening to every word as we conversed in hushed whispers out in the foyer.

Cypher's plan was relatively simple, considering we were fully aware that he only needed a few lackeys to complete it. The strategy he proposed was for us to go down into the launch bay and detach the power coupling to the lab and link it to the fuel cells of the prototype shuttle; all while avoiding any weepers in the area. He needed Beatrice to assist with granting security access to the power panel on the blue level to allow the encrypted security protocols to disengage.

"And how does he plan on convincing her to do that?" Thorn asked with a tone of doubt, knowing what kind of a stubborn fruitcake Betty could be at times.

"He is going to use that fragment we delivered as a 'primary core sample' or some such. Apparently, there had been a special room built to secure the meteor fragment, and introducing it into the system chamber will trigger a redundant program to reboot the development lab automations to start utilizing new test specimens directly from it," I repeated as best as I could what Cypher had related to me earlier.

The transition to the core specimen within that fragment would release the power lock and allow him to reroute the energy into the coils of the ship. Cypher would be employing us to do the dirty work, of course; but the offer to walk away with as many supplies as we could carry and a ride off this base was good enough for most of us. Then there was the question of who among us might want to go to the space station.

As much as I desired for time alone with him, it was news that simply could not wait. Thorn relayed the plan to Serena and the other girls in the break room who were picking through the last of the scraps of our dinner. It was a dicey plan, considering how large and dark that launch bay was. From what we saw, it had appeared like a giant maze from the window of the conveyor belt. None of us knew crap about space ships or energy coils, so we were leaving those details for Cypher to work out for us.

A new type of robotic servant equipped with several mechanical arms, rolled in and began cleaning up the table as we jumped out of its way, wary of how dangerous they could be. This time it stopped in front of me and a panel popped open from its torso, presenting a strange wristband with an elongated bar of black glass attached to it. With hesitation, I finally grabbed it; whereupon the panel promptly snapped shut and the robot resumed its duties cleaning up our dinner mess.

The rest of the crew looked at me peculiarly with an air of anticipation, which persuaded me to strap the device on. After a moment, a glitter of pixels lit up on the black panel and began to stack upon one another as little lights around the edge of the glass tapered towards them. A holographic screen materialized on my wrist with Cypher's dull face staring back at me. It soon switched to a red screen showing a topical floor plan outlining a direct path to the power coupling located at the center of the launch bay.

"Good, I see you got my gift," Cypher stated before the display switched, "we will use this device for communication during your jaunt downstairs so I can help guide you to your destination. In the meantime, get some rest and I suggest that you keep this little toy hidden from Beatrice." At that, the display blinked out and we settled down for the evening. Thankfully, the break room lights dimmed as we laid down to rest, and I wrestled with the strangest dreams that night.

I woke up next to Thorn on the floor in the foyer, which was certainly not the place I had fallen asleep. It was already late morning and he began to stir the moment I sat up. Quite dazed and confused as to why we were lying next to the window.

"How did I get out here?" I yawned in confusion while glancing out the tall windows to the gray clouds above.

"You were having nightmares and were talking in your sleep

last night," Thorn confessed as he petted my hair, and then plopped back down into the blanket crumpled upon the hard floor, "so I helped you out here because you were waking the others."

I felt a little embarrassed about that, but I certainly didn't remember getting up and coming out here. It was all a blur. I had a lingering feeling of something unpleasant but also a strange sense of relief. I blamed it on the stress; this day was starting off on an unusual note.

A chime came over the loudspeakers throughout the entire floor followed by Cypher addressing us, that breakfast would be served shortly and that we should all assemble in the break room. Large stainless steel bowls with extra gallons of water and a few towels were carted in by another automaton; allowing us to bathe to some extent. I made a mental note to try to follow one of those robots sometime to find out where they were coming from since Tasha had reported that all the other doors she had located were locked tight. Any attempt to bypass them would likely be thwarted, as Cypher was watching every move we made.

Another serving of high-quality rations was presented for us to gorge ourselves on; though notably, there was no alcohol provided this time. Thorn revealed that he had already spoken with the rest of our companions the previous evening while letting me sleep out by the entryway. Curiously enough, Betty didn't join us out in the break room for our morning meal. It was interesting to discover that both Serena and the child were more than eager to go to the Space Station when we completed our mission. Tasha and her friends were still undecided, but were leaning toward staying and were thinking about being dropped off somewhere by the coast.

Thorn did not immediately answer when I asked him about his plans. I didn't know why he was keeping it a mystery and felt a little dismissed by his avoidance to give me a clear answer. For some reason, I began to feel slightly guilty because I may have come across a little too anxious to follow his decision. I rolled up my sleeve to reveal the hologram communicator when it began to make a soft ticking sound. Cypher addressed the group on the holo-screen when it popped up.

"I've made preparations for the scheduled exercise this morning in the launch bay," he affirmed without pause, "is everyone ready to begin?"

"We haven't even made our final decisions yet about our plans afterward," Thorn responded, a little annoyed that Cypher was presuming we were all going to cooperate with his plan.

"I overheard your discussions last night, and believe I can provide each of you the final destinations you were considering. I assure you there is plenty of room on the Mirage Station for anyone else, including Serena and the child ...whose name I still didn't quite get?" Cypher paused in question.

"Neither did we," Thorn responded in kind, but Cypher was lost on the personal joke.

"I had a stack of rations and other useful odds and ends of supplies delivered to the cargo hold in the shuttle this morning," our host casually mentioned as he referred to the prototype ship, "The elevator will be opened at the end of the hour to take you down, please take the time to prepare yourself for the mission ahead," Cypher instructed and was about to sign off just before I caught him with a question.

"So, what's the plan with Beatrice, anyhow; what are we supposed to tell her?" I inquired.

"She slept in her Lab last night, and I informed her that I would release the meteor sample to her care so she may continue her research here at this base where she would be safe and all of her needs provided for," he added, "and in turn, she agreed to give me her full cooperation. She will join you at the elevator at the end of the hour," he finished and signed off.

Cypher left us wondering if that was merely some sort of ruse on his part since he was effectively disconnecting her lab from the power supply; but it was likely just a temporary matter until the ship launched. Whatever his ploy was, this really didn't sound like the greatest of ideas. At least the small wrist radio stayed on; displaying a rough digital map of the route we were to follow to get to the power conduit we needed to transfer.

We assembled when the hour passed and made our way to the elevator to find the meteor sample sitting in the center of the floor inside. Moments later, Beatrice arrived, flashing an arrogant smile that was quite out of character considering her attitude the previous evening. Cypher came over the intercom to ready us for what would lie ahead. With decisive grace, he colored in explanations for the few key questions we had.

There was a floor above the mainframe that was our first stop, which was our lead destination where we were to escort Betty and the asteroid fragment. Once there, she was to install the sample into the bio-matrix to initiate the new testing sequence of the purified strain. The automations would take over from there. He refrained from having a robotic unit deliver the volatile sample to the location itself, as hordes of weepers were known to attack the drones whenever they were patrolling the lower levels. Even though it would be a safer strategy, in this case, it wasn't worth the risk of losing the meteor sample.

Leaving Betty there, the rest of our team were to make our way to the launch chamber to reset the power coil from the supply conduit. We had been previously instructed to keep quiet about that part of the plan and follow Cypher's lead about what he meant by 'resetting' the coupling. Regardless, Beatrice didn't make a remark about it in question to our relief. With that, we checked our weapons again as the elevator began its long descent.

Serena felt bad about having to stay behind to watch the boy, even though Cypher had offered to watch over him and had assured us that the child would be kept safe. Still, her wound had not yet fully healed and she didn't want to leave the kid alone. Our host had promised that the elevator would be returned to take them both to the bay level once we had cleared the way. Cypher had related to us earlier that it would be best if Beatrice was not informed that there was a functioning ship located on the pad, lest she might attempt to interfere with its power supply.

Dropping to the lower levels, we came to a halt upon a secured floor. Betty had to wave her hand across the panel so her clearance could be read by the scanner. The doors slid open and the six of us flooded into the short corridor. Beyond its edge, there extended a metal walkway from the main structure out across the exposed wall of the massive launch chamber. We looked down from the high floor at the dark labyrinth we were about to enter in the moments to follow.

At the far end of the catwalk rested a thick ominous door of brushed steel. It appeared far more secure than any others we had seen on the site thus far. With an iron grip on the handle of the capsule, Betty lugged the core sample container over to the portal; now it was her show. She placed her hand upon the template, which scanned the data on her implant chip.

With protest from hidden hydraulics, the door parted from its interlocking sections and folded away. The interior revealed a surprisingly small chamber; lit from floor to ceiling. A slot, barely larger than the size of the containment sample box, sat embedded on the far wall. Two blinking screens on either side of the opening still displayed the active fail-safe protocol which had been initiated all those years ago.

Betty approached the digital keyboard and punched in a code, whereupon the shield door to the slot slid open with a hiss. With a moment of hesitation, she admired the stone in the reflecting light, and finally placed it within the niche. Back at the control panel, she engaged the device that locked the casing in place which sprayed it with a burst of sterilizing gas to sanitize the outer container. Just as quickly, a mechanical laser began to cut a hole in the protective glass of the box, spraying red sparks as it seared through the containment shield.

With a countdown ticking, a clock replaced the lit screens as a new bar displayed acceptance of the asteroid fragment. It only gave us a mere twelve-minute window prior to the ejection of the rock sample from its casing before it was deposited into the automation testing rig. That wasn't much time considering where we were heading. We had not bargained for such a narrow timeframe to get this done.

"Twelve minutes?" Ava exclaimed in dismay, "Why didn't you tell us that was all the time we had to get down there?" she demanded towards the old woman while I kept my communicator with Cypher hidden under my sleeve.

"I didn't know what it was set for," she spat back in defense as the timer ticked down to the system reboot, "Cypher said you need to get down to the coupling to make sure we don't lose power to the lab by securing it during the transition," she advised. This we already knew, but our actual mission was to disengage the power supply completely and redirect it to the fuel coils of the shuttle. He had tricked her with a lie.

"What are you going to do while we are down there?" Tasha asked Beatrice, who stood monitoring the screen while a faint growl of countless weepers echoed up from below from the noise of the countdown blaring over the speakers throughout the bay.

"I will be fine," she granted, "this vault door will close behind me and nothing can get in here without security access. Just make sure to collect me on your way back up top," Beatrice scolded with her finger.

Another glance at the monitor screen while the clock ticked relentlessly lower only served to fuel our level of anxiety. We rushed back to the open elevator as the door to the chamber folded shut once again, sealing the old woman within. Once inside the lift, I heard a tick click from my wrist and rolled up my sleeve to expose the radio device. Now uncovered, the holographic screen sprung to life.

"My data screens show that the introduction of the specimen sample has been confirmed," Cypher concurred, "and it appears you now have a limited time span to reach the conduit located on the pad, to transfer the connection."

"Yeah, it sure would've helped if you had fucking told us about that!" Ava shouted over my shoulder towards the small screen.

"As I've mentioned before, that system is protected by a firewall; there was no way of telling how long it would take the infusion cycle to commence," he admitted, "that said, I would suggest a measure of haste and less arguing at this point," he snapped back at her.

"Why do we need to do this at the exact time of the reboot, why not just manually detach and reconnect the power cable into the ship and be done with it?" Kel inquired, as we were not clear on the specific details. It was a question that Haiti or Felix could have answered, but they were no longer with us.

"One cannot simply disconnect that many Terawatts of

energy," Cypher explained, "for one, you would not be able to disengage it from the primary conduit, and the recoil of separation would cause an electrical chain reaction. Believe me, this exercise would be much simpler if we were able to shut down the hydrogen generators at their source ...but that is not an option," he offered with a condescending tone.

A lighted bar ran through the wire-frame graph on the screen, mapping our way. Unfortunately, due to the new time limit, Cypher had to recalculate a last-minute detour to get us there before the countdown elapsed. The new route took us through a portion of the crumbling construction platforms. The way was dark and we really did not want to risk such a hazardous course.

When the elevator doors opened on the bay level, we decided to split up, giving us two chances to make it to the target on time. Tasha and Ava could move faster, so they would go the long way. They took the briefest of moments to memorize the path on my hologram display and took off running. As Kel's wounded leg left her handicapped, she decided to climb the tallest construction rig near us to help provide cover fire from a vantage point with her sniper rifle.

Thinking out of the box, I had wondered why Cypher didn't just open the bay doors and let the sunlight in so we could have better visibility. As it turned out, there were certain steps in the system's launch protocol that needed to be tripped in sequence before that could happen. The bay doors would not open without the ship prepped for launch, and that tier wouldn't initiate until the vehicle was fully fueled; and of course, we couldn't fuel up the energy coils until the electrical matrix was realigned.

The timer on my fancy wrist radio showed we had less than ten minutes left. Thorn and I made for the new detour while Kel scrambled up the nearest platform crane. Weepers in the bottom level began to stir, and we heard their growls and errant shrieks echoing from the dark shadows. My heart started pounding and I began to wonder if this whole endeavor had been a huge mistake.

The floor level had a mixed stench of rusted steel and ozone. To make matters worse, a light mist clung to the floor, hampering our view. After crawling on our bellies under a pair of pressure tanks, we scurried up a building crane and made a risky jump to a construction platform that creaked and swayed precariously as we landed upon it with our combined weight. We could tell that the weepers in this section had caught our scent as their glowing eyes reflected in the floodlights began to turn our way from the darkness of the shadows. Strapping our rifles to our backs, we had to make a jump for an exposed undercarriage and we swung across.

"You've got to be fucking kidding me," I breathed aloud as I looked below while Thorn took the lead.

Beneath us, a group of infected began to swarm, reaching out for us as they growled from the gloom below. That was incentive not to slip, which I nearly did more than once on the slick rusted steel. This course required the athletic tone of a marathon runner, which I was not; and I certainly wasn't accustomed to such demanding acrobatics. Thorn caught me on the far side as we landed onto a turnstile that left us just out of reach of the ground.

I had to glance at the holo-screen once again to figure where we were supposed to head next. For lack of any buttons on the wristband, I waved my hand through the hologram in desperation to reach Cypher.

"Hey!" I pleaded towards the communicator, trying not to excite the weepers weaving through the maze of machinery towards us, "Are you there? Where do we go now?" I pleaded as Thorn and I could not make sense of the new route etched on the small screen. From here, we could see the central bay and the secondary shuttle, which was secured by a thick restraining clamp. Twenty yards from it sat a raised hub, with several wires and cables that snaked away in various directions off the platform, one of which led to the rear of the shuttle.

"Give me a moment," Cypher answered in return. Just then, a huge mechanical arm from a nearby crane swung around at disturbing speed and landed with a thud at the edge of the turnstile to act as our bridge towards the launch platform. It was difficult to climb up its enormous curved claw, and even more so across its structural arm to the far end where another similar crane moved as its immense servos whined while it reached out to connect our path midair, which effectively kept us out of reach of the mass of weepers swarming below.

Not far away, Ava and Tasha were making a sprint for the conduit on their own path. Tasha took the front lead with a set of double pistols, gunning down weepers to clear the way as they bolted ahead. These poor souls were still wearing the tattered remains of their uniforms, some donning jumpsuits or stained lab coats of their former stations. There were still hundreds of infected lingering here, many of them huddled in dark corners or shambling aimlessly about, on whom they didn't bother to waste their ammunition.

The green spotlights in the launch chamber made the eerie glowing eyes of the weepers appear even more sinister. It made me wonder if even a small piece of their minds lamented, knowing that they had become victims by their own hand. Rifle shots cracked the still air as Kel sniped at stray weepers from her nested position far above, helping to clear a safe path for us. With the timer now under five minutes, we had to make a dash for the conduit.

Dropping hard onto the narrow ledges of the robotic crane, we found ourselves on the far edge of the tarmac. Cypher's alternate route had not given consideration for any delays, such as the dozen looming figures that had crawled up upon the launch pad before us, blocking our way. Shots rang out, but at this distance, more of Kel's strikes missed as bullets ricocheted off the concrete deck. Around us, we heard the low whir of enormous winding servos.

Giant metal arms reached out to pluck the weepers up one by one, as huge robotic pincers snapped at the infected creatures. We dodged their swooping arms while hoping that Cypher possessed a finer control of these hulking automations than it currently appeared. After we barely missed being crushed by the cranes more than once, we dared to skirt the outer edge while we took potshots at any weeper that tried to grasp at our legs as we ran across the ledge. Those ghouls who had who had managed to scale the upper platform, led chase behind us.

Out of breath, I turned to see weepers being flung high into the air by the wildly swinging arms of the crane, which were inherently slow and lacked the subtle dexterity for picking off their moving prey. Even so, they were deadly allies when they found their mark. Infected blood sprayed across the deck whenever a weeper was squashed to a pulp by a mechanized clamp or had its body severed in two while the lower half kept walking a few awkward steps before collapsing, spilling its entrails. The entire launch platform had been transformed into a gallery of death.

We made it to the conduit with only a minute to spare and took cover behind the hub, shooting down any weeper that escaped Kel's sniper rounds or the reach of the construction claws under Cypher's control. Tasha and her friend were gaining ground on us when the clock finally ticked to zero. With that, the power in the entire bay flickered, with only the red emergency beacons of the upper conveyer belt tram left shining into the bay. With a dying hum, the lights on the conduit itself blinked out as the power draw terminated and the system began its reboot. Thorn and I looked at one another and hastily dropped our guns to the floor as we took our positions on either side of the power hub; knowing we only had a few moments to complete what needed to be done.

Square in the center of the exposed hub was a manual reset switch. Around the edge of the platform, Tasha and Ava were making their approach through the stray weepers being drawn by the sound of their gunfire. Thorn manually uncoupled the feed marked for the Development Lab, while I traced the line to the ship and connected it in its place. We stood there in silence wondering what to do next while the crane arms locked in frozen silence without power, as more of the infected began to creep upon our position. Cypher popped up again on the holo-screen on my arm to give us additional instructions.

"Caitlin, as the power begins to cycle back on, you will need to activate the reset switch on the center column," he advised, "you must only do so while it is within the shown safety range of the meter, before it reaches maximum load."

Thorn suddenly snatched up his gun off the floor and brought his rifle to bear, to cut down the few weepers that made it through the forest of giant robotic arms, which had now slowly began to regain power while I was busy attending the switch. I noted the series of colored lights were aligned in the hardwired system when I grabbed the thick handle with both hands to push the lever into place when the levels hit the green bar of the meter. It was difficult pulling it back into activation when I met resistance, and grunted with the effort as I pulled on it with all my weight. To our relief, it snapped into place just a hair before exceeding the limit of the green bar.

Energy snaked through the cable to the ship as white dots of light appeared upon its outer housing. A set of flood lamps appeared below the underbelly of the ship as the giant clamp that secured it slowly transferred the shuttle vehicle into the center of the tarmac.

"T-minus fifteen minutes until launch. Secure all cargo," a computerized voice echoed through the bay. Thorn and I looked at one another in stunned disbelief, suddenly realizing that Cypher had shortchanged us on time yet again.

Launch

The noise blaring from the speakers roused every weeper in the structure as we heard moans and shrieks arise from the surrounding walls of the launch bay. The battling arms of the robotic cranes ceased shortly thereafter, leaving us to fend for ourselves. Shots continued to ring out as Kel attempted to compensate for the sudden lack of backup support the cranes had provided. Tasha and Ava were finally able to make their way to the top of the pad mere moments after we had finished resetting the power coupling.

With a jolt, a distant crane arm extended from the walkway along the wall support above us and swung out to breach the tip of the tarmac as it extended. This was unexpected, but we had failed to anticipate how Cypher had planned to make it down from his gilded cage on the top floor to the dock of the ship. We kept cover fire as the expanding deck took its sweet time to bridge the gap between us.

We were expecting that Cypher had picked up Serena and the child on route as he had promised, but we were distressed to see Beatrice standing alone before us when the bridge gate door cycled open. She had an irritated look fuming in her eyes as though she was about to lose her temper. This was a confrontation we had readily expected at some point but weren't exactly ready to address at this very moment during a firefight. Luckily, we still had our firearms to keep the old woman in line.

A strange noise behind us made us all turn in unison when a hum of gears rotated up a single glowing cylinder from the center of the bay floor. It twisted once, and a smaller robot arm unfolded from the tarmac floor and promptly placed the illuminated rod into a secured hold within the ship.

"What the hell was that?" Tasha inquired, taking a moment to catch her breath between taking shots at any stray weeper that wandered within range.

"That was the primary sample!" Betty snapped in disbelief as she hastily unfurled her sleeve to expose an odd glass wristband, identical to the one I was wearing. Her eyes lifted to mine in bleak astonishment when she saw a duplicate one strapped to my wrist. It was then that we looked at one another and realized that Cypher had been playing us both.

"That bastard," I fumed under my breath, though loud enough for everyone to hear. Regardless, the irony of it took but a moment to set in, "...what did he promise you?" I demanded towards Betty as Thorn turned his rifle in her direction.

"Why is the power to my lab shut down?" She barked back with twice the antagonism I could muster. With a quick glance to the conduit, it only took her a few seconds to piece together that the coupling lying beside the hub, which had fed current to the Laboratory, had been disengaged.

"Well, that arrogant asshole still needs to get to his ship," Thorn noted the obvious, and that we would be there to stop him. It didn't seem like the smartest of tactics to betray both of us without having clear access to the shuttle after the fact.

"T-minus twelve minutes till launch. Cargo is secured. All unessential personnel are ordered to clear the area," the computer voice echoed through the dome. We passed a glare at one another in defiance, 'like hell we are.'

"Why would he put that fragment sample on the ship?" Ava demanded in confusion as to what had just transpired.

"He plans to use it for himself," Tasha finished, having connected the dots of his intricate ruse.

"Cypher had the fragment sample processed and verified for its prime DNA strain before it was resealed in a containment cylinder and transferred to that ship," Beatrice related as she pointed at the shuttle. Looking upwards, we noticed that the steel walkway, which had led directly to the processing chamber where we had left Betty, had doubled as a pedestrian ramp down to the launch pad.

"So, where is this fucktard, so we can have a word with him?" Ava offered with a snarky tone as she turned to take another crack shot, blowing a large hole in the head of a weeper that had clambered up onto the deck just a few yards away. The countdown voice echoed yet again as the green spotlights at ground level turned red, while a series of blue rotating strobe lights that lined the top edge of the bay blinked on.

"T-minus ten minutes until launch. All personnel are to report to their assigned stations," the announcement echoed from above. With that, there was an unnerving moment when the entire building creaked as the interlocking bolts on the silo hatch began to cycle, releasing their pins. With a horrible grinding wrench, the enormous bay doors dropped and began to slide open. Sunlight washed in like heavenly light, blinding us and weepers alike as it cut into the dark chamber. A shrill scream arose from the ghouls that were sensitive to the bright light having lived in consuming darkness for so long. Many quickly cowered and slunk away into whatever protective shadow they could find.

Although the sunlight was a welcoming sight, it came at a price. The top of the bay doors had not been cleared for the pre-launch but had been peppered with several stray military vehicles which had been left abandoned during the incursion many years ago. Trucks and jeeps, and fuel barrels, came tumbling down several stories, smashing onto the surrounding machinery and equipment. Weepers shrieked as they were crushed under tons of steel, spraying their infected organs and gore across the scaffolding. Floodlights exploded upon impact and ruptured tanks caught fire as thick clouds of soot bloomed with flames that rose into the misty morning light.

The percussion shook the launch pad as the shuttle swayed within the grip of its iron clamps. For a brief moment, the construction cranes had frozen in place; this led us to assume that Cypher was no longer at the controls in his glass penthouse, but on his way down to the ship. From the causeway where Beatrice had arrived, we heard Serena yelling, limping towards us in exhaustion, a look of despair shrouding her face. We could barely make out what she was shouting over the noise of bursting pipes and crashing equipment raining upon us; "The boy, he has the boy..."

While she was stumbling halfway along the catwalk, we peered up just as a large shadow momentarily blocked the glare of sunlight while the bay doors above opened ever wider. A large tanker truck had tipped over the edge directly above her position, the supporting asphalt beneath it now removed. At first, the engine carriage dangled and swayed precariously as we called out to Serena, who was unable to hear us over the noise of grinding metal. In desperation, I dropped my gun to run to her aid, seeing the danger looming above.

A strong arm yanked me back. I turned to see Thorn had grabbed my shoulder to stop me. My turquoise eyes looked into his, colored with confusion. The feeling of betrayal melted into dread that felt like my blood in my veins had turned to stone. Time seemed to slow as the tanker slipped over the edge with a shriek of metal and crushed the walkway were Serena had stood. After the impact, there was nothing left but smoke and twisted debris where she had been, the center of the bridge had buckled into a tangle of scrap steel and roaring flames.

Thorn clung onto my shoulder as tears welled in my eyes. She was gone. Serena had been alone on the bridge, yelling something about the child. Had he died too?

Upon the tarmac floor, a central ring in front of the ship lit up, expanding like a capsule from a shell layered within. In a flurry of thick steam, Cypher stepped out of the luminous tube. We should have guessed that the executive level would have its own private elevator passage to the launch floor. He took a step to one side, dragging the small boy out in front of him by the scruff of his ragged collar, with a gun in his other hand pointed at the child's head.

"Stay back, and he won't get hurt," Cypher warned as he tapped an electronic pad strapped to his cuff. When he did so, the giant robotic cranes once again came to attention, their enormous claws poised threateningly as Cypher inched his way towards the open shuttle door before him.

Even now, Cypher's germaphobe fears were apparent as he shuffled warily towards the boarding hatch while wearing a clumsy biohazard suit. A shot rang out from across the bay as the report struck the ship's hull next to him. Shocked by how close the sniper round had been, Cypher lost composure and turned towards the direction where the bullet had come from. He immediately eyed Kel who was steadying herself for another shot; cursing herself under her breath for having missed her first crack at him through the smoke and shadows of busted steel from across the bay.

With the touch of a button on his wrist, a robotic arm obeyed his command and twisted with haunting stealth towards Kel, snapping its giant claws at her angrily as its finite grasp was but a few yards out of reach. With a growl, Cypher tapped again at the controller on his wrist as the crane arm reacted and snatched a nearby pressure tank in its claws, ripping it up from its bolts. In one smooth motion, it launched the canister towards Kel, who was perched precariously in her sniper's nest on top of the construction platform. She raised her arms defensively in vain as if that would save her, only to breathe a sigh of relief as the heavy tank fell short.

It was a grim moment of tension as the pressure tank slammed into the ground at the base of the platform. With a hiss, it exploded. The percussion blew Kel high into the air and down onto the jagged supports, skewering her through. Her first breath was a cough of blood as she struggled to get to her feet.

Looking down, she touched the restraints of twisted metal spikes that had pierced through her body, gripping them in disbelief. Her eyes glazed over with a final sigh as she looked up through the black smoke that rose into the cloudy sky above. The bay doors snapped open and locked into place as the computer came over the speaker system when a siren horn signaled.

"T-minus five minutes until launch. Bay doors are clear for liftoff. Shuttle gate will lock in two minutes," its warning hail rang through the thick air.

Ava didn't waste the opportunity to raise her weapon while Cypher was distracted controlling the crane arm during his assault on Kel. Dropping to one knee, she brought up the scope of her rifle to be sure of her shot and not harm the child. Adjusting to aim high, she had his head in her crosshairs when she felt something suddenly yank her feet out from underneath her from behind, and she landed hard on her face. Nose bloodied, she reached for her rifle that lay on the bay floor, now several inches beyond her grasp.

Tasha turned to see her friend lying flat on her stomach and in the claws of a raging weeper, which was in the act of dragging her backward off the platform edge. Finding her magazine empty, she dropped her pistol to grab Ava's hand, straining to hold her back as the infected creature growled in defiance. Thorn and I turned to see what had happened, and he lunged for Tasha to anchor her from being pulled over the threshold and into the grasping arms of several weepers which had seized Ava's legs. I was torn, not knowing what to do; caught in the middle of having to choose between saving the young child or my friends.

Beatrice had no ethical margins to weigh her down, and she snatched up the rifle I had discarded just before Thorn had held me fast during my futile attempt to save Serena. All too eager to exact her revenge, the old woman barely bothered to take aim. Having never fired a rifle before, she pulled the trigger and lurched back, knocked off balance by the recoil. The shot passed inches from the little boy's face, grazing Cypher's wrist and the electronic band he wore.

Betty regained her poise again to take another shot just as Cypher turned towards her, his eyes grew wide in fear from behind the faceplate of his protective suit; now fogged by the moisture of his nervous breath. His grip loosened on the child, who jerked himself free from his grasp and dove into the protection of the open hatch of the nearby shuttle. A sour *'click-click'* met Betty's ears as she squeezed the trigger again and again, while a grimace fell across her lips as she realize the gun was out of ammo. Glancing down at the punctured suit and his own warm blood dripping onto the tarmac floor, Cypher dissolved into hysterics.

He was just as quickly silenced by a rifle butt to the side of the head that cracked open his faceplate and popped it free from its bindings. Beatrice was on him like a wildcat as he fell back onto the hard floor while she ripped the hood from his bio-suit, screaming like a banshee. Cypher was in a frenzy as he tried to fend her off but he was no match for her unbridled fury. He shrieked and wailed at her to stop. In her rage, she grabbed a dismembered arm from a weeper lying within reach, which had been cast there from its previous encounter with a robotic crane; and she began to mercilessly beat him in the face with its stump, dark blood mashing everywhere.

I was so aghast at her savage attack, and that she would risk infecting herself without restraint. It was without merit; though I agreed that Cypher got what he deserved but I was still stunned by the method of his punishment. I rushed past her as she was beating him senseless and dove into the ship to find the child. Seconds dragged on as I searched for the boy within the cramped vessel.

The carnage outside seemed muffled and distant from within the confines of the insulated shuttle. Wiggling past a bulkhead, I finally found a pair of small feet tucked within a cramped compartment. I leaned over and looked into the boy's eyes for the very first time, which were a vibrant mixture of gray and green. They were large and glassy, and I read a great deal of his past within them in that still moment.

"We have to go, we can't stay here..." I started to comfort him, but still apprehensive to force him from his hiding spot. He just looked back at me in confusion, as if to ask 'where else can we possibly go?' His engraved doubt caught me off guard. The initial plan was to depart by this shuttle and head for the coast to drop off a few passengers, while Thorn and I were still deciding what we were going to do. In that heated moment, the boy had chosen to vault into the ship for safety to escape his assailant. The two of us never heard the ringing of the final hail from the loudspeaker outside.

"Shuttle doors sealed, T-minus three minutes until liftoff. All personnel are to clear the launch pad."

I had managed to lift the child off his feet by his willingness to take my hand and we made our way back to the hatch in haste, only to rush my last steps towards the door just as it pressure-cycled shut with a hiss. Through the portal window, I could see Beatrice; she stood up slowly over Cypher's limp body, his legs still twitching in spasms. She dropped the severed arm she had used to club him to death and looked up into the sky as she heard the words of the computer sound through the bay of the impending launch.

She turned towards me just as the hatch pins locked; an odd look of surrender and satisfaction damp within her eyes, her face dripping with infected blood. Her body suddenly jerked back; the shot that took her down muffled from the shielded walls of the ship. A moment later Thorn was there, his hand upon the window as the energy coils began to whir and the shuttle switched to an automatic pilot sequence. I stood there looking into Thorn's dark eyes on the far side of the thick glass of the portal as we shared a growing ache of despair.

I turned and rushed for the cockpit door to stop the launch, only to beat helplessly upon the locked hatch as I punched at it with my fists. Blue letters blinking across the panel 'Security access not recognized.' The chip I needed to gain entry to the cockpit was embedded within Betty's hand, laying mere feet outside the sealed portal. There was nothing I could do.

The coils powered up to a high pitch as I jumped back to the porthole window, Thorn and Tasha were standing farther away, shielding their eyes as the thrusters under the ship kicked in. Blast shields rose around the ship, directing the force into exhaust tubes, which explained the purpose of the massive heatsinks we had discovered lining the rail depot. There was no sign of Ava, her body had been drawn over the verge of the platform and the weepers had taken her. Tasha had put a merciful bullet to her head, as Ava had pleaded in her last moments before being torn apart. I stood there at the window and cried, helpless and afraid. I couldn't tell if Thorn could read my lips as I tried to find something ...anything to say.

"Don't forget me..." I uttered, torn with anguish.

The clamps that restrained the ship unbuckled as the leveling thrusters initiated, and we felt the ship rise. It hovered for a moment as a soft female voice began to count down thirty seconds. The little boy grabbed my shirt, tugging at me; but I didn't know what he wanted. He finally gave up and crawled past the bulkhead to where he had hidden before, tucking himself into the narrow crawlspace.

There were no seats in the hold, and it finally dawned on me that it had all been an act; Cypher had thoroughly deceived us about loading the shuttle with supplies and being able to transport us as passengers. Cypher had never intended to take any of us aboard when he escaped the lab; we were to be left behind and discarded.

Neon biohazard signs lined the walls along with numerous warning tags within the small cabin. This had never been a prototype model as Cypher had claimed; the sole function of this ship had been to deliver the secured pathogen to the space station. It was the designated transit vehicle to bring the dangerous microbe to the orbiting station without risking their key personnel, who were supposed to have arrived in the first shuttle launch, which Cypher had scuttled.

The view outside the small window became fogged as a white mist enveloped the ship. Tasha and Thorn made a run for cover from the blast as the crane arms lowered in unison while thick steel barriers folded out from the edge of the platform and locked into place. With an audible metal 'pop' the power cable detached, and with a horrendous scream the engine coils ignited. I felt the unyielding pull of gravity wrench me off my feet as a steel brace raced up to greet me, and everything went black.

* * *

My head ached terribly and I could feel the sore knot on my head when I awoke. I almost passed out again when I tried to stand up, noting that I felt lighter once I had finally gotten on my own two feet. I was still lingering in a state of shock as I called out for the boy; not finding him within his previous hiding place. My back throbbed with pain as I stumbled out of the open hatch and into a brightly lit corridor.

It was a strange change to be in a structure that was so sterile with walls covered in glossed metal and clean white panels. Still in a daze, I did not quite know where I was until I passed by a thick window that enveloped the night sky. It was strange, I thought, as it had been mid-morning when the shuttle had launched, just now noticing as my vision cleared how the blackness beyond was speckled with countless stars. I made my way through another doorway while noting that the air had a strange taste to it.

I found a ladder that took me to what appeared to be the main bridge of a ship. It wasn't the active panes or blinking lights, nor the numerous displays quietly graphing data that caught my attention, but the glowing image of the Earth that glared in through the port windows that left me mesmerized. I was on the Mirage Space Station gently gliding through space in orbit. From here, the world looked calm, quiet, and content. I knew it was a facade of course; for our planet was not at peace.

I didn't know if I should laugh or cry in that frozen moment, only realizing how easy it is to feel so detached when you've distanced yourself from the truth. The small boy strode into the room, distracted by something he was carrying in his tiny hands. He found me standing there alone on the bridge and took my hand, placing in my palm the stem of a small white flower with its lush green leaves intact. I gazed at it for a moment in respite, then placed the tiny blossom gently upon the console and looked down at the display. Though Cypher had cleansed the space station of its active personnel, it had remained fully operational all this time. The air was filtered and reprocessed by a self-sustaining terrarium that recycled the water supply. Clearly, the reclamation systems had been placed on automation long ago.

I followed the boy back to the terrarium where we found a jungle of plants of every species, growing in harmony, fed by an intricate system of biofilters into a lush botanical garden. Exploring the station further, there were scores of storage cells packed with untouched cargo and medical labs equipped with dozens of containment modules. I walked with the boy by my side among the empty chambers and maze of corridors lined throughout the superstructure that radiated a haunting sensation to its forgotten purpose. Touching my scalp, I noticed a trickle of blood and felt a persistent throbbing in my head that grew worse with every step.

The Mirage was a massive station equipped with a vast array of solar collectors that could sustain a crew of hundreds, supplied for all of our top leadership and the privileged elite, all of whom had never step foot here. We returned to the control room where I began feverishly searching the data screens for a spare ship or evacuation pod; any form of transport to get us back to the surface. With final submission, I realized there were none; Cypher had long since sabotaged them all in his previous efforts to purge the station.

Isolated from all the others on the bridge, a single red screen demanded my attention and I was drawn towards it while the child took a seat in a console chair next to me, quietly examined the tiny flower he had plucked from the station's greenhouse.

The blinking screen ceased when I finally placed my hand on the trimmed console, and its image widened to reveal that the MN4 viral package delivered from the shuttle had been assimilated into the system. It then occurred to me that this station wasn't just an asylum for the top brass, but had been developed with a bioweapon delivery system designed for warfare. Mirage had not been created to protect the best minds of our race, but as a disgraceful defense system they could employ to intimidate countries, or use to instigate preemptive strikes against any nation which failed to comply with their demands. Privileged with this power, they could enact global control far out of reach, where nobody could ever touch them.

As a safeguard, Cypher had evidently programmed a one-hour timer to be initiated after infusion of the purified KRI pathogen into the biodefense systems. He had planned to run this place alone, to act as God over the decaying world spinning below. The consoles themselves were unhindered in their function; for it didn't recognize that there were actually no generals here, no scientists, nor pompous bureaucrats, or oppressive government officials to run amuck in this flying ivory tower ...there was just a young nobody sitting at the controls.

Looking at the timer, there was now less than twenty minutes left on the countdown before it locked the system, the screen requesting a code to abort the sequence; but unfortunately, it was a code that only Cypher knew. The only choice the screen offered was between an offensive counterforce strike, or a full system purge of the deadly designer virus. Of course, this program was an alteration of the original protocols which

Cypher had initiated when he had finally taken control of the station's core systems.

I was mildly surprised when the little boy stepped over and pointed to one of the two tabs, as if to prompt my choice. He gazed out at the Earth below us and turned to look up at me with his soft green eyes, for they were strangely delicate, yet blooming with a sense of empathy for the twisting and conflicting emotions now swirling within me as if he was providing consent to the difficult decision I had to make, now wavering unsteadily under my hands, before I gently touched the switch.

A blue light lit the room as all systems suspended while a sleek cylindrical pod jettisoned from the center of the station and fired towards the cloud-filled planet below. A strange calm fell over me as I looked down at my hand in neither wonder nor surprise; only accepting the actions my subconscious had taken without further thought. The look in the little boy's eyes said everything, and I realized the child had persuaded me to do what I already knew should be done. Instead of purging the virus and destroying it, I had commenced a global strike.

Curiously, I felt no remorse as some might assume. There was no need to prolong the discomfort and contemplation any other person might take to question my actions. Most people would defend mankind and all its accomplishments over the countless millennium; our arts and science, our music and poetry, the fantastic and incredible inventions humanity had created, the things of beauty and pursuit of love; and yet I had ended it all without hesitation ...realizing that my final judgment to the fate of our world had already been decided long ago.

The payload of the missile deployed mere moments before it touched the atmosphere. I watched with cold resolution as a countless number of self-guided cluster missiles detached and sped towards every major metropolis across the globe. The modified super virus would spread unchecked, infecting every species of mammal with the toxic germ; there was little chance that anyone would survive the new pandemic that would follow in its wake, creating enhanced raging mutations that would ravage the planet and reset the ecosystem after the human race, as we knew it, had been erased from the world.

Mankind had proven itself a dangerous and unpredictable species, and thus, had chosen its destiny long ago; it was only our technology and our ability to advance to this point in history that we finally caught up with our own self-persecution.

I felt tired and numb as I felt warm blood began to trickle from the trauma to my head. It was from the injury that I had suffered during the launch and noticed my vision beginning to fade. I no longer had the luxury of time to think about the nameless child who sat quietly beside me in his innocence, nor how he might survive here abandoned and alone after I was gone. I slumped down onto the floor of the bridge feeling drained and sleepy; and though my head was throbbing, I felt a twinge pull at my heart like a distant ache as I thought about Thorn ...and what might have been.

As I closed my eyes a final time, I considered the lives of the countless survivors who had struggled and sacrificed so much of themselves just to live another minute of another day through the long unforgiving years since the catastrophic event that destroyed the arrogance of our toxic civilization. That time had passed, and through the eyes of a child, we had offered a gentle mercy. Like a broken mirror, we had been cursed these past seven years as the Earth was cleansed of our taint.

It was time for the human race to stop sifting through these splintered shards in such bitter desperation to only find fractured reflections of ourselves, and to finally accept that the dream of what mankind might have been was forever shattered, and could never truly be whole again.

Afterword

The MN4 asteroid event forecast in April 2029, is not so rare an occurrence as one might think; although it is the possible, yet probable circumstances, that give such a colorful twist to this tale. The sobering reality is that we live in a world that is vulnerable to face such cataclysms in many forms; yet our civilization still endures, though it mostly does so out of blissful ignorance.

The human race has climbed to a level of technology where we can harness the limitless energy of the sun, the global winds, and geothermal power to meet all our needs, and beyond, yet our species still wastes an unwarranted amount of energy and capital on trivial wars over foolish and phantom beliefs, antiquated borders, and nonrenewable resources. Each day, humanity destroys far more than it will ever create. Ironic as it is that we claim to possess the intelligence to create such wonders but lack even the most subtle measure of sensibilities when wielding our power over nature; and that we instead, choose to abuse such misguided potential against our fellow man for nothing more than pettiness and personal gain.

Though asteroid Apophis is bound to arrive, I wonder if by 2029 that our societies might ultimately crumble into the shadow of martial law as foretold within, where people are scared and intimidated in the name of compliance. It would also be interesting to conclude if digital ID and RFID implants might someday become commonplace, only to have our every word and movement recorded, and tracked under an umbrella of constant surveillance. Some may believe that it is a work of fiction that our global internet and media is manipulated and censored, where free communications are restrained and could be suspended in a time of crises by a secret kill-switch. Some may also regard this as a saga of conspiracy when government entities overplay their hand only to invade and occupy foreign nations on unsupported whims, and their fleeced citizens are routinely force-fed justifications for such immoral behavior and blind misconduct under the false disguise of their own security.

When might a story foretell of a dystopian age in the far future when people would be imprisoned and tortured without charges, or a culling of the masses on nothing but fabricated allegations and corralled into prison camps as forced labor, where food, medicine, and the most basic of freedoms are used as leverage against them. It would be a vibrant yarn that spins tales of Government forces resorting to covert military strikes as a means to an end, or exploiting finance branches that spread malware and forge encrypted trenches to commit currency racketeering aimed to cripple economies. This novel may be nothing more than a rich fable of such legal authorities, who stoop so disgracefully low and conspire together to promote their own continued existence and bloated budgets by inventing scenarios of scandal and conflict merely to unleash their own dark design, while it is the protected who become the prey.

If we should ever find ourselves in such a microcosm as these extraordinary circumstances and fictional characters within, where the world we once knew collapses and becomes blurred by relentless oppression that creates anarchy and civil unrest; a final question must be asked. Who among us will refuse to obey the mindless commands from ruthless tyrants who compel us to commit atrocities against one another? If ever a day should come, who among the waking world would take a stand for what is right while they pick through what splintered shards are left of our shattered world in hopes of finding an honest reflection of themselves, and take the time to dedicate their lives towards a deeper philosophy and uphold the fragile dream that there is a better way for us to live and coexist in peace, as we share this world together.

About the Author

Michel Savage has been devoted to writing throughout his career. If one reads between the lines, they will find his novels revolve around the reminder that we are only borrowing our small place on this planet but for a brief period of time, and to take responsibility for the environment, for one another, and all other living creatures with which we share this world. And in doing so, hopefully planting a seed in our conscience of the importance to preserve what is left of the wilds, our untainted woodlands, and ever-dwindling rain forests.

He has had the blessing of sharing his stories and artwork around the globe, which is a gift in itself, and would encourage others not to waste too much of their lives chasing someone else's dreams but to follow their own.

One of the most valuable lessons he has learned in his years is that there are far more important things in life than power and money, such as kindness, compassion, and consideration towards others.

...share that thought if you will.

Also by
Michel Savage

Outlaws of Europa

The 2nd moon of Jupiter has been turned into a prison planet. Where for several generations, robot drone ships have been dumping the scum of the universe and are patrolled by a ring of advanced security satellites that would destroy any vessel attempting to land. After a century of research, old core samples from the ice reveal that the frozen oceans of Europa hold the base element of an immortality drug that can extend the human lifespan several-fold. Now greedy military corporations race for the new fountain of youth, only to discover they can't disable the orbiting sentry which was programmed to protect itself at all costs.

It appears the Confederation has a problem. How do they get past a self-evolving AI that has appointed itself as Warden, and furthermore, retake a planet roaming with Earth's worst criminals who might well be immortal themselves...

Hellbot – Battle Planet

Tranquility was one of those out of the way planets in a system far out of reach from the normal space lanes. Loners, dreamers ...whoever they were, chose to colonize this world. Thirty cycles ago something went terribly wrong. It was rumored their terraformer reactor went critical, and few escaped the chain reaction that clouded the atmosphere with a planet-wide sand storm. A decade of hard labor evaporated overnight. What wasn't buried under the ocean of sand was left to fry under the twin suns.

Human explorers began to wander back into the forgotten zone. No one knew of the machines that had evolved, or the war that raged beyond the edge of the universe ...where mankind did not belong.

Shadoworld - Shadow of the Sun

On a distant, slowly rotating world, Bronze Age tribes must migrate thought their lives to avoid the long cold death of nightfall. As of late, strange events have been deeply troubling the tribal elders; revealing evidence perhaps, that something is lurking on the dark side.

As for a pair of young misfits, the ancient mystery was about to unfold; to reveal their peoples forgotten past, buried deep within the underworld, shrouded in the shadow of the sun.

Shadoworld - Veil of Shadows

Ash was an orphaned street urchin who grew up in the gutters of a desolate medieval city; his bitter youth spent picking pockets and snatching trinkets from the wealthy to survive.

Over the years his art for stealth and sharpened skills had drawn the attention of the Thieves Guild who took him into their folds. Little did they know that the boys tragic past would one day find itself woven within the treacherous schemes of a mysterious spider cult.

As of late, a series of chilling murders had befallen several nobles within the privileged upper districts. Their gruesome deaths had appeared to be centered around an ancient cursed skull, which had recently found its way into the hands of a rich collector. There were few who would trespass upon the strange realms of witchcraft and dark magic ...but a master thief does not fear those who dwell in darkness, for he is one with the shadows.

Shadoworld - Shadows Gate

Asra found himself alone in the middle of the barren sands, unable to remember who he was or how he had gotten there. Saved by a caravan of traveling gypsies, he entered into an exotic world of dancing acrobats, fortune tellers, and mystics who performed their skills for cheering crowds across the desert empires.

However, his destiny would change the day he stumbled upon a forbidden shrine to find a mythical creature entombed beneath its shattered ruins. Promises were whispered and a dark pact was made with the ancient demon; a bond of magic that would lead him on a perilous journey to reveal his forgotten past.

Forgotten Future

At the edge of the world an impossible relic from the fables of antiquity has risen from the frozen wastelands of Antarctica. Professor Logan and his exploration team rush to investigate this historic find, but this unique discovery puts their lives in peril when they unearth the remnants of a long forgotten civilization left buried beneath the ice.

Within the twisting labyrinths below the melting glaciers they uncover an ancient culture which had perished from a mysterious cataclysm. They soon realize it was a polar shift which had caused their destruction, and our world was presently facing the same fate.

Witchwood
The Harvesting

Every day around the world hundreds of people go missing without a trace. Year after year, their numbers add up to millions of lost souls who are never to be seen again; and their numbers keep climbing ...this is where many of them went.

Project EVE

In the late 1940s after the 2nd World War, a classified government program was created in order to explore the military use of psychics to gain an advantage for their soldiers during armed conflict. At a remote laboratory in the mountains, a secret compound comprised of several hundred test subjects were trained to enhance their abilities with the goal of achieving the skills of telepathy and mind control.

Assigned to investigate this covert project, Walter Grant found himself entangled in a web of conspiracy and deceit when he discovered that the residents of the colony were being held captive by the scientists who had hidden the ugly truth behind their dangerous experiments.

At the heart of the project was a girl named Eve, whose extraordinary mind held the key, a child who would prove to them why humanity could not handle such power.

The Faerylands Trilogy
I • The Grey Forest
II • Soulstorm Keep
III • Sorrowblade

Long, long ago the Faerie had roamed free, but for countless centuries now the fey themselves have remained unseen; hidden and withdrawn, shrouded within the boundaries of the Evermore. But just how they became imprisoned there was a mystery their own elders had forgotten or refused to speak of, and a subject of taboo among the ancients.

The Elvenborn had become a dying race, and now a strange and dreadful blight was encroaching upon their sanctuary. Ivy knew there was something terribly wrong with her world, something unspeakable her kind was hiding from. The Faerylands were vanishing, and she had to find out why.

Ivory
The Dreamkeepers

The Elvenborn were bestowed the task of healing their realm, a land left in chaos by the hands of men.

Limerick was but a simple bard who stumbled into an epic quest, one that would test his courage and take him beyond the edges of the Faerylands. High in the mountains sat the ruins of Aldana, where the spirits of the forest gathered to bring balance to the world and end the dreadful blight of the Craven.

Along this journey, the young bard would learn that everything is not as it seems, and that dreams are but a shadow of something real.

Artwork from the Faerylands series available online
Enter the Grey Forest

www.**GreyForest**.com

www.ingramcontent.com/pod-product-compliance
Lightning Source LLC
Chambersburg PA
CBHW060521260626
47161CB00003B/713